Panic!

Panic!

Bill Pronzini

Random House: New York

Library of Congress Cataloging in Publication Data
Pronzini, Bill.
Panic!
I.   Title.
PZ4.P9653Pan   [PS3566.R67]   813′.5′4   72-2900
ISBN 0-394-47491-0

Manufactured in the United States of America
by The Colonial Press, Clinton, Mass.

9 8 7 6 5 4 3 2
First Edition

For Bruni—with love
and
For Barry N. Malzberg—gifted, gloomy,
exasperating, and above all, a friend

What is the use of running,
when you are on the wrong road?

—GERMAN PROVERB

The First Day...

One

The desert surrounded the moving bus like an earthly vision of hell.

Heat shimmered in liquid waves on the polished black ribbon of the highway, in thick tendrils across the arid wastes extending eastward to the horizon, westward to a low stretch of reddish foothills. The noonday sun, in a charred cobalt sky, was a fiery yellow-orange ball suspended on glowing wires. Nothing moved beyond the dust-streaked windows except the heat; the only sign of life was a carrion bird, a black speck lying motionless above something dead or dying in the far distance.

Inside the bus, the air had the same furnacelike quality, smelling of dust, of sweat and cracked leather, of urine from the faulty toilet facility in the rear. It was not crowded. There were only five people riding in addition to the driver: two silent old ladies, with skin that had been dried and cured by twenty thousand appearances of the desert sun outside; a fat man, sleeping, snoring softly; a young, homely girl who sat with her legs splayed wide because the heat had chafed her inner thighs painfully; and, well in the rear on the driver's side, a lean, hollow-eyed man sitting slouched against the window, breathing through his mouth, thinking about nothing at all.

The hollow-eyed man's name was Jack Lennox, and he had long, shaggy black hair that hung lifelessly over a high, ascetic forehead, curled around large flat ears, partially draped the collar of a shapeless, sweat-stained blue shirt that had cost twelve dollars new two years before. There were deep, shadowed furrows etched into the once smoothly symmetrical planes of his face, a dissipated sheen to the once affluent healthiness of light olive skin. His eyes, sunken beneath thick, straight brows, were like green Christmas bulbs long burned-out, the whites tinged with a yellow that gave them a sour-buttermilk quality. He was thirty-three years of age, and he was an old, old man.

As he sat staring at the barren wasteland rushing past outside, he reached in an automatic gesture to the pocket of his shirt, fumbled, touched only the thin material and nothing more. He had smoked his last cigarette two hours before. He lowered his thin-fingered hands, untrimmed nails like black half-moons, and rubbed the slickness of them back and forth across the coarse material of his corduroy trousers; then, slowly, without turning his head from the window, he brought the hands up and dry-washed his face, palms grating lightly over the four-day growth of beard stubble there.

I wonder what time it is, he thought then. I wonder what day it is. I wonder where we are. But none of those things really mattered to him, and the questioning thoughts were rhetorical thoughts, requiring no answers. He stopped thinking again.

Outside, in the wavering distance, a second black ribbon had appeared, winding away from the main interstate highway through outcroppings of lava rock, dry washes, rocky and irregular land surface grown heavily with creosote bush and mesquite, porcupine prickly pear and ocotillo, giant saguaro cactus like lonely, entreating soldiers on a mystical battlefield. A moment later he could see the intersection between the county road and the main highway. A large post-supported sign stood there, with a reflectored arrow pointing eastward; below that:

| Cuenca Seco | 16 |
| Kehoe City | 34 |

They passed the sign, and the desert lay unbroken again, as ageless as time, as enigmatic as the Sphinx. Lennox turned from the window then and leaned forward slightly, clasping his hands tightly together in an attitude of imploring prayer and pressing the knot they formed up under his wishbone. The pain which had again begun there was alternately dull and acute, and he rocked faintly against the rigid coupling of his fingers, squeezing his eyes shut, waiting for the agony to ebb and subside. He knew it would be that way because he had experienced deep hunger on several occasions in the past nine months, and the pain came and went in approximately the same way each time. It had been almost two days now since he had last eaten anything of substance, fifteen hours since the three chocolate bars he had bought with his last quarter in the bus station, the bus station where he had gone to use the toilet, the bus station in—what town? what difference?—the bus station where he had gotten the ticket . . .

No.

He did not want to think about getting the ticket.

Jesus God, he did not want to think about that, but the old man—he could see the old man vividly in his mind—the old man standing there by the urinal, poor old man with a cane, zipping up his fly with gnarled and arthritic fingers, and the rectangle of pasteboard falling out of his baggy pocket and onto the floor, the old man not seeing it, moving away—and he himself moving forward, picking up the rectangle, one-way a long way and he wanted to move again, he wanted to get out of that town, get away from the Polack and the things the Polack had made him do, things like grinding stale bread and adding it to the raw hamburger to make it last longer, things like scraping the remains on the plates of recently departed customers back into the serving pots, things that nauseated and disgusted him.

And then the old man coming back, looking chagrined, looking lost, cane tapping on the tile floor, tapping, tapping, and seeing Lennox there with the ticket in his own trousers now, hidden in there.

"I lost my ticket," the old man said, "I lost it somewhere, it must have fallen out of my pocket. Have you seen it, son? Have you seen my ticket?"

"No," he answered, "no, I never saw any ticket."

"I got to go to my daughter, I got to have that ticket," the old man said. "She sent me the money, I don't have any money of my own. How can I get to my daughter now?"

"I don't know, old man, let me by."

"What about my ticket? What about my daughter?" pleading with him, eyes blinking silver tears, and he had walked away fast, leaving the old man there, standing there alone and leaning on his cane with the tears in his eyes and the lost look on his seamed old face, hurried out of there with the ticket burning in his pocket . . .

The pain went away.

It receded, faded into calm, and Lennox was able to sit up again. He rubbed oily sweat from his face, blanking his mind once more, shutting out the image of the old man, and leaned back in the seat; he sucked breath between yellow-filmed teeth, and the fetid and stagnant air burned like sulphur in his lungs.

There was a static, humming sound inside the bus now, and Lennox became aware that the loudspeaker system had been switched on. He raised his head, and the flat, toneless voice of the bus driver filtered out from a speaker on the roof above him. "There's a roadside oasis a few miles ahead, folks, and since it's past noon we'll be stopping there a half-hour for lunch. They've got hamburgers, assorted sandwiches, beer and soft drinks, reasonably priced . . ."

Lennox doubled forward again, pressing his forehead against the rear of the seat in front of him, his hands burrowing up under his wishbone. Violently and abruptly, the pain had come back.

Two

In a large city sixty miles to the north, in an air-conditioned downtown restaurant, a short, plump man sat in a corner booth and rubbed stubby fingers across his round paunch, cherubic face twisted into a momentary grimace.

The red-haired waitress standing before the booth said, "Is something the matter, sir?"

The plump man, whose name was Harry Vollyer, sighed audibly. "I've got a mild ulcer," he said. "Gives me trouble, every now and then."

"I'm sorry to hear that."

"Well, it's all part of the game."

"Game?"

"Life," Vollyer told her. "The greatest game of them all."

"I guess so," the waitress said. "Would you like to order now?"

"A grilled cheese sandwich and a glass of milk—cold milk."

"Yes, sir. And your friend?"

"He'll have a steak sandwich, no fries, and black coffee."

The waitress moved away, and Vollyer belched delicately, if sourly, and sighed again. He wore a tailored powder-blue suit and a handmade silk shirt the color of fresh grapefruit juice; his tie was by Bronzini, dark blue with faint black diamonds, fastened to his shirt by a tiny white-gold tack; his shoes were bench-crafted from imported Spanish leather, polished to a high gloss. On the little fingers of each hand he wore thick white-gold rings, with platinum-and-onyx settings in simple geometric designs. He had wide, bright blue eyes that gave him the appearance of being perpetually incredulous, and silvered hair that was cut and shaped immaculately to the roundness of his skull. The curve of his lips was benign and cheerful, and from the faint wrinkles at each corner you could tell that he laughed often, that he was a complacent and happy man.

There was movement from across the room, and Vollyer saw that Di Parma was finally coming back from the telephone booth. He smiled in a fatherly way. He had felt paternal toward Di Parma from the moment he met him, he didn't know exactly why; Livio was thirty-six, only fifteen years younger than Vollyer, but he gave the impression of being just a youth, of needing constant guidance and direction. It wasn't that his actions, his thoughts, were juvenile, it was just that he had this habitual look of being lost, of being about to burst into tears, which got right down and pulled at your heart. Vollyer liked Di Parma. He had only been working with him for eight months now, but he liked him considerably more than any of the others he had worked with over the years; he hoped that they could stay together for a while, that nothing would come up to necessitate a severance of their relationship. There were a lot of things he could teach Di Parma, and Livio was a willing student. It gave you a sense of well-being, of completion, when you had somebody like that to work with, somebody who didn't claim to know all the answers because he'd been around in some of the other channels for a while, somebody who could follow orders without back-talking or petulance.

Di Parma slipped into the booth across from him, a frown tugging at the edges of his mouth, corrugating the faintly freckled surface of his forehead. He was a very tall man with crew-cut brown hair and medium-length sideburns, dressed in a dove-gray suit that managed to look rumpled most of the time, in spite of the fact that it had cost as much money as Vollyer's powder-blue one. His shirt and tie were striped, colors harmonious, but he wore no clip or tack, no jewelry of any kind; he had an intense personal aversion to it and he refused to wear it, even refused to wear a wedding ring—a fact which never ceased to amaze Vollyer. He possessed a slender, aquiline nose that gave the illusion of turning up like an inverted fishhook when you faced him, and liquid brown eyes that conveyed the sense of bemusement which Vollyer found so appealing. His hands were oversized, spatulate, and he was self-conscious about them; he put them under the table now, because he had the inveterate feeling that everybody, even Vollyer, would stare at them if they were in plain sight, although Harry had told him on a number of occasions that his hands were not anywhere near as conspicuous as he imagined.

Vollyer smiled paternally and said, "Did you get through to Jean all right?"

"No," Di Parma answered, frowning, "no, she wasn't home. I called back twice but she didn't answer."

"Maybe she went out shopping."

"She does her shopping on Tuesdays and Fridays," Di Parma said. "This is Monday, Harry."

"A movie then, or a walk."

"Jean doesn't like movies, and she's been having this trouble with her arches. She's been to a podiatrist three times already this month." He worried his lower lip. "Damn, I don't know what to think."

"Livio, Livio, you just talked to her this morning. She was fine then, wasn't she?"

"Sure. Sure, she was okay."

"Then she's okay now, too," Vollyer said reasonably. "It's only been four hours."

"But she's not home and she's always home this time of day."

"Are you sure she didn't say something to you this morning about going out? Or maybe last night? Think about it, Livio."

Di Parma thought about it—and then he blinked and looked surprised and said, "One of the neighbors asked her to come over to some kind of luncheon. Us being new in the neighborhood and all."

Vollyer nodded tolerantly. "You see? Nothing to get excited about."

Di Parma was embarrassed. "Hell, Harry, I—"

"Forget it," Vollyer said. He made a dismissive gesture. "You're too tense all the time. Relax a little."

"Well," Di Parma said, and cleared his throat. "Did you order yet? I'm hungrier than I thought I was."

"All taken care of."

"A steak sandwich for me, no fries?"

"Just like always."

Vollyer settled back comfortably against the cool leather of the booth, folding his hands across his paunch. That Livio. Thirty-six years old, married a full five months now, and he went around like a kid on the third day of his honeymoon, calling Jean two and three times in a twenty-four-hour period whenever they were away from the city, worrying about her, talking about her incessantly. There was nothing wrong with love, Vollyer supposed, even though he had never experienced it and did not feel particularly cheated because he hadn't—there was nothing wrong with love but there *were* limits, and he could not understand how a grown man could become that hung up on a woman. Women had their purpose, Vollyer had never been one to put women down, but you had to treat them as simple equals—or inferiors if they deserved it; you just didn't put them up on pedestals like Roman goddesses or something.

Even though he could not understand Di Parma's constant preoccupation with his wife, he condoned it, he was indulgent of it. The thing was, Livio had not let this personal hang-up of his interfere in any way with the efficiency of his professional life; when he was working, he was cool and thinking, following orders, making all the right moves. That being the case, how could you put him down for a simple character flaw? Vollyer had decided that Di Parma's shortcomings were just a part of the game, and as such, had to be accepted, tolerated, because he liked Di Parma, he really did like Di Parma. He hoped that nothing would happen to change things; he hoped Livio would keep right on being cool and efficient when it counted.

The waitress came around with their lunch and set the plates down and went away again. Di Parma said, "What happens after we eat, Harry? Do we stay here or do we make the rest of the drive today?"

"Better if we stay here," Vollyer answered. "We'll find a motel, something with a pool and a nice lounge. We've only got sixty miles left, over the desert, and we can make that in an hour in the morning."

"What time do we leave?"

"Seven. We want to get there around eight."

"There shouldn't be much doing that early."

"We don't want *anything* doing."

"How soon do you figure we can get back home?"

"If everything goes okay, the day after tomorrow."

"I'll call Jean tomorrow night," Di Parma said. "She'll meet us at the airport. Listen, Harry, why don't you come out to the house then? You haven't seen the new house."

Vollyer had no particular desire to see the new house, but he smiled and said, "Sure, Livio, all right."

There was no getting around it, he really did like Di Parma.

Three

From the window of her room at the Joshua Hotel, Jana Hennessey stood looking down the length of Cuenca Seco's dusty main street to the spanning arch of the huge wooden banner marking the town's westward entrance. Even though the black lettering on the front of the sign was not visible from there, she had taken her yellow Triumph TR-6 beneath it late the previous afternoon

—after better than fifty miles of desert driving—and she remembered clearly what it said:

Welcome to Cuenca Seco
Gateway to a Desert Wonderland

As far as Jana was concerned, the wording was misrepresentational. The Wonderland it spoke of was little more than a dead sea sustaining grotesque cacti with spines like razor-edged daggers, a haven for vultures and scorpions and fat brown venom-filled snakes, an arid and polychromatic graveyard strewn with the very bones of time. And the Gateway—well, the Gateway was an anachronism in a world of steel-and-glass, of hurtling chrome-toothed machines, of great, rushing, ant-busy throngs of people; it was an elaborate set for an Old West movie, with too many false-fronted buildings and sun-bonneted women and Stetsoned men moving ponderously beneath a demoniacal sun, with dust-caked metal extras miscast in the roles of horses and carriages; it was make-believe that had magically become a reality, and been given an aura of antiquity that was somehow a little frightening.

Jana expelled a long, soft breath. The trouble with me is, she thought, I'm a big-city girl. I can't appreciate native Americana because I've never seen any of it face-to-face; I've never really been *out* of New York City until now. How much of the grass roots can you see in Brooklyn or Long Island or downtown Manhattan? It's not so easy to adjust to a different way of life, it's not so easy to surround yourself with nature instead of with people, with life-in-the-raw instead of life-insulated-by-luxury; it's not so easy to break away, to change, to forget.

To forget . . .

Abruptly, Jana turned from the window—tall and lithe in her mid-twenties, figure reminiscent of a lingerie model's, sable hair worn long and straight, with stray wisps falling over her shoulders, almost to the gentle swell of her breasts. A pair of silver-rimmed reading glasses gave her narrow face a quality of introspective intelligence that was enhanced by the prominence of delicately boned cheeks, by the firm set of a small, naturally pink mouth. Her eyes, behind the lens of the glasses, were an intense brown that contained, like an alien presence, a small dull glow of pain.

11

The room was small and hot, in spite of a portable air-conditioning unit mounted in the frame of the window; but since the Joshua Hotel was the only lodging in town—and since this was considered one of its finer accommodations—she had not had much choice in the matter. It contained a brass-framed double bed, two nightstands, a small private bathroom, and a child-sized writing desk; the walls were of a varnished blond wood, decorated with desert lithographs. The white bedspread depicted a stoic, war-painted Indian astride a pinto horse, a feathered lance in one hand.

Jana crossed the room, stood behind the desk, and studied the typewritten sheets laid out beside the portable Royal, the first two pages of the outline she had begun earlier that morning. Then she looked at the half-filled third page rolled into the platen of the machine, at the x-ed out lines there. She turned again and went to the bed and sat down, staring at the telephone on the nightstand nearest the door.

She had put off calling Harold Klein for a week now, and she knew that that had been a mistake. She hadn't wanted to talk to him because of the book, the fact that she hadn't even started it; and, more important, because he represented an integral part of the life in New York from which she had so completely severed herself. Time to think, uninterrupted, had been what she desperately needed during the two thousand five hundred miles she had driven this past week—time to sort things out in her mind so that she would be able to work again. And Harold would not have understood, would still not understand. Oh, he knew about Don Harper, of course—the bare facts of the affair—but that was all he knew. He was a fine agent, a good friend, but she had just never been able to talk to him on a personal level—and the things which had been on her mind of late were such that she would have found it almost impossible to discuss them with a priest, much less a man of Harold's uncomplicated nature.

But that did not alter the fact that her failure to call him had been a mistake. He was undoubtedly worried, and with good cause; he had done a lot for her, after all, had been responsible for a large percentage of her current success. He had a stake in her future—was a prospectively important part of her future—

and to continue to shun him would be, ultimately, to shun whatever prospects for renewed normalcy lay ahead of her.

She had been thinking about rectifying her mistake all morning, and now she knew that she would not be able to get back to her outline until she had done so. She picked up the phone and asked the desk clerk to dial Klein's personal office number in New York, nervously tapping short, manicured nails on the glass top of the table as she waited. What would she tell him? How would she—?

A soft click. "Harold Klein," his voice said distantly, metallically.

She drew a quiet, tremulous breath. "Hello, Harold, this is Jana."

Momentary silence—and then Klein said with deceptive calm, "Well, hello, Jana. How nice of you to call."

"Harold, I—"

"For God's sake," Klein interrupted, anger replacing the subtle sarcasm, "where have you been the past week? You just disappeared, without a word, without a trace. We've been so damned worried we were about ready to call in the police."

"I've been . . . traveling," she told him vaguely.

"Traveling where?"

"Cross country."

"Well, where are you now?"

She explained, briefly.

"What are you doing *there?*"

"Getting ready to write *Desert Adventure.*"

"You mean you haven't even started it yet?"

"No," she said.

"You're a week past deadline now," Klein said with exasperation. "I've gotten at least one phone call a day from Ross Phalen—"

"Ross Phalen is a pain in the ass," Jana said bluntly.

"That may be true, but his word is law at Nabob Press. Do you want to lose them, Jana? They're paying a hell of a lot more money than I can get you from any of the other juvenile publishers."

"I know that, Harold, and I'm sorry. But I've had some . . . problems the past month. I tried to work and I couldn't, and so I decided to come out here and see if the location would stimulate me."

"Problems? What sort of problems?"

"I'd rather not talk about it."

Klein exhaled audibly. "Don Harper, I suppose. Well, all right. How long will it take you to finish the book? I've got to have something to tell Phalen when he calls again."

"About a week," Jana said.

"And the illustrations?"

"Another week."

"Is that definite?"

"I think so, yes."

Klein sighed a second time. "When you get back to New York, girl, you and I are going to have a nice long talk about the facts of life. You've got to understand that running off unannounced this way—"

"Harold, I'm not coming back to New York."

"What?"

"I'm not coming back," Jana repeated.

Silence hummed over the wire for a moment, and then Klein said half-incredulously, "You're not serious."

"I'm very serious."

"For God's sake, *why?*"

"I've had it with New York, that's all, I'm sick to my soul of New York. I feel as if I'm . . . suffocating there."

"Where do you expect to go? What do you expect to do, a young girl alone?"

"I don't know," she said. "I'll travel, I'll go to Canada, to Mexico, I'll see some of the great wide world." She tried to make her tone light, but she had the feeling that her voice was strained and uncertain.

"Jana, I think you're making a rash and foolish decision. Your place is here, with people you know, with people you can equate with."

"Don't try to talk me out of it, Harold, I've made up my mind. Now I don't want to discuss it any more. I've got to get to work on *Desert Adventure* if you want a manuscript in a week."

"All right, we won't discuss it any more," Klein said, and Jana detected an irritating note of patronage in his voice.

"What's the name of the place where you're staying? The tele-phone number?"

She told him.

"I'll call you in a day or so, to see how you're coming along. Sooner, if anything urgent comes up."

"Fine."

"You won't go running off again, now?"

"No, I'll stay right here."

"Promise?"

"Promise."

They said parting words, and Jana put the receiver down quickly. The telephone conversation had gone about as she had expected it to, but it had upset her nonetheless. Harold meant well, but he was a prober, a man who tried to burrow his way into your soul, to examine each cell of your being in an effort to determine its relationship with every other cell. And that was exactly the kind of thing which frightened her, which she wanted desperately to avoid.

Harold must never know.

No one must ever know.

Hers was a private hell, and it could be shared by no one—no one at all.

Four

The roadside oasis was situated just outside the crest of a long curve in the main interstate highway, like a detached nipple on some gigantic contour drawing of a woman's breast.

It was set something over two hundred yards from the high-way, umbilically connected to it by a narrow, unpaved access road that blended into a rough-gravel parking area in front. There were, in actuality, three buildings: the main structure, old and sprawling, unpainted, with two weathered gas pumps under a short wooden awning; at the right edge of the parking area, a lattice-fronted, considerably smaller construction that obviously housed rest rooms; and a cabinlike dwelling set directly behind the main building—living quarters for the owner or owners. A large wooden sign, mounted on rusted steel rods on the roof of the main building, read *Del's Oasis* in heat-eroded blue letters.

Lennox saw all of this through dulled eyes as the bus turned off the black glass of the highway, onto the access road. It bounced jarringly, raising heavy clouds of dust, and he clutched at the armrests with both hands, his teeth clamped tightly together at the intensification of the pain which still burned deep within his belly. The bus slowed as it swung onto the surface of the parking lot, and the driver maneuvered it to parallel the gas pumps directly in front, switching off the diesel immediately. The doors whispered open, and heat-shrouded silence crept in.

Lennox got sluggishly out of his seat and followed the other passengers and the driver onto the gravel beneath the wooden awning. He saw that a screen door was set into the front of the structure, above which was a warped metal sign: *Café*. There were two windows, dust-caked, with green shades partially drawn inside, one on either flank of the door. In the left window was a Coca-Cola sign and a card that said *Open;* in the right was a shield advertising Coors beer.

The driver pulled open the screen door, and his passengers trooped in after him like a line of weary foot soldiers, Lennox entering last. It was not much cooler inside. There was an overt stuffiness in the barnlike interior that had not been dispelled by the large ceiling fan whirring overhead, or by the ice-cooler placed on a low table to one side. On the left was a long, deserted lunch counter with yellow leatherette-topped stools arranged before it; the remainder of the room was taken up with wooden tables covered in yellow-checked oilcloth, all of them empty now, and straight-backed chairs. The rough-wood walls were furbished with prospecting tools—picks, shovels, nugget pans, and the like—and faded facsimiles of venerable Western newspapers announcing the discovery of gold in California, silver in Nevada and Arizona. At the foot of the far wall, next to an open door leading to a storeroom, were a rocking cradle and portions of a wooden sluice box that a placard propped between them claimed to have been used at Sutter's Mill, California, circa 1850.

Panic!

Behind the lunch counter, dressed in clean white, a middle-aged, balding man with thick jowls stood slicing potatoes on a scarred sandwich board. To one side of him, tacked to the wall, was a square of cardboard: *We Accept All Major Credit Cards.* Lennox thought bitterly of the wallet full of credit cards he had destroyed months ago, because they had his name on them and were links with the dead past, because using them would be like leaving a clear, fresh trail to his current whereabouts, because he might never be able to pay the accumulated sums, and that was considered fraud and he did not want any more threats to his tenuous freedom. But Jesus, he should have kept just *one* card—Diner's or Carte Blanche—for emergencies like this, for the moments of burning hunger . . .

The balding man put down the heavy knife he was using as the string of customers—not Lennox—moved to the lunch counter and took stools in an even row; he wiped his hands on a freshly laundered towel, smiling professionally with thick lips that were a winelike red in the sallow cast of his face. "What'll it be today, folks?"

Lennox could smell the pungency of grilled meat hanging heavily in the hot, still air, and the muscles of his stomach convulsed. He backed to the door, turning, and stumbled outside, moving directly across to the bus, leaning unsteadily against the hot metal of its side. After a moment he re-entered the coach and took his small, cracked blue overnight bag from the rack above the seat. Then he crossed under the bright glare of the sun to the rest rooms.

Inside the door marked *Men,* he ran cold water into the lavatory basin and washed his face and neck, cupped his hands under the tap and rinsed his mouth several times; he resisted the urge to drink, knowing that if he swallowed any of the tepid, chemical-tasting liquid his contracted stomach would throw it up again immediately. From the overnight bag he took his razor and a thin sliver of soap; but the idea of shaving, which had been his intention, evaporated when he looked at himself in the speckled mirror over the basin. A close shave would have been incongruous with his unkempt hair, his sweat-dirty clothes, his hollow eyes—and he would still have looked like a derelict. To hell with it, he thought. To hell with all of it.

He returned the razor and soap to the bag, and then opened

the door to one of the two stalls, closing it behind him as he entered, and sat on the lowered lid of the toilet seat, his head in his hands. The pain, which had fluctuated into a muted gnawing as he splashed himself with water at the basin, again disappeared from his stomach; but he kept on sitting there, drinking air through his mouth.

Several minutes passed, and finally Lennox got weakly to his feet. He hoped to God that they would finish eating in the café before long. He wanted to get to some town, any town, a town where there were dishes to be washed or floors to be swept, a town where they had a mission or a Salvation Army kitchen; if he did not get something to eat very soon, he was afraid that he would collapse from lack of nourishment—you could die from malnutrition, couldn't you? How long could a man live without food? Three days, four? He wasn't sure, exactly; he was sure only of the pain which attacked his belly more and more frequently, more and more intensely, and that in itself was enough to frighten him.

He picked up his overnight bag and opened the door and went outside, blinking against the glinting sunlight. He moved toward the bus. As he came around on the side of it, he saw the driver lounging against the left front wheel, working on his teeth with a wooden pick. Lennox wet his lips with a dry tongue, pulling his eyes away, and put one foot on the metal entrance step.

The driver said, "Just a minute, guy."

Lennox stopped, and electricity fled along the nerve synapses in the saddle of his back. There was something—a terse authority—in the driver's voice that portended trouble. He turned, slowly, and faced the other man. "Yes?"

The driver was darkly powerful in his sweat-stained gray uniform, and there was a grim set to his squared jaw. He studied Lennox with small, sharp eyes, and the distaste at what he saw was clearly defined on his sun-flushed face. "I didn't see you inside the café," he said, and the tone of his voice made the words a question that demanded an acceptable answer.

"I . . . wasn't hungry," Lennox answered thickly. "I went to wash up."

"You've been riding with me since six this morning. You didn't eat when we took the rest stop in Chandlerville at eight, and you don't eat now. You don't have much of an appetite, is that it?"

"Yes, that's it."

"Well, maybe it is and maybe it isn't," the driver said. "Where are you going?"

"Going?"

"That's right: what destination?"

Lennox tried to remember the name of the city on the old man's ticket, but his mind had gone blank. He said, "I . . . the next town. The next stop."

"Let's have a look at your ticket."

"What for?"

"Let's see it," coldly.

Lennox got the pasteboard from his pocket, and the driver took it out of his nerveless fingers. He scanned it, his eyes narrowing. "That's what I thought," he said. "This is only valid to Gila River, and we passed through there two hours ago. You're riding on an expired pass."

He could not think of anything to say. What was there to say? He hadn't considered the possibility of the ticket being good only to one of the small towns along the bus route; he had been irrationally sure that the old man would be going to one of the larger border cities to the south, that that was where the daughter who had sent him the money would be living. The destination on the pasteboard had meant nothing to him originally, and he remembered only vaguely passing through Gila River; the name had sparked no recognition at that time. He stood there sweating, looking at the driver's shirt front, trying to think of something to do or say but not coming up with anything at all.

"You owe me four-eighty," the driver said. "That's the fare one way from Gila River to Troy Springs."

"I don't . . . have four-eighty," Lennox said woodenly.

"That's what I figured, too. You're nothing but a damned vag, and you're off my bus as of right now."

"Listen," Lennox said, "listen, you can't leave me here . . ."

"The hell I can't," the driver told him. "You're left, guy."

He turned abruptly and went to the café door, calling out to the passengers inside that they would be leaving now. He came back and got in behind the wheel, ignoring Lennox, and after a moment the other passengers filed out and entered the bus. The homely girl with the heat-chafed thighs looked at Lennox with a curious, mild hunger, but she did not say anything to him.

He stood there like a fool, feeling helpless, holding the overnight bag against his right leg. The homely girl pressed her face to the window glass and looked down at him with sad eyes. The bus began to move away, its diesel engine shattering the hot, dead stillness, and Lennox watched it swing around and start down the access road, raising clouds of dry, acrid dust. Sunlight gleamed feverishly off the silver metal of its body as it slowed and made the turn south, a sluggish armored sowbug disappearing along the curve of the highway. What now? he thought. What am I going to do now?

He heard movement behind him, and when he turned he saw that the balding man who had been behind the café counter had come outside. The balding man walked over beside Lennox and took a cigarette from the pocket of his white shirt and set it between his thick lips without lighting it. After a moment he said, "Put you off the bus, huh?"

"Yeah."

"How come?"

"I was riding on an expired ticket."

"These bus drivers can be bastards sometimes," the balding man said. "This is a hell of a place to strand a guy."

"A hell of a place," Lennox agreed dully.

The balding man studied him closely without appearing to do so. The heat was thick around the two of them, and from out of the barren plain to the east, something made a fluttering sound. Finally the balding man said, "You a little strapped for money, are you?"

"You could say that."

"Down on your luck or on the run?"

Lennox started. "What?"

"Cops looking for you?" the balding man asked matter-of-factly.

"No," he lied. "No."

"Were you heading any place special on that bus?"

"Just . . . drifting."

"Uh-huh. Well, I got some work if you could use it."

Lennox had been looking out over the desert, at the shimmering jagged floor of it, at the gaunt skeletal range rising on the horizon to the south, at the vast brittle emptiness lying motionless under the canopy of heat. He turned his attention to the balding man again and passed a hand across his mouth. "What kind of work?"

"This and that. A little painting, a little stock reshuffling, a little fixing up."

"Here?"

"That's right. I can't pay much—a few bucks—but you'll eat for three-four days and you can sleep on a cot in the storeroom. And you'll be able to buy another bus ticket out when you're through."

The pain was omnipresent in Lennox's stomach, gnawing, gnawing. He did not have to consider the offer at all. "All right," he said.

The balding man smiled briefly. "My name's Perrins, Al Perrins." He kept his hands at his sides.

"Mine's Delaney," Lennox said.

"Okay, Delaney. How about a couple of burgers? You can start work afterward."

Lennox made a dry clearing noise in his throat. His legs felt even weaker now, but it was the weakness of sudden relief. "Sounds good."

"The food ain't," Perrins said, and laughed. "But it'll fill your belly. Come on."

They turned and walked slowly inside the café. Lennox was thinking about the burgers Perrins had promised, and he felt nauseous with his hunger; he wondered if he would be able to keep any of the food down.

He was able to—most of it, anyway.

Five

When the young bright-face, Forester, finished his morning patrol and returned to the county sheriff's substation in Cuenca Seco, Andy Brackeen—the resident deputy-in-charge—went down to Sullivan's Bar to drink his lunch.

It had been a long morning, and Brackeen was badly hungover and very thirsty. He had gotten into a pointless argument with his wife, Marge, the night before and had driven over to Kehoe City in a huff; there had been a poker game in the back room of Indian Charley's, and he had lost heavily and drunk too damned much gin in the bargain. He still could not remember driving home, and that was very bad; he was hanging onto his job by a thread now, and the last stroke of the scissors would be a tag by one of the Highway Patrol units or cruising county cars for drunk driving in a county vehicle. He was a goddamned fool for getting into the gin like that; he couldn't handle gin, he had never been able to handle gin. It did things to his mind, blacked him out so that he could not recall what he had done after a certain point in the evening. But if he stayed with the beer, he was all right. He could drink beer with the best of them, and he was always in full control of his faculties; things were just fine if he stayed with the beer.

Brackeen had no illusions about himself. He knew what he was and why he was what he was. There had been a time when that knowledge had been heavy and consumptive within him, but that had been sixteen years ago, in another world named San Francisco—that had been before the desert and the beer, before Marge. Now the perception was only a dimly glowing ember resting on the edge of his soul.

He was a big man, thick-chested, and he had in his youth fought amateur bouts in the heavyweight class, almost but not quite qualifying for the Golden Gloves; but the once-powerful musculature of his body was now overlaid with a soft cushion of fat, and his belly swayed liquidly beneath his dark khaki uniform shirt, partially concealing the buckle of his Sam Browne belt, brushing across the checked grip of the .357 Colt Python Magnum on his right hip. Each of his forty-one years was grooved for all to see on the sun-blackened surface of his face, as the elements had carved the centuries on the desert land-scape he had made his home more than fourteen years before. Perpetually damp black hair, speckled with gray and pure white, was thickly visible beneath a deep-crowned white Stetson; gray eyes, red-rimmed and flatly expressionless, seemed as fixed as bright marbles solidified in lucite.

He was not particularly well-liked in the town of Cuenca Seco, but neither was he hated nor feared; he was, for the most part, simply tolerated and ignored. As he moved now along the heat-waved sidewalk toward Sullivan's Bar, walking slowly be-cause of the throbbing ache in his temples and because of the hot sun, he passed townspeople whom he knew—but there were no exchanges of greeting, no nods of recognition. He walked alone on the busy street, and it was the way Brackeen had come to want it; he could live with himself only as long as he was able to lock the secret of his disintegration as a man deep within, and he knew that friendships, liaisons, often brought probings which, if well-meaning, could still be ultimately destructive. He could never talk about it. He had never told anyone about it, not even Marge, even though she might have understood.

Sullivan's Bar was crowded with lunch trade, and Brack-een's eyes narrowed into thin slits at the sudden change in light as he entered. There was an air-conditioning unit behind the simulated kegs-and-plank bar, and the cool air was a salve on his pulsing temples, the feverish skin of his face. He moved across the wooden floor, up to the bar, and the men there made room for him without ceasing conversation, without looking at him, without acknowledging his presence in any way.

Sullivan came down immediately, no smile on his freckled Irish countenance. Brackeen said, "Mighty hot," the way he did every day when he came in, and took off his hat and put it on the bar face. He passed one of his big, knotted hands through his damp hair.

Sullivan said, "Yeah," ritualistically.

"Draw a pint, will you, Sully?"

"Sure."

"And put a Poor Boy in, I guess."

Sullivan went away and drew the beer and placed one of the foil-wrapped, ready-made sandwiches into the miniature electric oven on the back bar. He was an old-fashioned publican, and he scraped the foaming head off the glass of beer with a wooden spatula before serving it.

Brackeen wrapped both hands around the cold-beaded stein, lifted it, his eyes closing in anticipation. He drank in long, convulsive swallows, filling his mouth with the chill effervescence before letting it flow tingling through the burning passage of his throat and into the unsettled emptiness of his stomach.

The glass was empty. He put it down on the bar and rubbed the back of his hand across his mouth. Jesus, but he had needed that! And the next one, too. He didn't really want the Poor Boy at all, but he knew that when he had a hangover as bad as this one, he had to have something solid on his stomach; if not, he would conclude his tour at five o'clock by puking up stale beer, that was what had happened the last time he hadn't eaten with hell going.

Brackeen looked for Sullivan and caught his eye, lifting the empty stein. When it had been refilled, he drank more slowly, looking at his reflection in the mirror behind the bar. What he saw did not disturb him much. If he had been able, as a kid fresh out of the Police Academy, to look twenty years into the future and see himself as he was today, he would have been appalled at the vision; but as a kid, he had had ideals, dreams, he had had a lot of things that he no longer possessed. The fact that he had become a slob offended him not at all.

He ate the Poor Boy slowly, in mincing bites washed down with a third stein of draught. The beer was bringing him out of it, as it usually did. He called to Sullivan for a fourth draw, and while he waited for it he decided that he was strong enough to have a cigarette; he couldn't touch them in the mornings after a night like he'd had in Kehoe City.

He smoked two cigarettes, one each with the fourth and the fifth glasses of beer, and he was feeling straight with himself again, feeling pretty good. The headache had abated, and his gut was not giving him any more trouble. But it was time to get back, because Forester took his lunch at one-thirty and Forester had big eyes and a bigger mouth, being a bright-face. Brackeen didn't want to antagonize Forester, you had to pamper these young shits with their new-found authority, because if they went sour on you they could make a lot of trouble. And Forester

24

had never made a secret of the fact that he disliked—*disapproved* of—Brackeen.

He thought briefly about taking a couple of cans of beer back to the substation with him—Forester was going on patrol again, after his lunch—but he shelved that idea immediately. He had almost gotten caught with a half-quart in his hand that afternoon two months ago, when the county sheriff, Lydell, had come in unannounced. He had learned his lesson from that; there was no point in tempting fate, no percentage in raising already poor odds. He would be able to make it through the day now, with these five beers under his belt—and if he *did* begin hurting a little later on, maybe he could slip out for a couple of minutes and get back here for a bracer or two, as long as things remained quiet.

He eased off the stool and put his hat back on, adjusting the Magnum on his hip. "See you later, Sully," he said.

"Yeah, sure."

Brackeen smiled loosely and went out into the sweltering afternoon without touching his wallet—the final segment of the bitter ritual he and Sullivan enacted almost every day.

Six

Slowly, inexorably, the desert sun traversed its ardent path across the smoky blue heavens. When it reached the lip of the western horizon, it hung there for long minutes as if preparing itself for the descent, radiating, setting red-gold fire to the sky around it. Then, abruptly, it plunged, deepening the red haze into burnished brass, adding salmon and pink threads to the intricate color scheme of a desert sunset. The horizon swallowed it hungrily, and the empyrean modulated to blue-gray, to slate, to expanding black as the shining globe vanished completely.

The first papery whispers of the night wind stirred the mesquite, the bright gold flowers of the rabbit bush, and nocturnal animals—badgers, foxes, peccaries, coyotes, hooded skunks—

ventured tentatively from their lairs in search of food and water. Bats and horned owls filled the rapidly cooling air with the flutter of wings.

Darkness hooded the land in a black cloak, and the wind grew chill as the sharp and enigmatic reversal of desert temperature manifested itself. A pale gold moon appeared suddenly in the star-pricked velvet of the sky, as if it had been launched from some immense catapult, casting ghostly white shine across the silent landscape.

Night was full-born.

Another day had perished into infinity.

The Second Day . . .

One

I stand on the porch, supporting myself with my left hand on the stucco wall, and with my right I keep slapping the wood paneling of the door. Open up in there, damn you, I know you're in there, Phyllis. Open this goddamn door!

And the door opens and she looks out at me with that patronizing, superior expression curling her soft mouth—how could I ever have loved her, how could I ever have thought she was beautiful? Her silver-streaked blond hair is freshly coiffed, even though it is past ten o'clock at night; and the floor-length blue peignoir she wears has fur at the throat and on the sleeves. I know it is expensive, I have never seen it before, she bought it with my money—and she keeps looking at me that way, her eyes reducing me to a pile of soft odorous shit and I feel the rage burning down low in my groin, the flames of it already fanned by the liquor I've drunk since the court hearing.

I want to hit her. I want to slap that look away. I've never hit her before—any woman before—but God! I want to hit her now . . .

"Oh, it's you," she says with clear distaste. "I might have known it. What do you want, Jack?"

"Want to talk to you."

"There's nothing more to be said."

"Goddamn right there is, goddamn right!"

"You're drunk," she says, and starts to close the door.

I lean away from the wall and wedge my shoulder against

the wood. She frowns, nothing more. A sculpture fashioned of glacial ice. I push the door wide, moving her backward, and stagger inside, near falling, catching myself on the table in the hall, turning. She has gone out of focus. I shake my head and rub splayed fingers over my face, the nails digging harshly into the skin, and she shimmers, three of her into two into one.

"You're drunk," she says again.

"Who has a better right to be drunk, you tell me that."

"Jack, I don't want you in my house. Now say what you came to say and get out."

"Your house! You bitch, your house!"

"That's right. You heard what the judge said, didn't you?"

So sweet, so contemptuous, and I think of all the nights with her lying beneath me, warm, whispering, and inside nothing, despising me, playing out a not particularly demanding role while I burst in every way with love for her.

"It's my house!" I shout at her. "I built this goddamn house with my money!"

"Jack, what's the point of going over it again and again? It's settled now. We're divorced, the judge made a fair evaluation—"

"Fair! Oh my God, fair! He gave you everything, he gave you my guts, he made me a goddamn indentured servant!"

"You're being melodramatic, Jack," she says with that cold, empty rationality. "You always were childishly ineffective under stress."

"You frigging slut!"

"Jack, Jack, I've heard all the words before and they don't mean anything to me. Now please, won't you leave? If you don't, I'll have to call the police, and I really don't want to do that. Go home and go to bed. You shouldn't drink, either, you know."

I grow cunning. I take a step forward, with the room tilting slightly, and I point a finger at her as if it is the blade of a dagger, aiming squarely between the heavy white mounds of her breasts. "I'm not going to pay the alimony, Phyllis," I say softly, and I smile at her with the only side of my mouth which seems to respond.

"Oh, don't be absurd."

"I'm not going to pay it."

"If you don't, you'll go to jail."

"They have to catch me first."

"And just what is that supposed to imply?"

"What the hell do you think it implies, huh? I'm leaving town, I'm getting out of this state, I'm going as far away from you as I can go."

"I don't believe you. You won't quit your job, your precious job. Being Humber Realty's star salesman has always been your one shining ambition."

"I've already quit it," I say slyly. "I quit it at four this afternoon. Call Ed Humber if you want confirmation. Go ahead, call him."

She frowns again, and there is a faint touch of incredulity to the set of her mouth. Good! I'm getting through to her now, I'm getting to the core of her.

"I'll put the police on you if you do a silly thing like going away," she says coldly. *"I'll have you brought back and thrown in jail."*

"You think the police care about nonpayment of alimony? You think they'll make much of an effort to find me?"

"I won't let you deprive me of what's rightfully mine, Jack."

"No? How you going to stop me?"

"I'll stop you."

"No," I say, *"no, you won't, Phyllis,"* and I feel exultant. I've won! I've finally won! There are fissures in the ice shell now, I've penetrated, I've done what I came to do. I move forward, and a kind of loose, liquid laughter finds its way out of my throat, a strident, ecstatic mirth. Her face contorts, mottles, I've put it into you and broken it off, Phyllis, you bitch, and I reach out to put my hand on the doorknob.

She slaps me.

She brings her right hand around, palm open, and cracks it across my face with the stinging force of a whip. The sound reverberates through the house, bouncing off walls, coming back like a boomerang to pierce the soft buzzing in my ears. I jerk up convulsively, staring at her, at the cold flat mask of her face, the hatred in her eyes.

And she slaps me again.

I shake my head, and the momentary confusion within gives way to a rebirth of the burning rage which has sustained me all that day. I feel myself shaking, my hands curling into fists, and I open my mouth to tell her not to do it another time, but the words are stillborn in my throat because she slaps me again, and again and again, her hand whipping back and forth across my face like an arcing metronome. The fires consume all reason that the alcohol has not and I know what I'm going to do but I can't stop it, I bring my right fist up and I watch myself do so as if I have somehow shed the husk of my body, watch the fist come up as if in slow motion and join her face between the aristocratic tilt of her nose and the soft curve of her mouth, watch the lip split, the nose expand, watch blood spurt out to cover my hand, and then she is falling backward, crumpling against the wall by the door, her hands rushing up to cover her red-white face.

I stand frozen with shock, looking numbly at my right fist, and then the silent world in which all of this has happened no longer exists, the sound track comes on at full volume. I can hear Phyllis screaming between her hands, hear her flinging words at me which are not hysterical but merely a brief flare of the hidden emotions which rule her: "You won't deprive me of what I'm entitled to, you won't run out on me. I'll have a warrant sworn out against you for assault, I'll say that you came in here and beat me and threatened to kill me, the police care about that, Jack, they'll bring you back and put you in jail and you'll work in there to pay my alimony!"

She draws her bloodied hands away.

And she is half-smiling redly with her broken mouth.

I reach for the door, blindly, get it open, stagger onto the porch outside. I look wildly around me. Inside, Phyllis is still screaming. Lights begin to go on, one by one, in the neighboring houses, and the black night is consumed by sound. I don't know what to do, I'm scared, I'm going to be sick, and somebody shouts, moving across a lawn toward me, and then I know what I have to do, I know what I have to do to survive.

Run, Lennox.

Run.

Run.

RUN!

Panic!

Running . . .

Running . . .

Someone was shaking him, calling the name Delaney.

Lennox came out of the dream as he always did: spasmodically, his eyes snapping open but seeing nothing, his body slick with sweat. He sat up, put his palms flat on the wet, rumpled blanket of the cot, pure terror swiveling his head from side to side. He poised to bolt—and then his brain cleared, reoriented itself, and he blinked up at the lean form of Perrins standing over him in the bright early-morning sunlight.

"Christ," Perrins said, "that must have been some nightmare."

Lennox fell back on the cot and threw an arm over his eyes. He couldn't seem to regulate his breathing. "Was I making much noise?" he asked.

"Hell yes."

"Did I say anything?"

"Not that I could make out. Why?"

"I talk in my sleep sometimes, that's all."

"Yeah, well, it's after seven," Perrins said. "I open this place at eight. Go wash up, and I'll get you some breakfast. We've got plenty of work today."

"All right."

Perrins went out, and Lennox lay there with his arm over his eyes for a time, still trying to breathe normally. Oddly, there was the hangover aftertaste of alcohol in his mouth, even though he had not had a drink in several days, and his arms and the back of his neck ached stingingly with sunburn. Perrins had had him up on the roof late yesterday, repainting the weathered sign, and the desert sun, even fading into twilight, had been merciless.

He sat up again, finally, and dry-washed his face with his hands; he had shaved last night, before stretching out on the cot, but he had not done much of a job of it and he could feel the stubble on his chin already. He could smell himself, too, a sour, unhygienic odor that seemed to fold upward from his crotch; he wished vaguely that he had taken some kind of bath. But it had been more than a week now, and what the hell was another day? Like a lot of other once-important, once-carefully-attended-to small details, it no longer mattered very much.

Lennox got somewhat unsteadily to his feet and pulled on his pants and stepped into his shoes. Then he picked up his overnight bag, went through the dining room—Perrins had his back to him, working over the grill, the smell of frying bacon thick in there—and stepped out into the dusty parking area.

The sun, in spite of the early hour, hung low and bright on the eastern horizon. The air was already hot, and as Lennox walked slowly across to the rest rooms, his head began to throb, gently, steadily. He hoped Perrins did not have any more work to be done outside; there were people who were prone to sunstroke, and he had always been one of them, an indoor type, one of the night people, no aptitudes and no inclinations for nature or the elements.

He washed his face and hands in the john, and used a dampened paper towel to sponge over his groin, dispelling some of the sour odor, knowing it would return again long before the day was out. He put on the only white shirt he had—frayed, slightly soiled, with a urine-colored bleach stain on one of the tails—and ran a comb through his tangled hair carelessly. Then he went back inside.

Perrins had a plate of bacon and eggs, a glass of orange juice on the counter. Lennox ate silently, slowly, head bowed over his plate, not looking up. When he finished eating, Perrins came down from where he had been stocking the ice cooler. "All set, Delaney?"

"I guess I am," Lennox answered.

"First thing, I want you down in the storage basement. It's a mess down there, and I just haven't had the time to straighten it out myself."

They went into the storeroom, and behind several cartons of snack foods at the far end was an old-fashioned trap door with a ring-pull set through an iron eyebolt; Lennox had not noticed it before. Perrins dragged the door up and descended a set of stairs into a darkly musty vault that was only slightly cooler than the rooms upstairs. Following him, Lennox felt the eggs turn in his still-tender stomach—but he did not say anything.

Perrins clicked on a light set into one wall, revealing a rectangular area cluttered with cartons of beer and soft drinks, cases of tinned goods, a chipped enamel freezer for meat and other perishables, and various-sized containers of miscellany. He waved one of his thick arms. "Think you can handle it?"

"Sure," Lennox said listlessly. "How do you want it arranged?"

"Use your own judgment," Perrins told him. "Give me as much space as you can."

"Will do."

"Yell if you want anything."

Lennox nodded, and Perrins went back up the stairs and dropped the trap door heavily. It made a hollow, empty sound, like the door of a crypt being closed. Lennox held the eggs on the floor of his stomach with an effort of will, and looked around at the bare, sweating cement walls, the mélange which haphazardly filled the room.

What am I doing here? he thought. I deserve better than this. I fought all my life for position, for security, I made something out of myself and my dreams, and it isn't right, it isn't fair. Why me? Why not Phyllis, why not her, why not the bitches and the sons of bitches of this world? Why me?

Oh, goddamnit, why *me?*

Two

The desk clerk at the Joshua Hotel was a young man with luminous green eyes, dressed in Western garb; the eyes caressed Jana like fat, soft hands. He said, "Are you sure you want to go out into the desert alone, Miss Hennessey?"

"Yes, I'm quite sure," she answered. She wore a thin yellow blouse and stiff new Levis and high-laced desert boots; a wide-brimmed sombrero covered her pinned-up sable hair.

"Well," the desk clerk said, and shrugged. He took a dirt-creased map from a drawer beneath the counter and unfolded it. "Some place scenic, you said?"

Jana nodded. "I'm interested in unusual rock formations, or growths of flora, or panoramas."

"You a painter or something?" the clerk asked curiously.

"Or something."

"We get a lot of painters staying here. Photographers, too. Lot of unspoiled desert in this area."

"So I understand."

"Sure," the clerk said. His eyes were hungry on the swell of her breasts for a moment, and then, reluctantly, they shifted to the map he had spread out on the counter. He put a forefinger on a thin snakelike line which intersected the county road connecting Cuenca Seco with Kehoe City, just to the east of town; it meandered into the desert in a southwesterly—and then southern—direction some six or seven miles, by the map scale, fading out in the middle of empty white. "This is the road you want to take, Miss Hennessey. It's a dead end, as you can see, and not much of a road—railroad people built it back in the twenties, for a proposed water stop on the spur line to Kehoe City; but the spur was abandoned before they could finish it, and so they abandoned the road too. Still, you won't find any finer desert country in these parts."

"It sounds fine," Jana said.

"You want to take along some water, and make sure your car's gassed up before you leave. Road's not used much any more, and there's nothing out there but desert."

"I'll do that, thank you."

"Sure," feasting on her breasts again. "Have a nice time, Miss Hennessey."

Jana went out quickly and down the dusty steps into the bright white glare of the morning. She carried a large handbag which contained her sketch pad, a loose-leaf notebook, a tin of charcoal, and soft-lead pencils. She had finished the outline for *Desert Adventure* shortly past dark the night before, and when she had read it over this morning it had seemed to hold up rather decently; she was, in any case, satisfied with it. But before beginning work on the book, she had decided to make a venture into the desert early this morning. Some first-hand research and preliminary sketching would make composition simpler, and would help give the story more of an authentic flavor.

Jana was in somewhat better spirits than she had been after the call to Harold Klein the previous day, and she supposed it was because she had immersed herself so completely in the making up of the outline for *Desert Adventure* as to be physically exhausted by the time she had finished. When she had gone to bed and immediately to sleep, there had been no dreams, no subconscious intrusion of the affair with Don Harper and . . . the other thing. For the first time in weeks she had gotten a full night's rest.

She walked along the street to a market just opening, and bought a bottle of mineral water, some cheese and crackers for lunch. Then she returned to where she had parked the TR-6 and drove rapidly out of Cuenca Seco, to the east.

She had no difficulty locating the road the desk clerk had pointed out to her on the area map. It was unpaved, narrow, rutted, and as she turned onto it in second gear, the sports car's tires raised thick alkali dust. As early as it was, the sun was a radiating yellow sphere that bathed the surrounding desert in hot, shimmering luster.

Nothing moved on the barren reaches, and as she drove deeper into them Jana had the brief, disquieting thought that she was traveling across a landscape void of life, of movement of any kind—an explorer set down alone on an alien world long dead. And then, on her left, she saw a small covey of Gambel's quail scurrying into a thick clump of mesquite to take refuge from the gathering heat—and overhead, a red-tailed hawk gliding smoothly against the lush blue backdrop—and she smiled ironically, thinking: City-bred girls, not to mention professional writers, who keep having profound literary thoughts are most definitely pains in the ass. Far larger pains in the ass than publishers like Ross Phalen, to be sure.

Three

The dark blue rented Buick Electra passed the intersection of the state highway and the county road leading to Cuenca Seco at four minutes past eight. Harry Vollyer shifted his weight lightly on the passenger side of the front seat, yawned, and said, "We're almost there."

Di Parma nodded silently, hands firm on the wheel, eyes unblinking as he watched the retreating ribbon of the highway. Vollyer looked at him fondly. Livio was all business today, just the way he should be; hell, he hadn't even called his wife before they left the motel that morning—and that fact filled Vollyer with satisfaction. Di Parma was a good boy when the chips were down, when the job was close at hand, and you could count on him not to make mistakes, not to let personal matters interfere. A good kid, all right. Damn, just a fine kid.

Smiling, Vollyer leaned forward and withdrew the small black leather case from beneath the seat. He lifted it onto his lap, worked the catches. Inside, wrapped in chamois, were two Smith & Wesson Centennial Model 40 snub-nosed revolvers, .38 caliber; and a modified Remington XP-100, chambered for the Remington .221 Fireball and mounted with a Bushnell 1.3X Phantom scope. The latter weapon looked like nothing so much as one of those ray-gun blasters Flash Gordon used to carry in the movie serials Vollyer had seen as a youth, but for all its ludicrous appearance, he was inordinately proud of the gun, of its capabilities; it was the best long-range handgun-scope combination made, as far as he was concerned, and he had put in long hours practicing with it, mastering the difficult cross-arm method of accurate shooting. He had had the Remington for more than two years now, and he had had occasion to use it only once on a job—in a suburb of Kansas City, eleven months ago. But he carried it on each assignment nonetheless. He liked to be well prepared for any situation he might encounter, any unexpected occurrence, any potential emergency. That was why he was one of the best in the country, and why he commanded the kind of fee he did; when you brought in Vollyer, you were guaranteed results—one hundred percent.

He let his fingers caress the rough-textured grip of the Remington for a moment; then, quickly, he removed the twin .38s and refastened the case, sliding it under the seat again. He handed one of the belly-guns, butt first, across to Di Parma, watched as Livio took it, dropped it into the pocket of his suit coat without taking his eyes from the road. Vollyer put the other weapon into the pocket of his own jacket, an off-white cashmere, and peered ahead through the windshield.

Even with the smoke-tinted sunglasses he wore, the reflected glare from the already bright-hot desert sun irritated the sensitive membranes of his eyes. He wondered, as he had begun to do of late, if he needed glasses, and he made a mental note to get in to see an optometrist as soon as they got back home. In a profession like his, perfect vision was vital; you didn't want to screw around where your eyes were concerned.

The buildings of the roadside oasis appeared as faint specks in the distance, gained size, took on discernible dimensions. They were nearing the access road. Automatically, Di Parma took his foot off the accelerator, slowing, as Vollyer studied the oasis.

"No cars," Vollyer said.

"We go?"

"We go."

They turned onto the access road, proceeding slowly. Di Parma asked, "How do we work it?"

"Stop the car off on the side," Vollyer told him. "I'll go inside. You check the rest rooms there, on the right, and then go around and look into the cabin in back, where he lives. If he's alone, and if the highway is clear when you come inside, we make the hit."

"And if he's not alone?"

"We get something to drink and walk out," Vollyer said. "We drive south a couple of towns, get a motel, and come back again tomorrow morning."

"Okay."

Di Parma took the Buick up near the rest rooms and shut off the engine. The two of them got out. Wordlessly, Di Parma moved away toward the lattice-fronted building. Vollyer watched him for a moment, nodding, pleased; then, straightening his jacket, he walked quickly across to the screen door, opened it with his shoulder, and stepped inside the café.

The tables, the lunch counter were deserted. The target was behind the counter, cutting pie into wedges. He looked up, put on a professional smile, and Vollyer returned it.

"Morning," the target said.

"Morning," Vollyer answered cheerfully. He moved several steps into the room, his eyes searching it without seeming to do so. He noticed a door partially ajar at the far end of the room, apparently leading to a storeroom, and he walked casually in that direction. He put his head around the half-open door. Storeroom, all right. Stacked cartons. Cot pushed up against the wall beneath an open window. Empty. Vollyer turned and went up to the lunch counter.

The target was frowning. "Looking for something, mister?"

"The john," Vollyer said apologetically. He was the picture of guilelessness.

"Outside," the target told him.

"Oh. Well, thanks."

"Something I can get for you?"

"A glass of milk," Vollyer said. "Nice and cold."

"Coming up."

Vollyer leaned against the counter and watched the target open a refrigerator unit, take out a bottle of fresh milk, pour from it into a tumbler. The bottle went back into the refrigerator, and the tumbler was set before Vollyer on the counter top. He lifted it, tasted, drank deeply. There was nothing like a cold glass of milk in the morning, especially on a hot morning like this one.

The door opened and Di Parma came inside. He crossed to where Vollyer stood, looked at the target, and then said, "Okay."

"No cars?"

"Nothing."

"Clean in here," Vollyer said. "Let's get it done."

The two men backed off several steps, and their hands went down to the pockets of their jackets. The target had his mouth open to ask Di Parma if he wanted anything, but when he saw the expressions on the faces of the two men, he pressed his lips

40

together. His eyes narrowed, and his forehead wrinkled into deep horizontal lines.

Vollyer and Di Parma took out their guns.

The target made a half-step backward, involuntarily, and his buttocks came up hard against the refrigerator unit. His eyes bulged with understanding, and a thin stream of saliva worked its way out over his lower lip and trailed down along his chin. "Oh Jesus," he said. "Oh Jesus."

The two guns were steady on him, and he couldn't run, there was no place for him to go. He knew he was going to die, and the knowledge released his sphincter muscles; the odor was strong and sour in the hot, still room.

"No," he said, "no, there's some kind of mistake."

"No mistake," Vollyer said quietly.

"Listen, please, they promised me it was all right. They said I could get out; they said nothing would happen. Listen, I'm clear, I'm out of it, I never said a word, I'm no fink. Listen, don't you understand? For Christ's sake!"

"All right, Livio," Vollyer said.

"No!" the target screamed. "No, no, no, no!"

They shot him six times, three times each, the bullets transcribing a five-inch radius on his upper torso. The target died on his feet, the way he was supposed to die, without making another sound.

Four

Lennox finished stacking crates of tinned goods against the near wall of the storage basement, and rubbed sweat from his eyes with the back of one arm. It was close in there, the air thick with fine particles of dust. The back of his throat felt hot and parched.

He tried to work saliva around inside his mouth, but the ducts seemed to have dried up. A spasm of brittle coughing seized him, and he pushed away from the wall to stand in the middle of the still-cluttered room. His mind felt sluggish, and yet somehow claustrophobic. He had an irrational impulse to rush headlong into one of the walls and pound it with his fists. He wanted to cry. The need to vent the deep brooding futility in some tangible way, to rid himself of the pressure building in heavy waves within the shell of him, was almost overpowering.

He thought: What's happening to me? Why can't I get straight with myself any more?

He dragged air into his lungs in open-mouthed suckings, and the paroxysm of coughing subsided. The impression of crushing entrapment retreated with it, and he felt a little better, a little more in control. His hand trembled only slightly when he raised it to wipe away the fresh sheen of sweat on his forehead.

Phyllis, you bitch, he thought.

And then he wondered if Perrins would let him have a beer. Christ, he needed one; his throat was so dry it was abrasively sore. Well, why wouldn't Perrins let him have one? He was working for wages, wasn't he? If he couldn't get one gratis, then let the bastard take it out of his salary.

Lennox drew a shuddering breath and moved slowly to the set of stairs. He climbed them, working the rough edge of his tongue over his lips, and pushed the trap door up; its hinges were new, oiled, silent. Once in the storeroom, he lowered the trap, stepped around the cartons toward the door leading into the café—a soft-moving man by nature, creating no sound on his rubber-soled shoes.

He heard Perrins' voice just before he reached the door. "Listen," it said, "don't you understand? For Christ's sake!"

The tone, the inflection, of those words caused Lennox to pull up next to the door, concealed by it but close enough so that he could lean forward and look around it into the café. He did that curiously, cautiously. He saw Perrins standing there behind the lunch counter, face the color of buttermilk, and he saw two neatly dressed men positioned in front of the counter, partially turned away from him. But their faces were clear in profile, hard and impassive, faces carved in stone, and he heard one of them say "All right, Livio," and he saw Perrins put up his hands as if to ward off a blow, heard him begin screaming "No!" again and again. Lennox saw the guns then, for the first time, saw them

42

and understood, in that fraction of a second before the room became filled with smoke and explosive sound, just what kind of scene was being enacted before him.

He watched in a kind of numbed horror as the deafening echo of the gunshots faded and red blossoms appeared on the front of Perrins' white shirt, trailing down like thickly obscene tear streams over the white apron, the white trousers. Perrins stopped jerking with the impact of the bullets and stood very still for a long, uncertain moment—and then he fell, like a tree, like a small and not particularly significant tree cut down by a woodsman's saw, straight, rigid, toppling sideways, disappearing with a sound that was not very loud at all.

The two men put their guns away, and Lennox watched one of them—the fat one—nod and motion to the other, watched that one move across to the door, look out through the window. The fat one was smiling. He went over to the counter, wiped off a half-filled glass of milk with a pocket handkerchief, and then looked down at the slats behind. He was still smiling when he straightened up again.

Lennox pulled his head back. He wanted to vomit. *Cold blood, they shot him down, killers and they, God what if, search they'll search and they'll find me and they'll, oh God God God*

He shook his head, and shook it again. No. No! He had to get out of there, they couldn't find him, he had to get away from there. His head swiveled wildly, and his eyes touched the open window, the window, and beyond—the desert.

Slowly he backed away, staring at the door, and the sweat broke and ran like water from skin blisters the length of his body. Cheeks gray-white, hands palsied, he reached the window, swung one leg over the sill, and nobody came through the door. The other leg, soft now, hurry, hurry, and he was outside, shoes sibilant on gravel, careful, moving away, moving to safety, the desert out there big and empty, hot, the sun spilling fire down on the grotesque cacti, the spindly brush, the strange and awesome formations of rock—waiting for him.

Run, Lennox.

Run!

Five

Di Parma said, "All clear," and stepped away from the window.

Vollyer brushed a speck of something from the sleeve of his cashmere jacket and went over to join him at the door. They passed through the fly screen, letting it bang shut behind them, the sound like a faint, tardy echo of the gunshots a few moments earlier. Neither of them looked back.

They walked out from under the shade of the wooden awning into the white radiance of the sun. Vollyer blinked rapidly against the hot, strong glare which penetrated the smoky lens of his sunglasses; he was going to have to see an optometrist, all right. Nothing to worry about, of course, like with the mild ulcer—all part of the game—but you still had to be careful, you still had to observe the basic rules.

When they reached the car, Vollyer started quickly around to the passenger side. He had gotten to the rear deck when Di Parma said sharply, "Harry!"

Vollyer stopped, turned, and Di Parma was pointing off toward the stretch of desert behind the café, visible between there and the rest rooms. The harsh light made Vollyer's eyes sting as he followed the extension of Di Parma's arm—and then he saw what Livio was pointing at, on high ground a few hundred yards distant.

There was somebody out there.

Somebody running.

Di Parma said, "What the hell?" as Vollyer hurried up beside him. "What the hell, Harry?"

Vollyer did not answer. Behind the sunglasses, his eyes glittered in their watered sockets. The runner was gone now, vanished on the other side of the high section—but Vollyer's quick, sharp mind had registered several facts from his single prolonged glimpse: white shirt, long sleeves rolled up, tails pulled out and fluttering over dark blue trousers; lean, agile, but not particularly young, he didn't move like a kid; long, shaggy dark hair.

Vollyer stared intently at the empty, rugged landscape. No flash of white, no movement. The terrain grew steadily rougher in the distance, sprinkled thickly with formations of rock, heavy with prickly pear, creosote bush, giant saguaro. There were hundreds of places to hide out there—and conversely, the irregularity of the land made an effective shield to cover continued flight.

Di Parma moistened his lips, put his right hand into the pocket of his jacket. "Where did he come from? Christ, we checked everything here."

"He wasn't running for the exercise," Vollyer said. "He came from here, all right."

"You think he saw us make the hit?"

"Maybe."

"Harry, we've got to go after him."

"Soft now, soft," Vollyer said. "There's no cause to panic. You take the car and pull it around behind the café, up close against the building so it can't be seen from the highway. Then you go out there and see if you can find him. I don't think there's much chance of it now, but maybe you'll get lucky. Fifteen minutes, and then you come back. Understood?"

Di Parma nodded. "Where'll you be?"

"Back inside."

"What for?"

"Move, Livio, move."

Di Parma hesitated for a moment; then he brought his lips into a flat line and slipped in under the wheel. Vollyer was already moving across the sun-baked lot, pulling on a pair of thin doeskin gloves, when Di Parma jerked the Buick into gear and drove it around behind the café.

A little spice to liven up a routine assignment, Vollyer thought as he pulled open the fly screen and stepped inside again. The game takes on added dimensions, added excitement. His eyes still glittered, and there was a half-smile on his plump mouth.

Moving quickly, not looking at the buzzing ring of flies circling hungrily above the lunch counter, he reversed the placard in one of the windows so that it read *Closed* facing outward; then he pulled the shades down and switched off all the lights at a fuse box located to one side of the counter. He set the bolt lock on the door, crossed through the half-gloom—his steps echoing hollowly in the heavy, oppressive silence—to where a pay phone was located on the rear wall. He cut the cord on it with a penknife from his pocket, put the knife away, and entered the storeroom.

His eyes prowled the interior briefly before he went to the open window and looked out. He could see the Buick pulled in close to the rear wall of the building, and when his gaze swept over the desert Di Parma was moving along the high ground in quick, jerky steps. Nothing else moved on the radiant terrain.

Vollyer turned from the window, and as he did so, his eyes drifted down to the cot which was pressed up against the wall beneath it. The edge of something, a small bag, protruded slightly from under the cot. He knelt and pulled the bag out and zippered it open: soiled laundry, a shaving kit, a few miscellaneous items. And, at the bottom, a small flat manila envelope.

The envelope contained a full-color portrait photograph, 5x9 size, of a man and a woman. They were smiling at one another, hands entwined, and in the background was a table piled with brightly wrapped presents, a crystal punchbowl containing a burgundy-colored liquid and slices of citrus fruit, a double-tiered anniversary cake. The woman was slim, fair, with blond hair streaked in silver; the man was lean, dark-haired, vaguely handsome. He was the right size and coloring to be the one running out on the desert.

Vollyer turned the photograph over. Across the top, in light blue fountain ink, was written: *The Lennoxes, Two Down and Forty-Eight to Go.* Below that was a photographer's stamp—Damon Studio—but no listing of city or state.

He put the portrait in his pocket, rezipped the bag, and returned it beneath the cot. Then he straightened, glancing around again. After a moment he went to the large stack of cartons on the far side of the storeroom—and behind it, he found the lowered trap door.

There was no need for him to raise the door. He knew what would be beneath it, and he knew now where he and Di Parma had made their mistake. Well, no, not a mistake exactly, how could you figure the target putting up a transient just prior to their arrival? They had been careful; it was just one of those things. All part of the game.

Vollyer retraced his steps to the window, climbed out ponderously, and pulled the sash down after him. When he turned,

he saw that Di Parma was coming back now, running awkwardly across the stark earth. He went down to the corner of
the building and looked at the highway, and it was still void of
traffic; then he moved out to meet Di Parma.

Livio's face was dust-streaked, and there was a three-cor-
nered tear in the sleeve of his suit coat. He was tired and
sweating and strung up tight. He said grimly, unnecessarily,
"There's no sign of the son of a bitch."

Vollyer inclined his head speculatively. The fact that Di
Parma had not flushed Lennox—the odds were good that it *was*
this Lennox—indicated that the runner had kept on running,
that he hadn't chosen to hide in the rocks, waiting to make his
way back to the oasis after Vollyer and Di Parma had gone. Of
course, there was still the possibility that he *had* been hiding out
there, was at this moment hiding, and that Livio had overlooked
him; but Vollyer knew something about human nature, and as
far as he was concerned, the runners would always run, the hid-
ers would always hide, the fighters would always fight. People
reacted in the same way time after time; they were predictable.
This Lennox was obviously not a fighter, and he was obviously
not a hider; if he had been either one, he would have remained
out of sight in the storeroom or in that cellar until he had the
place to himself—and then he would have gone directly to the
cops to volunteer help or he would have gathered up his belong-
ings and slipped out of there quickly and quietly. But instead, he
had run; and that made him a runner, and the bet a safe one that
he was *still* running.

This fact made him no less dangerous to the two of them;
but the way Vollyer saw it, he and Di Parma had time—just how
much time he could not be sure, but enough so that he was not
particularly worried, not yet. In fact, the challenge of the situation seemed to stimulate him in an oddly perverse way; it was at
times like this that the game really became intriguing, when you
were forced to use every bit of knowledge and strategy at your
disposal in order to emerge the winner, again the winner.

He told Di Parma what he had done inside the café, what he
had found there, how it figured to give them some time and an
edge to find this Lennox. He told him not to worry. He told him
things were going to be just fine.

Di Parma was not convinced. He said, "Harry, if that guy gets to the cops—"

"He's not going to get to the cops."

"We'll never find him out there."

"Maybe not."

"Then what do we do?"

Vollyer said, "We go take a look at that map we've got in the car."

Six

The rock formation was a small, oblique confusion of wind- and sand-eroded granite, situated some two hundred yards to the south of the little-used dirt road, six and a half miles out from Cuenca Seco. At one end of the formation, a tapered flat-topped extremity pointed accusingly at the sky; in the shadow of this, Jana finished spreading out a heavy blanket from the trunk of the TR-6 and looked out over the desert.

In the distance, an irregular blue coloration, darker than the sky itself, appeared like a gigantic wet spot across the horizon— the reflection of the bright blue sky off the surface of a highway, the most common of all desert mirages. Except for the wavering of distant mountains in the blur of heat, movement seemed not to exist. Less than twenty feet away, a giant saguaro stood tall and majestic, like a patriarch overseeing his vast holdings, its accordion-pleated trunk dotted with holes made by Gila woodpeckers in search of insect larvae. To the left, dense stands of rabbit bush carpeted a wide swath of the desert floor in a brilliant mantle of gold; to the right, several clusters of ocotillo, their thorny stalks reminiscent of bundles of sticks tied at the bottom, grew in regulated rows, as if planted by the hand of man. There was reddish soil and bluish basalt rock and small black lava cones; there were natural bridges, arches, mounds, knobs, shapes of every description—a fairyland or a nightmare, depending on the direction of the viewer's imagination. And to

Jana's continuing surprise, there were few totally barren patches, and no sand dunes at all.

As she watched, a sudden flurry of activity occurred almost directly in front of her. A small dun-colored roadrunner, moving with great speed, flashed out of a clump of mesquite, raced thirty or forty yards across the rocky earth, and then struck with a slashing motion of its long sharp bill; its feathered head jerked up a moment later, a gecko lizard held firmly by the head, struggling in vain. The roadrunner carried its prey off quickly, vanishing as rapidly as it had appeared.

Jana repressed a shudder and went to where she had parked the Triumph a few yards away. From inside, she took the handbag with her sketch pad, notebook, and writing and drawing implements—and the sack containing the food and water she had purchased in Cuenca Seco. She arranged these on the blanket and sat down in the exact center of it, Indian fashion, with the sketch pad open across her lap.

Well, she thought, here we are. The wide-open spaces. Nature in the raw. The Wild, Wild West. Beats the stifling, sweating, polluted canyons of New York City all to hell, doesn't it?

Sure it does.

You bet.

She picked up a piece of thick charcoal and began to draw the patriarchal saguaro with rapid, fluid strokes.

Seven

The runner, running:

There, among the pinnacles of rock, the element-polished stone like slick glass beneath his feet, stumbling, falling now and then, the palms of his hands cut by razor-edged chunks of ancient granite. There, looking over his shoulder, eyes afraid, face coated with dry alkali dust through which flowing sweat has created meandering streams. There, emerging from a profusion of rocks momentarily to cross a shallow wash, churning legs digging up small geysers from the sand, half-blind with the sweat and the constant yellow-white glare of the sun. There, among rocks again, knee lancing painfully off a projection of sandstone, elbow scraping another projection, looking over his shoulder again, tripping again, falling again, getting up again, single thought, single purpose.

The labored gasping of his breath, the raging beat of his heart, the hammering pulse of his blood fill the tiny vacuum in which he moves with nightmarish sound, even though he is surrounded by stillness. His body is a mass of twisted nerve ends and small aches, and his eyes are painful under heat-inflamed lids. How much longer can he keep moving? How much further can the blind panic carry him?

Not long, not far. Less than five minutes has elapsed when he falls again, and this time he cannot seem to regain his feet. He kneels on the rough ground, resting forward on his hands, his head hanging down and his mouth open to drink of the burning air. As he crouches there, animal-like, the urgency begins to suddenly die in him—as it had finally died that night he struck Phyllis; exhaustion has dulled the sharp, bright edge of the panic, and the urge to flight is no longer indomitable within his brain.

He mewls for breath until the pace of his heart decelerates, until the blood ceases throbbing in his temples, his ears. Then he turns his body and looks behind him and sees nothing; there is nothing but the rocks and the heat and the desert vegetation. He allows his weight to fall wearily onto his right hip, but the lambent rays of the sun burn his face, burn his neck, and the stones there in the direct shine are like bits of molten metal. He drags himself a few feet distant, to where an arched and delicately fanned sandstone ledge, like a giant ostrich plume, offers shade; it is cooler there, and the intense glare of light diminishes.

Lennox wipes sweat from his aching eyes, and again looks back the way he has come. Emptiness. He does not know how far he has run, or where he is in relation to the oasis, or how long he has been running. His thoughts are sluggish from the grip of terror, from the heat, and he tries to shape them into coherency.

The first thing he thinks of is his overnight bag.

A fresh tremor of fear spirals through him. He knows exactly what is in that bag, he knows the photograph is there, the photograph of Phyllis and him and what is written across the back—Jesus, why hadn't he gotten rid of it a long time ago, what was he trying to do to himself keeping it as he had? If the two men, the killers, searched the storeroom they had found the bag, they had found it and—what? They hadn't seen him running away, had they? They didn't know anybody was there, or they wouldn't have killed Perrins as they had—why *had* they? They hadn't known he was there, maybe they'd think the bag belonged to some customer, forgotten there, articles were always being left at cafés, weren't they? Yes, that is what they would think *if* they searched the storeroom, *if* they found the bag. He shouldn't have panicked like that, he shouldn't have run . . .

Well, he's all right now, he's in control now, and he doesn't have anything to—oh Christ, oh sweet Christ, the police, the cops, they'll come eventually and if the killers didn't find the bag the cops will, the bag and the photograph and his name and maybe he had left his fingerprints there, they would check and they would find out he was wanted, a fugitive, his bag there and Perrins lying behind the lunch counter, murdered, shot, maybe they would think he had killed him! Maybe they would put that up against him, too, and what if they caught him and he couldn't make them believe he was innocent . . . ?

No, no, they won't catch him, he'll get away, he'll get out of this desert, steal a car if he has to, he knows enough about them to be able to hot-wire an ignition. Yes, that's the answer, that's the only answer, because he can't go back, the two killers might still be there, they might have seen him after all and they might be looking for him right now, and even if they were gone the cops might have come, a motorist might have stopped, he can't go back, he has to keep running, he has to get out.

Think, Lennox, plan your moves, figure out what to do next.

And he thinks—and remembers. He remembers the furnacelike interior of the bus the day before, and the desert landscape rushing past the dust-stippled window, and the junction of the county road extending to the east, and the sign in the fork there, the sign: CUENCA SECO 16 mi. There is a town in the vicinity then, sixteen miles from the highway at that point, but is that county road straight, does the town lie due east or to the south or to the north? How far is he from the town now, from the county road, from any other road that might lead to safety? East by northeast, that has to be the direction, and he looks up into the burning sky, looks for the sun climbing slowly toward the zenith. Rises in the east, sets in the west, rises in the east, there, over there, east by northeast.

Lennox gets shakily to his feet, stands for a moment in the shade of the overhanging arch. He drags fluttering breath into his quieted lungs, shields his eyes, looking up, and steps out. The sun covers him with a canopy of fire as he begins hurrying once again over the rocky terrain, toward the glowing ball, keeping to cover, looking furtively over his shoulder as he has done so many times before.

The runner: still running.

Eight

Vollyer had the area map he and Di Parma had picked up the day before spread open on the Buick's front seat; he scanned it without haste, his thick forefinger touching the long curve of the highway, the location of the oasis at the head of the curve, the black dot that was Cuenca Seco, the county road leading there, the dead-end road that—from above the town—led to the southwest and then hooked gradually to the south. His moving finger followed the thin line that was the dead-end road, beginning to end, back again.

He thought: If he knows the area, he'll make directly for the town, for this Cuenca Seco. If he doesn't know it, he'll run more or less in a straight line to put as much distance between himself and the oasis as he can. Either way, the odds are good that he'll hit this dead end at some point on a three- or four-mile radius.

Vollyer was aware that several other possibilities existed as well: the area to the south, southeast and part of the southwest was unbroken desert, and Lennox could conceivably become lost out there, wandering aimlessly; he could move to the north, either by design or by accident, and eventually encounter the county road—although due north from there, deep canyons bordered the road on the near side; he could arc back, again either by design or by accident, and reach the intrastate highway above or below the oasis. But Vollyer had to play the percentages, because he and Di Parma had no way of covering every one of the potentialities, and the percentages had Lennox, runner that he surely was, moving east or northeast—and coming on that dead-end trail.

Strategy, that was the name of this particular aspect of the game: move and countermove, anticipate your opponent, put yourself inside his mind. And you had to be bold, you had to take the offensive; only the losers played defense, only the losers failed to employ tactical gambits. You had to make your decision, and quickly, without reservations. That was the winning way, the only way.

Vollyer made his decision.

He refolded the map, returned it to the glove compartment, and went to where Di Parma was stationed at the corner of the building, watching the highway. He said, "Still clear?"

"So far," Di Parma told him. His large hands were nervous, agitated, like grotesque and misshapen wings. "Harry, when are we going to get out of here?"

"Pretty soon now."

"What are we waiting for?"

"Stay cool, Livio."

Vollyer turned again and moved quickly past an old dirty-white Chevrolet to the small cabin. The door was locked. He broke a pane of glass with the butt of the .38 and slipped inside. He spent four minutes in there, the first thirty seconds to locate the second telephone and cut its wires. When he came out again, he had a pair of Japanese-made, high-powered binoculars, a pocket compass, and a small canvas knapsack. He tossed the binoculars into the rear seat of the Buick, looked down at Di Parma; when Livio nodded continued clearance, Vollyer crossed to the storeroom window, slid it up, and climbed back over the sill.

Three minutes this time. The knapsack was now filled with six plastic bottles of water, a few pieces of fresh fruit, and some key-open tins of meat and fish. He took the sack to the Buick, dropped it onto the back seat with the binoculars.

Di Parma said urgently, "Car coming!"

Vollyer hurried to the corner of the building. A dusty late-model Ford was approaching along the access road, dust like rolling clouds of smoke billowing up on either side of it. There were no official markings on the car. As it drew closer, he could see that there were two people inside, a man and a woman, the man driving.

"Goddamn it!" Di Parma said.

"Easy. They'll leave when they see it's closed up."

"What if they don't? What if they're out of gas or something, and they come nosing around back here?"

Vollyer looked at him sharply. Come on, he thought, don't go rattled on me now. He said, "Just keep your head."

"But what if they come around here?" Di Parma insisted.

"Then we kill them," Vollyer said, and shrugged.

The Ford pulled onto the parking area and drew up near the pumps. Vollyer could no longer see it. He heard one of the doors slam in the hot quiet morning, and then only heavy silence. Standing next to him, Di Parma was sweating profusely; but Vollyer's own face was dry, and his eyes were flat and hard. He listened intently, watching, waiting, his right hand on the .38 revolver in his jacket pocket.

A long minute passed, and then the car-door sound was repeated. The Ford's engine made a loud, growling roar, a sign of the driver's displeasure, and there was the harsh grating of tires spinning on gravel; the car came into view again, moving onto the access road, a moment later making the turn south on the highway.

Di Parma said, "Christ!"

Vollyer gave him an indulgent smile. "Come on, it's time to move out."

At the Buick, Di Parma looked into the rear seat at the items Vollyer had taken from the cabin and the café. "What's all this, Harry?"

"Insurance," Vollyer told him.

"I don't follow."

"You will, Livio, you will."

Di Parma drove out from behind the café and along the access road to the now-deserted highway. Vollyer told him to turn north, and then leaned back and closed his eyes. There were faint liquid sun patterns behind the lids, pulsating, and the balls themselves felt too large for their sockets. Damned bright glare.

He hoped his aim wouldn't be affected if he had the opportunity to use the Remington a little later on.

Nine

Brackeen was half-dozing in his partitioned office when Forester radioed in shortly before noon.

He was in good spirits. The hangover of the day before had all but disappeared by five o'clock, when he'd gone off duty, and four beers before supper had chased the last remnants of it. Later, he'd made up with Marge—damn, but she was still fine in bed, she was a hell of a lot better and hotter at forty than any of those young whores he'd had in Kehoe City—and he'd gotten a good night's sleep for a change. This morning had been quiet; he'd done half an hour's paperwork, looked into a minor vandalism complaint, and spent most of the rest of the time leafing through circulars from the FBI and State Police. When Bradshaw, the clerk and radio man, came in to tell him Forester was calling, he had been working up a mild thirst sleepily thinking of Sullivan's and the upcoming lunch hour.

He got ponderously out of his chair, his soft belly swaying, and followed Bradshaw out to the PBX unit in the main room of the substation. He scratched himself sourly. Forester was due in pretty soon, and him calling now meant he'd gotten onto something—Christ only knew what piddly-ass thing it was—and that in turn meant that Brackeen was probably going to get a late lunch.

He sighed and took the hand mike Bradshaw proffered. He said, "Brackeen."

Forester's voice said excitedly, amid gentle static, "Listen, we've got a murder."

A half-formed yawn died on Brackeen's mouth. "A what?"

"A murder, a murder!"

"The hell you say. Where?"

"Del's Oasis, out on the Intrastate."

"Who's dead?"

"Al Perrins, the guy bought Del out about six months back."

"How do you know it's murder?"

"Well, Jesus Christ, he's got six bullet holes in his chest," Forester snapped. "What else would you call it?"

Oh, these goddamn snotty bright-faces. "Any sign of who did it?"

"No. But I haven't had the chance to go over the place yet."

"You find Perrins yourself?"

"Yeah. I was cruising the area, and I thought I'd stop in for a quick Coke to take the edge off the heat, like I sometimes do."

A Coke, Brackeen thought. You silly bastard, you.

Forester went on, "But the place was dark, all shut up, and the *Closed* sign was in the window. It didn't figure for Perrins to be closed up on a weekday like this, and I thought maybe he was sick or something. I went around back, to that cabin he lives in, and the door glass had been broken in. The place was empty, but the phone wires had been cut and it had been gone through a little; hard to tell if anything was taken. I found the rear window to the café storeroom open, and crawled in to have a look around. Perrins was lying in a pool of blood behind the lunch counter."

They're always lying in a pool of blood, Brackeen thought. If you looked at ten thousand violent-homicide reports made by bright-faces like Forester, you'd find that in nine thousand of them the victims were found quote lying in a pool of blood unquote. He said, "All right, hang loose. I'll be out there in about twenty minutes."

Forester didn't respond immediately, and Brackeen took satisfaction in the knowledge that the idea didn't appeal to him. Finally Forester said, "Maybe you'd better get the county people and State Police out here."

"Sure," Brackeen said. "Twenty minutes, Forester."

He gave the mike back to Bradshaw and told him to put the news of the homicide on the air to the county sheriff's office—and to the Highway Patrol office—in Kehoe City. Then he lo-

Panic!

cated his Stetson and went out to where his cruiser was parked in front. He drove very fast, the way he liked to drive, windows down and the hot, thick air blowing against the textured leather of his face; the siren, shrill and undulatory, turned heads and cleared away the few cars which dotted the streets of Cuenca Seco and the county road beyond.

Brackeen felt a faint, half-forgotten stir of excitement as he sent the cruiser hurtling along the heat-spotted road. There had been a time when the commission of a crime such as murder set the juices flowing warm and deep within him, a time when his position as a representative of the law—of Justice—had inspired grim determination, a need to protect the citizenry from the lawless and the desperate. That time was long dead now—let the bright-faces inflate themselves with righteous vigor—but still, he could not help being interested in what Forester had had to report. A murder, any violent death, was an unheard-of occurrence in Cuenca Seco and environs, the last one having taken place in 1962 and that a husband-wife thing resulting from a protracted drought and flaring tempers, and a revolver kept too handy and too well supplied with bullets; in fact, any kind of overt crime was so rare as to be virtually nonexistent. There was no challenge to the job of law enforcement in Cuenca Seco, and that was the way Brackeen wanted it; but the fact remained that he had been a trained city cop once, dedicated in his own way, and a murder was something he couldn't take with his usual indifference. That was why he was going to the scene personally, instead of letting Forester and Lydell and the State Highway Patrol have it all to themselves . . .

Forester was waiting for him under the wooden awning in front when Brackeen arrived at Del's Oasis. He had a slender, athletic build and ash-blond hair and intense eyes the color of forged steel; in spite of the heat, his khaki uniform was fresh and crisp except for patches of dust on the trousers that he had apparently gotten from climbing through the storeroom window. He stood officiously, unmoving, watching the approach of his immediate superior without expression.

Brackeen parked his cruiser behind Forester's, stepped out into the wash of heat from the perpendicular desert sun. He pushed his hat back and crossed under the awning. Forester nodded curtly, his sharp eyes now registering disapproval at what they beheld; he said, "The county and state people coming?"

"They'll be along," Brackeen answered. He moved past Forester and entered the oppressive warmth of the café. The shades had been pulled up and the lights were on; the air was thick with flies, buzzing angrily, circling. Brackeen went to the lunch counter and around behind it. Forester had apparently found a blanket somewhere and had used it to cover Perrins; the dead man lay sprawled on his back, one leg twisted under him, arms outflung. Wedging his big buttocks against the shelving beneath the counter, Brackeen knelt and drew the blanket back. Pool of blood, hell; there wasn't much blood at all. Well, that figured. But the guy had been shot six times, all right, you could count each one of the scorched holes in the dark-spotted front of Perrins' shirt.

Brackeen frowned slightly. Each of the holes was on the upper chest, left side and middle, over and around the heart, with maybe five inches between the two outside wounds. Some nice shooting—or some careful shooting. He replaced the blanket, stood up, and came out from behind the counter.

Forester was watching him from just inside the screen door. Brackeen looked at him and asked, "You go over the premises?"

"Naturally."

"Find anything?"

Forester hesitated, and then shrugged, and then said, tight-lipped, "I think so."

"What?"

"In the storeroom."

Brackeen followed him across and into the storeroom. Near the window, a cot was pressed against the wall; on top of the cot, the handle of a broom wedged through two leather carry loops, was a battered overnight bag, zippered open.

Forester said, "Found that bag under the cot. Probably prints on it."

"Probably," Brackeen agreed dryly.

"Clothing and some other stuff inside. Clothes are too small to belong to Perrins."

"All right," Brackeen said. "Let's hear it."

"Hear what?"

"Your theory."

Forester smiled grimly. "I figure the bag belongs to a transient, a guy Perrins put up for the night, maybe had do some work around here. The sign up on the roof is freshly painted."

Well, the bright-face was observant, at least. Brackeen said, "And so you think this transient shot Perrins."

"That's right."

"Where did he get the gun?"

"Could have had it with him. Maybe stolen."

"And the motive?"

"Robbery—what else?"

"Register cleaned out, is it?"

"Well, no, but that doesn't have to mean much."

The hell it doesn't, Brackeen thought. But he said only, "Why not?"

Forester said, "Maybe the transient didn't intend to kill Perrins. Maybe he only wanted to intimidate him with the gun. But Perrins could have tried to take it away from him, and the transient panicked and emptied all six loads into Perrins' chest. Then he ran, so damned shook up he forgot his bag and the money. Panic does that to a man."

What the hell do you know about panic? Brackeen thought with sudden, vicious anger. You son of a bitching wet-nose, what do you know about anything? Your theory is piss-poor, it's got holes shot all through it. I was studying law enforcement when you were still crapping your diapers, and even on my first day on the force I could have told you no man in panic ever put six bullets within five inches of each other in another man's chest. Whoever this transient is, if he exists at all, had nothing much, if anything at all, to do with Perrins' death. You want to know what this thing looks like? It looks like a professional hit, a contract job, six slugs placed like that is the kind of bull's-eye shooting hired sluggers go in for—but you're such a smart-assed one you don't even see it for your own self-importance.

Brackeen's eyes smoldered as he looked at Forester—but then, as abruptly as it had come, the anger drained out of him. The old, comfortable apathy returned at once, and he thought: Oh Christ, what's the use? As contemptuous as he was of Forester, he remembered that he did not want to antagonize him, not with his job hanging the way it was; and the quickest way to give a bright-face like that a potentially disastrous hard-on for him would be to explode his nice pat little theory.

But a small perversity made him press it just a little. "How do you explain the place being shut up the way it was? And the phone wires being cut? A guy jammed up with panic doesn't take the time to do those things."

Forester had an answer for that. "He could have done them first, maybe forced Perrins to close up at the point of the gun. He probably figured to tie Perrins up, and leave him here in the closed café. That would buy him enough time to get away."

"Was the front door locked?"

"From the inside. He went out through the storeroom window, looks like—same way I got in."

"How do you think he left here?"

"On foot."

"Where? Up to the highway?"

"Sure, looking to hitch a ride."

"Did Perrins have a car?"

"Naturally."

"Is it here now?"

"Around back, by the cabin."

"Then why didn't this transient take the car?"

"Well, maybe he planned to," Forester said, and there was anger in his voice now. "But it's not running. I talked to Perrins yesterday, and he was working on it in his spare time. Listen, what's the idea of all these questions? If you've got a better idea about what happened here today, why don't you say so?"

Brackeen subsided. If he pushed it any further, Forester was liable to get peeved and put Lydell down on him for fair. Lydell was one of these Bible-thumping bigots, and a political hack on top of that, and he demanded harmony in his office and between his men—not to mention what he considered strict moral and ethical behavior; he wasn't particularly fond of Brackeen to begin with, and it would not take much prodding to open his eyes all the way and then to make that final cut of the thread. So the hell with it; Lydell could chew up the bright-face's presumptions, if he cared to, though he was such a goddamned incompetent that that wasn't likely. Or maybe the State Highway Patrol investigators, who were pretty facile if too bloody plodding for Brackeen's taste, might deflate him a little later on. In any case, the thing for Brackeen to do was to keep his mouth shut and fade into the background, especially when Lydell arrived.

He said, "No, I don't have a better idea, Forester. I'm sorry; I didn't mean to start interrogating you."

Forester looked at him steadily for a moment, and then made a magnanimous gesture that almost contemptuously reversed their roles. "Sure," he said. "Sure, that's all right."

They went outside again, and Forester resumed his former position under the awning, waiting for the county units and the Highway Patrol, ready to send any arriving and curious citizens on their way. Brackeen left him and wandered around behind the café. The ground was rough and graveled there, but he could make out what looked to be faint tire impressions up close beside the rear wall. So it could be this transient of Forester's had a car, he thought. Or it could be Perrins had some broad out recently to spend the night.

Or it could be a professional slugger parked his car around here just this morning, for one reason or another.

He went to the cabin and stepped inside. It had been gone through, for a fact, but the job had been a methodical one. Guys under panic, or pressure of any kind, didn't conduct searches as neat and businesslike as this one had obviously been; guys looking for money, valuables, were always in a hurry, always sloppy. The only ones who were careful, unhurried, were the professionals, after a particular item or items. Transient, Forester's skinny ass. A pro—one, possibly two. Why? Well, maybe Perrins had a past. Maybe Perrins had been hooked in with the Organization, or some independent outfit, in one way or another. Maybe Perrins had been dangerous to somebody.

Any way you wanted it, a professional hit.

And the hell with it.

Brackeen went out and around to the front again, and two county cars and two Highway Patrol cars and an ambulance had arrived from Kehoe City. Lydell was there, fat, sixtyish, as officious as Forester, eyes brightly excited at the prospect of his involvement in a violent death. A man named Hollowell was there, a special investigator attached to the sheriff's office—short, balding, jocular, carrying two camera cases and a large bag which contained, as he made a point of explaining to Brackeen and Forester, the latest in fingerprinting and evidence-gathering equipment. Two plain-clothes State Highway Patrol investigators were there; their names were Gottlieb and Sanchez—which did not particularly endear them to Lydell—and they were both tall and dark and stoic.

All of them went inside and looked at the body, and Forester recounted how he had discovered it and showed them the overnight bag and told them what he thought had happened. Hollowell snapped several photographs of Perrins, from different angles, and then took his fingerprints; Gottlieb signed a release, and the ambulance attendants removed the body for Kehoe City. Sanchez prowled around and Gottlieb prowled around and Hollowell began lifting prints off suitable surfaces in the café and storeroom. Forester had Lydell in one corner, talking animatedly to him. Brackeen sat on one of the stools at the lunch counter and smoked and tried to look alert; he was wishing he had a cold beer.

Gottlieb and Sanchez went out and poked through the cabin in the rear and came back and said nothing to anyone. They ignored Forester when he tried to give them his theory again. Hollowell discovered a couple of clear latents off the handles of the overnight bag, and another off the window frame in the storeroom; the prints did not belong to Perrins. He told Lydell, and Gottlieb and Sanchez, that he would run them through the state and FBI files as soon as they got back to Kehoe City.

Brackeen stood it as long as he could, and then he went to Lydell and respectfully told him that he thought it was about time he returned to Cuenca Seco. Lydell, preoccupied, looking important, agreed that that was a good idea and dismissed him perfunctorily. No one paid any attention to Brackeen when he left.

He drove back to Cuenca Seco and parked the cruiser in front of the substation. The small perversity was with him again. He entered, told Bradshaw he was taking his lunch break, and walked down to Sullivan's. He drank the first beer to Forester and the second to Lydell and the third to Hollowell and the fourth to Gottlieb and Sanchez and the fifth to crime.

He felt lousy.

And for the first time in a long time, he felt curiously empty.

Ten

The sun is fire above, and the rocks are fire below. The heat drains moisture from the tissues of Lennox's body, drying him out like a strip of old leather, swelling his tongue, causing his breathing to fluctuate. It is almost three o'clock now, and the floor of the desert wavers with heat and mirage; midafternoon is the hottest part of the day out here, temperatures soaring to 150 degrees and above, and there is no sound.

The mind wanders.

He is nine years old, walking home from school, and in his right hand he holds clenched two dozen baseball cards which he has traded for that afternoon. He has several Dodgers and this particularly delights him, the Dodgers are his favorite team— Pee Wee Reese and Billy Cox and Carl Furillo; and he has a rare Bob Feller, too.

He walks quickly, because he wants to get home and arrange these cards with the others he has, he is very close to the complete set, perhaps he even has it now with these new acquisitions. He turns the corner, and Tommy Franklin is there, hands on pudgy hips, scowling.

A tremor of fear rushes through him and he stops. "Hey, Lennox," Franklin yells at him, and advances several steps. "You got my baseball cards."

"These are mine," he shouts back. "I traded for them."

"No, they're mine, I was supposed to get 'em first and you butted in and now I want 'em."

"It's not fair, it's not fair . . ."

"You better give me my cards, Lennox. I'll beat you up if you don't give me my cards."

He tries to stand his ground. He tries to tell himself he can lick Tommy Franklin. But the fear is too strong within him. He chokes back the sob that rises in his throat and flings the cards down on the sidewalk—Pee Wee Reese and Billy Cox and Carl Furillo and the rare Bob Feller, scattered out like bright leaves.

And he turns and flees, with Tommy Franklin's derisive laughter ringing in his ears.

He runs all the way home.

How many hours has it been now? Five, six, a dozen? He does not know. He knows only that the skin of his neck and face and arms is painfully blistered, knows only that a burning thirst rages in his throat, knows only that the sun has swollen his eyelids to mere slits and the dusty sweat streaming in is like an acid-based astringent blurring and distorting his vision.

He has no idea where he is, the terrain all looks the same to him, he could be wandering in endless circles and yet he has been following the sun, angling toward it until it climbed to the center of the amethyst sky, and then moving away from it, keeping it at his left shoulder, as it began its descent. East, he knows he has been moving that way even though he has never been much good at directions—east, not in a circle, he is not lost.

And yet—where are the roads? Where is the town? He should have come upon them by now, he should have found help by now, maybe he *is* lost, oh God, maybe he'll never find his way out, maybe he'll die out here with the juices of his life sucked out of him by that monstrous sphere overhead—

The panic rears up inside him again, a flashing burst of it, and he cries out softly between lips that have long ago cracked and bled and dried and cracked and bled again. But the exhaustion, the dehydration of his flesh prevent him from plunging into headlong flight. He stumbles sideways, into a long shadow cast by a protuberance of granite, and clings to the hot stone with clawed fingers until the fear ebbs and leaves him weak and breathless.

The desert shimmers, shimmers, and a memory dances once more across the surface of his mind.

He is seventeen and very drunk. He and some of his friends are drinking beer in the prewar Ford which his father has bought him, road-racing in an abandoned development known as Happy Acres north of town. The radio is playing Presley and Jerry Lee Lewis and Fats Domino, and empty bottles fly periodically out of the open windows, and scrawny little Pete Tamazzi is telling this story about how he got into Nancy Collins the week before, Nancy Collins being a very proper Catholic girl and president of the Student Body and obviously a virgin and obviously intending to stay that way, Pete being full of bullshit as usual and as usual the others urging him on to more and more graphic lies.

He sends the Ford into a sliding curve, and over his shoulder he shouts to Hal Younger, "Crack me another one, bartender."

Hal opens a bottle and starts to pass it forward, and suddenly the interior of the car is filled with eerily flashing red light. He looks up at the rear-view mirror, and laughter dies on his lips and the beer turns sour in his stomach. "Oh Christ!" he says.

The others are looking out through the rear window, and Pete says "Cops" and begins to hiccup.

"Well," Hal says, "we're screwed, guys."

He knows he should stop. The police car is not far behind them, coming fast, the red light swirling hellish shadows over the black weed-tossed development, turning the faces of the boys in the car into demonic caricatures, visions in a nightmare.

He knows he should stop—and yet his beer-numbed thoughts are those of blue uniforms with shiny brass buttons, and small barred cells, and his mother crying and his father shouting. His hands grip the wheel and his foot bears down on the accelerator. The Ford has been modified, bored and stroked, three jugs, Mallory ignition, but it is no match for the new Chryslers the local police are using and he knows it. Still, he can't stop himself, he can't slow down, and now there is the sound of a siren to splinter the night around them, feeding his need to escape, to be free of these sudden pursuers.

He fights the wheel into a turn, gearing down, switching off the headlights. There is a pale moon, but it does not shed enough light by which to see sufficiently. But he knows the crosshatched roads in Happy Acres, he has been here many times with Cassy Sunderland and Karen Akers and with Hal and Pete and the others . . .

"Jack, what are you doing, for God's sake!" Hal shouts.

And Gene Turner's voice: "You can't outrun them, you'll kill us all!"

And Pete's: "Jack, those are cops, they're cops!"

He hears the voices and yet they are meaningless, they do not penetrate the thick haze of desperation which seems to have gained control of him. The Ford spins wildly forward under his guiding hands, rocking, pitching, engine whining, plunging through darkness into darkness, gear down, gear up, skid right, fishtail left, shortcut across that flat grassy stretch, and now he can see the road, the Western Avenue Extension. He looks into the rear-view mirror—and suddenly there are no stabbing white cones seeking out the Ford, no crimson wash to the landscape. He's lost them, he's beaten them, he's won!

Exhilaration sweeps through him. He down-shifts into second as he reaches the Extension, slowing, but instead of turning right, toward town, he turns left and drives two thousand yards and swings down a rutted tractor lane; the lane borders a grassy-banked stream in which he had once picked watercress when he was younger, and there is a small grove of willows there. He takes the Ford in amongst the low-hanging branches, cuts the engine, and the black of the night enfolds them.

He turns to look at the others then, grinning, and their faces seem to shine whitely through the ebon interior of the car. The smile fades. He is looking not at admiration, not at gratitude— he is looking at trembling anger.

"You crazy bastard!" Hal says thickly.

"What the hell?" he says. "I saved you guys, didn't I? Those cops were too far back to get a clear look at the car or the license. They don't know who it was. If I'd stopped we'd be busted now, on our way to jail."

"You could have killed us, you could have rolled this car right off the road," Pete says.

"And suppose they'd caught us?" Gene snaps. "It would have gone twice as bad for trying to run away."

He stares at them. "Listen," he says, "we did get away. We had to get away and we got away. That's all that matters. Don't you see that, you guys? That's all that matters, getting away."

But they do not answer, and they do not speak again even after he leaves the willows a half-hour later and drives them slowly back to town.

Lennox pushes away from the granite profusion, again into the blinding glare of the sun. The few moments in the shade have helped his vision, and he can see again in a wavering focus. His eyes sweep the terrain: strange outcroppings of rock, tall cacti, mesquite and creosote bush and cat-claw, thick clumps of cholla climbing halfway along a volcanic cone—

What's that?

There, there, off to the right?

Something . . . bright yellow, fiendishly reflecting the rays of the sun. Something made of metal—a car? the hood of a car? Is there a road over there? Are there people? A car means both, a car means help, a car means escape—*is that a car?*

Lennox feels the welling of relief, but tempered by the dim reminder of mirage, of other possible explanations for the brilliant reflection, of shattered hope. He fights down the urge to fling himself in that direction; it is a half-mile or more to where he sees the glare and he cannot run a half-mile, not now. Steadily, that is how he has to move, steadily.

But it is no more than a hundred yards before he breaks into a staggering and painful run . . .

Eleven

For Jana, it had been a quiet day.

Her sketch pad was now, in late afternoon, half full with charcoal and pencil drawings of the stark landscape which lay spread out before her, and she had made several notes and observations to be incorporated into the text of *Desert Adventure.* The intense heat had bothered her considerably after a while, and she had had to periodically relocate the blanket and her position in order to remain in one of the shifting patches of shade; but there had been nothing else to disturb her work—no inquisitive visitors, animal or human—and in spite of her mild aversion to her surroundings, she had immersed herself in the day's project as completely as she had immersed herself in the outline yesterday.

Sitting now in the shadow of an oddly humped outcropping of granite, she laid the sketch pad aside and drank from the bottle of mineral water. Then she sat leaning back on her hands, feeling hot and drowsy, not quite ready to make the drive back into Cuenca Seco. She allowed her thoughts to drift, and when the image of Don Harper materialized, she did not recoil from it.

Detachedly, as if she were a disinterested third party clinically examining a relationship between two other people, she placed him mentally against a changing background of memories: Washington Square in the Village, gray sky, fluttering pigeons, leafless trees like skeletal fingers reaching upward, his cheeks flushed from the bitter-cold winter wind, laughing; an off-Broadway theatre with no name, a dramatic production with a forgotten title, sitting intently forward, brow creased, eyes shining, totally absorbed in the illusion being enacted under the floodlights below; the sparkling blue of Long Island Sound, streaked with silver afternoon light, cold salt spray flecking his cheeks as the bow of the sleek white sailboat glides through gentle swells, one large soft hand competent on the tiller, the other possessively on her hip, shouting merriment into the wind . . .

It was good then, she thought, it was fine then, but only because I was in love then. I was in love with fun and with excitement and with handsomeness and with charm and with sophistication—but not with Don Harper, the real Don Harper, the man. I didn't know him, then, and maybe I wouldn't have cared if I had. But it could never have lasted, I can see that now, it could never have been for us. Don has no depth, he has a tremendous surface but it is only a thin, thin veneer laid across an empty vacuum. He loves being a hedonist, he loves being an important account executive, he loves *things*—but not people, I don't think so. He doesn't love his wife, his poor wife, he never once mentioned loving her even after he told me about her. No, it was his position that he did not want to jeopardize, his pursuit of pleasure. He cared for me only as a decoration, public on his arm and private in his bed; and when the decoration began to take root, he threw it coldly and carelessly back into the jungle where he had first discovered it.

Lord, she wished she had been able to analyze Don and herself and the affair as objectively then as she seemed to be able to do now. The bitterness might not have been as overwhelming inside her, she might not have been so utterly demoralized, she might not have been so susceptible to—

Jana roused herself sharply. All right now, girl, that's enough of that. You're having a quiet day and you don't want to

spoil it by slipping back into the dark caverns of the past and there you go again with those damned literary images you silly broad. Shape up, look at that desert out there, look at that
man?

man out there?

Startled, Jana pulled onto her knees, onto her feet, staring intently at the child-sized figure which seemed to be staggering toward her across the rocky ground. My God! she thought, and then she did not know what to think. She felt a vague apprehension, a tiny cold cube of fright beginning to form in her stomach. Who was he? What was he doing out there? What did he want?

Her first impulse was to conceal herself in the rocks, perhaps he wouldn't see her; then she thought of gathering up the blanket and the other things and running to the car and driving away very quickly. And then it was too late to do any of those things, even if she had been able, because he was waving his arms awkwardly, loosely above his head—he had seen her, he was coming to her.

Jana moved back against the rock, watching his approach, and as he grew from a child into an adult, his features became clearly defined. He was thin and his face, his clothes, his hair were caked with dust and sweat; he ran as if in great pain, blistered mouth open wide, the dry gasping of his breath audible in the desert stillness.

He came up to her, stopping several yards away, and knuckled his swollen eyes. He seemed to sway slightly, and Jana thought for a moment that he was going to fall. Compassion pressed at the edges of her anxiety, diminishing it. She relaxed somewhat, standing her ground; but she was still ready to bolt at the first sign of provocation.

"Who are you?" she said to him. "What happened to you?"

His mouth formed words, but he had no voice for them. He sank to his knees in the soft sand and braced his hands on his thighs, looking up at her. Relief and entreaty were apparent in his gaze, and the last vestiges of Jana's wariness transformed into concern. Swiftly she caught up the bottle of mineral water —a little more than half full—and ran to where the man knelt watching her. She extended the bottle. He pulled it from her hands, making a sound that was almost a whimper. Head thrown back, holding the bottle in both hands, he sucked greedily at the neck of it. Water spilled out in his haste and washed away some of the thick dust on his lips, revealing them to be cracked and beaded with flecks of dried blood. Jana looked away.

He finished drinking, allowed the empty bottle to fall into the sand and drew the back of one sun-reddened arm gingerly over his mouth. Then, painfully, he pulled one leg under him and gained his feet, stumbling, finding his balance. Jana took an involuntary step backward, watching him now, but he made no move toward her. One corner of his mouth trembled, and all at once she realized that he was trying to smile.

"Can you talk now?" she asked him.

Soft, shuddering breath. "I . . . I think . . ."—testing his dust- and heat-parched vocal cords—"I think so."

"How long have you been out there, under that sun?"

"All day. Years."

"What happened?"

"My car quit running," he said. "And I got lost. I'm not much of an outdoors man."

"You should have stayed on the highway."

"I wasn't on a highway. I was out in the middle of nowhere. I'm a . . . rock hunter, you see. That's my hobby."

"You must be an amateur to go hunting rocks dressed the way you are."

"Well . . . this is my first time on the desert."

"Mine, too, as a matter of fact."

"You don't live in this area?"

"No. I'm just a tourist."

"Are you alone here?"

Her tentative smile faded slightly. "Why?"

"I don't know. I just thought you might be. I saw the sun reflecting off your car, and then I saw you . . ." He ran a hand through his dusty hair, and looked beyond her to where the roadbed was visible through the rocks. "Where does that road lead?"

"To Cuenca Seco."

"What about the other direction?"

"It's a dead end."

"How far to Cuenca Seco?"

"About seven miles."

"Can you take me there? Right now?"

"Well . . ."

"I've got to get to a service station or a garage—some place that has a wrecker for my car."

Jana considered it. He seemed harmless enough, an even worse tenderfoot that she was; and he hadn't even looked at her as a woman, only as a savior, a beacon in a sea of arid heat. She couldn't very well refuse him, not after what he had obviously been through today. He looked exhausted, and those blisters and skin cracks and sunburned patches needed medication. She was being too cautious—overreacting. This was the desert, not the streets of New York City. There was a different set of rules applicable out here.

"All right," she said. "I'll take you in."

"Thanks, Miss—"

"Hennessey, Jana Hennessey."

"Thanks, Miss Hennessey."

"What's your name?"

"Delaney," he said. "Pete Delaney."

Jana turned and began gathering up the blanket and the other things. She said, "You probably haven't eaten all day, have you?"

"No," he answered. "Nothing."

"There's some crackers and cheese in my bag. You're welcome to what's left."

"Thanks," he said again, softly, and followed her across to the waiting Triumph . . .

Twelve

Di Parma didn't like what they were doing.

He didn't like it one single damned bit.

What was the matter with Harry, anyway? He was acting like this was a picnic or something, sitting over there grinning in that funny little way of his, his eyes all bright. Vollyer was the best in the business, everybody said that, and he was a nice guy, too, and a friend. It was a real pleasure to work with him. You learned a lot from Harry, there was no doubt about that. But what kind of thing was this?

They had been on this damned twisting dirt road all day now, driving back and forth at ten miles an hour and all they had seen was some kid in a jeep chasing jackrabbits a half-mile from the county road—and him three hours ago. This guy, this Lennox, wasn't going to show up around here, Harry was crazy if he thought that's what was going to happen. The son of a bitch was long gone by now, he had made it back to that oasis or to the intrastate highway to flag down a car. Oh sure, Harry sitting there telling him about percentages and how you had to put yourself in Lennox's shoes, but it still didn't make any sense. Di Parma couldn't see it at all.

What they should have done, they should have cut out. They should have hit the highway and driven straight back to the state capital and caught the first plane home. That's what they should have done. So all right, the guy saw them make the hit. Maybe it wasn't as bad as they had first thought. Lennox didn't know their names, maybe he hadn't even seen their faces clear enough to make a positive identification. Maybe he wouldn't even go to the cops at all. A drifter like that, he wouldn't want to get involved in any killing, he'd probably move out fast if he was a runner the way Harry kept saying he was. It was crazy to hang around on a dirt road in the middle of nowhere. When the cops found the target's body, they'd be leery of any strangers who had no good reason for being in the area. Christ, they were asking for it, they were just asking for it, it was crazy.

Di Parma reached down and turned the air conditioner up a little higher. It was hot inside the Buick, the bitch heat got through the windshield and through the other windows and the sun was so bright it was like having needles poked into your eyes after a while. He had a throbbing headache.

He didn't want to be here, he wanted to be on that plane, he wanted to be home with Jean. He wanted to be in bed with her, holding her close, telling her how much he loved her. Oh Jesus, he loved her! He was crazy for her, to touch her, to be near her. She was beautiful. She was the most beautiful thing in the world. Her hair was like silk; he ran his fingers through her hair and he thought of silk and kitten fur and everything soft that he had ever touched. And her skin like rich cream and her body so perfect, and her laugh—oh, that laugh she had! Like music playing, sweet and low and warm. She loved him too, she told him that almost as often as he told her. She wanted to give him a kid. Imagine him with a kid; he'd never liked kids much but now he wanted one, he wanted to have one with Jean. A little girl. A little girl that looked like her, sweet and soft, and they would call her Jeannie, what else?

God, he wished he was with Jean!

Di Parma turned to look at Vollyer, and Harry was sitting there with that little smile, that damned little smile, sucking on an orange and looking out at the desert. He would tell Di Parma to stop any minute now, like he'd done a dozen times before, and then he would get out with those binoculars he'd taken from the target's cabin and he would sweep the desert with them and he wouldn't see anything this time either. It was crazy, it was just plain crazy.

"Harry," he said impulsively, "Harry, haven't we been out here long enough? He's not going to show, Harry. I tell you, he's not going to show."

"We'll give him a little more time," Vollyer said, and it was the same thing he had said five or six times already. "You can't make it five miles across the desert in a couple of hours, Livio."

"You don't know that's what he's doing," Di Parma said.

"That's right, I don't know it."

"And what if he is? What if he does reach this road like you figure? Maybe he won't walk right along it. Maybe he'll hide in the rocks when he sees a car. How do you know he didn't spot this one back at the oasis? He might recognize it, keep to ground."

"It's a chance we're taking," Vollyer said evenly. "He's a runner, Livio."

"What difference does that make?"

"Runners don't think, they just react."

"Harry—"

"Stop the car," Vollyer said suddenly.

"What?"

"Stop the car!"

"For Christ's sake," Di Parma said. He touched the brakes.

Vollyer had the door open before the Buick came to a complete standstill, pulling off his sunglasses and raising the binoculars to his eyes. He was looking straight ahead, down the length of the road.

"There's a car coming," he said. "See the dust down there?"

Di Parma stared through the windshield. "Yeah, I see it."

"Pull off in those rocks there. Hurry it up, Livio."

Di Parma took the Buick off the road on the left, out of sight behind a jagged formation of sandstone that arched skyward thirty feet or more. Vollyer swung out, the binoculars in one hand, the Remington scope handgun in the other. Di Parma shut off the engine and followed him.

The sandstone arch was smooth and gently sloped on its backside, and Vollyer climbed it hastily, face bright red from the exertion. When he reached the top, he stretched out prone and stared along the road at the growing dust cloud.

Di Parma dropped down beside him. "It's just another kid in a jeep."

"Maybe."

"Who else would it be?"

"Does that matter? We don't want to be seen out here."

"Why the gun, Harry?"

"Just in case."

"We're taking a hell of a lot of chances."

"At this point, that's the name of the game."

"Harry, this is no goddamn game!"

Vollyer turned his head slowly and looked at Di Parma. "Shut up, Livio," he said softly.

Di Parma could not see Vollyer's eyes behind the smoky lens of the sunglasses, but the set of his mouth was hard and white. Harry was wound up tight, that was for sure. He'd never seen him wound up this tight before. His own guts were roped into a knot, because even if he didn't like to admit it to himself, he was afraid of Vollyer. He had heard stories about what Harry was like when he was strung out, and they weren't stories you liked to hear about your partner. If he got Harry down on him, he was begging for trouble he might not be able to handle. The thing for him to do was to go along with Vollyer, whether he liked it or not—to trust him as he had in the past. Harry would snap out of it pretty soon; you didn't stay on top in this kind of business for twenty-five years by making the wrong moves. But this whole assignment had turned into a bummer, and there was no telling what would happen next when the luck was running sour. He *had* to get out of this, for Jean's sake; she could never know what he really did for a living, never. She thought he was a salesman for farm tools. He hated lying to her, but it was the only way, she would never have understood—

Vollyer caught his arm. "Sports car," he said.

Di Parma looked along the road, and the machine was nearing them rapidly. It was a sleek yellow Triumph with New York plates; the dust cloud billowed out behind it like a gigantic duncolored parachute attached by invisible wires. Di Parma squinted against the glare of the sun, and he could see two people inside, a woman driving and the passenger a man sitting hunched forward on the seat.

The Triumph drew parallel to them, and Vollyer and Di Parma were far enough away and at enough of an angle to be able to look through the open window on the passenger side. They saw the dust-streaked, sunburned face of the man, saw it clearly, and it was the same face smiling out from the portrait photograph in Vollyer's pocket—it was him, Lennox, the witness. Di Parma, staring, was incredulous. Harry had been right, he had been backing a winner after all. Jesus, the guy *had* come straight across the desert and hit this road . . .

Vollyer reacted instantly at the moment of recognition. He pulled off his sunglasses and gained his knees, turning slightly, planting his left foot at an angle out from his body to brace himself. He extended his left arm, crooked horizontally, and rested the long barrel of the Remington on his forearm, squinting through the Bushnell scope. The Triumph was pulling away, fifty yards beyond them, and Di Parma sucked in his breath, watching Vollyer, thinking: Squeeze off, squeeze off, Harry, for Christ's sake!

Vollyer waited a moment longer. And fired.

Again.

Rolling echoes of sound fragmented the brittle late-afternoon stillness. Di Parma saw a hole appear in the dusty plastic of the Triumph's rear window, saw the spurt of air and dust as the left rear tire blew. The little car began to yaw suddenly, its rear end snapping around, and Di Parma thought for an instant that it was going to roll. But it remained upright, plunging off the road on their side, hurtling through thick clumps of creosote bush, skidding sideways as the girl fought the wheel and the locked brakes, tilting, rear end folding in on itself as it slammed into a chunk of granite, caroming off, a second tire blowing now, driver's door scraping another boulder, front end fishtailing again to point at still another outcropping, meeting it with a glancing blow and finally coming to a shuddering halt better than a hundred yards off the road.

Vollyer was already halfway down the slope, not looking back. Di Parma scrambled after him, and there was elation soaring through him. We're all right! he thought. We're going to come out of it just fine, Jean baby, I'll be home in the morning . . .

Thirteen

Inside Lennox, the panic was a living, screaming entity.

It had been reborn the instant the angry, whistling pellet slashed through the rear window and imbedded itself in the dashboard, narrowly missing the girl. He had twisted in the seat and then the tire had blown and Jana had cried out, a keening sound that was a knife blade prodding the belly of the panic, enraging it, spiraling it out of control. The world spun and tilted crazily, and he felt himself thrown forward, felt sharp pain above his right eye as his head struck the windshield, felt blood flowing down to further distort the spinning montage outside the vehicle. Impact, grinding of metal, impact, the girl crying out again, impact, impact, and through it all the bright, hot panic clawing at the cells of his brain. He was not dazed, he was not confused. He knew what had happened, or the fear within him knew it; the equation was so very simple. They had found him: the killers had known about him all along and they had been looking for him and they had found him; he had no idea how, the *how* was not important, only the *why* was important and he knew the why.

Even before the car stopped moving, he was preparing flight.

And when it did stop, and the surrealistic movement became once again a motionless desert landscape, his hand was on the door handle, shoving it down, leaning his weight against it. Metal protested, binding, and he kicked at the door savagely, *run, run,* sweat commingling with the blood to half-blind him, and the girl was moaning words now, saying "My God, oh my God!" He looked at her—even with the panic he looked at her and she was the color of old snow, eyes glazed, still clinging to the wheel, repeating over and over, "My God, oh my God!"

Lennox kicked again at the door, and it gave finally and opened wide with a rending sound, *run!* and he was half out now, one foot on the ground, and his head jerked around, eyes searching through the dim red haze for the road, locating it. They were there, just as he had known they would be. Sunlight gleaming off metal extensions of their hands. Coming for him. Bringing death.

Run!

He levered his body up, supporting himself on the sprung door, and behind him the girl was still saying "Oh my God!" Suddenly, acutely, Lennox was fully aware of her. He looked at her, sitting rigidly in momentary shock, staring at nothing. *Run, run,* but something held him back, the girl held him back as if by some subconscious telepathy. He couldn't leave her here, they would kill her, and even with the panic screaming there inside him, he couldn't allow it to happen. He was responsible for her, he had gotten her into this, she was innocent. He had to take her with him. There was no inner debate, no real decision, it was simply a thing he was compelled to do.

Lennox reached back inside, and he had developed awesome strength. He locked his fingers on her arm and pulled her out of the seat, out from under the wheel, out of the car. She cried out in pain as a sharp edge of metal gashed her leg, and then he had her on her feet and he was staggering away from the car, half-dragging her behind, feeling her resist in spite of her shock and refusing to yield, dimly hearing her moan something at him but listening only to the shrill, clear voice of the panic now.

Into the rocks, near-falling, gasping, and a long way off a dull cracking sound, and another, and he knew they were shooting without really knowing it—keep moving, dodging, hang onto the girl, get away, get away, escape, fear shriveling his groin, fear gagging his throat, fear clamped onto his brain like a parasitic slug. And through the numbing wash of terror, a disjointed and yet intense feeling that it had always been this way for him, that his entire life had been one headlong flight; but like a wild thing in a wheel, he had never really escaped anything and never really would—and like that same wild thing, he would die running blind and running scared without ever having stopped running for even a little while . . .

Fourteen

Di Parma raised his arm and fired a third shot from the reloaded .38, but Lennox and the girl had vanished into the jagged mosaic of rocks. Vollyer yelled at him, "Save your ammunition! Think, Livio, think!"

He was a few steps ahead and to one side of Di Parma as they passed the damaged Triumph and plunged into the rocks. In his right hand was the other belly gun; the Remington was tucked into the waistband of his trousers now. It was only a two-shot, and the rest of the ammunition he had brought for it was in the case under the Buick's front seat.

Pinnacles and arches and knobs jutted up from the sandy earth on all sides of them, and there were sharp-thorned cacti and thick growths of mesquite. They fanned out, probing the terrain with slitted eyes, but there were a thousand hiding places here, a thousand barriers to camouflage flight. They saw nothing. There were small sounds—shoes scraping stone, a muffled cry—but when they pursued they found nothing.

Deeper into the craggy patchwork, moving more slowly

now, listening. Silence. The startled cry of a martin. Something reptilian slithering beyond a boulder. A soft, rattling sound—dislodged pebble—directly ahead of them. They converged on the spot, just in time to see a small brown rock squirrel scamper into a crevice; it gave off a high-pitched, frightened whistle and was quiet.

They spent another ten minutes searching—futilely. At the end of that time they paused in the shade under a rocky ledge and Di Parma rubbed at his mouth with his free hand. His face was screwed up as if he were about to cry, lower lip trembling faintly. Vollyer, looking at him, thought that he resembled a pouting little boy; but there was no fondness, no paternal tolerance, in the image now. You're getting to be an albatross, Livio, he thought. Don't let it happen. Don't wind yourself around my neck.

Di Parma said, "Not again, Harry. Goddamn it, not again."

"We'll find them."

"How did they get away? How?"

"They haven't gotten away."

"But we had them. We had them cold."

"Even losers get lucky for a little while."

"Who do you think that girl is?"

"Does it matter?"

"No. No, I guess not."

Vollyer was thinking, calculating. "You keep looking, keep moving around. But don't get lost."

"All right."

"If you see them, fire a shot."

Moving in an awkward run, Vollyer made his way back to the sandstone formation and the Buick; it was undetectable from the road, if anyone chanced by, and he decided to leave it where it was. From the briefcase, he removed the spare ammunition for the Remington and the box of shells for the .38s and slipped them into the knapsack he had taken from Del's Oasis. The binoculars were on the front seat, and he looped them around his neck. Then, carrying the knapsack, he closed the door and returned to where the battered Triumph had finally come to rest.

He stood beside it, letting his eyes sweep the area. Five hundred yards distant, angling sharply into the rocks, was what looked to be an arroyo. He hurried there and saw that the wash was thirty or forty feet deep and another fifty feet wide, with a boulder-strewn bottom sustaining ironwood and mesquite. He went back to the Triumph, pausing to listen; he heard only silence.

The driver's door was jammed shut, and he had to move around to the passenger side to get into the car. Wedged behind the front seat was a handbag with a sketch pad and a notebook inside, and Vollyer took a moment to shuffle through them. The keys hung from the ignition lock. He switched it on and pressed the starter. At first, from the dull whirr, he thought that the car was inoperable, that it would have to be pushed out of sight instead; but on his fourth try, the engine caught and held feebly.

Vollyer went through the gears experimentally, and found that the transmission had not been damaged. He let out the clutch slowly, and the car thumped backward on its blown tires, the rims grating sharply, metallically over the rock. He backed and filled, skirting the stone formations at a crawl until he located a clear path to the edge of the arroyo. Once there, he set the hand brake just enough to prevent the car from rolling forward of its own volition, and then slipped out on the passenger side and went around to the rear. He leaned his weight against the crumpled deck, grunting as his soft muscles dissented, and managed to edge the lightweight machine forward until its front wheels passed the rim; momentum took care of the rest.

The Triumph slid in a rush down the steep wall of the arroyo. The front bumper struck a shelf of rock three-quarters of the way down, and the car flipped over and landed on its canvas top, crushing it, filling the air with the reverberation of breaking glass and twisting metal. One of the wheels turned lazily in the bright glare of the falling sun; stillness blanketed the landscape again.

Vollyer returned for the knapsack, which he had placed on the ground before entering the Triumph, and a few moments later Di Parma came out of the stone forest to join him. He had a small wedge of yellow material in his left hand, and he extended it to Vollyer. "Found this on a cactus in there. It must be from the girl's blouse."

"No sign of them otherwise?"

"No."

"You know where you found this?"

"Yeah, I think so."

Vollyer nodded and gave him the knapsack. "Put this on," he said. "We've got water, food, and shells in there—and three guns and a compass and a pair of binoculars. They don't have a damned thing. We'll get them, sooner or later."

"It had better be sooner," Di Parma said grimly. His big red hands were nervous at his sides. "I'm no good at chases, Harry. I don't like anything about this."

They moved forward into the rocks.

Fifteen

Jana and the man she knew as Pete Delaney were on higher ground, running parallel to the dry wash toward a low butte in the distance, when they heard the echoing crash somewhere behind them. It was a brittle and metallic sound, the kind a car would make upon impact with something hard and unyielding— the sound of ultimate destruction.

He stiffened and stumbled to a halt, looking past her, still holding roughly to her wrist. But there was nothing for him to see. He started forward with her again, but Jana held back, fighting breath into her lungs. Her temples pounded rhythmically, and the inside of her head felt as if it were layered in thick cotton. The effects of the shock which had gripped her following the Triumph's wild flight off the road still lingered, and she could not seem to compose her thoughts; they were sluggish, like fat weevils in the cotton bunting.

She knew that it was no accident that they had gone off the road; she had heard the bullet humming just over her right shoulder, slamming into the dash, had heard reports behind them just before the rear tire exploded. Someone had shot at them, *shot* at them! But *why?* Pete Delaney? And those two men on the road running after them—more gunshots? She could not remember, she had been so dazed. Running, the rocks and the cacti, the fingers like steel bands on her wrist. The fear. She could feel it rise within her of its own volition, and, as well, seem to enter her body like an electrical current emanating from this man, Delaney. He radiated fear, it seeped from his pores like an invisible and noxious vapor. His face was a mask of it: gaffed mouth, protuberant eyes, throbbing veins.

She tried, now, to claw her wrist free of his painful grasp. He refused to let go. "You're . . . you're hurting me!"

He did not seem to hear her. His eyes made a furtive ambit of the area; ground cover was thinner here, less concealing. He looked into the wash. It hooked sharply to the left several hundred yards ahead, vanishing into more thickly clustered rocks, and its bottom offered sanctuary in the form of boulders and paloverde and an occasional smoke tree.

Jana tried again to free herself, vainly, as he pulled her down the inclined but not steep bank of the wash. She fell when they reached the rocky floor, crying out softly, putting another tear in her Levis and a gash in the flesh just below her knee; tears formed in her eyes as he jerked her to her feet, and she began to sob in broken, gasping cries.

He ran with her to the closest of the smoke trees and drew her down behind the twisted, multi-trunked base; over their heads, the blue-gray twigs on its thorny branches—nearly leafless now—looked like billows of smoke against the fading blue of the sky. He released her wrist then, and there were angry red welts where his fingers had bitten into her skin. Jana rubbed at the spot gently with her other hand, turning her face away, drinking air hungrily. She was still sobbing, more softly now.

Lying flat on his stomach, the man she knew as Delaney peered through the humped bottom branch of the smoke tree, looking down the wash for a time and then upward, along its western bank to the rocks through which they had come moments ago. Nothing moved. He pulled himself into a sitting position, air whistling painfully through his nostrils, facing Jana. He seemed less wild-eyed now, more in control; the mask of panic had smoothed.

"We can rest a minute," he said thickly. "Not long. Are you all right?"

"What's happening?" she said. "I don't understand what's *happening.*"

82

"They shot us off the road, those two men."

"Why? Who are they?"

"They're killers."

"What?"

"Killers, professional killers."

"Dear God! What do they want with you? Who *are* you?"

"I'm not anybody, I'm just . . . Pete Delaney."

"Then what do they want with you?"

"I saw them murder a man," he said. "This morning, at the oasis stop on the highway. That's why I was on the desert. I ran away but they found me somehow. They'll kill me if they catch me. They'll kill both of us now."

Jana shook her head numbly, disbelievingly. Professional killers? She had always thought they were something conjured up from the imaginations of fiction writers. Murder? Death? Just words, more fiction, a sympathetic shudder at a morning newspaper headline—things that never touched your life, that were somehow not even real. And she felt a sense of unreality sweep over her, as if she were a player in a melodrama, in one of those turgid mystery puzzle things her drama instructor at N.Y.U. had loved to produce. The concept of her life being in danger, of death and menace, was utterly alien. It had all happened so fast, too fast; she had been sucked into a vortex and she no longer had control of her own destiny. She was trapped, helpless, she was terrified.

He said, "We've got to keep running. We can't stay here. As long as we keep moving, we've got a chance."

Jana stared at him, and suddenly she hated him, she wanted to strike out at him, it was his fault that this was happening to her, it was *him*. "You bastard!" she said, and she slapped him with the open flat of her palm. "Oh, damn you, you bastard, damn you, damn you!"

He caught her wrist as she raised it again, covering her mouth with his other hand. Jana struggled, but he held her tightly. He said, his voice trembling, "Stop it, for God's sake, stop it! Don't get hysterical, do you want them to find us?"

As abruptly as it had come, the rage abated within Jana and she slumped loosely in his grasp. She felt the hot tears flooding from her eyes again, and she tried to think, tried to understand, but the cotton had thickened inside her head, filling it completely. Vaguely she felt herself being lifted, felt him steady her with a corded arm about her shoulders. And then they were moving again, moving along the sandy floor of the wash, scattering an army of huge jet-black pinacate beetles which had emerged from their burrows, frightening a sinister-looking but harmless horned lizard.

Jana no longer tried to resist as they ran, and there was soon little moisture remaining in her for tears. Her head pulsated viciously, and the muscles in her thighs and ankles screamed in protest at the stumbling, accelerated movement.

They paused for brief moments of rest when their lungs threatened to burst, and Jana thought once of death—her death —and cried out fearfully; but then the tiny rift in the cotton mended and there were no more thoughts, there was only the running. Up out of the dry wash, through more rocks, across a short open space, veering away from the bluff in the distance, veering back to it, high ground, low ground, rocks and pebbles and sand, heat but not so intense now as afternoon faded into dusk, as a sky they did not see slowly and inexorably changed from blue to a deep, almost grayish violet.

Sixteen

The freshly born night wind blew softly, sibilantly through the low-hanging branches of the willow tree growing in Andy Brackeen's front yard, and billowed the white front-window curtains in the simple frame cottage beyond. Beneath the willow, settled into an old wooden rocker, Brackeen balanced a can of beer on one thick thigh and held his face up to the fanning caress of the breeze.

Sunset was an hour away, and he had been sitting there, drinking beer, since he had come off duty a few minutes past five. The empty feeling with which he had come back from Del's Oasis had lingered throughout the afternoon, and it was present in him now. He knew what it was, all right—it was this Perrins murder, the kind of thing he knew it to be—but the knowledge did nothing except increase the inner restlessness he felt.

I should have said something, he thought. I should have said something to Lydell and those state boys, and to hell with Forester. That stupid bastard. It was a professional job, for Christ's sake, anybody ought to be able to see that, and him playing up to Gottlieb and Sanchez with that cockeyed theory about the drifter. And those two: methodical and noncommittal, just like the goddamn state government, like any goddamn politician you could think of. Wait and see. Check this, look into that, put it all together with a pencil and a slide rule and two weeks of horseshit across an air-conditioned office. That wasn't police work, that was fat-assed bureaucracy in action. By the time anybody got around to doing anything, the slugger or sluggers could be shacked up with a pair of cooch dancers in the Bahamas and the trail would be ice-cold.

And this poor drifter, whoever he was, was going to take the shaft for it, sure as hell. They had his prints—what they figured were his prints—in Washington now, since the state check had been negative, and as soon as they identified him there would be a pickup order out on him five minutes later. Which was all right, if the thing was handled right—but Brackeen didn't think that it would be; when they picked this guy up, they would hammer at him on the killing and turn deaf ears to anything else he had to say. There was nothing wrong with slapping a guy around if you figured he was holding out, Brackeen thought this Supreme Court/civil rights/police brutality stuff was so much puckey, but you had to keep an open mind nonetheless, you had to listen to what was being said and figure maybe there was an angle you were overlooking. That was what made a good cop. A good cop had an open mind, and there wasn't a good cop in this whole bloody state that Brackeen had met in the entire time he had been here.

This drifter—why had he run? Well, you could figure it simply enough: he had seen something. And what had he seen? Perrins getting hit? The guy or guys who did the job? It could be, too, that he had stumbled on the body after the shooting and thought that he might be tagged for it and cut out for that reason; but if that was the case, why had he left his overnight bag there, and fingerprints on a dozen surfaces?

Figure he saw something, then, figure he saw the hit. So he runs. Where does he run? He doesn't have a car; that doesn't add. Would he go to the highway the way Forester had it? Or would he head into the desert? Circumstances. If he saw something, and got away clean, he'd head for the highway because that was the quickest potential way out of the area. But if he was spotted by the sluggers, the desert would be his choice; there were innumerable hiding places out there, as long as you had the guts—or enough fear—to risk snakes and the sun and the badlands themselves.

And if that was the case, what would the hit men do? Go after him, in one way or another? It had to be that way: no pro was going to leave a witness, not under any circumstances. If all of this was accurate thinking—and the chances of it were good enough to preclude light dismissal—then maybe the killers of Perrins were still somewhere in this area. And maybe the drifter was, too. If they hadn't caught him. If he was still alive.

Well, Jesus, this whole thing was giving him a headache. Had it been up to him, he'd have had helicopters out and a couple of roadblocks set up two hours after he'd seen the way things were at the Oasis. But it hadn't been up to him, he was out of it, he was just a resident-in-charge with his job hanging by a thread and a yen for noninvolvement. The thing for him to do was let it alone, forget about it, but he could not seem to do it; he wanted to be shut of it, he wanted the old status quo, and yet it would not let him alone, it kept eating at him and eating at him . . .

Brackeen lifted the beer on his thigh and drained it and put the can on the ground beside the rocker. There were six cans there now and he was as sober as he had been when he arrived home. He looked at the house and shouted, "Marge! Marge, bring me another beer!"

The front door opened after a time and a big woman with dark blond hair came out on the porch. She had huge, soft breasts and firmly wide hips and thick thighs that vibrated sinuously when she walked; her face was round and well-tanned, and the age lines were faint, pleasant trails crosshatching its contours. Brackeen, watching her come down the steps toward him, felt the same stirring hunger deep in his loins that he had felt the first time he saw her, here in Cuenca Seco, those many years ago. She was a lot of woman, you couldn't deny that—a kitten when you wanted it one way and a hellion when you wanted it the other, a listener instead of a talker, a rock, a wall, uncomplaining and unquestioning, always there, always waiting. She was the kind of woman he had desperately needed after what had happened in San Francisco, the kind of woman he had to have in order to maintain his sanity; he owed a lot to Marge, he owed a hell of a lot to her.

Marge handed him the beer she carried, and then stood looking down at him. "What's the matter tonight, Andy?" she asked at length.

"Why?"

"Something's bothering you."

"It's nothing, babe."

"It's that murder today, isn't it?"

"You heard about that, did you?"

"The whole town's talking about it."

"All right, so they're talking."

"Are you investigating?"

"Christ, no."

"Well, what do you think happened?"

"What difference does it make what I think?"

"Do you think that drifter did it?"

"The hell with the goddamn drifter," Brackeen said.

"God, you're in a mood," Marge said.

"So I'm in a mood, so what?"

"So come in the house and I'll see what I can do about it."

"It's too hot for screwing."

"You didn't think it was too hot last night."

"That was last night."

"You really are in a mood," Marge said. She turned and went up on the porch again, moving her hips. When she got to the door, she looked back, but Brackeen was sitting there in the rocker with his eyes focused on the base of the willow tree. She shrugged and went inside and shut the door softly.

Brackeen drank from his fresh beer, and smoked a cigarette, and the night wind blew cool and feathery across his seamed face. After a while he decided that maybe it wasn't too hot. He got up from the rocker and went into the house, and Marge was waiting for him just the way he had known she would be.

Seventeen

When the last burning edge of the sun vanished in the flame-streaked sky to the west, the harsh desert landscape softened into a serene and golden tableau. Gradually, almost magically, the horizon gentled into a wash of pink and the pale sphere of the moon rose, the desert turning vermilion now—as if infrared light were being cast over it. Shadows lengthened and deepened, and there was an almost reverent hush across the land.

Vollyer stood on a high shelf of rock, the binoculars fitted to his eyes, and turned in a slow pirouette until he had described a one-hundred-and-eighty-degree turn. It was like looking at a particularly vivid three-dimensional painting: the motionlessness was absolute. He lowered the glasses finally, reluctantly, and climbed down to where Di Parma sat drinking from one of the plastic water bottles.

Wordlessly, Vollyer sat beside him and pressed his hand up under his wishbone. The ulcer was giving him trouble again, not enough to hamper him seriously but just enough to be annoying —like an omnipresent but not especially painful toothache. As if that wasn't enough, his eyes still ached, and even now, with darkness approaching rapidly, they were still watering. Ruefully, he looked down at the dusty, torn material of his expensive trousers and shirt, the now-filthy-gray cashmere of his jacket lying with Di Parma's suit coat and the knapsack in the dust at their feet. I must look like hell, he thought; I must look like something off the Bowery in New York. I wonder what Fineberg, the tailor, would say if he could see me now—or one of those bow-and-scrape waiters in the restaurants along the Loop back home. No man can be cultured or refined or genteel—or even respectable—when there's dirt on his face and a rip in his pants. One of the game's little axioms.

Di Parma said, "Nothing, right?" in a dull voice.

"Nothing," Vollyer answered.

"Now what do we do?"

"We don't have much choice, Livio."

"You mean we spend the night out here?"

"That's right."

"Oh shit, Harry."

"We've come too far to backtrack to the car now."

"Snakes come out at night," Di Parma said, and his voice was that of a complaining child. "I don't like snakes."

"You haven't seen any snakes yet, have you?"

"They don't move around during the day. Night's when they hunt. It's too hot in the daytime."

"Tell me some more about the desert."

"I don't know anything about the desert."

"You know about the snakes."

"I told you, I don't like the goddamn things," Di Parma said, as if that explained it.

"You can see a long way on the desert at night, isn't that right?" Vollyer said. "When the moon is up, it can get to be just as bright as day, isn't that right?"

"I don't know," Di Parma said.

"It's right," Vollyer told him. "We'll sleep in shifts. Because of the snakes and because Lennox and the girl might try moving after dark, figuring to cross us up."

Di Parma drank again from the water bottle. He said, without looking at Vollyer, "How long are we going to stay out here looking?"

"Until we find them."

"That could take a week, a month."

"It won't take another full day."

"I don't see how you can be so sure."

"We found where they'd been in that arroyo," Vollyer said. "We found where they left it again. We're on their trail."

"Maybe," Di Parma said doubtfully. "But I still say they could be anywhere. They could've doubled back to the road by now."

Vollyer looked out over the desert again. A faint glow lingered on the horizon, prolonging the twilight, but the sky directly above them was dark and clear, speckled with the indistinct and precursory images of what would soon be crystal-bright stars. "They're out there," he said softly. "Hiding now, maybe, but not any longer than dawn. He's a runner, Livio, and runners have to run."

"He's got the girl with him. Maybe she'll change his mind, if she hasn't already."

"I don't think so."

Abruptly, Di Parma stood, picked up his jacket, and walked a few feet away. He put the jacket on and buttoned it and slid his large hands into the pockets.

He said, "It cooled off in a hell of a hurry."

"One of nature's little games."

"You think the Buick will be okay where we left it?"

"It's well hidden from the road."

"Suppose somebody sees it?"

"Then they'll figure it to belong to sightseers. Or hikers."

"Our suitcases are in the trunk, Harry."

"There's nothing in them but a couple of changes of clothes."

"The girl's car—what about that?"

"It'll sit for months in that wash before it's found."

"Not if she had somebody waiting for her in town," Di Parma said. "Not if she's reported missing and the cops put out a search party. We don't know what she was doing out here all alone."

"She was sketching," Vollyer said.

"What?"

"There was a sketch pad behind the front seat, full of desert landscapes."

"That doesn't change the fact that she could have been expected somewhere."

"Maybe. But she was alone today. She could be alone, period."

"Damn it, Harry, that's only a guess. How do we know who she might have told she was coming out here? How do we know what friends she might have?"

Vollyer's stomach had begun to throb painfully. "Livio," he said, "Livio, you're pushing me, Livio, you're getting on my nerves, Livio. I'm in charge, I'm giving the orders here and you're taking them and I don't want to hear any more bitching or any more back-talk, Livio. This is business, this is *my* business, you're just a punk kid in my business. Do you understand, Livio? Livio, do you understand?" Voice calm, almost gentle, face showing no emotion at all.

Di Parma opened his mouth, closed it again, and then lowered his eyes. His shoulders were hunched inside his jacket. He took his hands out of his pockets and looked at them and put them away again. Almost inaudibly he said, "I understand, Harry."

It was the right answer.

Eighteen

Drenched in moonlight, the eroded, multishaped formations of granite and sandstone and occasional lava had a ghostly, other-world look and the desert held the chilling enchantment of a graveyard at midnight. Overhead, the stars burned in a brilliant display against the backdrop of silken blackness. To the east, under the great pallid gold moon, the yellowish spines of vast clusters of cholla seemed to glow like distant lights, beckoning false sanctuary. The stillness was less acute now, with the first venturings of the night creatures—a horned owl made a questioning lament in silhouette against the moon, a coyote bayed querulously, a small and harmless yellow-breasted chat emitted a wailing shriek that sounded more as if it had been made by some giant beast. And the temperature dropped with almost startling rapidity, ultimately as much as fifty or sixty degrees.

Near a deep, wide wash, in the ineffectual shelter of a kind of natural rock fort, Lennox sat hugging his knees, shivering occasionally when the whispering night wind touched him with cold fingers. He felt weak, feverish, and the inflamed skin of his face and neck and arms burned with a hellish intensity; there was pain in his head, in the muscles and joints of his legs, in the cracked, swollen blisters that were his lips. He kept trying to work saliva through the arid cavern of his mouth, but there was no moisture left within him; his throat was a sealed passage that made swallowing impossible.

But his mind, curiously, was clear. It had been clear from the time he had stopped and hidden behind the smoke tree in that other wash; the panic had abated then, the consuming force of it at least, and the running since that time had been a calculated if desperate thing. There had been more rest stops than he would have liked—because of the girl and because of his own flagging strength—but they had seen no sign of their pursuers. Lennox had not deluded himself, however; he knew they were behind somewhere, and because of the urgency of his flight with the girl, there had been no time to cover their trail; the two men, city-bred or not, would not have had much difficulty in following, especially across the unavoidable open ground they had encountered from time to time.

He and Jana had been here in the rock fort since dusk. He had wanted to continue, to keep running well into the night, but both of them were exhausted. You could run only so far in a single day, and then you had to have rest; you could run only so far . . .

There had been no conversation between them. Jana had sprawled out, face down in the sandy bottom of the fort, and sleep had claimed her immediately. Lennox had found a crevice which allowed a wide view of their backtrail, and he had sat there until just a few minutes ago, when darkness came. Would the two men keep looking in the bright white shine of the moon? He didn't think so; they would need rest, too, and they would not want to take the chance of missing a sign in the deep pools of shadow the moonlight did not reach. Too, they would figure him and the girl to be exhausted, to seek out a hiding place for the night. No, they were safe now, until morning. And then—

And then.

He did not know what to do. If they kept running as they had today, blindly, they would be no better off than they were now; but he did not know where they were, or how far away the town of Cuenca Seco was—and the killers would be expecting them to move in that direction anyway. Could they double back to the road? Maybe—but there was no guarantee they would not stumble right into the arms of the men who pursued them; and he was not sure any longer in which direction the road lay. They could stay where they were, hidden here in the fort, hope that they were passed by, and then run in the opposite direction; but if their backtrail led to here, and the killers were able to follow it, they would be waiting in self-dug graves—they had no weapons, they could not make a stand. There was only one thing for them to do, then.

Panic!

Keep running.

Lennox raised his head and glanced over at the girl. She was awake now, sitting up, working at a cactus thorn which had broken off in her ankle. Her face, under its layering of dust, was a grimace of pain. He looked at her—really looked at her for the first time—and he saw that she was very pretty. He remembered her poise, the fluid grace of her movements when he had first stumbled upon her, and he wondered vaguely if she was a model of some kind in New York; the car had had New York plates. But no, her hips were too prominent, her breasts too large; no, she was something else but she was big-city beyond any doubt; she had known the bright lights and the supper clubs and the Broadway opening nights, she had known elegance and luxury. You could see it, even now, even under the coating of alkali dust and dried sweat—like sensing a hotel was grand and proud and ultra-respectable despite a façade of city-produced soot and cinders.

And yet, she had stamina too—she had guts. She had not gone completely to pieces when the car went out of control, or when he had pulled her out of the wreckage and into the rocks, or when he had told her there in the wash what all of this was about; in spite of her shock, her horror at the knowledge of the situation she had suddenly been thrust into, she had not been a hindrance, a danger to his chance for survival as well as to her own.

But he felt responsible for her. If it had not been for him, she would be safe now, in Cuenca Seco or wherever it was that she had been staying in this area. God, he wished now that he had obeyed the transitory impulse which he had felt when he first came upon her. He had thought, then, of simply taking her car, stealing it, leaving her there to walk back to Cuenca Seco; it would have been a quicker, more positive method of escape, he had thought, than trying to find some way out of the town when she dropped him off there. If he had done that, she would be free of this; he would still be alone. But he had not wanted to hurt her in repayment for her kindness, had not wanted her safety on his conscience. And now—ironically, bitterly—her safety weighed far heavier on his mind than it would have if he had followed that original impulse.

The wind seemed to blow colder, murmuring, and across

from him Jana hugged herself. A great stillness had settled over the desert now, and her head was cocked slightly to one side, as if she were listening for the next sound. Lennox thought she looked very small and very vulnerable.

In a voice that was cracked and brittle, like glass breaking a long way off, he said, "How are you feeling?"

She stared at him with dull, silent hatred.

"Look," he said, "I'm sorry for you. I'm sorry you had to get involved in this."

"That's a great deal of consolation." The dry tremble of her own voice softened the bitterness of the words.

"Do you think I wanted any of this?" he said. "Do you think I wanted to be a witness to a murder?"

She looked away, at the bright face of the moon. A lone, tattered cloud drifted eerily across the lower half of it, giving it for a brief moment a whiskered, ancient appearance. After a long pause she said in what was almost a whisper, "I'm afraid."

"I know," Lennox said. "I know."

"And thirsty. I've never been this thirsty in my life."

"Don't think about it. It only makes it worse if you think about it."

"What are we going to do?" softly, plaintively. "How long can we keep running away from them?"

"As long as we have to."

"I don't know how much further I can go."

"You'll feel better in the morning."

"Will I? Will the thirst and the fear be gone then?"

"I'm sorry," Lennox said again.

"You're sorry, oh God, you're sorry."

She sat rigidly, her face in profile and soft in the moonlight. Lennox felt strangely drawn to her in that moment, to this woman about whom he knew nothing but to whom he was bonded by a bitter quirk of fate. Since his discovery of the kind of cold and calculating bitch Phyllis was, he had mistrusted women; except for a plump divorcée he had picked up in a bar outside of Reno, and a waitress in a hash joint he had worked in Utah—two biologically initiated liaisons which had left him depressed and unfulfilled on both occasions—he had had little to do with them since the night he had begun running in earnest. But it was not a physical thing, this attraction he felt for the girl named Jana Hennessey. It was, instead, an innate recognition deep within himself that their common bond was far more basic than the immediacy of their plight, that they shared a kind of kinship; he saw something of himself in her, something dark and lonely and empty, and he could not explain what it was.

Impulsively he said, "Tell me about yourself, Jana."

Her head moved slowly until she was facing him again. "Why?"

"I'd like to know."

"What difference does it make, now?"

"You come from New York, don't you?" he said.

She did not answer.

"Jana?"

"Yes, I come from New York," she said wearily.

"What do you do there?"

"I write books."

"What kind of books?"

"Children's books."

"Is that why you're out here?"

"I . . . yes. Yes."

"What were you doing all alone today? Research?"

"I was making some sketches."

"You do your own illustrating?"

"Yes."

"It must be a fine thing to have artistic talents."

"It's a lot of hard work."

"Where do you live in New York? Greenwich Village?"

"I don't live in New York any more."

"Well, where do you live? Out here? This state, I mean?"

"Oh God," she said, "what *difference* does it make? We're going to die on this desert, you know that, don't you?"

"We're not going to die," Lennox said.

"How are we going to get away?"

"I don't know. We'll get away."

"No," she said, "no, we won't."

He had a sudden thought, and hope touched him faintly, clinging. "*Are* you living here? Or are you just staying in the area—with friends, maybe?"

"In a hotel," Jana answered. "Why?"

"In Cuenca Seco?"

"Yes."

"Does anyone know you came out here today?"

She frowned. "The desk clerk. He showed me how to get here on a map."

"Anyone else?"

"I don't think so."

"Did the clerk seem interested in you?"

"His eyes were all over me, if that's what you mean. What are you getting at?"

"I was thinking that when you didn't come back tonight, he might have gone to the police and reported you missing. And that they might send out some men to look for you."

"Why should he go to the police if I don't come back right away? He'd be a fool to do that."

"It's a chance, that's all."

"Is it the only chance we have?"

"No. No, not the only one."

"What will we do when we leave here? Keep running the way we did today?"

"I don't know. I'm trying to think what to do."

The wind whistled in a gentle monotone between the rocks and stroked Jana with chill intimacy; she hugged herself again, shivering. "God, it's cold. I had no idea it got this cold on the desert at night."

Lennox watched her rocking slightly and he felt very sorry for her. He crawled stiffly across to her, raised himself up on his knees. "We'd better huddle together for warmth," he said softly, and put a tentative arm about her shoulders. "If we don't—"

She pulled away from him viciously, pushing him off balance, so that he fell on his right elbow. Her eyes, in the moonshine, were wide, flickering pools. "Don't touch me!" she said. "Damn you, don't you touch me!"

He stared at her. "I was only thinking—"

"I don't care what you were thinking."

"For God's sake," Lennox said, "I only wanted to make it a little easier for you, for both of us."

"Leave me alone, just leave me alone."

"You don't have to be afraid of me."

"Just keep your hands off me, that's all. I don't like to be touched. I don't want you to touch me."

96

"All right."

"All *right.*"

She lay down in the sand, facing toward him but not looking at him, her body pulled into a fetal position, her arms folded tautly over her breasts. He stared at her for a long time, but she did not move and her eyes did not close; finally he rolled onto his back and covered his own eyes with his arm, shielding out the moonlight, embracing the darkness.

What's the matter with her? he thought. I only wanted to make her warm.

And then he thought: I wonder if I can sleep?

And slept.

The Third Day . . .

One

It had been this way for Brackeen in San Francisco:

A patrolman with an impressive record in his four years on the force, one soft step from a promotion to plain clothes and an inspectorship, he had been teamed with another good, young officer, Bob Coretti. Their cruise beat was the Potrero District, and the industrial and waterfront area extending from China Basin to Hunters Point; it was not the safest or the cleanest patrol in the city, but they knew it well and they functioned well in its jungle of streets and alleys and dark old buildings. They were known, even respected, as tough but decent heat—and as a result they had even built up a small but dependable stable of informants who would put them on to minor rumbles for a few dollars' cash.

It was one of these tipsters, a pool hustler named Scully, who gave them the line on Feldman.

They were cruising on South Van Ness, a few minutes before ten of a bleak Thursday in early February. It had been a quiet night, like you can get in early winter, the sky filled with a biting wind and a thin rain; the heater in their patrol car was not working, and Coretti, who was driving, had been complaining about the fact for the past hour. He was telling Brackeen that he was tempted to fix the damned thing himself and send the city a bill for repair costs, when Scully came out of one of the bars along the strip and gave them the high sign.

They met him ten minutes later, in a deserted parking lot,

and he told them what the grapevine had. According to the rap, he said, this Feldman was a parlor collector for a string of books in Southern California, who had lost the battle with the obvious temptation. Scully didn't know exactly how much he'd gotten away with, but since the betting had been unusually heavy at Caliente on Saturday, his guess was five figures. The tip was that Feldman had come into San Francisco, and was grounding in a tenement hotel—room 306—a couple of blocks off Third, near Hunters Point.

Brackeen gave Scully ten bucks, and then he and Coretti went to check it out. They didn't say much on the ride over, nor did they radio in to Dispatch their destination and mission, as they should have done. They were tense and excited; both of them knew that taking this Feldman might be the lever they needed to get out of a patrol car and into the General Works Detail at the Hall of Justice. They did not want to share this one— not until they had Feldman in custody. Neither of them even considered the possibility that they might not be able to handle it.

The hotel Scully had named stood between a storage warehouse for one of the interstate truck lines and an iron foundry, midway on the block; it was a three-story wooden affair, well over half a century old, cancerous and dying and yet clinging to its last few years with a kind of bitter tenacity. A narrow alley separated it from the iron foundry on the right. Inside, the sparse lobby contained the strong musty smell of age—the smell of death wrapped in mothballs—and little else; there was no one behind the short desk paralleling the wall on the right.

Brackeen said, "No use making announcements. We'll do this nice and slow and quiet."

Coretti nodded, and they went across to a set of bare wood stairs and climbed carefully and soundlessly to the third floor. They stopped in front of 306, and without speaking, moved one on either side of the door, drawing their service revolvers. When they were set, Brackeen reached out with the barrel of his gun and rapped sharply on the door panel.

Momentary silence. And then a faint creaking of bedsprings. The only sound in the hallway was their quiet breathing. Brackeen knocked on the door again, and again there was silence. They looked at one another, and Coretti shrugged and

Brackeen moved away from the wall, stepped back to get leverage, and then slammed his foot against the thin wood just above the knob. The lock held. He drove his foot forward a second time, viciously, and the lock pulled from the jamb with a protesting screech of rusted metal and the door kicked inward heavily. Feldman was at the far window, one leg over the sill, and he had a tan pasteboard suitcase in his left hand and a big Colt automatic clenched in his right. He froze momentarily as the door gave; then his arm lifted and the gun jumped once, twice, three times, billowing flame.

Brackeen was the first into the room, and he threw himself to the floor as Feldman fired, landing on his right shoulder and spoiling the shot he had. Coretti was half in and half out of the open doorway, a clear target, but Feldman's shot was wild, showering plaster dust from high in the wall above the open door. Coretti ducked back into the hallway.

Brackeen gained his knees, brought his service revolver up and on the window—but by then Feldman was just a dim shadow seen through the pelting rain on the fire escape outside. He snapped a quick shot that shattered the window glass, and shards fell and broke on the sill and floor with a sound like the ringing of tiny discordant bells; the bullet whined off into the night and he thought he could hear Feldman's heavy shoes retreating on the iron rungs of the fire escape.

He turned to yell to Coretti to get downstairs, to block the alley, but Coretti had thought of that already; he was pounding down the stairs at the end of the hall. Adrenalin flowed through Brackeen in a hot, thick rush and he turned back to the window. They couldn't let Feldman get away, not this one, not the big feather that was going to get him the promotion he'd worked for so long and so hard. Without thinking further, moving on reflex, he ran to the window, threw one leg over the sill, and started out onto the fire escape.

Feldman was standing there, on the second rung down, and the bore of the automatic in his hand was centered on Brackeen's face.

He couldn't move. The unexpectedness, the shock of it, petrified him, and in that single instant Feldman—thin face white, frightened, homicidal—squeezed the trigger. The sound of the hammer falling was a deafening explosion in Brackeen's ears and he thought *Oh God, I'm going to die, I'm dead* and the sudden fear was like a wiggling, slime-cold thing in his groin and his rectum and his belly, penetrating to the very core of him, touching the soul of him, and a scream that had no voice echoed through every cell and nerve-ending in his body. He looked at death, seemed to look beyond it to a terrible darkness, and his horror was pure and primeval. The second explosion, the ultimate explosion, was monstrously loud and he felt the bullet tear into his face, shattering bones, spurting blood, ending his life, ending the world.

And yet, it was all in his mind.

The explosion, the pain, was illusion. The automatic jammed, miraculously it jammed, and there was only the rain and the great mushrooming sound inside Brackeen's head. Feldman looked at the gun in disbelief, and then he turned and fled down the slippery metal steps, almost falling, not looking back.

It was not until then that Brackeen realized he was still alive.

The realization came slowly, and at first he refused to believe it. *I'm dead,* he thought, and felt the cold rain on his face and a sliver of glass cutting into his thigh, sending faint signals of pain from his clouded mind. *I'm dead,* and his eyes cleared and he could see Feldman reach the bottom of the fire escape—one of those old-fashioned ones that ended flush with the pavement—and start running wildly across the slick alley floor. *I'm dead, I have to stop him,* two confused and conflicting thoughts, and he tried to raise the gun in his right hand. He had no strength. He felt incredibly weak, worse than he had as a kid after a bout with double pneumonia, but he was alive—accepting it now, the miracle of it—he was alive; and the trembling started. He straddled the window sill, shaking like a malaria victim, and through dulled eyes he saw Feldman disappear into the solid darkness between the hotel and the iron foundry at the alley mouth.

A moment later there was the sound of a shot. And then silence. And then another shot. The rain drummed hollowly on the metal of the fire escape, and the wind hurled itself against the walls of the narrow canyon like a caged thing. Somewhere in the building, a woman shouted querulously. A long way off, the moan of a siren punctured the wet blackness of the night.

104

Panic!

Brackeen sat there for what seemed like an eternity before he was able to move again. When he stood up finally on the iron-slatted platform, the weakness buckled his knees and he nearly fell, bracing himself against the cold wood of the hotel wall. Going down, he held onto the railing with both hands, the service revolver back in his holster although he did not remember putting it there. He reached the alley below and walked toward the gray-black of its mouth; his gait was shuffling, awkward, like one of the wet-brains he had seen on Skid Row. When he reached the street, he saw that several people in various stages of undress were huddled around something on the sidewalk, murmuring and fluttering like sparrows. He went there and looked down.

It was Coretti, and he was dead.

He had been shot in the face.

Brackeen turned away and stumbled back into the alley and puked in the rain until there was nothing left, until another patrol car arrived on the scene. He was better then, and the trembling, though still noticeable, was less violent; the homicide inspectors who came a few minutes later attributed it to nervous reaction and simple shock. Brackeen did not tell them what had happened on the fire escape. He did not tell them how, in a sense, he was responsible for Coretti's death. He made his report and he let them take him back to the Potrero precinct to change and then he went home and stayed there for three days, thinking about what had happened, examining it, and each time he relived the scene—saw the black hole of the automatic staring at him, death staring at him—he broke out in a cold sweat and began trembling and felt the fear squeezing painfully at his genitals. He took out his gun two dozen times in those three days and held it in his hands two dozen times, and two dozen times he had to put it away because the sight of it, the feel of it, made him sick to his stomach. And when he slept, he dreamed of a scythe blade descending and fleshless fingers beckoning and Coretti pointing at him, saying his name again and again through the gaping, bleeding hole in what had once been his face . . .

Brackeen went back on duty the fourth day—the day Feldman tried to shoot it out with a team of detectives from the Fresno force and died with nine bullets in his head and torso and a .32 Iver-Johnson back-up gun in his pocket, which a later ballistics report proved was the weapon that had killed Coretti. But it was no good. He could not face his fellow workers any more than he had been able to face himself, despite their sympathy or perhaps because of it. He stuck it out for two weeks, and at the end of that time he knew he was finished as an efficient big-city cop, knew that he would never again be able to face a gun—perhaps not even to use one in any kind of tight situation—without the shaking and the sweating and the petrifying fear. He was a coward, deep down where a man lived he was rancid jelly, and Coretti's death was a crushing weight on him; he could not take the chance of crapping out in some future crisis, and possibly having the blood of another good cop on his hands and on his soul. He loved police work, he had been born to it; but knowing what he now knew about himself, he simply could not continue.

And so he resigned from the force, quietly, and everyone seemed to understand without anything being said. After a few aimless months in the Bay Area, during which he found and lost several jobs—always for the same reason: listlessness and inattentiveness and disinterest—he drifted south. A year in Los Angeles working the produce market, six months in Dago as a hod carrier, and then, finally, the desert and Cuenca Seco and Marge and marriage. He worked in the freight yards in Kehoe City for a while, and when Marge's uncle offered him a job in his feed store, Brackeen accepted that.

He had no intention of taking on the resident deputy's position when it came up. Marge had managed to pry loose from him at one time or another the fact that he had once been a cop, but that was all of his past he would reveal to her; she told her uncle ·about it, and the uncle had some kind of political pull with the county and offered to finagle the job for Brackeen if he wanted it. Brackeen said no, and he meant it at first; but they worked on him, Marge and the uncle, reminding him of how unhappy he was at the feed store, chipping away at his resistance in a dozen little ways. He began to think about it, and the cop in him—a thing that, like the shame and the guilt, had not died over the years—forced him eventually into doing some checking on the resident's duties. They consisted, he learned, mostly of sitting behind a desk, making routine patrols, and administering traffic tickets—no hassles, no problems, no crises to face, no partners to watch out for. He wondered if he could wear a gun again. He went with the uncle to the substation in Cuenca Seco and strapped one of the Magnums on and took it out and held it in his hands. Something stirred deep within him, but he did not tremble and he did not sweat and he did not feel sick at his stomach. As long as he wasn't forced to use it, he thought, he might be all right.

He took the job.

And here he was.

Brackeen lay in the early-morning darkness, the warm pressure of Marge's hip against his thigh, and thought it all through again for the first time in a decade.

He did not want to think about it, and yet his mind dwelled on it just the same. There was no pain now; time had put a thick skin over the wound even though it had failed to heal it. But what there was, was a deep feeling of incompletion, a kind of vague hunger that seemed to have always been there, unfulfilled. The same emptiness he had experienced that afternoon in Sullivan's Bar. The past was touching him again, as it had not touched him in a long time, and the ghosts of pride and manhood haunted him vaguely, like wraiths half-felt in the darkness, never quite manifesting themselves and yet never quite vanishing either.

It was this goddamn killing that was responsible; he couldn't get it out of his head, he couldn't combat the perverse mental involvement in it. It was as if, strangely, it was a personal thing, demanding his intervention, demanding a commitment on his part that he had been unable and unwilling to make since that cold, wet February night when a part of him died along with Bob Coretti. And he didn't know why; the reason for it was an enigma that he could not solve.

Brackeen turned his head on the pillow and looked at the luminescent dial of the clock on the bedside table. Five A.M. Another hour and a half before the alarm would ring. Another three hours before he was due at the substation to assign Forester some innocuous paperwork. This was one of the days, of which there were two in each week, when county policy dictated a reversal of roles: the bright-face would sit behind a desk and Brackeen would make the routine patrols. The idea was to give the assistant deputies a taste of office duty, while the residents kept abreast of their districts on the outside. Brackeen had always disliked the patrolling—it reminded him, in an ephemeral but uncomfortable sense, of the days and nights he and Coretti had cruised the Potrero in San Francisco—and the prospect of it on this day was even more unappealing. He wanted to know what was happening in Kehoe City and in the capital on the Perrins thing; he wanted to know what the fingerprint and personal background checks had turned up; he wanted to tell Lydell and the State Highway Patrol investigators what he thought and to make some recommendations and to hell with rocking the boat. Damn it, he wanted to be *involved* in it.

Even though he did not want to be involved in it.

The ambivalence was so strong in him, so frustrating in him, that it was almost like physical pain.

Two

Dawn.

On the desert, the first light is silvery and cold. The moon and the stars fade as darkness recedes, and the quiet is absolute, almost eerie. Then, slowly, magically, the silver becomes gold and the sun peeks almost shyly between distant mountain crests. There is warmth in the air again as the long shadows of towering saguaros stretch across the desert floor, as the grotesquely beautiful rock formations turn the color of flame.

Once again the light changes, becoming a brilliant yellow-white, as the sun reveals more of itself on the eastern horizon. The stillness is broken now by the chattering of quail, by a half-muffled burst of machine-gun fire that is nothing more than the cry of a cactus wren. The desert begins to shimmer with heat and mirage, and as the temperature rises with the sun and the glare increases, human vision once again blurs and there is no more softness, no more beauty, no more serenity to the land.

Panic!

Illusion is consumed by reality, and reality is a middle-aged whore at high noon: coarse, ugly, and uncompromising.

The runners are there, running there, running since that first silvery light, running now through a sea of cactus—barrel, agave, saguaro, prickly pear, cholla, beavertail. Thorns like tiny needles, like slender jade daggers, like gleaming stilettos rip at their skin, at their clothing, inflicting painful but half-noticed scratches and punctures that bleed for a moment and then dry up almost immediately. They are three-quarters of the way across, and their momentary objective—a low butte—looms reddish-brown and barren in the climbing sun.

They are no longer running blind, they have a direction now. North. Cuenca Seco or the county highway or perhaps even the dead-end road. It is the best choice in spite of the fact that it is the obvious one, this is what Delaney—is that really his name? —told Jana in the fort this morning. She does not know if he is right but she has to believe in him because there is no one else to believe in in the suddenly miniaturized confines of her world. She no longer hates him. Like her, he is here as a result of cruel and bitter circumstance; the fault is not his, there is no fault. She does not want to be alone and she does not want to die out here, even though she is very certain that she *is* going to die out here. But hope is the foundation of sanity, and there is hope even in the most fatalistic of men if that man is sane. Let the fearful be allowed to hope. To the last breath, to the bitter end, to the final revelation. Ovid said it and Aristotle said it and the New Testament said it and now Jana Hennessey is saying it.

I'm keeping the faith, baby; I've got hope.

Her mind is touched by these random thoughts, and random others, as she runs. She wonders what Harold Klein will say when she learns of her death. What Don Harper will say. Even what Ross Phalen at Nabob Press will say. She wonders if there will be much pain or if it will be over quickly. She wonders if God is alive and if He is, what Heaven is like; she has sinned, yes, many times in many ways but she does not believe in the existence of an orthodox Hell, fire and brimstone and all that nonsense, only the truly wicked—which she is not—are unforgiven at the Judgment and their souls are destroyed instantaneously rather than having to suffer eternal damnation.

109

She wonders what kind of man this Delaney, this drifter, is. She wonders why he asked her about herself last night. She wonders why she was unable to control the violent reaction to his touch, to his offer of warmth, when it was so obviously genuine. She had almost frozen, lying there with the wind chilling her, wanting to go to him and the warmth of him and yet afraid, afraid of the maleness of him, afraid of her own actions—immediate and ultimate. Her loneliness, magnified by the coldly brittle stars, the fat white moon, the velvet blackness, had been immense; and yet, the other thing, the fear of herself, had been stronger. Even with death so apparently imminent, she could not and cannot bring herself to face the question which has been in her mind for the past few weeks, the root of her flight from New York. She would rather die with the question unanswered; it would be better that way.

More thoughts come and go, fleetingly, like subliminal messages on the surface of her brain. Some of them make little sense.

Listen, it's too bad they took the cigarette commercials off television. You could do one where these two beautiful people are running in slow motion through the desert instead of through a grassy meadow. They stop beside a dry stream bed and light up, holding hands, laughing, and two men jump out with guns and shoot them. Very symbolic, you see. The American Cancer Society would love it.

Do you know what happens when you drink too much water? Well, what happens is, you keep having to pee. And if you have to stop to pee, how can you keep on running? Ergo, not drinking any water allows you to keep on running, and not eating any food—well now, let's not get vulgar, remember that writers of children's books must never be vulgar. That's what Ross Phalen says and I wonder what Ross Phalen would say if he knew just how vulgar writers of children's books could get. He would crap, excuse me, Ross, he would have a bowel movement or would you prefer defecate, he would crap in his pants and I'm so tired, oh God, I'm so tired. And thirsty, I'm so thirsty my tongue has dried up and fallen out of my mouth like, like, come on, Jana, what's a writer without his similes and meta-

110

*phors, like a pistil from a withered flower, there now I knew you
could do it . . .*

Delaney—somehow, Jana feels that is simply not his real
name—stops abruptly and bends into the shadow of a cactus.
When he straightens again, he holds in his hand a long, slender
piece of granite, smooth and rounded on one end, flared and
sharply pointed on the other. It resembles a hunting knife, and it
shines wickedly in the sun.

Jana finds words. "What good is that thing?"

"I don't know," he answers. "It's something, at least."

"I have to rest pretty soon, I can't go much further without
some rest."

"When we get around that hill." He puts the granite knife
into his belt on the left side.

She tries to compose her thoughts as they run again, but the
heat and the malevolent cactus thorns and the hunger and the
thirst are anathema to coherent reasoning. The disjointed images come and go as the butte, promising momentary respite,
looms larger ahead of them.

*Bad guys chasing the hero and heroine across the barren
wastes. The situation appears hopeless, all appears lost. But
wait—what's that? Hoofbeats? A bugle? We're saved! It's Roy
and Trigger, Gene and Champion, Batman and Robin; it's Su-
perman and Sam Spade and the boys from* Bonanza. *Here we
are, gang! Look here, over here! Do you see us, do you see us
over here . . . ?*

Three

Vollyer saw them.

He was standing on an outcropping, scanning the desert
with the binoculars as he had done several times that morning,
sweeping through a long, flat expanse grown thickly with

cactus. His eyes had been bothering him since sunrise and the returning glare—they watered heavily, aching, causing him moments of double vision—and he almost missed the rapid movement in the shining green and brown. He snapped the glasses back, and after a moment he saw them, running toward a craggy mesa or butte or whatever the geological term for a desert hill was. They were a long way off, well out of range of the Remington, but the important thing was their exact location had finally been pinpointed.

There was no excitement in Vollyer as he watched Lennox and the girl. The excitement was in the machinations, the maneuvers, of the game—not in the final and assured victory. But the fatigue he had begun to feel as a result of the draining heat and the rough terrain, the throbbing in his stomach which the few hours' rest and the last of the fresh fruit had failed to quiet, the burning ache behind his eyes, were each of them forgotten.

He lowered the binoculars, half-smiling, and climbed down to where Di Parma stood waiting.

Four

Brackeen found the wrecked Triumph TR-6 a few minutes before noon.

He had spent the morning cruising the area west and north of Cuenca Seco, and making periodic radio checks with Bradshaw on the Perrins thing. If the state or county investigations had turned up anything, they were not letting it out, even to the substation in whose district the killing had occurred; Bradshaw had heard nothing at all. Brackeen knew that he was going to have to make a direct inquiry in order to get information—but the desire for both involvement and noninvolvement was still raging ambivalently inside him, and he could not seem to make up his mind one way or the other. He was early coming back in to Cuenca Seco for his lunch break, and he decided to conduct the weekly check of the abandoned dead-end road winding into the desert just east of town; it was always quiet and deserted out there, and you could be alone with your thoughts.

He drove the full length of the road, U-turned, and started back. He still didn't know what he wanted to do. The indecision continued to anger and frustrate him, and he was mentally absorbed in it so deeply as to be oblivious to his surroundings, driving mechanically. It took the blinding reflection, from well to one side of the road—like a huge blood ruby catching and refracting the sun's rays—to jerk him out of it.

Brackeen slowed, frowning, and then stopped the cruiser. Instinctive curiosity, a trait police officers learned very early in their careers if they weren't born with it, made him step out into the harsh glare of midday and cross to where the object glinted in the sunlight near a large boulder; as he approached, he saw that it was a piece of red taillight glass, lying cupped upward in the rocky soil. It did not have a filming of dust, he noticed, as it would have if it had been there for any length of time. No accidents had been reported in this vicinity, and if Forester was as good as he liked you to believe, he would have investigated the reflection had it been here the week previous.

More than curious now, Brackeen began to prowl the area. He saw faint impressions that might have been tire tracks, erratic and irregularly shaped, such as a car would leave if it had gone out of control. He found a streak of yellow paint on one of the boulders nearby. He found another broken section of taillight. And when he saw no sign of a vehicle amongst the granite and sandstone and extended his prowling to the dry wash in the distance, he found the Triumph.

He stood for a moment on the bank, looking down at the battered wreckage, and then made his way carefully into the wash. The convertible top was crushed badly on the passenger side, but when he got down on his knees on the driver's side, and looked beneath, he could see that it was empty. And he could see, too, where a large-caliber bullet had gouged a deep hole in the dash panel.

A faint excitement stirred inside him. He straightened and walked around the car and saw that it could be righted without a great deal of exertion. He braced his body against the chassis, finding handholds, and the muscles which had once been prominent responded under the layers of soft fat; in less than a minute he had the Triumph tilted crookedly against one of the rocks, on its axles and what was left of its tires.

Brackeen sifted through the tangled metal. He located a rounded hole in the crumpled plastic of the rear window, at the very top, and it was obvious to him that it had been made by the same bullet imbedded in the dash panel. From the angle of trajectory, he determined that it had been fired from a height of several feet. There were no bloodstains in the interior, at least none that he could find, and it seemed reasonable to assume that no one had been seriously wounded either by bullets or in the crash. It was hardly likely that anyone could have crawled out of the Triumph if he had been in it when it went into the wash; the way it looked, the shooting had taken place over on the road and the car had gone off it there, fishtailing into the one boulder where he had found the taillight shard, scraping another and leaving the streak of yellow paint. The TR-6 had been driven or pushed into the wash later on. But by whom? And for what reason?

The car was unfamiliar to Brackeen, and the New York license plates told him the reason for that. There was no registration holder attached to the steering column, nothing in the glove compartment—anywhere in the car—to point to the owner. Behind the front seat, he discovered a bag with a notebook and a sketch pad inside; some of the pages in each were crumpled and torn, but the descriptive notes in the one and the stark desert sketches in the other were discernible. He was no expert, but the handwriting in the notebook appeared to be feminine, and the drawings had a certain feminine quality—but he could be wrong and he knew it. The only things that seemed certain were that whoever owned the Triumph had spent some time out here on the desert, and not long ago.

And that he—or she—was now apparently and unexplainably missing.

Brackeen went over the car again and found nothing else of relevance. With his pocket knife, he dug the bullet out of the dash panel and examined it in the palm of his hand; it had been badly damaged on impact, and he wasn't able to identify it. He put the pellet in the pocket of his uniform shirt and walked slowly back to the cruiser.

Using a clean handkerchief, he toweled his face free of

114

sweat and then called Bradshaw on the car's short-wave radio. He gave him the TR-6's license number and told him to have it checked out; he also requested the services of Hank Madison and Cuenca Seco's county-maintained wrecker. After he had given the ten-four sign-out, he sat there in the heat-washed silence, pulling speculatively at his lower lip. Then, abruptly, he got out of the cruiser again and walked back to where he had found the first piece of broken taillight. From the direction of the tire impressions, it seemed probable that the Triumph had been traveling north, toward Cuenca Seco, when it had suddenly gone out of control. If you assumed that the shooting was what had been responsible, and it was a reasonable assumption, whoever it was had to have been anchored somewhere to the south and somewhere near the road and somewhere on an elevation of several feet.

Brackeen studied the terrain to the south, and then moved in that direction. Fifteen minutes later, five minutes before the wrecker arrived, he found the locked and deserted Buick Electra where it had been hidden behind a jagged sculpture of sandstone.

Five

Di Parma said, "Where are they? *Goddamn* it, where are they?"

Vollyer put the binoculars to his stinging eyes, blinking away sweat, and reconnoitered the area on all sides of them. Stillness. Wavering heat. Great pools of bluish water that were nothing more than layers of heated air mirroring the sky. They were on the far side of the craggy butte now, and the land here was both flat and roughly irregular, both rocky and barren. Cactus and ocotillo and creosote bush dominated the patches of vegetation. The silence was like that in a vacuum: almost deafening.

Slowly Vollyer lowered the glasses and touched his parched lips with the back of his free hand. He sank exhaustedly onto a granite shelf in the shade of an overhang. "I don't understand it," he said. "We should have found them by now. There aren't that many places they could have gone."

"Are you sure you saw them, Harry?"

"I saw them, all right."

"And this is where they were heading?"

"How many times do I have to tell you?"

"Your eyes can play tricks on you out here—"

"My eyes are fine, there's nothing wrong with my eyes."

"Okay," Di Parma said. "Okay." He sank to his knees in the shade near where Vollyer sat and pulled the knapsack off his shoulders. He got the last container of water from it and drank a little, resisting the urge to drink it all, knowing that Vollyer was watching him. His legs and arms felt awkward, as if he had only partial control of them, and there was a thrumming pain in his temples.

It was all wrong, this whole thing had a bad feel to it. Three times this Lennox had gotten away, twice with the girl, and it was like an omen, like something was trying to tell Harry and him that it was useless, warn them to give it up and get out while they were still able. He didn't like it, he was scared, he wanted civilization, people, a cool place to sleep, he wanted Jean— God, he wanted Jean! But the chase had become like an obsession with Harry, you couldn't reason with him, you couldn't talk to him; he'd tried that last night, and the way Vollyer had looked at him had been almost murderous, almost as if he was thinking about using the belly-gun or that frigging Remington. It had shaken him and he'd kept his mouth shut since, remembering those stories he had heard, remembering that look in Harry's eyes. Still, how long could they keep up the hunt? The water was almost gone, you couldn't live very long without water on the desert. Why didn't they just call it off? Lennox and the girl had been without water, without food, for almost two days now; they couldn't last much longer, the heat would do the job of silencing as effectively as they could . . .

Vollyer said, "Give me a little of that water, Livio."

Di Parma handed him the container and watched while he drank sparingly. When Vollyer handed it back to him, he asked, "What time is it, Harry?"

"After one."

"We've been out here almost twenty-four hours."

"I know it."

Di Parma lifted the tattered remains of his suit jacket and stared at it. Jean had picked it out for him; she said he looked very dashing—that was the word she used, dashing—in a light blue weave. He would have to throw it away now, and how was he going to explain the loss of it to Jean? Maybe he wouldn't have to, maybe he could replace it from one of the shops off the Loop before he went home; if they could match the style and color, she'd never know the difference—that was what he would have to do, all right.

He wondered what Jean was doing now and if she was okay. She would be worried about him, that was for sure, because he hadn't called her since yesterday morning and he always called her every night and every morning when he was on the road. He hoped she wouldn't be too upset, he hated to see her upset, when she cried it was like little knives cutting away at his insides and he felt big and helpless. The first thing he had to do when they got out of this desert, the very first thing was to call Jean and let her know that everything was fine, he could make up some story about entertaining a buyer to explain his silence. She would understand, she would accept his word without question; that was one of the beautiful things about Jean: she trusted him, she knew he would never violate that trust. He hated the lying to her, but there was no other way without hurting her and he would never hurt her.

Kneeling there, loving her, wanting her, Di Parma thought: Damn Lennox and that bitch from the Triumph! Damn them for keeping Jean and me apart . . .

Six

Exhausted, bodies puckered like raisins from the dehydrating sun, Lennox and Jana lay belly down in the shade tunnel created by a low, eroded stone bridge. The sand there was cool and powdery, soft against their fevered skin, and they had been lying in it for the better part of an hour. When they had reached the butte and skirted it at its base, Lennox had begun looking for a place to rest immediately, realizing the girl's near-prostration, knowing that he, too, was approaching collapse—but it seemed to have taken hours before they found the sanctuary here beneath the bridge.

Lennox stirred now, rolling painfully onto his back, and he wondered vaguely if his legs would support him when he tried to stand again. The familiar burning pangs of hunger stabbed harshly at his belly, intensified by the added bodily deprivation of liquids, and he knew that unless they found food shortly—at the very least, some water—they would be physically unable to continue. It was a small miracle that they had managed to come this far; and it was amazing how much the human body could endure if put to a major test.

He moved his head, looking at Jana. She had slept—passed out?—the moment she was prone in the sand, and she lay motionless now, her face somehow pale beneath the dust and the sweat and the sunburned mosaic of red and brown patches, and for a moment he had the feeling that she was dead. He sat up convulsively, leaning toward her. One of her hands twitched then, like the slim paw of a sleeping kitten, and he knew a sense of relief. The protectiveness, the responsibility, he felt toward her was an odd sort of thing; he had never really committed himself, he thought with a kind of detached and yet vivid insight, to anyone *but* himself in all his thirty-three years—not even to Phyllis in the beginning, when he had loved her intensely, not even to Humber Realty except where it could further his own ends. Jack Lennox had been his entire life, his sole purpose—Jack Lennox's feelings, needs, triumphs, and defeats, pleasures and pains. No one else had ever really mattered, witness that poor old man in the bus depot, witness him. And now, inexplicably, a girl he barely knew, a girl who might die because of him, a girl who shared his pain and his loneliness, this girl mattered. She had, unwittingly, broken through to touch the core of him, and there was suddenly an awareness in him of his own self-centeredness, of his limitations and his failings, a vague understanding of what he was and why he was what he was. The revelation was not a pleasant one, but the sluggishness of his mind, while it refused to allow him to dwell on it, also refused to allow him to reject it.

Sitting with his legs splayed out in front of him, his hands folded between his knees, Lennox stared out at the bright, stark desert world. A line of ancient, element-carved rocks stretched away to the north—he had learned to read the sun like a compass in the past two days; interesting, the little tricks a running man picks up—and when he and Jana were able to move again, those rocks would serve as cover.

He became gradually aware, as he looked out at the silent emptiness, of a large cylindrical cactus, crowned with small scarlet flowers, growing just beyond the blanket of shade cast by the stone arch overhead. He gave it his attention, studying the striated, thorn-covered trunk, the greenness of it, and something—a scrap of knowledge, read or heard at some time in his life and then filed away in the archives of his brain—nudged at his consciousness, evanescent and yet demanding. He groped at it, retrieved it, held it grimly.

There was a kind of cactus which stored moisture in its pulp, enabling it to stay green longer than any of the other varieties. You could get liquid, drinkable liquid, from that pulp. Barrel cactus, that was the name of it. You sliced off the top of the barrel and the pulp was there inside . . .

Lennox pulled his legs under him and staggered to his feet, staring at the cactus growing that short distance away. It was barrel-shaped, all right, it looked like a barrel, all right, and he stumbled toward it, coming into the direct glare of the sun again, wincing as the furnacelike air struck him savagely across the face and neck. He fumbled at his belt and got the knife-contoured piece of granite free and stepped up to the cactus; he drove the pointed end into the barrel's trunk a few inches below the crown, plunging it deeply, sawing with it, unmindful of the needle-sharp spines jabbing at his hands and wrist and forearm, sweat streaming down into his eyes, his mind blank. The trunk was thick, but its fibers yielded to the desperate hackings and finally the top broke free and dropped to the sandy earth, resembling a fresh scalp with a vividly festooned bonnet, the flowers like splashes of blood in the brilliant light.

Lennox dropped the granite knife and reached inside the cactus with his hand cupped, touched cool wet pulp, seized it, pulled it out and up to his face, squeezing the juice past his parted and eroded lips. It was bitter, it was ambrosial, it dripped into the back of his throat and soothed the constricted passage and returned feeling to the swollen blob that was his tongue. Again and again he dipped out handfuls of the heavy pulp, and after a time he could swallow again, there was less complaint from the contracted muscles of his stomach.

He scooped out a double handful, then, and hurried back to where Jana lay prone in the shade. Using his knee, he turned her and held the barrel pulp low over her mouth, squeezing lightly, letting a few droplets fall on lips that were almost as deeply split as his own. She stirred immediately, her eyes fluttering open, and he said gently, "Open your mouth, Jana. I've found something we can drink."

Thickly, painfully: "What . . . what is it?"

"Cactus pulp. Open your mouth."

Obediently she parted her lips and he pressed out the juice carefully, trying not to waste any. When the pulp yielded no more, he tossed it aside and helped her into a sitting position. She swallowed and coughed dryly. "More," she said.

"Can you stand up? Can you walk?"

"I . . . don't know."

He drew her to her feet and supported her to the decapitated barrel cactus; she moved gracelessly, jerkily, like a wooden-jointed marionette, but she remained upright. Lennox scooped free another double handful of pulp and squeezed the juice into her mouth—a third and a fourth. She was better now, he could see that; there was an alertness to her eyes once more, and she could stand without assistance, without swaying.

He retrieved the granite knife and returned it to his belt. Then he and Jana each took handfuls of the pulp back into the shade and sat down cross-legged in the sand and drank. When there was no more moisture, they used the pith to rub some of the caked dust and sweat from their faces.

At length Lennox said, "How do you feel?"

"Light-headed," she answered.

"Can you go on?"

"Do we have any choice?"

"No."

120

"Then I can go on."

He touched her hand, fleetingly, with the tips of his fingers. "You've got a lot of courage," he said softly.

"Sure." She did not look at him. "Can we get juice from all the cactus like that one?"

"I think so."

"That's something, isn't it?"

"It's something."

"How did you think of it?"

"One of those scraps of knowledge you hear somewhere and file away and forget about. When the time is right, you remember it again."

"Do you know of some way to get food, too?"

"No—unless we could catch a squirrel or a jackrabbit or something. But we'd have to eat the meat raw if we did."

Jana shuddered faintly.

"Well, it doesn't matter anyway," Lennox said. "We'll be out of here before too much longer. Maybe by nightfall."

"You don't really believe that, do you?"

"I believe it."

"No," Jana said, and she was looking at him now. "No, you don't."

"Jana . . ."

"Do you know where we are? Do you have any idea at all where we are? Tell me the truth."

He wanted to lie to her, to reassure her, but he could not seem to do it; it was as if honesty was a vital thing between them now, as if their kinship had become so strong that lying was completely unnecessary. "No," he said, "I don't know where we are. And I don't think we'll get out of here by nightfall. I don't know if we'll ever get out of here."

She continued to look at him, and he saw a kind of confusion flickering across her features, as if a small, incomprehensible battle were being waged inside her. He wanted desperately to know what she was thinking in that moment; and as if a certain telepathic communion had been established between them, she put words to her thoughts, she said, "What's your real name? It's not Delaney, is it?"

And before he could consider consequences, before he could think anything at all, he answered, "No. No, it's Lennox, Jack Lennox . . ."

Seven

Seen through the substation's long front window, the main street of Cuenca Seco was dusty and quiet; the elongated shadows cast by buildings on both sides of the thoroughfare met in the exact center, touching one another and then merging like lovers unable to wait for darkness, finding magic in the golden stillness of late afternoon. But Brackeen, standing just beyond the front counter, listening intently to a crackling voice that originated in the state capital, was not in the least interested in what lay outside the window; he had far more important things on his mind than the capriciousness of shadows.

He had made his decision.

He was in it now, he was in it all the way.

The crackling voice stopped talking, finally, and Brackeen muttered a thanks and dropped the phone back into its cradle. He turned to look at the tall, rangy figure of Cuenca Seco's night deputy, Cal Demeter. "I'll take any calls that come in myself—for a while anyway. I'll be in my office."

Demeter nodded sourly. He did not care for Brackeen at all, and the less contact he had with him the better he liked it; but it was past six-thirty now, an hour and a half since Brackeen had officially gone off duty, and he was still hanging around, throwing out orders. It wasn't like Brackeen, not that slob. Neither was it like him to jump all over Forester the way he'd done at five o'clock, telling him he was a snot-nosed bright-face with a lot to learn about being a cop, telling him he was sick and tired of his half-assed opinions and smart-assed remarks, telling him to get the hell home and not to go out tonight because he wanted Forester on stand-by. And all because the kid had done a little more bragging about finding this dead guy, Perrins, at Del's Oasis the day before. That fat son of a bitch had something biting him, biting him so hard it was going to bite him right out of a job. Forester was one of Lydell's fair-haired boys, the kind of kid who could hold a grudge, too, and he didn't like Brackeen any more than Demeter did. Lard-belly had made a big mistake opening up to Forester like that, sure and sweet enough he had; wouldn't be long now before he'd have to find some other source besides the county to pay for his beer and his whores in Kehoe City . . .

Brackeen went into his partitioned cubicle across the office. He sat down behind his desk and lit a cigarette and stared at the clock on the wall without seeing it. He had enough facts now to be fairly sure of the validity of the conclusions he had formed earlier that afternoon, conclusions which had forced his decision to involve himself. Carefully, he went over all of it in his mind.

Item: one Triumph TR-6, registered to a Daryl Setlak in New York City. But Setlak was a college kid who had sold the Triumph three weeks before, for cash, to a Manhattan used-car dealer; it had obviously been purchased since then, but the bureaucratic red tape involved in any state or federal agency had delayed the entry into the records of the new owner. A telephone call to the used-car dealership had gone unanswered; with the three-hour time difference in the East, it had been past six there when Brackeen called and the place was obviously closed for the night. An appeal had been made to the New York police, but there was no report from them as yet; the current owner of the TR-6 was still unknown. And still missing. All he knew was that the car had been ambushed, fired upon with some kind of high-powered weapon. Later it had been pushed or driven into the dry wash, so as to hide it, apparently, from view of anyone passing on the road.

Item: one Buick Electra hardtop, current model, rented in the capital two days ago by a man named Standish, who had possessed a valid Illinois driver's license and other necessary identification. The name was being checked through Illinois channels; no report as yet. Except for a small empty case under the front seat, passenger side—and two expensive suitcases, containing quality men's clothing in two different sizes but nothing which could be used for immediate identification purposes—the car had been clean. Fingerprints were possible, but since Lydell had refused to listen to a request to send Hollowell and his equipment to Cuenca Seco, the interior had not been dusted as yet.

Item: a dead man who had used the name Al Perrins and whose effects had borne out that identity—but whose fingerprints were those of a man named George Lassiter, a native of St. Louis, two convictions for the sale and possession of narcotics, one in 1951 and the other in 1957. Lassiter was or had been a purported member of the Organization, but was rumored to have severed his affiliations recently by mutual consent. But he had been shot six times in the chest, all six bullets within a five-inch radius, and that was a mark of a contracted professional hit.

Item: a man named Jack Lennox, the drifter, whose fingerprints—taken from the oasis and the overnight bag found in the storeroom there—revealed him to be a fugitive from justice in the Pacific Northwest. He was wanted for assault and battery, and for assault with intent to commit murder, both charges having been filed by his ex-wife; he was also wanted for nonpayment of alimony to the same ex-wife. At present he, too, was still missing; law enforcement agencies had been alerted in a dozen western states, asking his detainment for questioning in connection with the Perrins/Lassiter murder, but there had been no reports to date on his possible whereabouts.

Item: the owner of the Triumph, gender unknown, presence in this area unknown but thought to be innocent—a tourist, or perhaps an artist or writer on assignment if the notebook and sketch pad discovered in the Triumph were indicative of profession. Current whereabouts also unknown.

Item: a man named Standish, hirer of the Buick. Presence in this area unknown. Current whereabouts unknown.

Add it all up and what did you get? A connection. A corroboration of the idea Brackeen had had all along that Perrins/Lassiter had been murdered by a pair—figuring two now, from the suitcases in the Buick's trunk—of professional sluggers. Extrapolating: Lennox had witnessed the killing of Lassiter, and had run, and had given himself away in the process. He had gone straight across the desert, maybe with close pursuit. Somewhere along the abandoned road he had met the Triumph's owner and talked him into a ride out. The sluggers had discovered this in some way and ambushed the TR-6, but the bullets and the subsequent crash had failed to do the job for them; Lennox and the car's owner had managed to escape, again with close pursuit. And now? Well, now they were somewhere out on the desert, all of them, the hunters and the hunted; that was why the Buick had still been there, hidden behind the rocks.

All of it made sense, all of it dovetailed—too perfectly to be a pipe dream. The only other possible answers involved heavy coincidence, and Brackeen did not trust coincidence on that level of occurrence. Every known fact substantiated his theory; there were no discrepancies.

The thing was, could he convince the State Highway Patrol boys—screw Lydell and the goddamn county—that he was right? Could he convince them to send out helicopters, search parties, before it was too late? He did not have the authority to do anything on his own; the most he could do, and he had already done that, was to post a special deputy at the junction of the county road and the abandoned road. If the sluggers came back for their Buick, they would find it gone and they would have no choice but to hike out. But Brackeen did not want that to happen. Because if it did, and if his previous knowledge of the operating code of the professional assassin still held true today, it would mean that Lennox and the Triumph's owner were certainly dead. As it stood now, one or both of them might still be alive, might still be saved—*if* he could juice the state investigators into acting as soon as possible.

That might not be easy, he knew. When he had finally come in off the desert, after two hours of abortive reconnaissance of the area where he had discovered the two cars, and the reaching of his decision to intervene, he had called Lydell for information —and the sheriff had told him to tend to his duties and to stay out of the murder investigation; it wasn't his problem, Lydell said, in spite of the fact that the killing had happened in his district. Brackeen had tried to argue, but Lydell had simply hung up on him. He had had to go around the old bastard, to a deputy he knew from the poker games at Indian Charley's, in order to obtain the information on Perrins/Lassiter and on Lennox. He had had no better luck when he'd called the Highway Patrol office. Neither Gottlieb nor Sanchez was there, and the sergeant on duty had referred him to the main investigative office in the capital. They had come through with the information on the rented Buick—that was what the call a few minutes previous had been about—but only because to them it had no bearing on the murder. When he had tried to press for facts on the case, they had told him the same thing as Lydell: stay out of it.

But now that he had committed himself, he couldn't stay out of it. There was anger in him again, and a sense of duty, and a sense of purpose. The emptiness was gone, and he felt whole again for the first time in fifteen years, he felt like a resurrection of the old Andy Brackeen, the proud one, the one with guts. And yet, it was not the kind of feeling that he could rejoice in, not with the source of his immediate rebirth unresolved.

He reached out for the telephone. And it rang just as his fingers touched the receiver.

He caught it up, said, "Sheriff's substation, Cuenca Seco. Brackeen."

"My name is Harold Klein, I'm calling from New York," a man's excited voice said. "I want to report a missing person."

"New York, did you say?"

"Yes, yes, that's right."

Brackeen gripped the handset a little tighter. "The name of this missing person?"

"Jana Hennessey. Miss Jana Hennessey."

"Is she a visitor in Cuenca Seco?"

"Yes, she's researching a book, she writes children's books, you see, I'm her agent, and I called this Joshua Hotel where she's staying just now and the clerk said she went out into the desert yesterday and hasn't come back, he didn't think anything of it, the damned fool, but I'm worried, she promised me faithfully she'd be working, she's just a girl . . ."

"What kind of car does she own?" Brackeen asked tightly.

"Car? A little yellow sports model, she bought it a couple of weeks ago . . ."

That's it, Brackeen thought, that's all I need. The bastards will listen to me now. He took Klein's number and told him he would be in touch; then he switched off and dialed the State Highway Patrol office in Kehoe City. And as he waited, his eyes, sunken in deep pouches of fat, were bright and alert and alive.

Eight

Di Parma almost stepped on the rattlesnake.

They were making their way to higher ground, into towering spires of rock, for a better vantage point of the vicinity. On their left, poised on the western horizon, the setting sun was a flaming hole in the pale fabric of sky, painting the landscape in golds and magentas. Vollyer, legs like thick needles thrusting pain at his groin and hips with every step, had dropped several paces behind; his breath whistled agonizingly in his throat, and there were skittering images playing at the corners of his eyes.

Face set grimly, Di Parma climbed with his shoulders hunched forward, arms swinging loosely at his sides. He came around a thrusting projection and his left foot was upraised for another step when he sensed the movement directly beneath him. He looked down then, and the rattler was there—a huge, pale, indistinctly marked diamondback, slithering out from beneath a rock, thick body gyrating sinuously, head coming around as it sensed danger, hooded, deadly eyes seeming to stare at him and a thinly forked tongue licking agitatedly at the air.

Di Parma recoiled in horror. He staggered backward, nausea rising in his throat, and his hand clawed at the pocket of his jacket draped over his left arm. The diamondback was beginning to coil, still seeming to stare at him, evil, evil, and the belly-gun was in Di Parma's hand now, triggered once, triggered twice; the snake's head snapped free of its body, now you see it and now you don't, and the body jerked, twisted, a hideous *danse macabre,* and then straightened and was still as the echo of the shots rolled like fading thunder through the quiet dusk. Shuddering violently, Di Parma turned away, stomach muscles convulsed, and vomited emptily.

It had happened very quickly, and Vollyer did not know what it was until he stumbled up and saw the body of the diamondback, spasming again, faintly, in the dust. Savage rage welled up inside him. He went to Di Parma and spun him upright and slapped him across the face, forehand, backhand, forehand, backhand. "You son of a bitch! You stupid shithead!"

There was a glazed look in Di Parma's eyes. "Oh my God," he said. "Oh my God, Harry."

"You let them know where we are. You couldn't have done a better job of it if you'd raised a signal flag!"

"Harry, the snake, did you see the snake . . ."

"I don't care about the bitching snake."

"It was coiling up, it was going to strike."

"The hell it was."

"It was, I tell you!"

"And you panicked."

"I didn't have any choice," Di Parma said whiningly. "God, you don't know how I hate snakes, Harry. They're the one thing I'm afraid of, I want to puke every time I see one."

"You'll puke, all right," Vollyer said. "You'll puke."

"Harry, for Christ's sake, I couldn't help it."

Vollyer stared at him, and it was as if Di Parma was a stranger, it was as if he had never seen him before in his life. The rage was ebbing, and there was no emotion whatsoever to replace it; he felt nothing for Livio now, no paternity, no friendship, no liking and yet no disliking. Just—nothing. Di Parma had been put to the test out here, and he had shown just what he was made of, and now, as far as Vollyer was concerned, he was a void, a stranger, a lump of clay. Nothing at all.

His hands still shaking, Di Parma put the .38 away in his jacket. He was unable to meet Vollyer's gaze. "Maybe they didn't hear the shots, Harry," he said. "Maybe they're too far away."

"They're not too far away," Vollyer said tonelessly. "And sounds carry a long way out here."

"They might not be able to tell where the shots came from."

"You'd better hope not."

"Harry, listen—"

"Shut up."

Di Parma looked at the sun-blistered face, its plumpness swollen almost grotesquely, and a tremor of fear caused another stomach paroxysm; Harry's eyes, in that moment, were those of the snake's—cold and hooded and deadly. He shook his head, sharply, and the illusion vanished. Vollyer turned then and started upward, and after a time—circling the dead rattler, avoiding it with his gaze—Di Parma followed on legs that had suddenly been weighted with lead.

128

Nine

When the two closely spaced gunshots sounded, Lennox pulled Jana behind a wall of rock and they crouched there breathlessly, listening. Silence prevailed again, heavy and unbroken.

She whispered, "That was gunfire, wasn't it?"

"Yeah."

"And not far off."

"Too close," he said. "Too damned close."

"They weren't shooting at us, were they? They're not that close, are they?"

"No, not at us. A snake, maybe. I don't know."

"We don't have much longer, do we?"

"What kind of talk is that?"

"I'm tired, Jack. I'm so tired."

"Listen, don't give up on me now."

"It seems so useless, all this running."

"Maybe, but I'm not quitting, I can't quit."

"Hope springs eternal," she murmured.

"What?"

"Nothing. I'm sorry."

"I won't let you quit either, Jana."

"All right."

"We'll have to find a place to spend the night," he said grimly. "We can't stay here, it's too open." His eyes moved over the surrounding terrain. "We'll follow these rocks to that high ground over there. Should be enough cover, if we're careful. It'll be dark pretty soon, and they won't be able to find us in the dark. They probably won't even try."

Jana nodded and he took her hand and she did not pull away; the dry, cracked surface of his palm seemed to comfort her somehow. There was a tenderness in him, a gentleness that she had not expected to exist in a man so obviously plagued by fear—fear that went deeper, went beyond that which their current predicament had generated. It was as if he had lived with fear of one kind or another for a long time, as if it had distorted the genuine qualities he possessed. She wondered again who he was and why he had not told her his real name until that afternoon, why he had hidden his true identity—and why he had finally decided to confide in her. She had wanted to ask him that, in the shade under the stone arch, but he had risen abruptly, telling her it was time to be moving again, they couldn't afford to stay there any longer.

Now, following him across the rough ground, Jana wanted to ask him again. It was somehow important that she know more about this man, this Jack Lennox who had unwittingly endangered her life, and then saved it—if only for a little while. Maybe, she thought, it's because he cares. And because he's the first person I've ever known who could possibly understand what it's like to live within the shell of oneself, lonely and afraid . . .

The last of the flaming sun had dropped beneath the horizon, and the sky was streaked in smoky pink and tarnished gold, when he found a night refuge for them.

It was a large, flat, sheltered area hollowed out between several sheer pinnacles, a natural water tank that would fill with cool, fresh rainwater during the wet months; seepage and gradual evaporation under the drying sun had left the surface cracked and powder-dry, and so it would remain until the rains came once again. There was only one entrance, a narrow cleft which Lennox had very nearly missed in the sheer rock facing. It would be virtually impossible to locate once darkness settled; even with the wash of moonlight, deep shadows would hide the entrance—the dry stream path which angled upward through the cleft, crested, and dropped away into the hollowed tank several feet below.

On level ground, where the path began its rise to the rock spires, a barrel cactus grew rounded and green. Once Lennox had discovered and cautiously examined the tank, and returned to tell Jana of what he had found, he used the granite knife to slice off the crown of the barrel; they dipped out pulp hurriedly, watching their backtrail, sucking greedily at the bitter droplets of cactus juice. Then, silently, they soothed the cool pith over their rawly burned faces and climbed into the tank.

They lay on the dry floor of it, weak and spent. Half forgotten in the urgency of their flight, pain came to them again, harsh and lingering—the pain of hunger, the pain of sunburn, the pain of blistered foot soles. Dozens of tears and tiny holes in their clothing marked the location of stinging cuts and abrasions and cactus bites, and their exposed arms and hands were tapestries of scabrous scratches. The cactus liquid had soothed their burning throats, and momentarily appeased the bodily cry for moisture; but they were badly dehydrated and their need had grown greater, would continue to grow greater, with each passing minute.

Darkness settled, erasing the polychromatic sunset from the sky, and the moon leaped high with that surprising desert suddenness. The stars began to burn like fired crystal. Outside the tank, a soft, silvery wraith slipped quickly in and out of shadows—a bushy-tailed kit fox, the size of a large house cat, prowling for wood rats and kangaroo rats and other nocturnal rodents. Overhead, owl wings made faint, faraway sounds in the ghostly silence.

It was pleasantly cool for a time, and the night wind salved Lennox and Jana, soft, gentle. But then it turned cold and disdainful, chilling them, and they stirred and awoke, almost simultaneously. After a moment, without speaking, they left the tank and returned to the barrel cactus and drank again of its pulp. The air, there below, was filled with a heady fragrance that came from a night-blooming cereus somewhere nearby—and if it had not been for the pain and the weakness and the fear that was theirs, the night might have held a deep magic allure.

In the tank again, they sat facing one another, close but without touching. Jana said softly, "Talk to me, Jack. I need something to keep my mind off how hungry I am, and what's out there behind us. And tomorrow—I don't want to think about tomorrow."

"What should I talk about?"

"I don't know. You—Jack Lennox."

"I don't think so," he said.

"Why not?"

"There's nothing to say."

"There's always something to say."

"Not in my case."

"Jack," she said simply, "I want to know."

"All right. I'm thirty-three years old, a native of the Pacific

Northwest, divorced and a gentleman of the road, as they used to say. I work when I feel like it, and play when I feel like it, and move on to new places when I feel like it."

"Is that all?"

"That's all."

She was silent for a time, and then, softly, "Are you involved with those men out there?"

"What?"

"That story you told me about seeing them kill somebody—is that really true?"

"Of course it's true."

"And that's why they're chasing you—us?"

"Yes. What did you think?"

"I don't know. You lied about your name . . ."

"That has nothing to do with this."

"What *does* it have to do with?"

"Nothing."

"You're running from something else, aren't you?" she said. "Something besides those men."

He stiffened slightly. "What makes you say that?"

"It's the truth, isn't it?"

"Suppose it is. What difference does it make?"

"None, I guess. I just want to know."

"Well, I don't want to talk about it."

"Why not—now?"

"You want my life history, but you won't say a thing about yourself," Lennox said. "Let's try that tack for a while."

"I told you all there is to know last night."

"Did you?"

"Yes."

Lennox studied her—and, slowly, he realized just what the bond was between them, the kinship he had intuited last night and today. "Maybe we've both got something to hide," he said. "Maybe you're running away from something else, too."

A kind of dark torment flickered across Jana's features, and then was gone. "Maybe I am," she said.

"Do *you* want to talk about it?"

"No. I couldn't if I wanted to."

"Why?"

"It's . . . I just couldn't, that's all."

132

"Any more than I can."

"Any more than you can."

They fell silent. Lennox wanted to say something more to her, but there did not seem to be anything to say. He thought: I wonder if it would do any good to bring it out into the open, I wonder if I *could* talk about it? He looked at her, bathed in the soft moonshine—the weary, pain-edged loveliness of her—and suddenly he was filled with an overpowering compulsion to do just that, to unburden himself, to lay bare the soul of Jack Lennox. He had wanted to do it, without consciously admitting the fact to himself, ever since he had impulsively confessed his real name to her that afternoon. It was as if the weight of his immediate past had become dead weight, too heavy to carry any further without throwing it off for just a little while. It had been coming to this for some time now, you can only dam it up inside you for so long, just so long, and then it has to come out; the levees of the human mind can hold it no longer. He was going to tell her. There was a fluttering, intense sensation in the pit of his stomach, the kind of feeling you get when you know you're going to do something in spite of yourself, right or wrong, wise or foolish, you know you're going to do it anyway. He was going to tell her, all right, he was going to tell her—

"Phyllis," he said. The word was thick and hot in his throat.

"What?"

"That's what I'm running from. A woman and a life and a hell named Phyllis," and it all came spilling out of him, floodgates opening, words rushing forth—all of it, from the beginning:

The night he had first met Phyllis at a cocktail lounge, she was new in his town then, a secretary with a Seattle firm that had opened a branch office there, and how he had fallen in love with her after their fourth Gibson, a major joke between them when the feeling had been fresh and good and clean in the beginning. The courtship and the love-making, the whispered endearments, the plans, the hopes, the dreams, the promises. The picnics and hikes through giant redwood forests. The afternoon they had gone swimming nude in the Pacific and he had been pinched by a sand crab on his left buttock, another fine private joke to be shared. The engagement, the marriage, the long hours at Humber Realty, the striving for growth and position and monetary security. The house he had built and the things he had bought to fill it. Phyllis' reluctance to have children—"why don't we wait a few years, darling, we're not ready for parenthood just yet." Her increasing awareness of social standing, her desire to belong to organizations and country clubs and in-groups, her attraction for expensive clothes, expensive appointments, expensive friends.

The change—or the realization of things having changed: The pushing and the pettiness and the mild rebukes of his manners, attitudes, feelings in public and in private that had soon become open ridicule. The breakdown of all communication. The taunting sexual denial. The emergence of a predator, demanding everything and giving nothing, shutting him out, using him, denying his worth as a man and a human being. The sudden, bitter understanding that the thing he had once thought was love in her was only sugared hate.

And, finally, the lover whose identity he had been unable to uncover and whose existence he could never prove except by her mocking eyes. The separation and the divorce. The court hearing. The complete victory she had won at the hands of a sympathetic judge, and the cold and triumphant smile she had given him as they left the courtroom. His decision to quit Humber and the town and the state, to deny her the alimony she so strongly coveted. The drunken late-evening visit to the house that he had built and paid for and which no longer belonged to him. The words and the slaps—the final insult, the last straw. His rage, and the result of that rage. Her words, flung at him through broken and bleeding lips. And his flight; the desperate need to run—the running itself, the panic, the desire to escape, the desire which had carried him along on a blind course through five states in the past nine months, carried him here, to this desert, to now, to *this* . . .

When he stopped talking, finally, Lennox felt as if he had undergone a massive catharsis. There was drying sweat on his forehead despite the cold night breeze. Jana sat motionless, looking at him, and the silence was absolute, pressing in on them from the surrounding rock walls, from the sweeping panorama above; she had not interrupted him while he talked, and she did not speak for a long while now. Then, at last, she stirred slightly in the sand and put her hands on her knees.

She said, "I've got no real right to ask you this, but—why did you decide to run away?"

Lennox raised his head. "I told you why. She made it plain what she was going to do, and she did it—oh yes, I know Phyllis and she did it. It wouldn't surprise me if she lied to the cops to make it look worse than it was. That's something she would do, all right."

"I didn't mean that," Jana said quietly. "I meant, why did you decide to run away *before* you went to see her that night? Why did you quit your job?"

"I told you that, too. I wasn't going to pay her that alimony on top of everything else. I just wasn't going to do it."

"You let her beat you, Jack."

"The hell I did. She didn't get her alimony, did she?"

"No," Jana said, "but she won, anyway. In the long run, she's the winner."

"I don't know what you're talking about."

"If you hadn't run, if you'd stayed there and paid her the money, you'd have beaten *her*. If what you told me about her is true, the thing she wanted at the end of it all was to destroy you completely. And she's doing that now."

"I'd have been her goddamn slave if I'd stayed and paid that alimony!"

"For a while, maybe. But then you'd have found somebody else, you'd have regained yourself, your spirit. And you'd have been the one who won out in the end, Jack."

"Oh Christ," Lennox said.

"What has the running gotten you?" Jana asked. "Are you happy, secure, have you forgotten Phyllis, have you regained your self-respect? What are you now, Jack? A drifter, a lonely man and a frightened one. Filled with hate that keeps on festering inside you. What kind of existence is that?"

He stared at her. He didn't want to believe what she was saying, what did she know about it, goddamn it, just from listening to him tell it in an encapsulated form? He didn't want to believe her—and yet, the last nine months, in sober retrospection, had been a nightmare of running and fearing and hating, just as she said. Filled with hate, yes, hate for Phyllis that was cold and complete; and filled with another kind of hate, too, hate for himself and what he was becoming and trying to

put all the blame on Phyllis when in reality a part of it was his—
no, that wasn't true, no, it was Phyllis, Phyllis, Phyllis—

"I don't care," he said. "Jesus Christ, I don't care any more,
do you hear me?"

"You care," Jana said. "If you didn't care, you wouldn't
keep running now. You care, Jack, you cling to life too desperately not to care."

I don't want to hear any more of this crap, Lennox thought
savagely. He said, "Listen, who are you to analyze what I am?
You're running, too, you're afraid of something, too. Well, why
don't you spit it up the way I just did, get it out into the open, let
me tell *you* some things then. What do you say, Jana?"

"No," she said, and she shook her head. "No, we're talking
about you—"

"Not any more, we're talking about you now. Come on,
what are you afraid of? Why are you running? Come on, Jana."

"No," she said.

"Yes, it's easy. Just open your mouth and say it, that's what
I did, let's play with your guts for a while."

"No. No."

Lennox moved closer to her. He felt confused and angry;
she had touched and opened something deep inside him with her
words and what he had glimpsed within that fissure was repul-
sive. He wanted to strike back at her, unreasoningly, childishly.
"Come on, Jana, talk to me, tell me all about it. I'm a good listener too, you know, I've got a good analytical mind—"

"No." Jana turned away from him, hugging herself, shivering in the cold wind that blew down into the tank. "No!"

He reached out and took her shoulders, firmly, and turned
her back to him. He was very close to her now, his eyes looking
into hers, his breath warm on her face, his hands pressing her
nearer so that her breasts almost touched the ragged front of his
shirt. "Tell me about it, Jana! Tell me what you're afraid of, tell
me!"

She struggled in his grip, and in the reflection of bright
moonlight he saw raw terror brimming in her eyes. A frown
creased his forehead and he released her. She fell away from
him, sprawling into the dust, and cradled her head in her arms;
her shoulders trembled as if she were crying, but she made no
sound.

136

The anger, the demand for retribution, left him and he felt an immediate return of the compassion that he had experienced throughout the day, the protectiveness; he didn't want to hurt her, not really, for God's sake, what was the matter with him? He moved to her side, and his fingers were gentle on her arms this time as he brought her over onto her side, exposing her face to the shine of the moon again. Her features were twisted, a veil of despair.

"Jana," he said in a low, soft voice, "Jana, what is it?"

He saw the word *no* form on her lips, but she did not put voice to it. It was, then, as if all her inner defenses crumbled, as if—as with him—the incubus had become too much and the levees had ceased to wall it in. A shuddering sob tremored through her body; and in a voice that was a half-whisper barely audible above the murmuring wind she said:

"I'm a lesbian. God forgive me, God help me, I'm a lesbian!"

Ten

It took Brackeen more than two hours to obtain a promise of action from the State Highway Patrol.

Most of that time was spent in locating Fred Gottlieb, the man in charge of the murder investigation; Gottlieb had all the facts, he was told by both Kehoe City and the main Patrol office in the capital, and there could be no authorizations based on speculative evidence—no matter how well it all dovetailed— without his approval. Once Brackeen found him, at the home of a married sister in a nearby community, and outlined the facts and the conclusions he had drawn from those facts, Gottlieb did not require much convincing. He listened attentively, asked several questions, confided that he and his partner, Dick Sanchez, had been looking into the possibility of Perrins/Lassiter's death being a contracted Organization hit, and agreed without reluctance that the theory had considerable merit. Brackeen's opinion of the State Highway Patrol went up considerably; he was dealing with a good, competent officer here, not fools like Lydell and the bright-face, Forester.

It was past dark by this time, and both men decided that there was not much that could be done until the daylight hours. Brackeen suggested an airplane or helicopter reconnaissance of the desert area to the east, south, and west of Cuenca Seco, and Gottlieb told him that he would have machines in the air at dawn. He said also that he would contact the county office in Kehoe City and have Lydell arrange for a team of experienced men on standby in Cuenca Seco, in the event the air reconnaissance uncovered anything; even if it didn't, Gottlieb concurred that a careful foot search should be made of the area surrounding the location of the wrecked Triumph and the rental Buick.

Brackeen said, "Will you be coming down yourself?"

"As soon as I can get back to Kehoe City and round up Sanchez," Gottlieb answered. "Where will you be?"

"Here in the substation."

"I might be pretty late."

"I'll be here."

"Okay," Gottlieb said. "Listen, Brackeen, you did a hell of a job putting all this together. We'd have got it eventually, but probably not in time; there may still be a chance, now, for Lennox and the Hennessey girl."

Brackeen said, "There are some things you can't forget."

"How's that?"

"Never mind. You going to want to take charge of things when you get here?"

"Officially, yes," Gottlieb said. "Unofficially, it's your district and you've got a free wheel."

"Thanks, Gottlieb."

"Sure. Later, huh?"

"Later."

Brackeen put down the phone and stared at it. He should have felt relieved now, or pleased, or satisfied, but he was more keyed up than he had been before the long-distance call from the girl's New York agent, Klein. He had proven something to the world, which did not matter—and something to himself, which did matter—but that was somehow not enough; this thing wasn't done with yet, none of it was done with yet, and he knew that the tenseness would not leave him until it was, if it was.

He picked up the phone and called Marge for the second time in the past several hours and told her he would not be home, that he was spending the night in the substation. She didn't protest; that was one thing about Marge, she never complained, never sat heavy on his back. Talking to her, he felt a trace of guilt—an emotion new to him—for all the times he had cheated on her with the plump young whores in Kehoe City. She was a good woman, she was too goddamn good a woman to have to put up with that kind of thing. Well, she wouldn't have to put up with it any more, he told himself. Not any more.

There was a lot of time between now and the arrival of Gottlieb and Sanchez—between now and dawn—and Brackeen felt nervous and edgy with inactivity. He left the cubicle, told Demeter that he was going out for a while, and picked up his cruiser. He drove east through the bright moonlight and stopped at the junction of the county road and the abandoned dead end; the special deputy he had stationed there several hours earlier was alert and eager, but he had seen nothing. Brackeen sat with him for a time, debating the idea of patrolling the abandoned road, and then decided against it; wherever they were on the desert, they would not be moving in the darkness—even with the drenching light from the moon. If Lennox and Jana Hennessey were still alive, they would be hiding now, waiting for dawn. Half dead from hunger and thirst, from the burning sun, from fear and from running.

If they were still alive.

Brackeen drove back to the substation to await the arrival of Gottlieb and Sanchez.

Eleven

Jana saw shock and disbelief register on Lennox's face, and she thought: No, no, I didn't want to say it, why did you make me say it? She pulled away from him again, rolling her body into a tight cocoon, withdrawing from the sick pain that the almost involuntary revelation had unleashed inside her. But the shell she had so carefully constructed these past ten days was cracked and broken now, irreparably, and she had no defenses. It was in the open now, the word—the fear—had been spoken, he knew, somebody knew. God, oh God, why had she pried into his soul and he into hers, they were like leeches sucking at one another, and for what reason? Strength? Succor? Or was it just that each of them sought to lessen his own misery by exposing that of the other?

She felt his hands touching her again and shrank from them, making a sound that was almost a whimper in her throat; but she was boneless, she was plastic, and he lifted her and held her upright. She would not look at him, she could not. I want to die now, she thought. I can't face it, I just can't face it, I was trying to run away from myself, just like Jack, and you can't escape from yourself—

"Jana," he said, "Jana, it's not true, I don't believe it."

"Oh yes," she said woodenly. "Oh yes. Don't you hate me now? Don't I disgust you?"

"Why? Because of some mistake you might have made? Jana, I don't hate you, I could never hate you."

"I'm a lesbian, don't you understand?"

"You're a normal woman, you couldn't be anything else."

"A lesbian! I am, I know I am."

"You know you are? Why do you say it like that?"

Don't tell him any more, don't talk about it, don't, Jana, don't—but what difference does it make now? He knows, you told him and he knows and what difference does the rest of it make?

"Jana?"

"I liked it, you see," she said, and her eyes were glazed, shining like bright wet stones. "I liked being with Kelly, I liked it the first time and I liked it the last time, I liked being in her arms, I liked her touching me, I liked—"

"Stop it!" Lennox shook her and it was like shaking Raggedy Ann. She did not hear him; she was listening to bitter memories now, and putting voice to them without conscious realization of it, lost and wandering in her own private hell.

"The first time I was drunk and I didn't know what Kelly was, she was just a casual friend who lived down the hall and I

140

thought she was being sympathetic because I had just broken up with Don and I was angry and soured at the rejection and we were sitting there, in my apartment, sitting there and talking and drinking and I started to cry and she held my head and whispered to me and I put my arms around her, it was all so natural, and then I went to sleep or passed out and when I woke up we were in bed together, my bed, and she was holding me and kissing me and telling me that she loved me and I . . . I couldn't stop her, it seemed so good to be loved after what Don had done to me . . ."

Lennox touched her hair, gently, almost delicately, the way you touch a sleeping child. Jana did not take notice. She no longer knew he was there; the words she was speaking were for herself, a volume-open replaying of a memory tape that had already been played a hundred, a thousand times before.

"The morning after that first night with Kelly, I was sick at what I had done and I thought for a while about taking sleeping pills or cutting my wrists, but I couldn't bring myself to do it. I thought about a psychiatrist but I couldn't call one, I couldn't tell anyone what I'd done, and then Kelly came and I didn't want to let her in but something made me let her in and she was contrite, she said she was sorry, she said she had been a lesbian for a long time and she hadn't been able to control herself and then she told me that she loved me, she said it just like that, 'I love you, Jana,' she said, and suddenly I couldn't hate her any more, I didn't want her to go away, I wanted her to stay with me, and we made love that night and a lot of nights afterward and I woke up one morning and looked at myself in the mirror and I thought: You're a lesbian now, too, you're turning into a lesbian just like Kelly. Then I went and vomited in the toilet, because I don't want to be a lesbian, I want to be normal, but I *liked* it with Kelly, I liked it every time, I liked it as much as I liked making love with Don. I knew I had to do something, I knew I had to stop myself before it was too late, divorce myself from Kelly and from New York, from everything that was turning me into what I didn't want to be turned into. I had to be alone, I had to have time to think, I had to plan for the future—just me, just Jana, keeping her mind occupied with *things,* and maybe if enough time goes by I'll be all right again, maybe if I don't let myself get involved with anyone, not with *anyone,* because I think I'm a lesbian now and if I am I'll reject any man, I'll be frigid with any man who tries to make love to me and if I have anything to do with a woman no matter how casual maybe I'll try to seduce her or maybe I'll let her seduce me, and then I'll know for sure, I'll *know*, and I can't face it yet, maybe not ever. I've got to be alone, I've got to be alone . . ."

The tape had run out now, and Jana's eyes lost some of their glassy quality. Lennox shook her again, less sharply this time, and when he was sure his words would penetrate, he said, "Jana, listen to me, you're all right now, don't you see that? You're free now. You broke away, and that proves—"

"It proves nothing. It's not Kelly and it's not New York any more. It's *me* I'm afraid of, it's *me* I can't face." She began to tremble, violently, and the cold wind was only a small part of the cause; her teeth chattered with little hollow clicking sounds. "It's me, it's me, it's me . . ."

Lennox put his arms all the way around her, drawing her close. "Jana," he said, "Jana."

She could feel the warmth of him, the solidity of him, she could feel his breath against her hair, the way his hands moved on her arms and her back, she could hear his soft, gentle voice. The tremoring began to subside, slowly, but there was something else now, a sensation, a curious inner quivering. "No," she said. "Oh no."

"It's all right," Lennox whispered. "Jana, it's all right."

"Oh my God, no, no."

Caressing, warm, solid, male, touching her, holding her, no, no, the thought there in her mind, growing, spreading, beginning to command, no no no, and the embers stirring and the fires sparking, a tightness in her chest, a catch to her breathing, a flowing warmth in her loins, oh no oh no, and she wants to pull free of his arms, she doesn't want this to happen, she can't let it happen, but he is so warm, his touch is so gentle, she is safe but no, no! she can't let it happen, she can't know, but it *is* happening, does that in itself mean something and is that enough, it is happening inside her, she is letting it happen, she wants it, she wants him, she wants *him*, him, him, him

and Lennox holds her, rocking, whispering, and he has never known a tenderness like the one which he feels for this

142

girl, this victim, this kin, her body is soft against his and she is still trembling but it is a different kind of trembling now, somehow he senses that and he holds her tighter and she says, "No, oh please," and her arms go around him and she is holding onto him now, too, she is pressing against him and moving against him and they fall sideways into the dust and fit their bodies tightly to one another, clinging, clinging

and Jana presses her face to the side of his neck, not wanting to press her face there, his pulse beat is soft and irregular against her ear, and she moves her hands along his back, not wanting to move them, and moves her hips against him, not wanting to move them, I don't want this, she thinks, *I don't want this*, and her loins are hungry and eager for the first sign of his arousal

and Lennox becomes aware of her body now, moving, the rippling of her muscles under his fingers, and he understands, he understands what must be happening inside her, the confusion, he doesn't want to hurt her but he doesn't know what will hurt her the most—capitulation or rejection, he wants to help, he wants to reassure her, he knows she is normal, he *feels* it, he has to communicate it to her and there is really only one way now, but he is so tired, the toll of the past two days has been too great, he can't, and he focuses on her movements, on her body, and his hand slips down and touches her buttocks and then he is lengthening, growing, impossibly and wondrously coming alive

and Jana feels him erect against her, oh no, no, and her hips move faster under his hand now, under his hand, *I don't want this*, "No, please no," and she is burning, she is burning, *Love me, no, love me love me love me*

and Lennox says her name, "Jana," and hears her moaning and wants her desperately and his fingers on her clothing are deft, quick, gentle

and Jana helps him, helps them both, the wind blowing cold over naked flesh, her eyes squeezed tightly shut, her lips saying "No" and her mind saying *Yes, yes!* and she is afraid, she is terrified, but he is whispering to her now, calming her, stroking her, and the fire, the need, the need

and they are one, murmuring, clinging, moving, and it is savage, it is tender—together, reaching upward, reaching the zenith, together, together, it happens together, incredibly, perfectly, the way it had to be . . .

They lie silent, holding tightly to one another, and there is no need for words. Jana knows, and inside she weeps—but the tears are clean and good, purging. Lennox knows, and inside there is a peace, unstable but rich and promising. They are one now, in many ways.

In many ways.

The Final Day . . .

One

Vollyer came awake just before dawn—and he was blind.

A soft, strangled cry bubbled in his throat; he sat up, pawing at his eyes. Darkness, darkness, with light shimmering faintly at the edges, with light flickering a long way off like candles at the end of a long, dark tunnel; but there were no images, no colors, there was only the light and pain, pain hammering behind the swollen lids, pain pulsating at the core of each eyeball. He shook his head and kept on shaking it, scratching wildly at the mucus-crusted sockets with the tips of his fingers.

Di Parma had been sitting on a rock nearby, watching the eastern horizon turn a dusty gray with the approach of dawn, eating the last of the tinned meat with chilled fingers. He came running over to Vollyer and knelt beside him. "Harry, what's the matter? Jesus, Harry, what is it?"

"Get away from me!" Vollyer snapped at him. Control, control, get control of yourself, don't panic, only the losers panic. Hands away from your eyes, only makes it worse rubbing at them, that's it, blink now, blink, blink, light growing brighter, yes, taking away the darkness, force those lids up all the way, blink, blink, the sky, you can see the sky now and Di Parma, fuzzy but it's Di Parma, concentrate, blink, his features, eyes, nose, mouth, blink, concentrate, blink, fuzziness fading, focus coming back, you're all right, you're not really blind, only temporary, bad strain that's all, you can see now, you can see as well as before . . .

147

Vollyer dragged cool air into his lungs and sat up again, looking around him. The solid objects had faint, dancing perimeter shadows until he stared at one in particular and then the shadow went away. His head ached massively, malignantly, and there were searing needles probing at the retinas of his eyes. He got shakily to his feet and held his hands out in front of him and stared at their backs; the hands were trembling, but there were only two of them and they had no dancing shadows.

Di Parma said, "Was it your eyes, Harry? Mine have been giving me hell, too. It's the glare of that sun . . ."

Vollyer said nothing. He walked slowly to the rock on which Di Parma had been sitting and took the binoculars from it and then went to where he could look out over the desert to the north. He lifted the glasses, squinting through the lens. The moon was gone now, the stars fading, and the landscape lay cold and starkly quiet under the retreating gray-black of the sky. He could see a long way, he could see cactus, rocks, bushy shrubs, distinct and identifiable forms. He released a long, soft breath, turning, calm again.

"Come on," he said to Di Parma. "It's time to be moving. We're close to them, I can feel it. Even with you shooting at that snake last night, we're close to them. It won't be long now . . ."

Two

Brackeen said, "I can't take any more of this sitting around. I'm going out and check with the deputy I posted at the junction."

"If he had anything to report, he would have radioed in," Gottlieb said. He sat across from his partner, Dick Sanchez, at one of the desks in the substation, drinking his tenth or eleventh cup of coffee and chain-smoking cork-tipped cigarettes. Both men owned tired eyes and disheveled suits, and they were playing two-handed pinochle with no enthusiasm at all.

Brackeen stood at the front counter, looking out through the window. The first pale, cold light of dawn touched the empty street beyond, an inchoate dissolution of the shadows resting in doorways and alleyways and at the corners of the false-fronted buildings. "I know that," he said without turning. "But I'm ready to climb the goddamn walls."

"Lydell will have those men I asked for here any minute now," Gottlieb told him. "Why don't you wait for him and we'll all go out together?"

"I'd feel better moving around, that's all."

"Go ahead, then."

"Radio when you're coming?"

"As soon as we leave."

"What time are the choppers going up?"

"They should be in the air any minute now."

"Then we'll have a report in another hour or less."

"About that."

Brackeen passed a hand across his face. There were deep circles etched into the puffy flesh beneath his eyes, and the lack of sleep had made the lids heavy and put a cottony taste in his mouth that was enhanced by the amount of coffee he had drunk and cigarettes he had smoked since last night. His nerves were raw-edged from inactivity, fatigue, caffein, nicotine. But his mind was clear and alert, kept that way by the prospect of movement and accomplishment, and by the presence of Gottlieb and Sanchez; the three of them had passed the hours since the arrival of the state investigators shortly after midnight in talking Brackeen's theory through, examining every possibility, planning the moves to be made on this day.

As Brackeen picked up his Stetson and crossed to the front door, Gottlieb said mildly, "Stay loose, huh?"

"As loose as the two of you," Brackeen said, and went out.

He drove to the junction and talked to the deputy again, and there was nothing to report. The sky was much lighter now, splashed with gold and deep red on the eastern horizon, and it would not be long before the rounded rim of the sun edged up there like a huge golden shield. A narrow wash paralleled the county road for a short distance here, beginning just beyond the rutted surface of the abandoned rail company road; a red-topped, black-and-white striped Gila woodpecker swooped low over it, shrieking maniacally all the while. There was no other sound; the county road was deserted at this hour of the morning.

Brackeen stood by his cruiser, looking up into the lightening heavens. The hell with this, he thought. He slid under the cruiser's wheel and entered the abandoned road, driving slowly, his head moving in careful quadrants from the road surface to the terrain stretching away to the east. He did not expect to see anything, but this was better than just sitting, waiting for Lydell to show up, waiting for the choppers to report.

A half-mile, by the odometer, beyond the place where he had found the rental Buick the day before, Brackeen U-turned and started back again. He passed the sandstone formation which had concealed the Buick, passed the dry wash where the wrecked yellow Triumph had lain, and followed the gentle curve in the road from due north to northeasterly. Less than a mile from the junction, he slowed, remembering the all but obliterated shortcut from the rail company road to the county highway several miles to the east of the junction; trucks carrying road-grading equipment and the men who operated it had made the cut across the flatland here in order to save some eight miles in the haul out of Kehoe City. Brackeen had been over the rutted surface several times. It skirted a long, deep arroyo, over which the railroad, in the early days of the century, had built a trestle for a proposed spur to Cuenca Seco; the trestle had long since collapsed into the arroyo, and there was little else remaining of the abortive line of tracks branching off the later-abandoned line to Kehoe City. The railroad had not had much luck in this area of the desert over the years.

Brackeen did not want to return to the junction just yet; it only meant more passive waiting. He swung the cruiser off the road, onto the creosote-choked flatland. It wouldn't do any harm to check the area out here, he thought; there was always the chance that he might spot something, and even if he didn't it would consume some time until the air reconnaissance could be made and Lydell could get off his fat ass and into Cuenca Seco with the team of men.

Slowly, dust blossoming in lazy plumes behind him, Brackeen drove toward the flaming brass light in the eastern sky.

150

Three

Lennox and Jana left the tank at the first fading of darkness, rested and with regathered strength, and began moving toward a long sloping rise to the north. The air was no longer cold, though still cool, and they went as swiftly as their stiffened, aching bodies would allow; they had drunk deeply of the pulp of another barrel cactus outside the tank, and the moisture would stay with them for a while, until the sun climbed into the sky and set fire to the desert again.

They had passed the long night wrapped in each other's arms, insulated against the biting wind, against the terror which lay without. The need for words had not come to either of them, and they had slept, and when they had awakened there was still no need to put voice to what they had shared. Jana had met Lennox's gaze when he looked at her, and smiled faintly and nodded, thanking him with her eyes, telling him that she was all right now, that she knew and accepted the truth about herself.

As they ran, Lennox found himself wondering how deeply his feelings for Jana were rooted—if he could possibly be in love with her. There was none of the wild, joyous exhilaration he had felt with Phyllis in the beginning, none of the electricity, the chemical magnetism that draws and fuses two individuals; there was only the peace she generated within him, the bond that was theirs, the tenderness that overwhelmed him each time he looked at her and touched her. Was that love? Or the beginnings of love? He didn't know, but he wanted to know. He wanted to know her better, he wanted her to know him, he wanted them to get out of this place, this trap, so that the understanding and the perception each seemed to have of the other's inner self could be nurtured and developed.

He gripped Jana's hand tightly, looking over his shoulder at her, trying to smile with his cracked mouth. She returned the pressure of his fingers, touching him with her eyes, and he knew that she felt some of the same things about him—and the knowledge filled him with hope and with pleasure and with urgency.

They approached the crest of the rise, threading their way between scattered boulders and thick clumps of mesquite; the sky was bright with the building haze of heat now, and Gambel's quail and an occasional jackrabbit scurried away before them, startled by their presence in a world that belonged to creatures instead of men. Finally, minutes later, they topped the rise, and Lennox stopped abruptly, staring at what lay beyond. "Oh God," he said softly.

Flat, semi-barren land stretched away from them, void of all but transitory cover; there was a line of rocky outcroppings to the west, but they were some distance away and he and Jana would have to cross a great expanse of open ground to get to them. Naked, they would be naked . . .

Jana said sharply, "Jack, look!"

"What is it?"

"Down there! Is that a road?"

Lennox followed her pointing arm with his eyes. Near the foot of the long slope falling away into the flatland was a pair of faintly discernible wheel ruts, obliterated in spots, grown over with brush in others, but ruts nonetheless, coming from around the rocks to the west, hooking eastward to parallel a wide arroyo cut deeply, like a jagged scar, into the dry, desolate plain. They would lead somewhere, they would lead to Cuenca Seco or to another road, they would lead *out*.

Lennox felt a surge of wild hope. He saw the same relief mirrored on Jana's face, the sudden brightness of her eyes, and she said, "Oh, Jack, a road, a road!" and then they were running down the slope, unaware now of the rocky, treacherous soil and the gleaming cactus needles and the multiple, clutching arms of the mesquite and ocotillo, forgetting the danger of exposure on the open flat, seeing nothing but the wheel ruts, the path to safety . . .

Four

The pain in the lids and sockets of Vollyer's eyes had become ex-
cruciating, and the shadows were back at the edges of solid objects, distorting them slightly, putting them vaguely out of
focus. The edge of the sun had crawled above the eastern horizon now, and the glare of daylight wavered over the landscape,
contracting the pupils, intensifying the agony.

They were coming on a long rise, and he stopped to catch
his breath, to rub gingerly at the swollen pits with his pocket
handkerchief. Di Parma said, "You sure your eyes are okay,
Harry? Jesus, they don't look too good—"

"There's nothing wrong with my eyes!"

"Harry, listen, we've got to call it off pretty soon. We can't
stay out here much longer, Harry, not without food and water.
We may have gone too far as it is, it'll take us a full day or more
to get back to the car—"

"Shut up, will you shut up?"

Di Parma caught his arm. "Listen, I'm telling you, I don't
want to die on this desert!"

Vollyer pushed him away savagely and swung the binoculars up. At first he could not see anything but blurred images
through the lens, and he thought: I can see, I can see, my eyes
are all right and I can see, clear up now, you bastards, clear up
so I can *see!* He blinked frantically, and the blur lessened and
there was substance, there were shapes; he tried to swallow into
a constricted throat, fighting the double vision that would not
completely dissipate, moving the glasses in a wide arc, west to
east, along the top of the rise—

*They were there, Lennox and the girl, standing there at the
crest and looking down to the other side, just standing there, five
hundred yards away.*

Vollyer jerked the glasses down, and the Remington scope–
handgun was in his right hand. He began to run up the slope. Di
Parma hesitated and then ran after him, reaching his side.
"Harry, what is it, did you see them?" but even as he said the
words, Di Parma was looking up at the crest of the rise and the
two figures standing there, looking at them for a brief instant

before they jumped forward to disappear on the other side. He had been carrying his jacket, and he fumbled the .38 out of the pocket, flung the garment down; his lips pulled away from his teeth, and the fingers of his huge hand were spasmodic on the sweating metal of the belly-gun.

They ran diagonally across the slope, toward the spot where Lennox and the girl had been standing. Vollyer gagged on each breath, running on legs that were like jagged edges of bone, and sweat poured acid agony into his eyes. He fell once and Di Parma slowed automatically and pulled him to his feet, and then they were at the crest and looking beyond and Lennox and the girl were almost to the bottom of the slope on that side, running to the west. Vollyer pawed away sweat, pawed away some of the shimmering blur, but he was still too far away for an accurate shot, he had to get closer, a little closer, and he plunged downward with Di Parma at his heels, slipping, sliding wildly on the incline, moving in a diagonal again to cut off the targets at the bottom.

Vollyer became aware, through the stinging obscurity of his vision, that there was some kind of road or cart track down there—that was what they were running for and they were looking at that, only that, they did not know that he and Di Parma were up here behind them and that was all the edge he needed, the game was definitely over now, no mistake now. The gap was closing, closing, two hundred yards, less, near enough, one bullet for Lennox and one for the girl, and he skidded to his knees on the slope halfway down, bracing himself, washing away sweat with the palm of his free hand, bringing the Remington up into the crook of his arm and sighting with the scope. Two of Lennox and two of the woman, oh you goddamn bastard eyes, blink, blink, concentrate, clear up, there now, there, finger closing on the trigger, steady, steady—

The first shot.

Pause.

And amid rolling vibrations of sound that filled the yellow-gold morning like distant thunder, the second shot . . .

Five

With the window rolled down, and the cruiser's speed held to a crawl, Brackeen heard clearly the deep, hollow reports and knew immediately what they were.

Reflexively, his foot bore down on the accelerator and the patrol car responded with instant power, rear tires spewing dust and pebbles. He clung grimly to the wheel, body tensed, eyes probing the flaming distance, trying to see beyond the line of rocks just ahead. The shots had come from somewhere on their far side, somewhere close, and he knew with the intuitive sixth sense of a born cop that it was not a kid potting at jackrabbits or quail, or one of the local settlers target-practicing at an early hour; he knew that this was it, that this was the showdown, that the waiting had come to an abrupt end and there would be no need for the helicopters any longer, no need for Lydell and his search party, knew that he would find all of them—Lennox and Jana Hennessey, dead or alive now, and the professional sluggers—waiting for him just a few seconds away . . .

Brackeen remembered the bullet he had found in the dashboard of the wrecked yellow Triumph, too badly mutilated for accurate identification but obviously of a high caliber; remembered, too, the dead body of Perrins/Lassiter and the six bullet holes within a five-inch radius on the upper torso, testimony to a deadly marksmanship. One man, possibly both, with a high-velocity weapon of some kind and more than likely the smaller handguns they had used on the hit, revolvers or automatics . . . automatics . . . automatics . . .

And Brackeen's mind was suddenly filled with a vivid reproduction of the rain-slick fire escape and the frightened white face of Feldman and the heavy automatic leveled upward, the huge black bore of the gun, the explosion and the destructive impact of the bullet which had seemed so real and yet had only been illusion; Coretti's face, alive and dead, smiling and bloodily pulped, alternating like shuffled *Before* and *After* photographs across the surface of his mind. Sweat flowed thickly, hotly over his face and under his arms and into his crotch, and there was fear in the center of his belly now, fear twisting at his vitals, the same kind of fear he had felt staring at Feldman's gun that night, staring at death and the terrible black void beyond.

I can't face a gun, he thought. I can't let it happen again!

And then he thought: But I have to, there's nobody else, if I back off and radio for Gottlieb and Sanchez, for help, it might be too late by the time they got here and Lennox and the Hennessey girl could still be alive right now, no, I've got to see it through, I can't crap out on them now . . .

The back of Brackeen's neck grew cold and bristling, then, and his thoughts became very clear and sharp. Understanding flowed through him, taking the edge off the building panic in his belly, quieting the stutter of his heart. He had to see it through. That was the way it had to be all right, that was the only way it *could* be. Because the commitment and the resurrection of Andy Brackeen had to be full and complete or else there was no real commitment and no true resurrection at all. You couldn't start living again halfway, with half-knowledge, and subconsciously he had known this from the very beginning. He had known there was a good chance it would come to this, to a confrontation, a showdown, and he had wanted it to be that way. Jesus Christ, he *wanted* to face the gun or guns out there, he had to face them—that was why he had come out alone this morning, that was why he had been so nervous with the waiting last night and today; he wanted it because without it he would still be half a man, and he had to know what Andy Brackeen really was, he had to know.

He caught up the hand mike on the cruiser's radio and called the substation. Demeter was there. Brackeen gave his position, and what he had heard, and asked for immediate assistance; then he signed out before any questions could be asked; there was no time for questions.

The line of rocks loomed directly ahead. Brackeen replaced the mike and drew the .357 Magnum from the holster at his belt, holding it on the seat beside him, palm sweating on the textured butt. His mind was blank now, relying on instinct and training to dictate his actions, and the fear that was in him was tempered with a kind of anticipation . . .

156

Six

The first bullet cut hot and burning through Lennox's right side, and the unexpectedness of it, the sudden biting pain, caused him to stagger, to lose his balance. He went down, rolling, his head striking a glancing blow on a rock, thinking fuzzily, *My God, my God, what,* and then there was billowing sound to take away the early-morning stillness and he knew what it was, he realized he had been shot, he realized that their luck had finally run out.

Panic, the old familiar shrieking panic, clutched at him and he reached out blindly and caught onto a heavily thorned prickly pear, slicing open the heel of his hand, slowing himself. And then Jana screamed, he could hear her screaming, he could hear more echoes of sound, and he managed to check his forward momentum, to twist his body so that he could see upward along the slope.

She was down, she was on her hands and knees and crawling toward him. Lennox felt the added emotions of hatred and rage and futility as he scrambled to his feet, looking up at Jana and beyond her, fighting down the urge to immediate flight, and the two of them were up there, scrambling down the slope, *you dirty sons of bitches, why don't you finish it, why don't you sit up there and get it over with!* He heard Jana cry his name, cry it again, and he ran to her and pulled her to her feet and there was no blood on her, there was only blood on him, blood soaking the remnants of his shirt, blood flowing down from his cut palm to drip thickly crimson from his fingertips. The second shot had missed her, it had been the shock of seeing him fall or the bad footing which had sent her to her knees; her eyes were huge puddles of terror, pleading mutely, and he flung his arm around her shoulders and dragged her with him down the slope.

There was no place to go, the rutted trail was useless, they were trapped; the avenue of escape had opened only briefly, to tempt them, and then it had closed and there was nowhere for them to go. It had all been for nothing, all the running and the hiding, and last night, too, the insight and moments of peace and ecstasy and salvation, the growing thing that might be love between them—all for nothing, all too late. Fate had played a monstrous joke on them, tantalizing them with a chance, a future, and then presenting them with nothing but a certain death . . .

Seven

"You missed them!" Di Parma screamed. "Damn you, damn you, you missed them both!"

He ran past Vollyer, arms flung wide, spitting obscenities in a release of the pent-up frustration he had known the past two days. They're not going to get away this time, they're not going to get away, oh you prick, Harry, damn your bad eyes and your boss-man superior attitude, you missed them, they should be dead now but they'll be dead pretty soon . . .

Vollyer was up and stumbling after him, frantically trying to chamber one of the .221 cartridges into the Remington, but Di Parma paid no attention to him. He was watching Lennox and the girl, watching them reach the wheel ruts below and start across them, a hundred yards away, just a hundred yards. He lengthened his strides, summoning all the strength left in his body, gaining on them, opening up his lead on the struggling Vollyer, and he was twenty yards from the trail when he became aware of the rumbling whine of an automobile engine coming out of the west, increasing in magnitude as the machine drew closer.

Di Parma turned his body without slackening his pace, looking toward the line of rocks in that direction, and then the car was there, he saw the car, he saw its unmistakable black-and-white markings, the red-glassed dome light, heard the deafening roar of its engine as it hurtled forward. He tasted momentary panic and his thoughts were sharply confused. Cops, oh Jesus, cops, how did they find us, I knew this was all wrong, I knew it!—and the cruiser veered off the road, coming straight at him, the gleaming chrome of its grill like bared teeth in the expanding brightness. He reversed himself, scrambling backward, eyes searching wildly for cover, not finding any, and the cruiser came to a shuddering stop nose up to a boulder fifty feet from where he was.

He dropped to his knees in the rocky soil, holding the .38 steadied in both hands, and opened fire.

Eight

Brackeen was through the driver's door, moving with amazing speed for his bulk, before the cruiser stopped rocking.

In the distance, he caught a glimpse of the two figures—a man and a woman, the drifter and Jana Hennessey—that he had seen running the moment he'd emerged from the rocks. He felt a grim, fleeting elation that he had been in time, that they were still alive.

He crouched along the front fender, the Magnum heavy in the wetness of his hand, and a bullet dug its way metallically into the far side of the car, another spiderwebbed the near corner of the windshield. He forgot the runners then, thinking: It's happening, it's happening, but that was all he thought. A curious sense of detachment spread over him, as if he were suddenly witnessing all of this from some distant place, as if he were not really part of it at ail.

Another bullet furrowed across the cruiser's hood, making a sound like fingernails being drawn across a blackboard. Brackeen knelt by the near headlight, looking around it, and the one he had taken out after with the cruiser was kneeling there fifty or sixty yards away. He was doing all the shooting. The other one, further up the slope, was running at an angle toward a thick-bodied cactus; something long and misshapen glittered in his hand.

The kneeling one fired again, and the headlamp in front of Brackeen exploded, spraying glass that narrowly missed his eyes, forcing him back. When he got his head up again, the slugger was on his feet, trying to run up the slope, clawing at the jagged earth with his free hand. Brackeen moved out a little, not thinking, setting himself at the edge of the bumper, and the Magnum recoiled loudly. Dust kicked up at the slugger's heels. He raised the muzzle and squeezed off again.

The shooter jerked, leaned forward, fell, and then slid backward on his belly with his arms spread-eagled.

One, that's one.

Brackeen looked up at the cactus for the other, swinging the Magnum over, and he saw the sunlight glinting again and there was, all at once, white agony in his chest and he toppled backward with thunder detonating in his ears and he was looking up at the bright, hot sky, jarred into thinking now, trying to understand. Roll over, get up, but his limbs would not obey the command of his brain; he wanted to touch his chest, he knew that there would be a hole there, that thick, warm blood would be there, that he had been shot and that he was badly wounded and yet, with all of it, he was strangely calm, the feeling of detachment still lingered. The pain spread malignantly through his body, numbing his mind now in a dark gray haze; but the sky was still hot, so blue and hot the morning sky, *what did he shoot me with? Not a rifle, what he was carrying was too small for a rifle—a handgun, then? Sure, with a scope sight, I should have known, but you can't figure all the angles, you've got to do the best you can and sometimes that's not good enough, but the important thing is doing your duty, the important thing is not crapping out—listen, I did it, didn't I? I did it, Coretti, I faced their guns and I didn't panic and I didn't freeze up, oh Marge, there's so much I have to make up to you, to both of us,* and the one who had shot him ran up and extended the scope-sighted handgun and blew away the side of Brackeen's head.

Nine

When they heard the oncoming car, Jana and Lennox checked their headlong flight, looking back. Shattered hope re-formed and re-cemented as they recognized the vehicle, saw it skid off the wheel ruts in a spume of dust and veer straight at the nearest of the two killers, saw the driver's door fly open and the big uniformed officer tumble out, saw the near one on the slope fall to his knees, heard the hollow, cracking sound of gunshots and the savage whine of bullets striking metal; they were, all at once, awed and breathless spectators, divorced from the unfolding drama, clinging to one another, held spellbound by the abrupt and inexplicable turn of events.

Jana felt the bunched muscles of Lennox's arm and shoulder, and his blood stained her fingers where they were caught in the front of his shirt. I love him, she thought, as she had thought lying in his arms last night, as she had thought waking in his arms this morning. It isn't possible, it isn't reasonable, but I love him. Part of it is a reaction to what happened between us, part of it is gratitude for giving me the courage to face myself and for helping me to understand the truth—and yet, it's more than that, it's deeper than that, it means much more than the wild, giddy infatuation I had with Don. I need him, he needs me, we can help each other, we can learn from each other, we can lean on each other. We can't die now, we simply can't die now . . .

She held him more tightly, careful of the wound in his side that her gently probing fingers told her was only superficial, watching the figures moving beyond through the shimmer of gathering heat, the thoughts spinning and sustaining her, blotting out the fear. She watched the one man get to his feet and begin to run up the incline, saw the second one scurrying higher above him. Then the officer stepped out to the front of the cruiser and a brief wisp of smoke spiraled out and up from his extended right hand and the near one jerked and fell amid the booming echo of the gunshot. Jana's heart seemed to hurl itself at the walls of her chest, *we're going to be all right!* and then she saw the officer reel and fall, heard a louder reverberation, and exultation instantaneously dissolved into returning horror.

"No," she said, "oh no, no, no!"

The remaining pursuer broke away from the cactus behind which he had taken refuge, from behind which he had fired, and began to stumble down the grade. Lennox said, "Jesus!" and spun Jana around and they were running again, running with panic again. She forced her legs to keep working, her slender body screaming against the renewed demands of it, and her mind chanted in a frenzied cadence, *Hope, no hope, hope, no hope,* because all of this was a hideous fluctuation, as if God could not make up His mind, as if He were ridden with indecision as to the outcome, and that made it so much more terrible, so much more of a nightmare . . .

Ten

Vollyer turned away from the dead cop, fitting another cartridge into the Remington, and looked along the wheel ruts at the fleeing forms of Lennox and the girl. He was facing directly into the half-revealed plate of the sun and its light was like burning embers thrust against the surface of his eyes; he still had only partial focus, the wavering shadows had broadened, and the two of them down there were indistinct images viewed through warped glass. He would just be wasting time and ammunition trying to pick them off from here, looking into that goddamn sun; he had missed them both at a closer range from the slope, hadn't he? Hitting the cop as he had, had been more luck than marksmanship, the way his eyes were now, and they were bad —there was no use in kidding himself any longer, they were very bad.

He started to the cruiser, and as he did so, he saw the slope through the swimming blur and Di Parma was there, on his feet, pitching down toward him. A gaping hole in his left shoulder, just under the collarbone, splashed blood in bright red streams over the front of his shirt and trousers as he moved, and his left arm flopped uselessly, almost comically, at his side. When Vollyer had run past him moments earlier, to make sure about the cop, Di Parma had seemed not to be moving and he had thought he was dead; now, seeing him still alive, Vollyer felt nothing at all. Di Parma was still a stranger, a nonentity, a lump of clay— alive or dead, it no longer made any real difference.

He came up and there was wildness in his eyes, a mixture of

pain and fright. He was whimpering, red froth at the corners of his mouth. "I'm hurt, Harry, I'm hurt bad, oh God, oh God, we've got to get out of here."

"Not yet," Vollyer said, "not until we get to Lennox and the girl."

From inside the cruiser, the short-wave radio crackled abruptly, angrily to life; a voice demanded acknowledgment. Di Parma looked at the car, looked back to Vollyer. "There's other cops around here, they'll be swarming all over this place in a few minutes!"

"We're going after the witnesses," Vollyer said. "Get in the car."

Di Parma's face contorted into a grimace of agony and rage. "You're crazy, I'm not listening to you any more, oh, you bastard, I'm hurt and I need a doctor, I need Jean, there'll be cops, I'm getting *out* of here!" and he pushed past Vollyer and staggered to the cruiser's open door.

Vollyer lifted the Remington and dispassionately shot him in the back.

The bullet shattered Di Parma's spine just above the kidneys. He screamed once, very briefly, a shrill, surprised feminine sound, and then pitched forward onto his face and lay dead there in the blood-spattered dust.

Pivoting, emotionless, Vollyer scrubbed at his eyes with his free hand and peered along the wheel ruts again. He could still see the girl and Lennox down there. Silence now, thick and brittle, save for the continued crackling of the short wave; but there was no sign, no sound, of approaching cars from either direction. He had time, he still had time. It would take only a couple of minutes to catch the two of them, and then he would drive out, get back to the Buick if he could or find a place to ditch the cruiser and pick up another car; but he had to get the two of them first, it was no good without getting them. You play all the way or you don't play, and he had always played all the way; that was why he was a winner and Lennox and the girl and Di Parma, too, were all losers.

He loaded the Remington once more and slid in under the wheel of the cruiser. The engine started on the first ignition turn. He backed the car away from the boulder and drove over Di Parma's legs, down to the wheel ruts, hunching forward, eyes slitted, and went after the running, shimmering, distorted figures on the flatland ahead.

Eleven

Looking back over his shoulder as they ran, Lennox watched the fat one kill two men in the space of a minute—the wounded police officer and, incomprehensibly, his partner, who had survived the bullet which had felled him on the slope. Vomit boiled up into Lennox's throat. What kind of man is that, he thought sickly, what kind of black union could have created a man like that?

He saw the fat one get into the cruiser, and he thought then: He won't come after us now, he'll know that poor cop isn't alone, that there have got to be others close by. He'll run, he doesn't have any choice now. He'll have to forget about us, he'll have to run, he'll have to let us alone.

But he didn't believe it. The brutal, senseless way the fat one committed murder, the relentless way he had pursued Jana and him until now made a false hope of Lennox's thoughts—and when he glanced back again and saw the patrol car bearing down on them along the rutted trail, he knew beyond any doubt that the situation was as critical now as it had been before the arrival of the single officer.

God oh God, where were the rest of the cops? It couldn't be just the one, there had to be others, they had to have figured out what had happened somehow, or else the one wouldn't be here. But if they didn't hurry they would be too late—where were they, where *were* they?

Lennox swung his head around again, holding onto Jana, trying to ignore the stabbing pain in his side where the bullet had creased him. No place to hide, no sanctuary, not enough time to cross the trail and try to re-climb the slope on the other side, nothing in front of them but a flat plane of cactus and sparse ground cover and the remains of a long-abandoned set of rail tracks—sections missing and grown with mesquite, sections collapsed or windblown into drunken angles—that came looping around the incline from the south, dissolved in favor of the trail, and then resumed in a straight run to the edge of the deep arroyo winding away on their left.

There was only one way for them to go, and Lennox altered their course in an abrupt quarter-turn toward the brink of the arroyo; if they could get down into that wash, out of the open, maybe they could hold out until more police arrived, *if* more police arrived. Slim chance, frail chance, but they had nothing else, nothing at all, and behind them the cruiser swerved sharply off the ruts, pursuing, the sound of its engine like the rumbling swell of an approaching earthquake in the quiet morning, the sun-baked soil beneath their feet seeming to ripple to complete the illusion. Lennox cast another wild look over his shoulder, saw the machine bouncing and swaying over the rough ground, gleaming metal leaping at them, a thing gone berserk, gaining in spite of the uneven terrain.

Dust choked his lungs, bringing on a spasm of coughing, as he dragged the faltering, panting Jana to the edge of the arroyo. It was some one hundred and fifty yards wide and forty feet deep at this point, with steep, layered shale walls that were treacherous but scalable, extending away on both sides, in both directions. Boulders and ironwood and mesquite littered its sandy bed, and a few yards beyond, below where the rail line crawled up to the edge of the wash, twisted chunks and lengths of rusted, disintegrating steel, sun-bleached bits of rotted wood that had once been ties formed heaps and piles and pyramids the width of the jagged incision—all that remained of a long-collapsed, long-forgotten trestle.

Lennox had the fleeting, disjointed image of a massive, grotesque display of Pop Art sculpture, created by the forces of nature long before man learned the dubious aesthetics to be found in the arrangement of junk and scrap metal. And then, without thinking any further, his ears filled with the rumbling, rattling howl of the cruiser, he turned Jana's face to his chest and took her over the edge.

Twelve

Thirty yards from where he had seen the girl and Lennox start down into the arroyo, Vollyer was forced to abandon the patrol car. The ground was too rough here, dotted with too many rocks and thickly grown vegetation, and the glare of the rising sun through the windshield was hellish on his eyes.

He scrambled out of the car, not hearing the demanding voice half garbled in static on the radio, not thinking about anything but the job he had to do. He had the Remington clenched in his right hand, and he pulled at his coat pocket with his left for the .38; he was taking no chances now, there was time, but very little of it, this particular game had gone as far as it could go.

He ran in a drunken wobble to the arroyo and ducked his head against his shoulder to clear away some of the astringent sweat, and then looked down into the fissure. He couldn't see them. Hiding, they were hiding; if they were still on the move he would have been able to pick them out easily from up here; there were plenty of places of concealment at the immediate bottom of the wash, but once you got fifty yards on either side you couldn't run very far without exposing yourself. And they hadn't had time to make it all the way across, to scale the bank on the opposite side. No, they were down there, all right, just down there, hiding, and it was only a matter of seconds now.

Vollyer transferred the Remington to his left hand, holding both guns up and away from his body, and dropped into a sitting position with his legs splayed out and pointing at an angle into the arroyo. He went down the bank that way, like a plump and begrimed child going down a long slide, using his right hand and the heels of his shoes to restrain momentum. A few feet from the bottom, an edge of rock bit painfully into the back of his left thigh, opening a deep gash, causing him to limp slightly when he struggled finally into an upright position on the dusty floor. The Remington back in his right hand, he moved forward, slowly, exhorting his eyes in mute viciousness to mend so that he could see clearly, exhorting in vain.

Something moved, a quick stirring, ahead and to his left.

Vollyer reeled around a steel-draped boulder, and the long rattled tail of a sidewinder swayed into the dimness at its base. Cautious of his footing, he backed away and crossed to where a stunted smoke tree offered possible cover. Nothing. A conglomerate of twisted steel. Nothing. He stopped, ducking his face into his shoulder again, and then squinted with myopic intensity on all sides of him. Nothing.

A high, flat-topped rock, with bonelike fragments of bleached wood strewn at its base, beckoned nearby. That was what he needed, a high vantage point in this proximity; if he could scale that rock, he might be able to locate their place of concealment. He went toward it, painfully, watchfully, listening to the ragged sound of his own breathing. It was otherwise very quiet. But they were close, he could sense their nearness; a tic jumped spasmodically along his right temple, and another pulled the left side of his mouth down crookedly.

They were very, very close . . .

Thirteen

The running was over.

Crouched with Jana in a right angle formed by a canted boulder and a mound of crumbling debris, Lennox knew that with sharp, crystal clarity. He could not run any more; he simply could not run any more. Whenever a crisis had arisen in his life, he had run away from it, he had taken the easy way out—as a child, as a teen-ager, as an adult, never standing firm, never meeting the crisis head-on, just letting the panic take possession of him, welcoming it, never fighting it. And each time he had run away—unnecessarily, foolishly—he had lost a little more of himself, abrogated a little more of his manhood. He knew now that this was what Jana had seen in him, what she had been trying to tell him last night; at long last he, too, was facing his weakness, just as she had faced hers, coming to terms with himself, understanding himself, realizing that if it had not been for

Jana and for the ordeal which was now reaching its culmination, he would have been irreclaimably destroyed by the poisons of his fear.

But now, if he had to die, he could die as a man, and he was very calm. He had felt the exorcism of the panic, the need and the capacity for flight, when he and Jana reached the bottom of the arroyo moments earlier. They could have tried to make it across to the far bank, they could have kept running and they could have died running, but with the understanding, he had instead brought Jana here, to the first concealment he had found. It was here they would make their final stand, if it was to be their final stand; he would fight, somehow, in some way, he would make a fight of it.

He looked at Jana and their eyes met, and he knew she was with him, all the way, unquestioning, undemanding, seeing the resolution in him and taking strength from it. Together, her eyes seemed to be saying. In life or in death, together.

He did not want her to die. He wanted her to live even more than he wanted to live himself—the first truly unselfish commitment of Jack Lennox to anything or anybody other than Jack Lennox—and anger rose in him, and hatred, cold and calculating, for the man-thing that thought of them not as human beings but merely as insensate objects, threats to his own warped existence. Lennox listened. Movement, soft, stealthy, coming from somewhere on the other side of the boulder, shoes sibilant on the sand, a deep wheezing of constricted breath. Jana heard it too, tensing slightly beside him, touching his arm. Lennox did not look at her; his full concentration was on the movement and the sounds beyond. Coming closer? Yes, closer, but not too close, not yet, there was still a minute or two.

A weapon, he had to have a weapon.

And he remembered the knifelike piece of granite.

His hand came up to touch his belt, where he had put the stone earlier—and it was gone. Damn, damn! It must have pulled free when the bullet skinned his side and he had fallen on the slope. He released a silent breath, passing his fingers over his split and puckered lips, looking around him, looking for another weapon, any weapon. His eyes touched small stones, a piece of decaying wood, an unwieldy section of rail—discarded them, moved on, restless, urgent, wanting something substantial, something heavy, something to throw, perhaps, or something sharp

and he saw the rusted splinter of steel.

It lay in the sand eight feet away from him, on open ground. Some two feet long, warped but otherwise unbent, it was a dull, cankered brown in the sunlight, its forward edge tapered into a point that appeared sharp, that appeared capable of penetrating flesh. Beside it was a long section of rail, the parent which had spawned it through metal fatigue or through impact in the collapse of decades past.

Lennox stared at the splinter, and he thought: Spear, it looks like some primitive spear, and there was a bitter irony in the association. Wasn't what was happening here, this battle for survival, a primitive thing too—as old as man, as old as life itself?

He had to have that spear. He had to take the chance of going out there to get it. That two feet of slim oxidizing steel represented the last remaining thread of hope, the battle lance, and without it they were naked—there could be no battle.

He put his lips to Jana's ear and breathed, "I'm going out after that piece of steel, stay here and keep down," and then, because this was perhaps the final goodbye and there was the need, just this once, to put it into words, "I love you, Jana."

He waited for her reply, the same three words, and when they were his he squeezed her hand and then moved out toward the splinter, the spear, lying in the sand beyond. He advanced in a humped, four-point stance, fingers splayed just ahead of his shoes, both sliding silently through the sand, his head turned to the left so that he could see the widening area around the boulder. He made a foot, another foot, coming out of the shade now, coming out of hiding, and from just beyond his vision there was a scuffling sound, leather scraping rock, pebbles tumbling, and he stopped moving and leaned forward, holding his breath, craning his neck, and twenty feet away, atop a high flat rock, the fat one, the killer, was pulling himself onto his feet, turned in profile, Death standing outlined against the bright, bright blue of the desert sky.

There was no quickening of Lennox's heart, no tightening of his groin, none of the symptoms of fear and panic and irresolution. Time had run out, there was no more time to brace himself with the lance, there was only time for one quick attack before the fat one turned and saw him, a single offensive and nothing more.

He thought: This is the moment, this is the judgment—and lunged toward the waiting spear.

Fourteen

Breath whistled asthmatically between Vollyer's lips as he straightened on top of the rock. He hunched forward, squinting, turning his body as he tried to fuse the dancing shadows below with the objects from which they sprang, cursing his eyes, screaming silently at his eyes. Sweat streamed down from his forehead, over his cheeks, and he lifted his left arm and in that moment he saw the movement, definite movement, independent of the shadows.

His body stiffened, the cords in his neck straining as he tried to focus on the source of the movement. It took shape for him, a man-shape, Lennox, Lennox, and the Remington came up in his right hand, jumping, roaring unsighted as the distorted figure ran across into the open. The bullet ricocheted off the boulder there, showering flakes of rock and dust, goddamn these eyes oh goddamn these eyes, and Lennox was bending down there in the sand, bending, two of him wavering, dancing. Vollyer dropped the Remington and the .38 slapped against his right palm and he fired and sand puffed up a foot wide, I missed him, you son-of-a-bitching eyes, I missed him, and then Lennox was coming up and moving forward, arm drawn back, something in his hand, and Vollyer squeezed the trigger again and again he missed, and Lennox's arm pistoned frontally and the something in his fingers broke free, a blur, a thin brown blur, he threw something at me, get out of the

impact, Jesus! sudden pain, blackness behind his eyes, fire spreading out molten from his stomach, no, no, what did he throw, my belly, oh oh my belly, and the gun clatters down onto the rock at his feet, he staggers, his hands come up and encounter coarse steel, a length of steel, imbedded there and deep deep inside him, sticky wet, blood, steel, a spear, he threw a steel *spear* at me but that's not right he's a runner he's not a fighter runners don't fight, and Vollyer's legs no longer support him, he falls to his knees, blind, fingers jerking desperately at the shaft penetrating the soft flesh just below his breastbone, trying vainly to pull it free

and he feels himself falling, blackness spinning all around him, dizzying within and without, his head strikes something, his arm strikes something, he is falling off the rock, and there is a solid jarring, an explosion of fresh pain that is still not as great as that in the core of his belly and the blackness becomes redness, flashing, pulsating, dissolves to blackness again and his hands flutter ineffectually at his stomach, the steel is gone now but the blood is there and the hole, the hole

dying, I'm dying, and he did it with a spear, a spear, what kind of thing is that, a goddamn spear, what kind of way is that to play the game . . .

Fifteen

Lennox had flung himself to the sand after releasing the steel splinter, looking up, preparing to roll toward a thick wooden tie if the hurtling shaft missed; but then he saw it strike flesh, saw the killer reel and stagger, the one gun drop, saw him topple off the rock into the sand at its base—and he allowed his body to go limp and his head to drop forward into the crook of his arms. He lay that way for a moment, finally lifted his head, and the fat one was still lying there in the sand, not moving. Lennox thought giddily: He shot at me point-blank, three or four times at point-blank range, and he missed every time and I had one primitive chance and I didn't miss, maybe there is a God after all . . .

And then Jana was there, kneeling in the sand beside him, holding his head, pressing his face between her breasts, trying to cry but finding no moisture for her tears. "I saw it all, I saw it, oh Jack, oh God, Jack, are you . . . ?"

"No," he said, "no, I'm all right."

A sobbing, almost hysterical laugh—a release of the spiraled tension inside her—spilled from Jana's throat. "It's over," she said, "we're all right, we're all right."

He felt tired, he felt incredibly tired. Hunger clawed just under his breastbone, and every inch of his body ached hellishly. He wanted to lie there and sleep, he wanted to lie with his head against Jana's warm breast and sleep for days, for weeks. His mind seemed to have gone blank, incapable in that moment of sustaining thought, and it was good that way, for just a little while; all the thinking that had to be done had already been done before this final confrontation—all the examining and understanding—and there was no need for introspection now. They had survived, they had found one another and they had found a future, and there was simply nothing else to think about in this moment.

"Jack," Jana said, "Jack, he's moving up there, he's still alive." There was a kind of sickness in her voice—but nothing more.

She released his head, and Lennox stared at the crumpled form lying a few feet away, saw it twitching in the sand. He got painfully to his knees, finally onto the enervated spikes that were his legs, and walked there cautiously, stopping to pick up a heavy rock on the way. But there was no need for caution; blood pumped in diminishing geysers from the wound in the fat man's round, soft stomach, and clawed fingers clutched uselessly at the earth. The eyes were open, but Lennox had the feeling that they were sightless, already sightless.

He felt no more hatred, he felt no emotion of any kind toward this dying lump of flesh. Rattling, liquid sounds began in the convulsing throat, the split lips opened, moved, as if trying to form words. He knows I'm standing here, Lennox thought, he knows I'm looking at him, and blood dribbled out at the corners of the small, broken mouth as it tried again to make intelligible sounds.

Lennox knelt, not knowing exactly why he knelt, and leaned close to the mottled, contorted face. Blood filled the mouth now, thick and red, overflowing, and Lennox felt nausea ascend in the pit of his stomach, intensifying the hunger pain there. He started to rise, to turn away, and then the rattling sounds became words, almost inaudible and yet very clear, forced through the bright blood along with a final, spasmodic exhalation—words that for Lennox had no meaning at all.

The words: "Fuck the winners."

They climbed out of the arroyo at the same point at which they had entered it, and just as they emerged, there came from the west the high-pitched scream of sirens. They stood on the flatland, and seconds later three cars came very fast along the rutted trail—two black-and-white county cruisers and an unmarked black hardtop. One of the cruisers slowed and stopped near the two bodies at the foot of the slope, and the other two machines continued along the ruts.

A chattering, whirring sound reached their ears, coming from the sky to the east, and when they looked up they saw a dark shape—a helicopter—flying just to the near side of the golden rim of the sun, like an insect moving away from a naked light bulb. They looked back to the wheel ruts as the cruiser and the black hardtop drew abreast of them, came to shuddering halts one behind the other. Doors were flung open, and men burst out and began to run toward them across the rocky flatland.

The helicopter was very close now, the sun reflecting off the transparent glass bubble beneath its rotors, coming directly overhead. The hot turbulence generated by its spinning blades was somehow soothing on Jana's face, billowing her dust-grimed hair, the tattered remains of her clothing. It really *is* over, she thought with a kind of wonder, it's finally over. And then her eyes turned to Lennox and she thought: No, it's just beginning.

He took her hand, held it tightly, and they started toward the approaching men.

Walking now.

Walking together.

About the Author

BILL PRONZINI is twenty-eight, currently a bachelor, and has been writing professionally for the past five years. He is an avid collector of pulp magazines, mystery novels, and magazine rejection slips, and his past occupations have included warehousing, office typing, car parking, and a part-time stint as a U.S. Marshals' guard. He is at present living and writing in Germany.

Piranha
to Scurfy

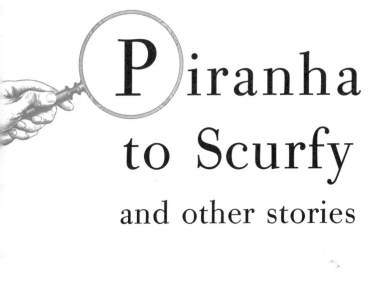

Piranha
to Scurfy
and other stories

BY RUTH RENDELL

Crown Publishers
New York

Published by Crown Publishers, New York, New York.
Member of the Crown Publishing Group.

Random House, Inc. New York, Toronto, London, Sydney, Auckland
www.randomhouse.com

Originally published in Great Britain by Hutchinson in 2000.

CROWN is a trademark and the Crown colophon is a registered trademark of Random House, Inc.

Printed in the United States of America

Design by Susan Maksuta

Library of Congress Cataloging-in-Publication Data
Rendell, Ruth
Piranha to scurfy / by Ruth Rendell.—1st ed.
Contents: Piranha to scurfy—Fair exchange—The wink—Catamount—Walter's leg—
The professional—The beach butler—The astronomical scarf—High mysterious union.
1. Detective and mystery stories, English.   2. Psychological fiction, English.   I. Title.
PR6068.E63   P57   2001
823'.914—dc21   00-043135

ISBN 0-609-60853-3

10   9   8   7   6   5   4   3   2   1

First American Edition

CONTENTS

PIRANHA TO SCURFY

I T WAS THE FIRST TIME he had been away on holiday without Mummy. The first time in his life. They had always gone to the Isle of Wight, to Ventnor or Totland Bay, so, going alone, he had chosen Cornwall for the change that people say is as good as a rest. Not that Ribbon's week in Cornwall had been entirely leisure. He had taken four books with him, read them carefully in the B and B's lounge, in his bedroom, on the beach, and sitting on the clifftop, and made meticulous notes in the looseleaf notebook he had bought in a shop in Newquay. The results had been satisfactory, more than satisfactory. Allowing for the anger and disgust making these discoveries invariably aroused, he felt he could say he had had a relaxing time. To use a horrible phrase much favored by Eric Owlberg in his literary output, he had recharged his batteries.

Coming home to an empty house would be an ordeal. He had known it would be, and it was. Instead of going out into the garden, he gave it careful scrutiny from the dining room window. Everything outside and indoors was as he had left it. The house was as he had left it, all the books in their places. Every room contained books. Ribbon was not one to make jokes, but he considered it witty to remark that while other people's walls were papered, his were booked. No one knew what he meant, for hardly anyone except himself ever entered 21 Grove Green Avenue, Leytonstone, and those to whom he uttered his little joke smiled uneasily. He had put up the shelves himself, buying them from Ikea. As they filled he bought more, adding to those already there until the shelves extended from floor to ceiling. A strange appearance was given to the house by this superfluity of books, as the shelves necessarily reduced the

3

size of the rooms, so that the living room, originally fifteen feet by twelve, shrank to thirteen feet by ten. The hall and landing were "booked" as densely as the rooms. The place looked like a library, but one mysteriously divided into small sections. His windows appeared as alcoves set deep in the walls, affording a view at the front of the house of a rather gloomy suburban street, thickly treed. The back gave onto the yellow-brick rears of other houses and, in the foreground, his garden, which was mostly lawn, dotted about with various drab shrubs. At the far end was a wide flower bed the sun never reached and in which grew creeping ivies and dark-leaved flowerless plants that like the shade.

He had got over expecting Mummy to come downstairs or walk into a room. She had been gone four months now. He sighed, for he was a long way from recovering from his loss and his regrets. Work was in some ways easier without her and in others immeasurably harder. She had reassured him; sometimes she had made him strong. But he had to press on—there was really no choice. Tomorrow things would be back to normal.

He began by ranging before him on the desk in the study—though was not the whole house a study?—the book-review pages from the newspapers that had arrived while he was away. As he had expected, Owlberg's latest novel, *Paving Hell,* appeared this very day in paperback, one year after hardcover publication. It was priced at £6.99 and by now would be in all the shops. Ribbon made a memo about it on one of the plain cards he kept for this purpose. But before continuing he let his eyes rest on the portrait of Mummy in the plain silver frame that stood on the table where used, read, and dissected books had their temporary home. It was Mummy who had first drawn his attention to Owlberg. She had borrowed one of his books from the public library and pointed out to Ribbon with indignation the mass of errors, solecisms, and abuse of the English language to be found in its pages. How he missed her! Wasn't it principally to her that he owed his choice of career, as well as the acumen and confidence to pursue it?

He sighed anew. Then he returned to his newspapers and noted down the titles of four more novels currently published in paperback, as well as the new Kingston Marle, *Demogorgon,* due to appear this coming Thursday in hardcover with the maximum hype and fanfares of metaphorical trumpets, but almost certainly already in the shops. A sign of the degeneracy of the times, Mummy had said, that a book whose publication was scheduled for May appeared on sale at the end of April. No one could wait these days; everyone was in a hurry. It certainly made his work harder. It increased the chances of his missing a vitally important novel that might have sold out before he knew it was in print.

Ribbon switched on his computer and checked that the printer was linked to it. It was only nine in the morning. He had at least an hour before he need make his trip to the bookshop. Where should it be today? Perhaps the City or the West End of London. It would be unwise to go back to his local shop so soon and attract too much attention to himself. Hatchard's, perhaps then, or Books Etc. or Dillon's, or even all three. He opened the notebook he had bought in Cornwall, reread what he had written, and with the paperback open on the desk, reached for the *Shorter Oxford Dictionary, Brewer's Dictionary of Phrase and Fable,* and *Whittaker's Almanac.* Referring to the first two and noting down his finds, he began his letter.

21 Grove Green Avenue
London E11 4ZH

Dear Joy Anne Fortune,

I have read your new novel *Dreadful Night* with very little pleasure and great disappointment. Your previous work has seemed to me, while being without any literary merit whatsoever, at least to be fresh, occasionally original, and largely free from those errors of fact and slips in grammar that, I may say, characterize *Dreadful Night.*

Look first at page 24. Do you really believe "desiccated" has two s's and one c? And if you do, has your publisher no copy editor whose job it is to recognize and correct these errors? On page 82 you refer to the republic of Guinea as being in East Africa and as a former British possession, instead of being in West Africa and formerly French, and on page 103 to the late General Sikorski as a one-time prime minister of Czechoslovakia rather than of Poland. You describe, on page 139, "hadith" as being the Jewish prayers for the dead instead of what it correctly means, the body of tradition and legend surrounding the Prophet Muhammad and his followers, and on the following page "tabernacle" as an entrance to a temple. Its true meaning is a portable sanctuary in which the Ark of the Covenant was carried.

Need I go on? I am weary of underlining the multifarious mistakes in your book. Needless to say, I shall buy no more of your work and shall advise my highly literate and discerning friends to boycott it.

Yours sincerely,

Ambrose Ribbon

The threat in the last paragraph was an empty one. Ribbon had no friends and could hardly say he missed having any. He was on excellent, at least speaking, terms with his neighbors and various managers of book-shops. There was a cousin in Gloucestershire he saw occasionally. Mummy had been his friend. There was no one he had ever met who could approach replacing her. He wished, as he did every day, she were back there beside him and able to read and appreciate his letter.

He addressed an envelope to Joy Anne Fortune care of her publisher (she was not one of "his" authors unwise enough to reply to him on headed writing paper), put the letter inside it, and sealed it up. Two more must be written before he left the house, one to Graham Prink pointing out mistakes in *Dancing Partners,* "lay" for "lie" in two instances and "may" for "might" in three, and the other to Jeanne Pettle to tell her that the plot and much of the dialogue in *Southern Discomfort* had been blatantly lifted from *Gone With the Wind.* He considered it the most flagrant plagiarism he had seen for a long while. In both he indicated how distasteful he found the authors' frequent use of obscenities, notably those words beginning with an *f* and a *c,* and the taking of the Deity's name in vain.

At five to ten Ribbon switched off the computer, took his letters, and closed the door behind him. Before going downstairs, he paid his second visit of the day to Mummy's room. He had been there for the first time since his return from Cornwall at seven the previous evening, again before he went to bed, and once more at seven this morning. While he was away his second greatest worry had been that something would be disturbed in there, an object removed or its position changed, for though he did his own housework, Glenys Next-door had a key and often in his absence, in her own words, "popped in to see that everything was okay."

But nothing was changed. Mummy's dressing table was exactly as she had left it, the two cut-glass scent bottles with silver stoppers set one on each side of the lace-edged mat, the silver-backed hairbrush on its glass tray alongside the hair tidy, and the pink pincushion. The wardrobe door he always left ajar so that her clothes could be seen inside, those dear garments, the afternoon dresses, the coats and skirts—Mummy had never possessed a pair of trousers—the warm winter coat, the neatly placed pairs of court shoes. Over the door, because he had seen this in an interiors magazine, he had hung, folded in two, the beautiful white and cream tapestry bedspread he had once given her but that she said was too good for daily use. On the bed lay the dear old one her own mother had worked, and on its spotless if worn bands of lace, her pink silk nightdress. He lingered, looking at it.

After a moment or two, he opened the window two inches at the top. It was a good idea to allow a little fresh air to circulate. He closed Mummy's door behind him and, carrying his letters, went downstairs. A busy day lay ahead. His tie straightened, one button only out of the three on his linen jacket done up, he set the burglar alarm. Eighteen fifty-two was the code, one eight five two, the date of the first edition of *Roget's Thesaurus*, a compendium Ribbon had found useful in his work. He opened the front door and closed it just as the alarm started braying. While he was waiting on the doorstep, his ear to the keyhole, for the alarm to cease until or unless an intruder set it off again, Glenys Next-door called out a cheery "Hiya!"

Ribbon hated this mode of address, but there was nothing he could do to stop it, any more than he could stop her calling him Amby. He smiled austerely and said good morning. Glenys Next-door—this was her own description of herself, first used when she moved into 23 Grove Green Avenue fifteen years before: "Hiya, I'm Glenys Next-door"—said it was the window cleaner's day and should she let him in.

"Why does he have to come in?" Ribbon said rather testily.

"It's his fortnight for doing the back, Amby. You know how he does the front on a Monday and the back on the Monday fortnight and inside and out on the last Monday in the month."

Like any professional with much on his mind, Ribbon found these domestic details almost unbearably irritating. Nor did he like the idea of a strange man left free to wander about his back garden. "Well, yes, I suppose so." He had never called Glenys Next-door by her given name and did not intend to begin. "You know the code, Mrs. Judd." It was appalling that she knew the code, but since Mummy had passed on and no one was in the house it was inevitable. "You do know the code, don't you?"

"Eight one five two."

"No, no, no." He must not lose his temper. Glancing up and down the street to make sure there was no one within earshot, he whispered, "One eight five two. You can remember that, can't you? I really don't want to write it down. You never know what happens to something once it has been put in writing."

Glenys Next-door had started to laugh. "You're a funny old fusspot you are, Amby. D'you know what I saw in your garden last night? A fox. How about that? In *Leytonstone*."

"Really?" Foxes dig, he thought.

"They're taking refuge, you see. Escaping the hunters. Cruel, isn't it? Are you off to work?"

"Yes and I'm late," Ribbon said, hurrying off. "Old fusspot" indeed. He was a good ten years younger than she.

Glenys Next-door had no idea what he did for a living, and he intended to keep her in ignorance. "Something in the media, is it?" she had once said to Mummy. Of course, "for a living" was not strictly true, implying as it did that he was paid for his work. That he was not was hardly for want of trying. He had written to twenty major publishing houses, pointing out to them that by what he did, uncovering errors in their authors' works and showing them to be unworthy of publication, he was potentially saving the publishers hundreds of thousands of pounds a year. The least they could do was offer him some emolument. He wrote to four national newspapers as well, asking for his work to receive publicity in their pages, and to the Department of Culture, Media and Sport, in the hope of recognition of the service he performed. A change in the law was what he wanted, providing something for him in the nature of the public lending right (he was vague about this) or the value-added tax. None of them replied, with the exception of the department, which sent a card saying that his communication had been noted—not signed by the secretary of state, though, but by some underling with an indecipherable signature.

It was the principle of the thing, not that he was in need of money. Thanks to Daddy, who, dying young, had left all the income from his royalties to Mummy and thus, of course, to him. No great sum but enough to live on if one was frugal and managing as he was. Daddy had written three textbooks before death came for him at the heartbreaking age of forty-one, and all were still in demand for use in business schools. Ribbon, because he could not help himself, in great secrecy and far from Mummy's sight, had gone through those books after his usual fashion, looking for errors. The compulsion to do this was irresistible, though he had tried to resist it, fighting against the need, conscious of the disloyalty, but finally succumbing, as another man might ultimately yield to some ludicrous autoeroticism. Alone, in the night, his bedroom door locked, he had perused Daddy's books and found—nothing.

The search was the most shameful thing he had ever done. And this not only on account of the distrust in Daddy's expertise and acumen that it implied, but also because he had to confess to himself that he did not understand what he read and would not have known a mistake if he had seen one. He had put Daddy's books away in a cupboard after that and, strangely enough, Mummy had never commented on their absence. Perhaps, her eyesight failing, she hadn't noticed.

Ribbon walked to Leytonstone tube station and sat on the seat to wait for a train. He had decided to change at Holborn and take the Piccadilly Line to Piccadilly Circus. From there it was only a short walk to Dillon's and a further few steps to Hatchard's. He acknowledged that Hatchard's was the better shop, but Dillon's guaranteed a greater anonymity to its patrons. Its assistants seemed indifferent to the activities of customers, ignoring their presence most of the time and not apparently noticing whether they stayed five minutes or half an hour. Ribbon liked that. He liked to describe himself as reserved, a private man, one who minded his own business and lived quietly. Others, in his view, would do well to be the same. As far as he was concerned, a shop assistant was there to take your money, give you your change, and say thank you. The displacement of the High Street or corner shop by vast impersonal supermarkets was one of few modern innovations he could heartily approve.

The train came. It was three-quarters empty, as was usual at this hour. He had read in the paper that London Transport was thinking of introducing Ladies Only carriages in the tube. Why not Men Only carriages as well? Preferably, when you considered what some young men were like, Middle-aged Scholarly Gentlemen Only carriages. The train stopped for a long time in the tunnel between Mile End and Bethnal Green. Naturally, passengers were offered no explanation for the delay. He waited a long time for the Piccadilly Line train, apparently because of some signaling failure outside Cockfosters, but eventually arrived at his destination just before eleven-thirty.

The sun had come out and it was very hot. The air smelled of diesel and cooking and beer, very different from Leytonstone, on the verges of Epping Forest. Ribbon went into Dillon's, where no one showed the slightest interest in his arrival, and the first thing to assault his senses was an enormous pyramidal display of Kingston Marle's *Demogorgon*. Each copy was as big as the average-sized dictionary and encased in a jacket printed in silver and two shades of red. A hole in the shape of a pentagram in the front cover revealed beneath it the bandaged face of some mummified corpse. The novel had already been reviewed, and the poster on the wall above the display quoted the *Sunday Express*'s encomium in exaggeratedly large type: READERS WILL HAVE FAINTED WITH FEAR BEFORE PAGE 10.

The price, at £18.99, was a disgrace, but there was no help for it. A legitimate outlay, if ever there was one. Ribbon took a copy and, from what a shop assistant had once told him were called "dump bins," helped himself to two paperbacks of books he had already examined and commented on in hardcover. There was no sign in the whole shop of Eric Owlberg's *Paving Hell*. Ribbon's dilemma was to ask or not to ask. The young woman behind the counter put his purchases in a bag, and he handed her Mummy's direct-debit Visa card. Lightly, as if it were an afterthought, the most casual thing in the world, he asked about the new Owlberg.

"Already sold out, has it?" he said with a little laugh.

Her face was impassive. "We're expecting them in tomorrow."

He signed the receipt B. J. Ribbon and passed it to the girl without a smile. She need not think he was going to make this trip all over again tomorrow. He made his way to Hatchard's, on the way depositing the Dillon's bag in a litter bin and transferring the books into the plain plastic holdall he carried rolled up in his pocket. If the staff at Hatchard's had seen Dillon's name on the bag he would have felt rather awkward. Now they would think he was carrying his purchases from a chemist or a photographic store.

One of them came up to him the minute he entered Hatchard's. He recognized her as the marketing manager, a small, good-looking blond woman with an accent. The very faintest of accents, but still enough for

Ribbon to be put off her from the start. She recognized him too, and to his astonishment and displeasure addressed him by his name.

"Good morning, Mr. Ribbon."

Inwardly he groaned, for he remembered having had forebodings about this at the time. On one occasion he had ordered a book, he was desperate to see an early copy, and had been obliged to say who he was and give them his number. He said good morning in a frosty sort of voice.

"How nice to see you," she said. "I think you may be in search of the new Kingston Marle, am I right? *Demogorgon*? Copies came in today."

Ribbon felt terrible. The plastic of his carrier was translucent rather than transparent, but he was sure she must be able to see the silver and the two shades of red glowing through the cloudy film that covered it. He held it behind his back in a manner he hoped looked natural.

"It was *Paving Hell* I actually wanted," he muttered, wondering what rule of life or social usage made it necessary for him to explain his wishes to marketing managers.

"We have it, of course," she said with a radiant smile and picked the paperback off a shelf. He was sure she was going to point out to him in schoolmistressy fashion that he had already had it in hardcover, she quite distinctly remembered, and why on earth did he want another copy. Instead she said, "Mr. Owlberg is here at this moment, signing stock for us. It's not a public signing, but I'm sure he'd love to meet such a constant reader as yourself. And be happy to sign a copy of his book for you."

Ribbon hoped his shudder hadn't been visible. No, no, he was in a hurry, he had a pressing engagement at twelve-thirty on the other side of town, he couldn't wait, he'd pay for his book. . . . Thoughts raced through his mind of the things he had written to Owlberg about his work, all of it perfectly justified of course, but galling to the author. His name would have lodged in Owlberg's mind as firmly as Owlberg's had in his. Imagining the reaction of *Paving Hell*'s author when he looked up from his signing, saw the face, and heard the name of his stern judge made him shudder again. He almost ran out of the shop. How fraught with dangers visits to the West End were! Next time he came up he'd stick to the City or Bloomsbury. There was a very good Waterstones in the Grays Inn Road. Deciding to walk up to Oxford Circus tube station and thus obviate a train change, he stopped on the way to draw money out from a cash dispenser. He punched in Mummy's pin number—her birth date, 1-5-27—and drew from the slot one hundred pounds in crisp new notes.

· · ·

Most authors to whom Ribbon wrote his letters of complaint either did not reply at all or wrote back in a conciliatory way to admit their mistakes and promise these would be rectified for the paperback edition. Only one, out of all the hundreds, if not thousands who had had a letter from him, had reacted violently and with threats. This was a woman called Selma Gunn. He had written to her, care of her publisher, criticizing quite mildly her novel *A Dish of Snakes,* remarking how irritating it was to read so many verbless sentences and pointing out the absurdity of her premise that Shakespeare, far from being a sixteenth-century English poet and dramatist, was in fact an Italian astrologer born in Verona and a close friend of Leonardo da Vinci's. Her reply came within four days, a vituperative response in which she several times used the f-word, called him an ignorant swollen-headed nonentity, and threatened legal action. Sure enough, on the following day a letter arrived from Ms. Gunn's solicitors, suggesting that many of his remarks were actionable, all were indefensible, and they awaited his reply with interest.

Ribbon had been terrified. He was unable to work, incapable of thinking of anything but Ms. Gunn's letter and the one from Evans Richler Sabatini. At first he said nothing to Mummy, though she, of course, with her customary sensitive acuity, could tell something was wrong. Two days later he received another letter from Selma Gunn. This time she drew his attention to certain astrological predictions in her book, told him that he was one of those Nostradamus had predicted would be destroyed when the world came to an end next year and that she herself had occult powers. She ended by demanding an apology.

Ribbon did not, of course, believe in the supernatural but, like most of us, was made to feel deeply uneasy when cursed or menaced by something in the nature of necromancy. He sat down at his computer and composed an abject apology. He was sorry, he wrote, he had intended no harm, Ms. Gunn was entitled to express her beliefs; her theory as to Shakespeare's origins was just as valid as identifying him with Bacon or Ben Jonson. It took it out of him, writing that letter, and when Mummy, observing his pallor and trembling hands, finally asked him what was wrong, he told her everything. He showed her the letter of apology. Masterful as ever, she took it from him and tore it up.

"Absolute nonsense," she said. He could tell she was furious. "On what grounds can the stupid woman bring an action, I should like to know? Take no notice. Ignore it. It will soon stop, you mark my words."

"But what harm can it do, Mummy?"

"You coward," Mummy said witheringly. "Are you a man or a mouse?"

Ribbon asked her, politely but as manfully as he could, not to talk to him like that. It was almost their first quarrel—but not their last.

He had bowed to her edict and stuck it out in accordance with her instructions, as he did in most cases. And she had been right, for he heard not another word from Selma Gunn or from Evans Richler Sabatini. The whole awful business was over, and Ribbon felt he had learned something from it: to be brave, to be resolute, to soldier on. But this did not include confronting Owlberg in the flesh, even though the author of *Paving Hell* had promised him in a letter responding to Ribbon's criticism of the hardcover edition of his book that the errors of fact he had pointed out would all be rectified in the paperback. His publishers, he wrote, had also received Ribbon's letter of complaint and were as pleased as he to have had such informed critical comment. Pleased, my foot! What piffle! Ribbon had snorted over this letter, which was a lie from start to finish. The man wasn't pleased; he was aghast and humiliated, as he should be.

Ribbon sat down in his living room to check in the paperback edition for the corrections so glibly promised. He read down here and wrote upstairs. The room was almost as Mummy had left it. The changes were only in that more books and bookshelves had been added and in the photographs in the silver frames. He had taken out the pictures of himself as a baby and himself as a schoolboy and replaced them with one of his parents' wedding, Daddy in air force uniform, Mummy in cream costume and small cream hat, and one of Daddy in his academic gown and mortarboard. There had never been one of Ribbon himself in similar garments. Mummy, for his own good, had decided he would be better off at home with her, leading a quiet sheltered life, than at a university. Had he regrets? A degree would have been useless to a man with a private income, as Mummy had pointed out, a man who had all the resources of an excellent public library system to educate him.

He opened *Paving Hell*. He had a foreboding before he had even turned to the middle of chapter 1, where the first mistake occurred, that nothing would have been put right. All the errors would still be there, for Owlberg's promises meant nothing, he had probably never passed Ribbon's comments on to the publishers; and they, if they had received the letter he wrote them, had never answered it. For all that, he was still enraged when he found he was right. Didn't the man care? Was money and a kind of low notoriety—for you couldn't call it fame—all he was interested in? None of the errors had been corrected. No, that wasn't quite true; one had. On page 99 Owlberg's ridiculous statement that the One World Trade Center tower in New York was the world's tallest building had been altered. Ribbon noted down the remaining mistakes, ready to write to Owlberg the next day. A vituperative letter it would be, spitting venom and catechizing illiteracy, carelessness, and a general disregard (contempt?) for the sensibilities of readers. And Owlberg would reply to it in his previous pusillanimous way, making empty promises, for he was no Selma Gunn.

Ribbon fetched himself a small whiskey and water. It was six o'clock. A cushion behind his head, his feet up on the footstool Mummy had embroidered, but covered now with a plastic sheet, he opened *Demogorgon*. This was the first book by Kingston Marle he had ever read, but he had some idea of what Marle wrote about. Murder, violence, crime, but instead of a detective detecting and reaching a solution, supernatural interventions, demonic possession, ghosts, as well as a great deal of unnatural or perverted sex, cannibalism, and torture. Occult manifestations occurred side by side with rational, if unedifying, events. Innocent people were caught up in the magical dabblings, frequently going wrong, of so-called adepts. Ribbon had learned this from the reviews he had read of Marle's books, most of which, surprisingly to him, received good notices in periodicals of repute. That is, the serious and reputable critics engaged by literary editors to comment on his work praised the quality of the prose as vastly superior to the general run of thriller writing. His characters, they said, convinced, and he induced in the reader a very real sense of terror, while a deep vein of moral theology underlay his plot. They also said that his serious approach to mumbo jumbo and such nonsense as evil spirits and necromancy was ridiculous, but they said it en passant and without much enthusiasm. Ribbon read the blurb inside the front cover and turned to chapter 1.

Almost the first thing he spotted was an error on page 2. He made a note of it. Another occurred on page 7. Whether Marle's prose was beautiful or not he scarcely noticed; he was too incensed by errors of fact, spelling mistakes, and grammatical howlers. For a while, that is. The first part of the novel concerned a man living alone in London, a man in his own situation whose mother had died not long before. There was another parallel: the man's name was Charles Ambrose. Well, it was common enough as a surname, much less so as a baptismal name, and only a paranoid person would think any connection was intended.

Charles Ambrose was rich and powerful, with a house in London, a mansion in the country, and a flat in Paris. All these places seemed to be haunted in various ways by something or other, but the odd thing was that Ribbon could see what that reviewer meant by readers fainting with terror before page 10. He wasn't going to faint, but he could feel himself growing increasingly alarmed. *Frightened* would be too strong a word. Every few minutes he found himself glancing up toward the closed door or looking into the dim and shadowy corners of the room. He was such a reader, so exceptionally well-read, that he had thought himself proof against this sort of thing. Why, he had read hundreds of ghost stories in his time. As a boy he had inured himself by reading first Dennis Wheatley, then Stephen King, not to mention M. R. James. And this *Demogorgon* was so absurd, the supernatural activity the reader was supposed to accept so pathetic, that he wouldn't have gone on with it but for the mistakes he kept finding on almost every page.

After a while he got up, opened the door, and put the hall light on. He had never been even mildly alarmed by Selma Gunn's *A Dish of Snakes,* nor touched with disquiet by any effusions of Joy Anne Fortune's. What was the matter with him? He came back into the living room and put on the central light and an extra table lamp, the one with the shade Mummy had decorated with pressed flowers. That was better. Anyone passing could see in now, something he usually disliked, but for some reason he didn't feel like drawing the curtains. Before sitting down again he fetched himself some more whiskey.

This passage about the mummy Charles Ambrose brought back with

him after the excavations he had carried out in Egypt was very unpleasant. Why had he never noticed before that the diminutive by which he
had always addressed his mother was the same word as that applied to
embalmed bodies? Especially nasty was the paragraph where Ambrose's
girlfriend, Kayra, reaches in semidarkness for a garment in her wardrobe
and her wrist is grasped by a scaly paw. This was so upsetting that Ribbon
almost missed noticing that Marle spelled the adjective "scaley." He had a
sense of the room being less light than a few moments before, as if the
bulbs in the lamps were weakening before entirely failing. One of them
did indeed fail while his eyes were on it, flickered, buzzed, and went out.
Of course Ribbon knew perfectly well this was not a supernatural phe-
nomenon but simply the result of the bulb coming to the end of its life
after a thousand hours, or whatever it was. He switched off the lamp,
extracted the bulb when it was cool, shook it to hear the rattle that told
him its usefulness was over, and took it outside to the waste bin. The
kitchen was in darkness. He put on the light and the outside light, which
illuminated part of the garden. That was better. A siren wailing on a
police car going down Grove Green Road made him jump. He helped
himself to more whiskey, a rare indulgence for him. He was no drinker.

Supper now. It was almost eight. Ribbon always set the table for himself, either here or in the dining room, put out a linen table napkin in its
silver ring, a jug of water and a glass, and the silver pepper pot and salt
cellar. This was Mummy's standard, and if he had deviated from it he
would have felt he was letting her down. But this evening, as he made
toast and scrambled two large free-range eggs in a buttered pan, filled a
small bowl with mandarin oranges from a can and poured evaporated
milk over them, he found himself most unwilling to venture into the dining room. It was at the best of times a gloomy chamber, its rather small
window set deep in bookshelves, its furnishings largely a reptilian shade
of brownish-green Mummy always called "crocodile." Poor Mummy only
kept the room like that because the crocodile green had been Daddy's
choice when they were first married. There was just a central light, a bulb
in a parchment shade, suspended above the middle of the mahogany
table. Books covered as yet only two sides of the room, but new shelves
had been bought and were waiting for him to put them up. One of
the pictures on the wall facing the window had been most distasteful to
Ribbon when he was a small boy, a lithograph of some Old Testa-

ment scene entitled *Saul Encounters the Witch of Endor*. Mummy, saying he
should not fear painted devils, had refused to take it down. He was in no
mood tonight to have that lowering over him while he ate his eggs.

Nor did he much fancy the kitchen. Once or twice, while he was sitting there, Glenys Next-door's cat had looked through the window at
him. It was a black cat, totally black all over, its eyes large and of a very
pale crystalline yellow. Of course he knew what it was and had never in
the past been alarmed by it, but somehow he sensed it would be different tonight. If Tinks Next-door pushed its black face and yellow eyes
against the glass, it might give him a serious shock. He put the plates on
a tray and carried it back into the living room with the replenished
whiskey glass.

It was both his job and his duty to continue reading *Demogorgon,* but
there was more to it than that, Ribbon admitted to himself in a rare burst
of honesty. He *wanted* to go on, he wanted to know what happened to
Charles Ambrose and Kayra de Floris, whose the emblamed corpse was,
and how it had been liberated from its arcane and archaic (writers always
muddled up those adjectives) sarcophagus, and whether the mysterious
and saintly rescuer was in fact the reincarnated Joseph of Arimathea
and the vessel he carried the Holy Grail. By the time Mummy's grandmother clock in the hall struck eleven, half an hour past his bedtime, he
had read half the book and would no longer have described himself as
merely alarmed. He was frightened. So frightened that he had to stop
reading.

Twice during the course of the past hour he had refilled his whiskey
glass, half in the hope that strong drink would induce sleep; finally, at a
quarter past eleven, he went to bed. He passed a miserable night, worse
even than those he'd experienced in the weeks after Mummy's death. It
was, for instance, a mistake to take *Demogorgon* upstairs with him. He
hardly knew why he had done so, for he certainly had no intention of
reading any more of it that night, if ever. The final chapter he had read—
well, he could scarcely say what had upset him most, the orgy in the
middle of the Arabian desert in which Charles and Kayra had both
enthusiastically taken part, wallowing in perverted practices, or the
intervention, disguised as a Bedouin tribesman, of the demon Kabadeus,
later revealing in his nakedness his hermaphrodite body with huge female
breasts and trifurcated member.

As always, Ribbon had placed his slippers by the bed. He'd pushed the book a little under the bed, but he couldn't forget that it was there. In the darkness he seemed to hear sounds he had never heard, or never noticed, before: a creaking as if a foot trod first on one stair, then the next; a rattling of the windowpane, though it was a windless night; a faint rustling on the bedroom door as if a thing in grave clothes had scrabbled with its decaying hand against the paneling. He put on the bed lamp. Its light was faint, showing him deep wells of darkness in the corners of the room. He told himself not to be a fool. Demons, ghosts, evil spirits had no existence. If only he hadn't brought the wretched book up with him! He would be better, he would be able to sleep, he was sure, if the book wasn't there, exerting a malign influence. Then something dreadful occurred to him. He couldn't take the book outside, downstairs, away. He hadn't the nerve. It would not be possible for him to open the door, go down the stairs, carrying that book.

The whiskey, asserting itself in the mysterious way it had, began a banging in his head. A flicker of pain ran from his eyebrow down his temple to his ear. He climbed out of bed, crept across the floor, his heart pounding, and put on the central light. That was a little better. He drew back the bedroom curtains and screamed. He actually screamed aloud, frightening himself even more with the noise he made. Tinks Next-door was sitting on the windowsill, staring impassively at curtain linings, now into Ribbon's face. It took no notice of the scream but lifted a paw, licked it, and began washing its face.

Ribbon pulled back the curtains. He sat down on the end of the bed, breathing deeply. It was two in the morning, a pitch-black night, ill-lit by widely spaced yellow chemical lamps. What he would really have liked to do was rush across the passage—do it quickly, don't think about it—into Mummy's room, burrow down into Mummy's bed, and spend the night there. If he could only do that he would be safe, would sleep, be comforted. It would be like creeping back into Mummy's arms. But he couldn't do it—it was impossible. For one thing, it would be a violation of the sacred room, the sacrosanct bed, never to be disturbed since Mummy had spent her last night in it. And for another, he dared not venture out onto the landing.

Back under the covers, he tried to court sleep by thinking of himself and Mummy in her last years, which helped a little. The two of them sit-

ting down to an evening meal in the dining room, a white candle alight
on the table, its soft light dispelling much of the gloom and ugliness.
Mummy had enjoyed television when a really good program was on:
Brideshead Revisited, for instance, or something from Jane Austen. She had
always liked the curtains drawn, even before it was dark, and it was his
job to do it, then fetch each of them a dry sherry. Sometimes they read
aloud to each other in the gentle lamplight, Mummy choosing to read her
favorite Victorian writers to him, he picking a book from his work, correcting the grammar as he read. Or she would talk about Daddy and her
first meeting with him in a library, she searching the shelves for a novel
whose author's name she had forgotten, he offering to help her and finding—triumphantly—Mrs. Henry Wood's *East Lynne.*

But all these memories of books and reading pulled Ribbon brutally
back to *Demogorgon.* The scaly hand was the worst thing and, second to
that, the cloud or ball of visible darkness that arose in the lighted room
when Charles Ambrose cast salt and asafetida into the pentagram. He
reached down to find the lead on the bed lamp where the switch was and
encountered something cold and leathery. It was only the tops of his slippers, which he always left just beside his bed, but he had once again
screamed before he remembered. The lamp on, he lay still, breathing
deeply. Only when the first light of morning, a gray trickle of dawn, came
creeping under and between the curtains at about six, did he fall into a
troubled doze.

Morning makes an enormous difference to fear and to depression. It
wasn't long before Ribbon was castigating himself for a fool and blaming
the whiskey and the scrambled eggs, rather than Kingston Marle, for his
disturbed night. However, he would read no more of *Demogorgon.* No
matter how much he might wish to know the fate of Charles and Kayra
or the identity of the bandaged reeking thing, he preferred not to expose
himself any longer to this distasteful rubbish or Marle's grammatical
lapses.

A hot shower, followed by a cold one, did a lot to restore him. He
breakfasted, but in the kitchen. When he had finished he went into the
dining room and had a look at *Saul Encounters the Witch of Endor.* It was
years since he had even glanced at it, which was no doubt why he had
never noticed how much like Mummy the witch looked. Of course
Mummy would never have worn diaphanous gray draperies and she'd had

all her own teeth, but there was something about the nose and mouth, the burning eyes and the pointing finger, this last particularly characteristic of Mummy, that reminded him of her. He dismissed the disloyal thought but, on an impulse, took the picture down and put it on the floor, its back toward him, to lean against the wall. It left behind it a paler rectangle on the ocher-colored wallpaper, but the new bookshelves would cover that. Ribbon went upstairs to his study and his daily labors. First, the letter to Owlberg.

21 Grove Green Avenue
London E11 4ZH

Dear Sir,
    In spite of your solemn promise to me as to the correction of errors in your new paperback publication, I find you have fulfilled this undertaking only to the extent of making *one single amendment.*
    This, of course, in anyone's estimation, is a gross insult to your readers, displaying as it does your contempt for them and for the TRUTH. I am sending a copy of this letter to your publishers and await an explanation both from you and them.

Yours faithfully,
Ambrose Ribbon

Letting off steam always put him in a good mood. He felt a joyful adrenaline rush and was inspired to write a congratulatory letter for a change. This one was addressed to: The Manager, Dillon's Bookshop, Piccadilly, London W1.

21 Grove Green Avenue
London E11 4ZH

Dear Sir or Madam,
(There were a lot of women taking men's jobs these days, poking their noses in where they weren't needed.)
    I write to congratulate you on your excellent organization, management, and the, alas, now old-fashioned attitude you have to your book buyers. I refer, of course, to the respectful distance and detach-

ment maintained between you and them. It makes a refreshing change
from the overfamiliarity displayed by many of your competitors.

Yours faithfully,

Ambrose Ribbon

Before writing to the author of the novel that had been directly
responsible for his loss of sleep, Ribbon needed to look something up: a
king of Egypt of the seventh century B.C. called Psamtik I he had come
across before in someone else's book. Marle referred to him as
Psammetichos I, and Ribbon was nearly sure this was wrong. He would
have to look it up, and the obvious place to do this was the *Encyclopaedia
Britannica.*

Others might have recourse to the Internet. Because Mummy had
despised such electronic devices, Ribbon did so too. He wasn't even on
the Net and never would be. The present difficulty was that Psamtik I
would be found in volume 8 of the Micropaedia, the one that covered
subjects from *Piranha* to *Scurfy.* This volume he had had no occasion to use
since Mummy's death, though his eyes sometimes strayed fearfully in its
direction. There it was placed, in the bookshelves to the left of where he
sat facing the window, bound in its black, blue, and gold, its position
between *Montpel* to *Piranesi* and *Scurlock* to *Tirah.* He was very reluctant
to touch it, but he *had to.* Mummy might be dead, but her injunctions and
instructions lived on. Don't be deterred, she had often said, don't be
deflected by anything from what you know to be right, not by weariness,
nor indifference, nor doubt. Press on, tell the truth, shame these people.

There would not be a mark on *Piranha* to *Scurfy*—he knew that—
nothing but his fingerprints, and they, of course, were invisible. It had
been used and put back and was unchanged. Cautiously he advanced
upon the shelf where the ten volumes of the Micropaedia and the nineteen of the Macropaedia were arranged and put out his hand to volume
8. As he lifted it down he noticed something different about it, different,
that is, from the others. Not a mark, not a stain or scar, but a slight loos-
ening of the thousand and two pages as if at some time it had been mis-
treated, violently shaken or in some similar way abused. It had. He
shivered a little, but he opened the book and turned the pages to the P's.
It was somewhat disappointing to find that Marle had been right. *Psamtik*
was right, but so was the Greek form, *Psammetichos I;* it was optional.

Still, there were enough errors in the book, a plethora of them, without that. Ribbon wrote as follows, saying nothing about his fear, his bad night, and his interest in *Demogorgon*'s characters:

21 Grove Green Avenue
London E11 4ZH

Sir,

Your new farrago of nonsense (I will not dignify it with the name of "novel" or even "thriller") is a disgrace to you, your publisher, and those reviewers corrupt enough to praise your writing. As to the market you serve, once it has sampled this revolting affront to English literary tradition and our noble language, I can hardly imagine its members will remain your readers for long. The greatest benefit to the fiction scene conceivable would be for you to retire, disappear, and take your appalling effusions with you into outer darkness.

The errors you have made in the text are numerous. On page 30 alone there are three. You cannot say "less people." "Fewer people" is correct. Only the illiterate would write: "He gave it to Charles and I." By "mitigate against" I suppose you mean "militate against." More howlers occur on pages 34, 67, and 103. It is unnecessary to write "meet with." "Meet" alone will do. "A copy" of something is sufficient. "A copying" is nonsense.

Have you any education at all? Or were you one of these children who somehow missed schooling because their parents were neglectful or itinerant? You barely seem able to understand the correct location of an apostrophe, still less the proper usage of a colon. Your book has wearied me too much to allow me to write more. Indeed, I have not finished it and shall not. I am too fearful of its corrupting my own prose.

He wrote "Sir" without the customary endearment so that he could justifiably sign himself "Yours truly." He reread his letters and paused a while over the third one. It was very strong and uncompromising. But there was not a phrase in it he didn't sincerely mean (for all his refusing to end with that word), and he told himself that he who hesitates is lost. Often when he wrote a really vituperative letter he allowed himself to sleep on it, not posting it till the following day and occasionally, though seldom, not sending it at all. But he quickly put all three into envelopes and addressed them, Kingston Marle's care of his publisher. He would take them to the box at once.

While he was upstairs his own post had come. Two envelopes lay on the mat. The direction on one was typed; on the other he recognized the handwriting of his cousin Frank's wife, Susan. He opened that one first. Susan wrote to remind him that he was spending the following weekend with herself and her husband at their home in the Cotswolds, as he did at roughly this time every year. Frank or she herself would be at Kingham Station to pick him up. She supposed he would be taking the one-fifty train from Paddington to Hereford, which reached Kingham at twenty minutes past three. If he had other plans perhaps he would let her know.

Ribbon snorted quietly. He didn't want to go, he never did, but they so loved having him he could hardly refuse after so many years. This would be his first visit without Mummy, or Auntie Bee as they called her. No doubt, they too desperately missed her. He opened the other letter and had a pleasant surprise. It was from Joy Anne Fortune and she gave her own address, a street in Bournemouth, not her publisher's or agent's. She must have written by return of post.

Her tone was humble and apologetic. She began by thanking him for pointing out the errors in her novel *Dreadful Night*. Some of them were due to her own carelessness, but others she blamed on the printer. Ribbon had heard that one before and didn't think much of it. Ms. Fortune assured him that all the mistakes would be corrected if the book ever went into paperback, though she thought it unlikely that this would happen. Here Ribbon agreed with her. However, this kind of letter—though rare—was gratifying. It made all his hard work worthwhile.

He put stamps on the letters to Eric Owlberg, Kingston Marle, and Dillon's and took them to the postbox. Again he experienced a quiver of dread in the pit of his stomach when he looked at the envelope addressed to Marle and recalled the words and terms he had used. But he drew strength from remembering how stalwartly he had withstood Selma Gunn's threats and defied her. There was no point in being in his job if he was unable to face resentful opposition. Mummy was gone, but he must soldier on alone. He repeated to himself Paul's words about fighting the good fight, running a straight race, and keeping the faith. He held the envelope in his hand for a moment or two after the Owlberg and Dillon's letters had fallen down inside the box. How much easier it would be, what a lightening of his spirits would take place, if he simply dropped that envelope into a litter bin rather than this postbox! On the other hand, he hadn't built up his reputation for uncompromising criticism and stern incorruptible judgment by being cowardly. In fact, he hardly knew why he was hesitating now. His usual behavior was far from this. What was wrong with him? There in the sunny street a sudden awful dread took hold of him, that when he put his hand to that aperture in the postbox and inserted the letter, a scaly paw would reach out of it and seize hold of his wrist. How stupid could he be? How irrational? He reminded himself of his final quarrel with Mummy, those awful words she had spoken, and quickly, without more thought, he dropped the letter into the box and walked away.

• • •

At least they didn't have to put up with that ghastly old woman, Susan Ribbon remarked to her husband as she prepared to drive to Kingham Station. Old Ambrose was a pussycat compared to Auntie Bee.

"You say that," said Frank. "You haven't got to take him to the pub."

"I've got to listen to him moaning about being too hot or too cold or the bread being wrong or the tea or the birds singing too early or us going to bed too late."

"It's only two days," said Frank. "I suppose I do it for my uncle Charlie's sake. He was a lovely man."

"Considering you were only four when he died, I don't see how you know."

Susan got to Kingham at twenty-two minutes past three and found Ambrose standing in the station approach, swiveling his head from left to right, up the road and down, a peevish look on his face. "I was beginning to wonder where you were," he said. "Punctuality is the politeness of princes, you know. I expect you heard my mother say that. It was a favorite dictum of hers."

In her opinion, Ambrose appeared far from well. His face, usually rather full and flabby, had a pasty, sunken look. "I haven't been sleeping," he said as they drove through Moreton-in-Marsh. "I've had some rather unpleasant dreams."

"It's all those highbrow books you read. You've been overtaxing your brain." Susan didn't exactly know what it was Ambrose did for a living. Some sort of freelance editing, Frank thought. The kind of thing you could do from home. It wouldn't bring in much, but Ambrose didn't need much, Auntie Bee being in possession of Uncle Charlie's royalties. "And you've suffered a terrible loss. It's only a few months since your mother died. But you'll soon feel better down here. Good fresh country air, peace and quiet—it's a far cry from London."

They would go into Oxford tomorrow, she said, do some shopping, visit Blackwell's, perhaps do a tour of the colleges, and then have lunch at the Randolph. She had asked some of her neighbors in for drinks at six; then they would have a quiet supper and watch a video. Ambrose nodded, not showing much interest. Susan told herself to be thankful for small mercies. At least there was no Auntie Bee. On that old witch's last visit with Ambrose, the year before she died, she had told Susan's friend from Stow that her skirt was too short for someone with middle-aged knees, and at ten-thirty informed the people who had come to dinner that it was time they went home.

When he had said hello to Frank she showed Ambrose up to his room. It was the one he always had, but he seemed unable to remember the way to it from one year to the next. She had made a few alterations. For one thing, it had been redecorated, and for another, she had changed the books in the shelf by the bed. A great reader herself, she thought it rather dreary always to have the same selection of reading matter in the guest bedroom.

Ambrose came down to tea, looking grim. "Are you a fan of Mr. Kingston Marle, Susan?"

"He's my favorite author," she said, surprised.

"I see. Then there's no more to be said, is there?" Ambrose proceeded to say more. "I rather dislike having a whole shelfful of his works by my bed. I've put them out on the landing." As an afterthought, he added, "I hope you don't mind."

After that, Susan decided against telling her husband's cousin the prime purpose of their planned visit to Oxford the next day. She poured him a cup of tea and handed him a slice of Madeira cake. Manfully, Frank said he would take Ambrose to see the horses and then they might stroll down to the Cross Keys for a nourishing glass of something.

"Not whiskey, I hope," said Ambrose.

"Lemonade, if you like," said Frank in an out-of-character sarcastic voice.

When they had gone Susan went upstairs and retrieved the seven novels of Kingston Marle's that Ambrose had stacked on the floor outside his bedroom door. She was particularly fond of *Evil Incarnate* and noticed that its dust jacket had a tear in the front on the bottom right-hand side. That tear had certainly not been there when she put the books on the shelf two days before. It looked too as if the jacket of *Wickedness in High Places* had been removed, screwed up in an angry fist, and later replaced. Why on earth would Ambrose do such a thing?

She returned the books to her own bedroom. Of course, Ambrose was a strange creature. You could expect nothing else with that monstrous old woman for a mother, his sequestered life, and, whatever Frank might say about his being a freelance editor, the probability that he subsisted on a small private income and had never actually worked for his living. He had never married nor even had a girlfriend, as far as Susan could make out. What did he do all day? These weekends, though only occurring annually, were terribly tedious and trying. Last year he had awakened her and Frank by knocking on their bedroom door at three in the morning to complain about a ticking clock in his room. Then there had been the business of the dry-cleaning spray. A splash of olive oil had left a pinpoint spot on the (already not very clean) jacket of Ambrose's navy blue suit. He had averred that the stain remover Susan had in the cupboard left it untouched, though Susan and Frank could see no mark at all after it had been applied, and insisted on their driving him into Cheltenham for a can of a particular kind of dry-cleaning spray. By then it was after five, and by the time they got there all possible purveyors of the spray were closed till Monday. Ambrose had gone on and on about that stain on his jacket right up to the moment Frank dropped him at Kingham Station on Sunday afternoon.

The evening passed uneventfully and without any real problems. It was true that Ambrose remarked on the silk trousers she had changed into, saying, on a slightly acrimonious note that reminded Susan of Auntie Bee, what a pity it was that skirts would soon go entirely out of fashion. He left most of his pheasant en casserole, though without comment. Susan and Frank lay awake a long while, occasionally giggling and expecting a knock at their door. None came. The silence of the night was broken only by the melancholy hooting of owls.

• • •

A fine morning, though not hot, and Oxford particularly beautiful in the sunshine. When they had parked the car they strolled up the High Street and had coffee in a small select café, outside which tables and chairs stood on the wide pavement. The Ribbons, however, went inside, where it was rather gloomy and dim. Ambrose deplored the adoption by English restaurants of Continental habits totally unsuited to what he called "our island climate." He talked about his mother and the gap in the company her absence caused, interrupting his own monologue to ask in a querulous tone why Susan kept looking at her watch.

"We have no particular engagement, do we? We are, as might be said, free as air?"

"Oh, quite," Susan said. "That's exactly right."

But it wasn't *exactly* right. She resisted glancing at her watch again. There was, after all, a clock on the café wall. So long as they were out of there by ten to eleven they would be in plenty of time. She didn't want to spend half the morning standing in a queue. Ambrose went on talking about Auntie Bee, how she'd lived in a slower-paced and more gracious past, how, as much as he missed her, he was glad for her sake she hadn't survived past the dawn of this new, and doubtless worse, millennium.

They left at eight minutes to eleven and walked to Blackwell's. Ambrose was in his element in bookshops, which was partly, though only partly, why they had come. The signing was advertised in the window and inside, though there was no voice on a public-address system urging customers to buy and get the author's signature. And there he was, sitting at the end of a table loaded with copies of his new book. A queue there was, but only a short one. Susan calculated that by the time she had selected her copy of *Demogorgon* and paid for it she would be no farther back than eighth in line, a matter of waiting ten minutes.

She hadn't counted on Ambrose's extraordinary reaction. Of course, she was well aware—he had seen to that—of his antipathy to the works of Kingston Marle, but not that it should take such a violent form. At first, the author and perhaps also the author's name, had been hidden from Ambrose's view by her own back and Frank's and the press of people around him. But as that crowd for some reason melted away, Frank turned around to say a word to his cousin and she went to collect the book she had reserved, Kingston Marle lifted his head and seemed to look straight at Frank and Ambrose.

He was a curious-looking man, tall and with a lantern-shaped but not unattractive face, his chin deep and his forehead high. A mass of long, dark womanish hair sprang from the top of that arched brow, flowed straight back, and descended to his collar in full, rather untidy curves. His mouth was wide and with the sensitive look lips shaped like this usually give to a face. Dark eyes skimmed over Frank, then Ambrose, and came to rest on her. He smiled. Whether it was this smile or the expression in Marle's eyes that had the effect on Ambrose it apparently did, Susan never knew. Ambrose let out a little sound—not quite a cry, more a grunt of protest. She heard him say to Frank, "Excuse me—must go—stuffy in here—can't breathe—just pop out for some fresh air," and he was gone, running faster than she would have believed him capable of.

When she was younger she would have thought it right to go after him, ask what was wrong, could she help, and so on. She would have left her book, given up the chance of getting it signed, and given all her attention to Ambrose. But she was older now and no longer believed it was necessary inevitably to put others first. As it was, Ambrose's hasty departure had lost her a place in the queue, and she found herself at number ten. Frank joined her.

"What was all that about?"

"Some nonsense about not being able to breathe. The old boy gets funny ideas in his head, just like his old mum. You don't think she's been reincarnated in him, do you?"

Susan laughed. "He'd have to be a baby for that to have happened, wouldn't he?"

She asked Kingston Marle to inscribe the book on the title page: *For Susan Ribbon.* While he was doing so and adding *with best wishes from the author, Kingston Marle,* he told her hers was a very unusual name. Had she ever met anyone else called Ribbon?

"No, I haven't. I believe we're the only ones in this country."

"And there aren't many of us," said Frank. "Our son is the last of the Ribbons, but he's only sixteen."

"Interesting," said Marle politely.

Susan wondered if she dared. She took a deep breath. "I admire your work very much. If I sent you some of my books—I mean, your books—and put in the postage, would you—would you sign those for me too?"

"Of course. It would be a pleasure."

Marle gave her a radiant smile. He rather wished he could have asked her to have lunch with him at the Lemon Tree instead of having to go to the Randolph with this earnest bookseller. Susan, of course, had no inkling of this and, clutching her signed book in its Blackwell's bag, she went in search of Ambrose. He was standing outside on the pavement, staring at the roadway, his hands clasped behind his back. She touched his arm and he flinched.

"Are you all right?"

He spun around, nearly cannoning into her. "Of course I'm all right. It was very hot and stuffy in there, that's all. What have you got in there? Not his latest?"

Susan was getting cross. She asked herself why she was obliged to put up with this year after year, perhaps until they all died. In silence, she took *Demogorgon* out of the bag and handed it to him. Ambrose took it in his fingers as someone might pick up a package of decaying refuse prior to dropping it in an incinerator, his nostrils wrinkling and his eyebrows raised. He opened it. As he looked at the title page his expression and his whole demeanor underwent a violent change. His face had gone a deep mottled red and a muscle under one eye began to twitch. Susan thought he was going to hurl the book in among the passing traffic. Instead he thrust it back at her and said in a very curt, abrupt voice, "I'd like to go home now. I'm not well."

Frank said, "Why don't we all go into the Randolph—we're lunching there anyway—and have a quiet drink and a rest. I'm sure you'll soon feel better, Ambrose. It *is* a warm day and there was a quite a crowd in there. I don't care for crowds myself, so I know how you feel."

"You don't know how I feel at all. You've just made that very plain. I don't want to go to the Randolph, I want to go home."

There was little they could do about it. Susan, who seldom lunched out and sometimes grew very tired of cooking, was disappointed. But you can't force an obstinate man to go into a hotel and drink sherry if he is unwilling to do this. They went back to the car park, and Frank drove home. When she and Frank had a single guest, it was usually Susan's cour-

teous habit to sit in the back of the car and offer the visitor the passenger
seat. She had done this on the way to Oxford, but this time she sat next
to Frank and left the back to Ambrose. He sat in the middle of the seat,
obstructing Frank's view in the rear mirror. Once, when Frank stopped
at a red light, she thought she felt Ambrose trembling, but it might only
have been the engine, which was inclined to judder.

On their return he went straight up to his room without explanation
and remained there, drinkless, lunchless, and, later on, tealess. Susan
read her new book and was soon totally absorbed in it. She could well
understand what the reviewer had meant when he wrote about readers
fainting with fear, though in fact she herself had not fainted but only felt
pleasurably terrified. Just the same, she was glad Frank was there, a large
comforting presence, intermittently reading the *Times* and watching golf
on television. Susan wondered why archaeologists went on excavating
tombs in Egypt when they knew the risk of being laid under a curse or
bringing home a demon. Much wiser to dig up a bit of Oxfordshire, as a
party of archaeology students were doing down the road. But Charles
Ambrose—how funny he should share a name with such a very different
man!—was nothing if not brave, and Susan felt total empathy with Kayra
de Floris when she told him one midnight, smoking *kif* on Mount Ararat,
"I could never put my body and soul into the keeping of a coward."

The bit about the cupboard was almost too much for her. She decided
to shine a torch into her wardrobe that night before she hung up her
dress. And make sure Frank was in the room. Frank's roaring with laughter at her she wouldn't mind at all. It was terrible, that chapter where
Charles first sees the small, dark, *curled-up* shape in the corner of the
room. Susan had no difficulty imagining her hero's feelings. The trouble
(or the wonderful thing) was that Kingston Marle wrote so well.
Whatever people might say about only the plot and the action and suspense being of importance in this sort of book, there was no doubt that
good literary writing made threats, danger, terror, fear, and a dark nameless dread immeasurably more real. Susan had to lay the book down at
six; their friends were coming in for a drink at half past.

She put on a long skirt and silk sweater, having first made Frank come
upstairs with her, open the wardrobe door, and demonstrate, while shaking with mirth, that there was no scaly paw inside. Then she knocked on
Ambrose's door. He came at once, his sports jacket changed for a dark

gray, almost black suit, which he had perhaps bought new for Auntie Bee's funeral. That was an occasion she and Frank had not been asked to. Probably Ambrose had attended it alone.

"I hadn't forgotten about your party," he said in a mournful tone.

"Are you feeling better?"

"A little." Downstairs, his eye fell at once on *Demogorgon*. "Susan, I wonder if you would oblige me and put that book away. I hope I'm not asking too much. It is simply that I would find it extremely distasteful if there were to be any discussion of that book in my presence among your friends this evening."

Susan took the book upstairs and put it on her bedside cabinet. "We are only expecting four people, Ambrose," she said. "It's hardly a party."

"A gathering," he said. "Seven is a gathering."

For years she had been trying to identify the character in fiction of whom Ambrose Ribbon reminded her. A children's book, she thought it was. *Alice in Wonderland? The Wind in the Willows?* Suddenly she knew. It was Eeyore, the lugubrious donkey in *Winnie-the-Pooh*. He even looked rather like Eeyore, with his melancholy gray face and stooping shoulders. For the first time, perhaps the first time ever, she felt sorry for him. Poor Ambrose, prisoner of a selfish mother. Presumably, when she died, she had left those royalties to him, after all. Susan distinctly remembered one unpleasant occasion when the two of them had been staying and Auntie Bee had suddenly announced her intention of leaving everything she had to the Royal National Lifeboat Institute. She must have changed her mind.

• • •

Susan voiced these feelings to her husband in bed that night, their pillow talk consisting of a review of the "gathering," the low-key, rather depressing supper they had eaten afterward, and the video they had watched, which failed to come up to expectations. Unfortunately, in spite of the novel's absence from the living room, Bill and Irene had begun to talk about *Demogorgon* almost as soon as they arrived. Apparently, this was the first day of its serialization in a national newspaper. They had read the installment with avidity, as had James and Rosie. Knowing Susan's positive addiction to Kingston Marle, Rosie wondered if she happened to have a copy to lend, when Susan had finished reading it, of course.

Susan was afraid to look at Ambrose. Hastily she promised a loan of the novel and changed the subject to the less dangerous one of the archaeologists' excavations in Haybury Meadow and the protests it occasioned from local environmentalists. But the damage was done. Ambrose spoke scarcely a word all evening. It was as if he felt Kingston Marle and his book underlying everything that was said and threatening always to break through the surface of the conversation, as in a later chapter in *Demogorgon,* when the monstrous Dragosoma, with the head and breasts of a woman and the body of a manatee, rises slowly out of the Sea of Azov. At one point a silvery sheen of sweat covered the pallid skin of Ambrose's face.

"Poor devil," said Frank. "I suppose he was cut up about his old mum."

"There's no accounting for people, is there?"

They were especially gentle to him the next day, without knowing exactly why gentleness was needed. Ambrose refused to go to church, treating them to a lecture on the death of God and atheism as the only course for enlightened mankind. They listened indulgently. Susan cooked a particularly nice lunch, consisting of Ambrose's favorite foods— chicken, sausages, roast potatoes, and peas. It had been practically the only dish on Auntie Bee's culinary repertoire, Ambrose having been brought up on sardines on toast and tinned spaghetti, the chicken being served on Sundays. He drank more wine than was usual with him and had a brandy afterward.

They put him on an early-afternoon train for London. Though she had never done so before, Susan kissed him. His reaction was very marked. Seeing what was about to happen, he turned his head abruptly as her mouth approached, and the kiss landed on the bristles above his right ear. They stood on the platform and waved to him.

"That was a disaster," said Frank in the car. "Do we have to do it again?"

Susan surprised herself. "We have to do it again." She sighed. "Now I can go back and have a nice afternoon reading my book."

• • •

A letter from Kingston Marle, acknowledging the errors in *Demogorgon* and perhaps offering some explanation of how they came to be there, with a promise of amendment in the paperback edition, would have set everything to rights. The disastrous weekend would fade into oblivion and those stupid guests of Frank's with it. Frank's idiot wife, good-looking, they said, though he had never been able to see it, but a woman of neither education nor discernment, would dwindle away into the mists of the past. Above all, that lantern-shaped face, that monstrous jaw and vaulted forehead, looming so shockingly above its owner's blood-colored works, would lose its menace and assume a merely arrogant cast. But before he reached home, while he was still in the train, Ambrose, thinking about it—he could think of nothing else—knew with a kind of sorrowful resignation that no such letter would be waiting for him. No such letter would come the next day, or the next. By his own foolhardy move, his misplaced *courage,* by doing his duty, he had seen to that.

And yet it had scarcely been all his own doing. If that retarded woman, his cousin's doll-faced wife, had only had the sense to ask Marle to inscribe the book "For Susan," rather than "For Susan Ribbon," little harm would have been done. Ribbon could hardly understand why she had done so, unless from malice, for these days it was the custom, and one he constantly deplored, to call everyone from the moment you met them, or even if you only talked to them on the phone, by their first names. Previously, Marle would have known his address but not his appearance, not seen his face, not established him as a real and therefore vulnerable person.

No letter had come. There were no letters at all on the doormat, only a flyer from a pizza takeaway company and two hire-car cards. It was still quite early, only about six. Ribbon made himself a pot of real tea—that woman used *tea bags*—and decided to break with tradition and do some work. He never worked on a Sunday evening, but he was in need of something positive to distract his mind from Kingston Marle. Taking his tea into the front room, he saw Marle's book lying on the coffee table. It was the first thing his eye lighted on. The Book. The awful book that had been the ruin of his weekend. He must have left *Demogorgon* on the table when he'd abandoned it in a kind of queasy disgust halfway through. Yet he had no memory of leaving it there. He could have sworn he had put it away, tucked it into a drawer to be out of sight and therefore of mind. The dreadful face, fish-belly white between the bandages, leered at him out of the star-shaped hole in the red-and-silver jacket. He opened the drawer in the cabinet where he thought he had put it. There was nothing there but what had been there before, a few sheets of writing paper and an old diary of Mummy's. Of course there was nothing there, he didn't possess two copies of the horrible thing, but it was going in there now . . .

The phone rang. This frequent event in other people's homes happened seldom in Ribbon's. He ran out into the hall where the phone was and stood looking at it while it rang. Suppose it should be Kingston Marle? Gingerly he lifted the receiver. If it was Marle he would slam it down fast. That woman's voice said, "Ambrose? Are you all right?"

"Of course I'm all right. I've just got home."

"It was just that we've been rather worried about you. Now that I know you're safely home, that's fine."

Ribbon remembered his manners and recited Mummy's rubric. "Thank you very much for having me, Susan. I had a lovely time."

He would write to her, of course. That was the proper thing. Upstairs in the office he composed three letters. The first was to Susan.

21 Grove Green Avenue
London E11 4ZH

Dear Susan,

I very much enjoyed my weekend with you and Frank. It was very enjoyable to take a stroll with Frank and take in "the pub" on the way. The ample food provided was tip-top. Your friends seemed charming people, though I cannot commend their choice of reading matter!

All is well here. It looks as if we may be in for another spell of hot weather.

With kind regards to you both,
Yours affectionately,
Ambrose

Ribbon wasn't altogether pleased with this. He took out "very much" and put in "enormously," and for "very enjoyable" substituted "delightful." That was better. It would have to do. He was rather pleased with that acid comment about those ridiculous people's reading matter and hoped it would get back to them.

During the weekend, particularly during those hours in his room on Saturday afternoon, he had gone carefully through the two paperbacks he had bought at Dillon's. Lucy Grieves, the author of *Cottoning On,* had meticulously passed on to her publishers all the errors he had pointed out to her when the novel appeared in hardcover, down to "on to" instead of "onto." Ribbon felt satisfied. He was pleased with Lucy Grieves, though not to the extent of writing to congratulate her. The second letter he wrote was to Channon Scott Smith, the paperback version of whose novel *Carol Conway* contained precisely the same mistakes and literary howlers as it had in hardcover. That completed, a scathing paean of contempt if ever there was one, Ribbon sat back in his chair and thought long and hard.

Was there some way he could write to Kingston Marle and *make things all right* without groveling, without apologizing? God forbid that he should apologize for boldly telling truths that needed to be told. But could he compose something, without saying he was sorry, that would mollify Marle—better still, that would make him understand? He had a notion that he would feel easier in his mind if he wrote to Marle, would sleep better at night. The two nights he had passed at Frank's had been very wretched, the second one almost sleepless.

What was he afraid of? Afraid of writing and afraid of not writing? Just afraid? Marle couldn't do anything to him. Ribbon acknowledged to himself that he had no absurd fears of Marle's setting some hit man on him or stalking him or even attempting to sue him for libel. It wasn't that. What was it then? The cliché came into his head unbidden, the definition of what he felt: a nameless dread. If only Mummy were here to advise him! Suddenly he longed for her, and tears pricked the backs of his eyes. Yet he knew what she would have said. She would have said what she had that last time.

That *Encyclopaedia Britannica* volume 8 had been lying on the table. He had just shown Mummy the letter he had written to Desmond Erb, apologizing for correcting him when he wrote about "the quinone structure." Of course he should have looked the word up, but he hadn't. He had been so sure it should have been "quinine." Erb had been justifiably indignant, as writers tended to be, when he corrected an error in their work that was in fact not an error at all. He would never forget Mummy's anger, nor anything of that quarrel, come to that; how, almost of their own volition, his hands had crept across the desk toward the black, blue, and gold volume...

She was not here now to stop him, and after a while he wrote:

Dear Mr. Marle,

With reference to my letter of June 4th, in which I pointed out certain errors of fact and of grammar and spelling in your recent novel, I fear I may inadvertently have caused you pain. This was far from my intention. If I have hurt your feelings I must tell you that I very much regret this. I hope you will overlook it and forgive me.

Yours sincerely,

Reading this over, Ribbon found he very much disliked the bit about overlooking and forgiving. "Regret" wasn't right either. Also he hadn't actually named the book. He ought to have put in its title but, strangely, he found himself reluctant to type the word *Demogorgon*. It was as if, by putting it into cold print, he would set something in train, spark off some reaction. Of course, this was mad. He must be getting tired. Nevertheless, he composed a second letter.

Dear Mr. Marle,

With reference to my letter to yourself of June 4th, in which I pointed out certain errors in your recent and highly acclaimed novel, I fear I may inadvertently have hurt your feelings. It was not my intention to cause you pain. I am well aware—who is not?—of the high position you enjoy in the ranks of literature. The amendments I suggested you make to the novel when it appears in paperback—in many hundreds of thousand copies, no doubt—were meant in a spirit of assistance, not criticism, simply so that a good book might be made better.

Yours sincerely,

Sycophantic. But what could be more mollifying than flattery? Ribbon endured half an hour's agony and self-doubt, self-recrimination, and self-justification too, before writing a third and final letter.

Dear Mr. Marle,

    With reference to my letter to your good self, dated June 4th, in which I presumed to criticize your recent novel, I fear I may inadvertently have been wanting in respect. I hope you will believe me when I say it was not my intention to offend you. You enjoy a high and well-deserved position in the ranks of literature. It was gauche and clumsy of me to write to you as I did.

With best wishes,
Yours sincerely,

    To grovel in this way made Ribbon feel actually sick. And it was all lies too. Of course it had been his intention to offend the man, to cause him pain, and to make him angry. He would have given a great deal to recall that earlier letter but this—he quoted silently to himself those hackneyed but apt words about the moving finger that writes and having writ moves on—neither he nor anyone else could do. What did it matter if he suffered half an hour's humiliation when by sending this apology he would end his sufferings? Thank heaven only that Mummy wasn't here to see it.

    Those letters had taken him hours, and it had grown quite dark. Unexpectedly dark, he thought, for nine in the evening in the middle of June, with the longest day not much more than a week away. But still he sat there, in the dusk, looking at the backs of houses, yellow brick punctured by the bright rectangles of windows, at the big shaggy trees, his own garden, the square of grass dotted with dark shrubs, big and small. He had never previously noticed how unpleasant ordinary privets and cypresses can look in deep twilight when they are not clustered together in a shrubbery or copse, when they stand individually on an otherwise open space, strange shapes, tall and slender or round and squat, or with a branch here and there protruding like a limb, and casting elongated shadows.

    He got up abruptly and put the light on. The garden and its gathering of bushes disappeared. The window became dark, shiny, opaque. He switched off the light almost immediately and went downstairs. Seeing *Demogorgon* on the coffee table made him jump. What was it doing there? How did it get there? He had put it in the drawer. And there was the drawer standing open to prove it.

It couldn't have got out of the drawer and returned to the table on its own. Could it? *Of course not.* Ribbon put on every light in the room. He left the curtains open so that he could see the streetlights as well. He must have left the book on the table himself. He must have intended to put it into the drawer and for some reason not done so. Possibly he had been interrupted. But nothing ever interrupted what he was doing, did it? He couldn't remember. A cold teapot and a cup of cold tea stood on the tray on the coffee table beside the book. He couldn't remember making tea.

After he had taken the tray and the cold teapot away and poured the cold tea down the sink, he sat down in an armchair with *Chambers Dictionary.* He realized that he had never found out what the word *Demogorgon* meant. Here was the definition: "A mysterious infernal deity first mentioned about A.D. 450 (Appar Gr *daimon* deity, and *gorgo* Gorgon, from *gorgos* terrible)." He shuddered, closed the dictionary, and opened the second Channon Scott Smith paperback he had bought. This novel had been published four years before, but Ribbon had never read it, nor indeed any of the works of Mr. Scott Smith before the recently published one, but he thought this fat volume might yield a rich harvest, if *Carol Conway* were anything to go by. But instead of opening *Destiny's Suzerain,* he found that the book in his hands was *Demogorgon,* open one page past where he had stopped a few days before.

In a kind of horrified wonder, he began to read. It was curious how he was compelled to go on reading, considering how every line was like a faint pinprick in his equilibrium, a tiny physical tremor through his body, reminding him of those things he had written to Kingston Marle and the look Marle had given him in Oxford on Saturday. Later he was to ask himself why he had read any more of it at all, why he hadn't just stopped, why indeed he hadn't put the book in the rubbish for the refuse collectors to take away in the morning.

The dark shape in the corner of Charles Ambrose's tent was appearing for the first time: in his tent, then his hotel bedroom, his mansion in Shropshire, his flat in Mayfair. A small, curled-up shape like a tiny huddled person or small monkey. It sat or simply *was,* amorphous but for faintly visible hands or paws, and uniformly dark but for pinpoint malevolent eyes that stared and glinted. Ribbon looked up from the page for a moment. The lights were very bright. Out in the street a couple went by, hand in hand, talking and laughing. Usually the noise they made would have angered him, but tonight he felt curiously comforted. They made him feel he wasn't alone. They drew him, briefly, into reality. He would post the letter in the morning, and once it had gone all would be well.

He read two more pages. The unraveling of the mystery began on page 423. The Demogorgon was Charles Ambrose's own mother, who had been murdered and whom he had buried in the grounds of his Shropshire house. Finally, she came back to tell him the truth, came in the guise of a cypress tree that walked out of the pinetum. Ribbon gasped out loud. It was his own story. How had Marle known? What was Marle—some kind of god or magus that he knew such things? The dreadful notion came to him that *Demogorgon* had not always been like this, that the ending had originally been different, but that Marle, seeing him in Oxford and immediately identifying him with the writer of that defamatory letter, *had by some remote control or sorcery altered the end of the copy that was in his, Ribbon's, possession.*

He went upstairs and rewrote his letter, adding to the existing text: "Please forgive me. I meant you no harm. Don't torment me like this. I can't stand any more." It was a long time before he went to bed. Why go to bed when you know you won't sleep? With the light on—and all the lights in the house were on now—he couldn't see the garden, the shrubs on the lawn, the flower bed, but he drew the curtains just the same. At last he fell uneasily asleep in his chair, waking four or five hours later to the horrid thought that his original letter to Marle was the first really vituperative criticism he had sent to anyone since Mummy's death. Was there some significance in this? Did it mean he couldn't get along without Mummy? Or, worse, that he had killed all the power and confidence in himself he had once felt?

He got up, had a rejuvenating shower, but was unable to face breakfast. The three letters he had written the night before were in the postbox by nine, and Ribbon on the way to the tube station. Waterstones in Leadenhall Market was his destination. He bought Clara Jenkins's *Tales My Lover Told Me* in hardcover, as well as Raymond Kobbo's *The Nomad's Smile* and Natalya Dreadnought's *Tick* in paperback. Copies of *Demogorgon* were everywhere, stacked in piles or displayed in fanciful arrangements. Ribbon forced himself to touch one of them, to pick it up. He looked over his shoulder to see if any of the assistants were watching him and, having established that they were not, opened it at page 423. It was as he had thought, as he had hardly dared put into words. Charles Ambrose's mother made no appearance; there was nothing about a burial in the grounds of Montpellier Hall or a cypress tree walking. The end was quite different. Charles Ambrose, married to Kayra in a ceremony conducted in a balloon above the Himalayas, awakens on his wedding night and sees in the corner of the honeymoon bedroom the demon curled up, hunched and small, staring at him with gloating eyes. It had followed him from Egypt to Shropshire, from London to Russia, from Russia to New Orleans, and from New Orleans to Nepal. It would never leave him; it was his for life and perhaps beyond.

Ribbon replaced the book, took up another copy. The same thing: no murder, no burial, no tree walking, only the horror of the demon in the bedroom. So he had been right. Marle had infused this alternative ending into *his* copy alone. It was part of the torment, part of the revenge for the insults Ribbon had heaped on him. On the way back to Liverpool Street Station a shout and a thump made him look over his shoulder—a taxi had clipped the rear wheel of a motorbike—and he saw, a long way behind, Kingston Marle following him.

Ribbon thought he would faint. A great flood of heat washed over him, to be succeeded by shivering. Panic held him still for a moment. Then he dived into a shop, a sweetshop it was, and it was like entering a giant chocolate box. The scent of chocolate swamped him. Trembling, he stared at the street through a window draped with pink frills. Ages passed before Kingston Marle went by. He paused, turned his head to look at the chocolates, and Ribbon, again almost fainting, saw an unknown man, lantern-jawed but not monstrously so, long-haired but the hair sparse and brown, the blue eyes mild and wistful. Ribbon's heartbeat slowed; the blood withdrew from the surface of his skin. He muttered, "No, no thank you," to the woman behind the counter and went back into the street. What a wretched state his nerves were in! He'd be encountering a scaly paw in the wardrobe next. Clasping his bag of books, he got thoughtfully into the train.

•   •   •

What he really should have done was add a P.S. to the effect that he would appreciate a prompt acknowledgment of his letter. Just a line saying something like "Please be kind enough to acknowledge receipt." However, it was too late now. Kingston Marle's publisher would get his letter tomorrow and send it straight on. Ribbon knew publishers did not always do this, but surely in the case of so eminent an author and one of the most profitable on their list . . .

Sending the letter should have allayed his fears, but they seemed to crowd in upon him more urgently, jostling each other for preeminence in his mind. The man who had followed him along Bishopsgate, for instance. Of course he knew it had not been Kingston Marle, yet the similarity of build, of feature, of height between the two men was too great for coincidence. The most likely explanation was that his stalker was Marle's younger brother, and now, as he reached this reasonable conclusion, Ribbon no longer saw the man's eyes as mild but as sly and crafty. When his letter came Marle would call his brother off but, in the nature of things, the letter could not arrive at Marle's home before Wednesday at the earliest. Then there was the matter of The Book itself. The drawer in which it lay failed to hide it adequately. It was part of a mahogany cabinet (one of Mummy's wedding presents, Ribbon believed), well polished but of course opaque. Yet sometimes the wood seemed to become transparent and the harsh reds and glaring silver of *Demogorgon* shine through it as he understood a block of radium would appear as a glowing cuboid behind a wall of solid matter. Approaching closely, creeping up on it, he would see the bright colors fade and the woodwork reappear, smooth, shiny, and *ordinary* once more.

In the study upstairs on Monday evening he tried to do some work, but his eye was constantly drawn to the window and what lay beyond. He became convinced that the bushes on the lawn had moved. That small thin one had surely stood next to the pair of tall fat ones, not several yards away. Since the night before it had shifted its position, taking a step nearer to the house. Drawing the curtains helped, but after a while he got up and pulled them apart a little to check on the big round bush, to see if it had taken a step farther or had returned to its previous position. It was where it had been ten minutes before. All should have been well, but it was not. The room itself had become uncomfortable, and he resolved not to go back there, to move the computer downstairs, until he had heard from Kingston Marle.

The doorbell ringing made him jump so violently he felt pain travel through his body and reverberate. Immediately he thought of Marle's brother. Suppose Marle's brother, a strong young man, was outside the door and when it was opened would force his way in? Or, worse, was merely checking that Ribbon was at home and, when footsteps sounded inside, intended to disappear? Ribbon went down. He took a deep breath and threw the door open. His caller was Glenys Next-door.

Marching in without being invited, she said, "Hiya, Amby" and explained that Tinks Next-door was missing. The cat had not been home since the morning, when he was last seen by Sandra On-the-other-side sitting in Ribbon's front garden eating a bird.

"I'm out of my mind with worry, as you can imagine, Amby."

As a matter of fact, he couldn't. Ribbon cared very little for songbirds, but he cared for feline predators even less. "I'll let you know if I come across him. However"—he laughed lightly—"he knows he's not popular with me, so he makes himself scarce."

This was the wrong thing to say. In the works of his less literate authors Ribbon sometimes came upon the expression *to bridle*: "she bridled" or even "the young woman bridled." At last he understood what it meant. Glenys Next-door tossed her head, raised her eyebrows, and looked down her nose at him.

"I'm sorry for you, Amby, I really am. You must find that attitude problem of yours a real hang-up. I mean socially. I've tried to ignore it all these years, but there comes a time when one has to speak one's mind. No, don't bother, please, I can see myself out."

This was not going to be a *good* night. He knew that before he switched the bedside light off. For one thing, he always read in bed before going to sleep. Always had and always would. But for some reason he had forgotten to take *Destiny's Suzerain* upstairs with him, and though his bedroom was full of reading matter, shelves and shelves of it, he had read all the books before. Of course he could have gone downstairs and fetched himself a book, or even just gone into the study, which was lined with books. Booked, not papered, indeed. He *could* have done so, in theory he could have, but on coming into his bedroom he had locked the door. Why? He was unable to answer that question, though he put it to himself several times. It was a small house, potentially brightly lit, in a street of a hundred and fifty such houses, all populated. A dreadful feeling descended upon him as he lay in bed that if he unlocked that door, if he turned the key and opened it, something would come in. Was it the small thin bush that would come in? These thoughts, ridiculous, unworthy of him, puerile, frightened him so much that he put the bedside lamp on and left it on till morning.

Tuesday's post brought two letters. Eric Owlberg called Ribbon "a little harsh" and informed him that printers do not always do as they are told. Jeanne Pettle's letter was from a secretary who wrote that Ms. Pettle was away on an extended publicity tour but would certainly attend to his "interesting communication" when she returned. There was nothing from Dillon's. It was a bright sunny day. Ribbon went into the study and contemplated the garden. The shrubs were, of course, where they had always been. Or where they had been before the large round bush stepped back into its original position?

"Pull yourself together," Ribbon said aloud.

Housework day. He started, as he always did, in Mummy's room, dusting the picture rail and the central lamp with a bunch of pink and blue feathers attached to a rod, and the ornaments with a clean fluffy yellow duster. The numerous books he took out and dusted on alternate weeks, but this was not one of those. He vacuumed the carpet, opened the window wide, and replaced the pink silk nightdress with a pale blue one. He always washed Mummy's nightdresses by hand once a fortnight. Next his own room and the study, then downstairs to the dining and front rooms. Marle's publisher would have received his letter by the first post this morning and the department that looked after this kind of thing would, even at this moment probably, be readdressing the envelope and sending it on. Ribbon had no idea where the man lived. London? Devonshire? Most of those people seemed to live in the Cotswolds; its green hills and lush valleys must be chock-full of them. But perhaps Shropshire was more likely. He had written about Montpellier Hall as if he really knew such a house.

Ribbon dusted the mahogany cabinet and passed on to Mummy's little sewing table, but he couldn't quite leave things there, and he returned to the cabinet, to stand, duster in hand, staring at that drawer. It was not transparent on this sunny morning and nothing could be seen glowing in its depths. He pulled it open suddenly and snatched up The Book. He looked at its double redness and at the pentagram. After his experiences of the past days he wouldn't have been surprised if the bandaged face inside had changed its position, closed its mouth or moved its eyes. Well, he would have been surprised—he'd have been horrified, aghast. But the demon was the same as ever; The Book was just the same, an ordinary, rather tastelessly jacketed cheap thriller.

"What on earth is the matter with me?" Ribbon said to The Book.

He went out shopping for food. Sandra On-the-other-side appeared behind him in the queue at the checkout. "You've really upset Glenys," she said. "You know me, I believe in plain speaking, and in all honesty I think you ought to apologize."

"When I want your opinion I'll ask for it, Mrs. Wilson," said Ribbon.

Marle's brother got on the bus and sat behind him. It wasn't actually Marle's brother; he only thought it was, just for a single frightening moment. It was amazing really what a lot of people there were about who looked like Kingston Marle, men and women too. He had never noticed it before, had never had an inkling of it until he came face to face with Marle in that bookshop. If only it were possible to go back. For the moving finger, having writ, not to move on but to retreat, retrace its strokes, white them out with correction fluid and begin writing again. He would have guessed why that silly woman, his cousin's wife, was so anxious to get to Blackwell's; her fondness for Marle's works—distributed so tastelessly all over his bedroom—would have told him, and he would have cried off the Oxford trip, first warning her on no account to let Marle know her surname. Yet—and this was undeniable—Marle had Ribbon's home address, since the address was on the letter. The moving finger would have to go back a week and erase "21 Grove Green Avenue, London E11 4ZH" from the top right-hand corner of his letter. Then, and only then, would he have been safe . . .

Sometimes a second post arrived on a weekday, but none came that day. Ribbon took his shopping bags into the kitchen, unpacked them, went into the front room to open the window—and saw *Demogorgon* lying on the coffee table. A violent trembling convulsed him. He sat down, closed his eyes. He *knew* he hadn't taken it out of the drawer. Why on earth would he? He hated it. He wouldn't touch it unless he had to. There was not much doubt now that it had a life of its own. Some kind of kinetic energy lived inside its covers, the same sort of thing that moved the small thin bush across the lawn at night. Kingston Marle put that energy into objects, he infused them with it, he was a sorcerer whose powers extended far beyond his writings and his fame. Surely that was the only explanation why a writer of such appallingly bad books, misspelled, the grammar nonexistent, facts awry, should enjoy such a phenomenal success, not only with an ignorant illiterate public but among the cognoscenti. He practiced sorcery or was himself one of the demons he wrote about, an evil spirit living inside that hideous lantern-jawed exterior.

Ribbon reached out a slow wavering hand for The Book and found that, surely by chance, he had opened it at page 423. Shrinking while he did so, holding The Book almost too far away from his eyes to see the words, he read of Charles Ambrose's wedding night, of his waking in the half-dark with Kayra sleeping beside him and seeing the curled-up shape of the demon in the corner of the room. . . . So Marle had called off his necromancer's power, had he? He had restored the ending to what it originally was. Nothing about Mummy's death and burial, nothing about the walking tree. Did that mean he had already received Ribbon's apology? It might mean that. His publisher had hardly had time to send the letter on, but suppose Marle, for some reason—and the reason would be his current publicity tour—had been in his publisher's office and the letter had been handed to him. It was the only explanation, it fitted the facts. Marle had read his letter, accepted his apology, and, perhaps with a smile of triumph, whistled back whatever dogs of the occult carried his messages.

Ribbon held The Book in his hands. Everything might be over now, but he still didn't want it in the house. Carefully, he wrapped it up in newspaper, slipped the resulting parcel into a plastic carrier, tied the handles together, and dropped it in the waste bin. "Let it get itself out of that," he said aloud. "Just let it try." Was he imagining that a fetid smell came from it, swathed in plastic though it was? He splashed disinfectant into the waste bin, opened the kitchen window.

He sat down in the front room and opened Tales My Lover Told Me, but he couldn't concentrate. The afternoon grew dark; there was going to be a storm. For a moment he stood at the window, watching the clouds gather, black and swollen. When he was a little boy Mummy had told him a storm was the clouds fighting. It was years since he had thought of that, and now, remembering, for perhaps the first time in his life he questioned Mummy's judgment. Was it quite right so to mislead a child?

The rain came, sheets of it blown by the huge gale that arose. Ribbon wondered if Marle, among his many accomplishments, could raise a wind, strike lightning from some diabolical tinderbox and, like Jove himself, beat the drum of thunder. Perhaps. He would believe anything of that man now. He went around the house closing all the windows. The one in the study he closed, then fastened the catches. From his own bedroom window he looked at the lawn, where the bushes stood as they had always stood, unmoved, immovable, lashed by rain, whipping and twisting in the wind. Downstairs, in the kitchen, the window was wide open, flapping back and forth, and the waste bin had fallen on its side. The parcel lay beside it, the plastic bag that covered it, the newspaper inside, torn as if a scaly paw had ripped it. Other rubbish—food scraps, a sardine can—were scattered across the floor.

Ribbon stood transfixed. He could see the red-and-silver jacket of The Book gleaming, almost glowing, under its torn wrappings. What had come through the window? Was it possible the demon, unleashed by Marle, was now beyond his control? He asked the question aloud, he asked Mummy, though she was long gone. The sound of his own voice, shrill and horror-stricken, frightened him. Had whatever it was come in to retrieve the—he could hardly put it even into silent words—the *chronicle of its exploits?* Nonsense, nonsense. It was Mummy speaking, Mummy telling him to be strong, not to be a fool. He shook himself, gritted his teeth. He picked up the parcel, dropped it into a black rubbish bag, and took it into the garden, getting very wet in the process. In the wind the biggest bush of all reached out a needly arm and lashed him across the face.

He left the black bag there. He locked all the doors, and even when the storm had subsided and the sky cleared he kept all the windows closed. Late that night, in his bedroom, he stared down at the lawn. The Book in its bag was where he had left it, but the small thin bush had moved, in a different direction this time, stepping to one side so that the two fat bushes, the one that had lashed him and its twin, stood close together and side by side like tall, heavily built men gazing up at his window. Ribbon had saved half a bottle of Mummy's sleeping pills. For an emergency, for a rainy day. All the lights blazing, he went into Mummy's room, found the bottle, and swallowed two pills. They took effect rapidly. Fully clothed, he fell onto his bed and into something more like a deep trance than sleep. It was the first time in his life he had ever taken a soporific.

In the morning he looked through the yellow pages and found a firm of tree fellers, operating locally. Would they send someone to cut down all the shrubs in his garden? They would, but not before Monday. On Monday morning they would be with him by nine. In the broad daylight he asked himself again what had come through the kitchen window, come in and taken That Book out of the waste bin and, sane again, wondered if it might have been Glenys Next-door's fox. The sun was shining, the grass gleaming wet after the rain. He fetched a spade from the shed and advanced upon the wide flower bed. Not the right-hand side, not there, avoid that at all costs. He selected a spot on the extreme left, close by the fence dividing his garden from that of Sandra On-the-other-side. While he dug he wondered if it was a commonplace with people, this burying of unwanted or hated or threatening objects in their back gardens. Maybe all the gardens in Leytonstone, in the London suburbs, in the United Kingdom, in the world, were full of such concealed things, hidden in the earth, waiting...

He laid *Demogorgon* inside. The wet earth went back over the top of it, covering it, and Ribbon stamped the surface down viciously. If whatever it was came back and dug The Book out, he thought he would die.

• • •

T hings were better now that *Demogorgon* was gone. He wrote to Clara Jenkins at her home address—for some unaccountable reason she was in *Who's Who*—pointing out that in chapter 1 of *Tales My Lover Told Me* Humphry Nemo had blue eyes and in chapter 21 brown eyes; Thekla Pattison wore a wedding ring on page 20 but denied, on page 201, that she had ever possessed one; and on page 245 Justin Armstrong was taking part in an athletics contest, in spite of having broken his leg on page 223, a mere five days before. But Ribbon wrote with a new gentleness, as if she had caused him pain rather than rage.

Nothing had come from Dillon's. He wondered bitterly why he had troubled to congratulate them on their service if his accolade was to go unappreciated. And more to the point, nothing had come from Kingston Marle by Friday. He had the letter of apology—he must have, otherwise he wouldn't have altered the ending of *Demogorgon* back to the original plotline. But that hardly meant he had recovered from all his anger. He might still have other revenges in store. And, moreover, he might intend never to answer Ribbon at all.

The shrubs seemed to be back in their normal places. It would be a good idea to have a plan of the garden with the bushes all accurately positioned so that he could tell if they moved. He decided to make one. The evening was mild and sunny, though damp, and of course, at not long past midsummer, still broad daylight at eight. A deck chair was called for, a sheet of paper, and, better than a pen, a soft lead pencil. The deck chairs might be up in the loft or down here, he couldn't remember, though he had been in the shed on Wednesday evening to find a spade. He looked through the window. In the far corner, curled up, was a small dark shape.

Ribbon was too frightened to cry out. A pain seized him in the chest, ran up his left arm, held him in its grip before it slackened and released him. The black shape opened its eyes and looked at him, just as the demon in The Book looked at Charles Ambrose. Ribbon hunched his back and closed his eyes. When he opened them and looked again he saw Tinks Next-door get up, stretch, arch its back, and begin to walk in leisurely fashion toward the door. Ribbon flung it open.

"Scat! Get out! Go home!" he screamed.

Tinks fled. Had the wretched thing slunk in there when he'd opened the door to get the spade? Probably. He took out a deck chair and sat on it, but all heart had gone out of him for drawing a plan of the garden. In more ways than one, he thought, the pain receding and leaving only a dull ache. You could have mild heart attacks from which you recovered and were none the worse. Mummy said she had had several, some of them brought on—he sadly recalled—by his own defections from her standards. It could be hereditary. He must take things easy for the next few days, not *worry,* try to put stress behind him.

• • •

Kingston Marle had signed all the books she sent him and returned them with a covering letter. Of course she had sent postage and packing as well and had put in a very polite little note, repeating how much she loved his work and what a great pleasure meeting him in Blackwell's had been. But still she had hardly expected such a lovely long letter from him, nor one of quite that nature. Marle wrote how very different she was from the common run of fans, not only in intellect but in appearance too. He hoped she wouldn't take it amiss when he told her he had been struck by her beauty and elegance among that dowdy crowd.

It was a long time since any man had paid Susan such a compliment. She read and reread the letter, sighed a little, laughed, and showed it to Frank.

"I don't suppose he writes his own letters," said Frank, put out. "Some secretary will do it for him."

"Well, hardly."

"If you say so. When are you seeing him again?"

"Oh, don't be silly," said Susan.

She covered each individual book Kingston Marle had signed for her with plastic wrap and put them all away in a glass-fronted bookcase, from which, to make room, she first removed Frank's *Complete Works of Shakespeare*, Tennyson's *Poems*, *The Poems of Robert Browning*, and *Kobbe's Complete Opera Book*. Frank appeared not to notice. Admiring through the glass, indeed gloating over, her wonderful collection of Marle's works with the secret inscriptions hidden from all eyes, Susan wondered if she should respond to the author. On the one hand a letter would keep her in the forefront of his mind, but on the other it would be in direct contravention of the playing-hard-to-get principle. Not that Susan had any intention of being "got," of course not, but she was not averse to inspiring thoughts about her in Kingston Marle's mind or even a measure of regret that he was unable to know her better.

Several times in the next few days she surreptitiously took one of the books out and looked at the inscription. Each had something different in it. In *Wickedness in High Places* Marle had written, "To Susan, met on a fine morning in Oxford" and in *The Necromancer's Bride*, "To Susan, with kindest of regards," but on the title page of *Evil Incarnate* appeared the inscription Susan liked best: "She was a lady sweet and kind, ne'er a face so pleased my mind—Ever yours, Kingston Marle."

Perhaps he would write again, even if she didn't reply. Perhaps he would be *more likely* to write if she didn't reply.

• • •

On Monday morning the post came early, just after eight, delivering only one item. The computer-generated address on the envelope made Ribbon think for one wild moment that it might be from Kingston Marle. But it was from Clara Jenkins, and it was an angry, indignant letter, though containing no threats. Didn't he understand her novel was fiction?

You couldn't say things were true or false in fiction, for things were as the author, who was all-powerful, wanted them to be. In a magic-realism novel, such as *Tales My Lover Told Me,* only an ignorant fool would expect facts (and these included spelling, punctuation, and grammar) to be as they were in the dreary reality he inhabited. Ribbon took it into the kitchen, screwed it up, and dropped it in the waste bin.

He was waiting for the tree fellers, who were due at nine. Half past nine went by; ten went by. At ten past the front doorbell rang. It was Glenys Next-door.

"Tinks turned up," she said. "I was so pleased to see him I gave him a whole can of red sockeye salmon." She appeared to have forgiven Ribbon for his "attitude." "Now don't say what a wicked waste, I can see you were going to. I've got to go and see my mother—she's fallen over, broken her arm, and bashed her face—so would you be an angel and let the washing-machine man in?"

"I suppose so." The woman had a mother! She must be getting on for seventy herself.

"You're a star. Here's the key, and you can leave it on the hall table when he's been. Just tell him it's full of pillowcases and water and the door won't open."

The tree fellers came at eleven-thirty. The older one, a joker, said, "I'm a funny feller and he's a nice feller, right?"

"Come this way," Ribbon said frostily.

"What d'you want them lovely leylandiis down for, then? Not to mention that lovely flowering currant?"

"Them currants smell of cat's pee, Damian," said the young one. "Whether there's been cats peeing on them or not."

"Is that right? The things he knows, guv. He's wasted in this job, ought to be fiddling with computers."

Ribbon went indoors. The computer and printer were downstairs now, in the dining room. He wrote first to Natalya Dreadnought, author of *Tick,* pointing out in a mild way that "eponymous" applies to a character or object which gives a work its name, not to the name derived from the character. Therefore it was the large, blood-sucking mite of the order Acarina that was eponymous, not her title. The letter he wrote to Raymond Kobbo would correct just two mistakes in *The Nomad's Smile,* but for both Ribbon needed to consult the *Piranha* to *Scurfy* volume. He was pretty sure the Libyan caravan center should be spelt "Sabha," not "Sebha," and he was even more certain that "qalam," meaning a reed pen used in Arabic calligraphy, should start with a *k*. He went upstairs and lifted the heavy tome off the shelf. Finding that Kobbo had been right in both instances—"Sabha" and "Sebha" were optional spellings and "qalam" perfectly correct—unsettled him. Mummy would have known; Mummy would have set him right in her positive, no-nonsense way, before he had set foot on the bottom stair. He asked himself if he could live without her and could have sworn he heard her sharp voice say, "You should have thought of that before."

Before what? That day in February when she had come up here to—well, oversee him, supervise him. She frequently did so, and in later years he hadn't been as grateful to her as he should have been. By the desk here she had stood and told him it was time he earned some money by his work, by a man's fifty-second year it was time. She had made up her mind to leave Daddy's royalties to the lifeboat people. But it wasn't this that finished things for him, or triggered things off, however you liked to put it. It was the sneering tone in which she told him, her right index finger pointing at his chest, that he was no good, he had failed. She had kept him in comfort and luxury for decade after decade, she had instructed him, taught him everything he knew, yet in spite of this, his literary criticism had not had the slightest effect on authors' standards or effected the least improvement in fiction. He had wasted his time and his life through cowardice and pusillanimity, through mousiness instead of manliness.

It was the word "mousiness" that did it. His hands moved across the table to rest on *Piranha to Scurfy;* he lifted it in both hands and brought it down as hard as he could on her head. Once, twice, again and again. The first time she screamed, but not again after that. She staggered and sank to her knees and he beat her to the ground with volume 8 of the *Encyclopaedia Britannica*. She was an old woman: she put up no struggle; she died quickly. He very much wanted not to get blood on the book—she had taught him books were sacred—but there was no blood. What was shed was shed inside her.

Regret came immediately. Remorse followed. But she was dead. He buried her in the wide flower bed at the end of the garden that night, in the dark without a flashlight. The widows on either side slept soundly—no one saw a thing. The ivies grew back and the flowerless plants that liked shade. All summer he had watched them slowly growing. He told only two people she was dead, Glenys Next-door and his cousin Frank. Neither showed any inclination to come to the "funeral," so when the day he had appointed came he left the house at ten in the morning, wearing the new dark suit he had bought, a black tie that had been Daddy's, and carrying a bunch of spring flowers. Sandra On-the-other-side spotted him from her front-room window and, approving, nodded somberly while giving him a sad smile. Ribbon smiled sadly back. He put the flowers on someone else's grave and strolled round the cemetery for half an hour.

From a material point of view, living was easy. He had more money now than Mummy had ever let him have. Daddy's royalties were paid into her bank account twice a year and would continue to be paid in. Ribbon drew out what he wanted on her direct-debit card, his handwriting being so like hers that no one could tell the difference. He had been collecting her retirement pension for years, and he went on doing so. It occurred to him that the Department of Social Security might expect her to die sometime and the bank might expect it too, but she had been very young when he was born and might in any case have been expected to outlive him. He could go on doing this until what would have been her hundredth birthday and even beyond. But could he live without her? He had "made it up to her" by keeping her bedroom as a shrine, keeping her clothes as if one day she would come back and wear them again. Still, he was a lost soul, only half a man, a prey to doubts and fears and self-questioning and a nervous restlessness.

Looking down at the floor, he half-expected to see some mark where her small slight body had lain. There was nothing, any more than there was a mark on volume 8 of *Britannica*. He went downstairs and stared out into the garden. The cypress he had associated with her, had been near to seeing as containing her spirit, was down, was lying on the grass, its frondy branches already wilting in the heat. One of the two fat shrubs was down too. Damian and the young one were sitting *on Mummy's grave,* drinking something out of a vacuum flask and smoking cigarettes. Mummy would have had something to say about that, but he lacked the heart. He thought again how strange it was, how horrible and somehow wrong, that the small child's name for its mother was the same as that for an embalmed Egyptian corpse.

In the afternoon, after the washing-machine man had come and been let into Glenys Next-door's, Ribbon plucked up the courage to phone Kingston Marle's publisher. After various people's voice mail, instructions to press this button and that, and requests to leave messages, he was put through to the department that sent on authors' letters. A rather indignant young woman assured him that all mail was sent on within a week of the publisher's receiving it. Recovering a little of Mummy's spirit, he said in the strongest tone he could muster that a week was far too long. What about readers who were waiting anxiously for a reply? The young woman told him she had said "within a week" and it might be much sooner. With that he had to be content. It was eleven days now since he had apologized to Marle, ten since his publisher had received the letter. He asked tentatively if they ever handed a letter to an author in person. For a while she hardly seemed to understand what he was talking about. Then she gave him a defiant "no"; such a thing could never happen.

So Marle had not called off his dogs because he had received the apology. Perhaps it was only that the spell, or whatever it was, lasted no more than, say, twenty-four hours. It seemed, sadly, a more likely explanation. The tree fellers finished at five, leaving the wilted shrubs stacked on the flower bed, not on Mummy's grave but on the place where The Book was buried. Ribbon took two of Mummy's sleeping pills and passed a good night. No letter came in the morning; there was no post at all. Without any evidence as to the truth of this, he became suddenly sure that no letter would come from Marle now—it would never come.

He had nothing to do, he had written to everyone who needed reproving, he had supplied himself with no more new books and had no inclination to go out and buy more. Perhaps he would never write to anyone again. He unplugged the link between computer and printer and closed the computer's lid. The new shelving he had bought from Ikea to put up in the dining room would never be used now. In the middle of the morning he went into Mummy's bedroom, tucked the nightdress under the pillow and quilt, removed the bedspread from the wardrobe door, and closed the door. He couldn't have explained why he did these things; it simply seemed time to do them. From the window he saw a taxi draw up and Glenys Next-door get out of it. There was someone else inside the taxi she was helping out, but Ribbon didn't stay to see who it was.

He contemplated the back garden from the dining room. Somehow he would have to dispose of all those logs, the remains of the cypresses, the flowering currant, the holly, and the lilac bush. For a ten-pound note the men would doubtless have taken them away, but Ribbon hadn't thought of this at the time. The place looked bleak and characterless now, an empty expanse of grass with a stark ivy-clad flower bed at the end of it. He noticed, for the first time, over the wire dividing fence, the profusion of flowers in Glenys Next-door's, the bird table, the little fishpond (both hunting grounds for Tinks), the red-leaved Japanese maple. He would burn that wood; he would have a fire.

Of course he wasn't supposed to do this. In a small way it was against the law, for this was a smokeless zone and had been for nearly as long as he could remember. By the time anyone complained—and Glenys Next-door and Sandra On-the-other-side would both complain—the deed would have been done and the logs consumed. But he postponed it for a while and went back into the house. He felt reasonably well, if a little weak and dizzy. Going upstairs made him breathless in a way he never had been before, so he postponed that for a while too and had a cup of tea, sitting in the front room with his feet up. What would Marle do next? There was no knowing. Ribbon thought that when he was better he would find out where Marle lived, go to him and apologize in person. He would ask what he could do to make it up to Marle, and whatever the answer was he would do it. If Marle wanted him to be his servant he would do that, or kneel at his feet and kiss the ground, or allow Marle to flog him with a whip. Anything Marle wanted he would do, whatever it was.

Of course, he shouldn't have buried the book. That did no good. It would be ruined now and the best thing, the *cleanest* thing, would be to cremate it. After he was rested he made his way upstairs, crawled really, his hands on the stairs ahead of him, took *Piranha* to *Scurfy* off the shelf, and brought it down. He'd burn that too. Back in the garden he arranged the logs on a bed of screwed-up newspaper, rested volume 8 of *Britannica* on top of them, and, fetching the spade, unearthed *Demogorgon*. Its plastic covering had been inadequate to protect it, and it was sodden as well as very dirty. Ribbon felt guilty for treating it as he had. The fire would purify it. There was kerosene in a can somewhere; Mummy had used it for the little stove that heated her bedroom. He went back into the house, found the can, and sprinkled kerosene on newspaper, logs, and books, and applied a lighted match.

The flames roared up immediately, slowed once the oil had done its work. He poked at his fire with a long stick. A voice started shouting at him but he took no notice; it was only Glenys Next-door complaining. The smoke from the fire thickened, grew dense and gray. Its flames had reached The Book's wet pages, the great thick wad of 427 of them, and as the smoke billowed in a tall, whirling cloud an acrid smell poured from it. Ribbon stared at the smoke, for in it now, or behind it, something was taking shape, a small, thin, and very old woman swathed in a mummy's bandages, her head and arm bound in white bands, the skin between fish-belly white. He gave a small choking cry and fell, clutching the place where his heart was, holding on to the overpowering pain.

· · ·

The he pathologist seems to think he died of fright," the policeman said to Frank. "A bit fanciful that, if you ask me. Anyone can have a heart attack. You have to ask yourself what he could have been frightened *of.* Nothing, unless it was of catching fire. Of course, strictly speaking, the poor chap had no business to be having a fire. Mrs. Judd and her mother saw it all. It was a bit of a shock for the old lady—she's over ninety and not well herself. She's staying with her daughter while recovering from a bad fall."

Frank was uninterested in Glenys Judd's mother and her problems. He had a severe summer cold, could have done without any of this, and doubted if he would be well enough to attend Ambrose Ribbon's funeral. In the event, Susan went to it alone. Someone had to. It would be too terrible if no one was there.

She expected to find herself the only mourner, and she was very surprised to find she was not alone. On the other side of the aisle from her in the crematorium chapel sat Kingston Marle. At first she could hardly believe her eyes. Then he turned his head, smiled, and came to sit next to her. Afterward, as they stood admiring the two wreaths, his and hers and Frank's, he said that he supposed some sort of explanation was in order.

"Not really," Susan said. "I just think it's wonderful of you to come."

"I saw the announcement of his death in the paper with the date and place of the funeral," Marle said, turning his wonderful deep eyes from the flowers to her. "A rather odd thing had happened. I had a letter from your cousin—well, your husband's cousin. It was a few days after we met in Oxford. His letter was an apology, quite an abject apology, saying he was sorry for having written to me before, asking me to forgive him for criticizing me for something or other."

"What sort of something or other?"

"That I don't know. I never received his previous letter. But what he said reminded me that I *had* received a letter intended for Dillon's bookshop in Piccadilly and signed by him. Of course I sent it on to them and thought no more about it. But now I'm wondering if he put the Dillon's letter into the envelope intended for me and mine into the one for Dillon's. It's easily done. That's why I prefer E-mail myself."

Susan laughed. "It can't have had anything to do with his death, anyway."

"No, certainly not. I was going to mention it to him in Blackwell's but—well, I saw you instead and everything else went out of my head. I didn't really come here because of the letter—that's not important. I came because I hoped I might see you again."

"Oh."

"Will you have lunch with me?"

Susan looked around her, as if spies might be about. But they were alone. "I don't see why not," she said.

FAIR EXCHANGE

You're looking for tom dorchester, aren't you?" Penelope said.

I nodded. "How did you know?"

"I've been expecting you to ask. I mean, he's always been at this conference in the past. Quite a fixture. This must be the first he hasn't come to it in—what? Fifteen years? Twenty?"

"He's not here, then?"

"He's dead."

I wanted to say, "He can't be!" But that's absurd. Anyone can be dead. Here today and gone tomorrow, as the saying goes. Still, the more full of vitality a person is the more you feel he has a firmer grasp on life than the rest of us. Only violence, some appalling accident, could prize him loose. And Tom was—had been, I should say—more vital, more enthusiastic, and more interested in everything than most people. He seemed to love and hate more intensely, especially to love. I remember him once saying he needed no more than five hours' sleep a night, there was too much to do, to learn, to appreciate, to waste time sleeping. And then his wife had become ill, very ill. Much of his abundant energy he'd devoted to finding a cure for her particular kind of cancer. Or trying to find it.

I said, stupidly, I suppose, "But it was Frances who was going to die."

Penelope gave me a strange, indecipherable look. "I'll tell you about it, if you like. It's an odd story. Of course I don't know how much you know."

"About what? I wouldn't have called Tom a close friend, but I'd known him for years. I know he adored Frances. I mean, I adore Marian but—

well, you know what I mean. He was like a young lover. To say he worshiped the ground she trod on wouldn't be an exaggeration."

Penelope took her cigarettes out of her handbag and offered me one.

"I've given it up."

"I wish I could, but I know my limitations. Now, d'you want the story?"

I nodded.

"You may not like it. It's pretty awful one way or the other. He killed himself, you know."

"He *what? Tom Dorchester?*"

"Did away with himself, committed suicide, whatever."

There was only one possible event that could make this believable. "Ah, you mean Frances did die?"

Penelope shook her head. She took a sip of her drink. "It was June or July of last year, about a month after the conference. You'll remember Tom only came for two days because he felt he couldn't leave Frances any longer than that, though their younger daughter was with her. They had two daughters, both married, and the older one has three children. The eldest child was twelve at the time."

"I had dinner with Tom," I said. "There were a couple of other people there, but he mostly talked to me. He was telling me about some miracle cure they'd tried on Frances but it hadn't worked."

"It was at a clinic in Switzerland. They dehydrate you and give you nothing but walnuts to eat, something like that. When she came back and she was worse than ever, Tom found a healer. I actually met her. Chris and I went around to Tom's one evening and this woman was there. Very weird she was, very weird indeed."

"What do you mean, weird?"

"Well, you think of a healer as laying on hands, don't you? Or reciting mantras while using herbal remedies, something like that. This woman wasn't like that. She did it all by talk and the power of thought. That's what she said, the power of thought. Her name was Davina Tarsis and she was quite young. Late thirties, early forties, very strangely dressed. Not that sort of floaty, hippy look, Oriental garments and beads and whatever, not like that at all. She was very thin—only a very thin woman could have got away with wearing skin-tight white leggings and a white tunic with a great orange sun printed on the front of it. Her hair was long and dyed a deep purplish red. I don't know why I say 'was.' I expect she's still got purple hair. No makeup, of course: a scrubbed face and a ring in one nostril—not a stud, a ring.

"Tom thought she was wonderful. He claimed she'd cured a woman who had been having radiotherapy at the same time as Frances. Now, the odd thing was that she didn't talk much to Frances at all—I had a feeling Frances didn't altogether care for her. She talked to Tom. Not while we were there, I don't mean that. I mean in private. Apparently they had long sessions, like a kind of mad form of psychotherapy. Chris said maybe she was making a play for Tom, but I don't think it was that. I think she really believed in what she was doing and so did he. So, my God, did he.

"She taught him to believe that anything you wished for hard enough you could have. He told me that—not at the time, but when it was all over."

"What do you mean," I said, " 'when it was all over'?"

"When Tom had got what he wanted."

"Presumably, that was for Frances to be cured."

"That's right. He got very emotional with me one night—Chris was out somewhere—and he started crying and sobbing. I know men do cry these days, but I've never known a man to cry like Tom did that night. The tears poured out of his eyes. There was quite a long time when he couldn't speak, he choked on the words. It was dreadful. I didn't know what to do. I gave him some brandy, but he'd only take a sip of it because he was driving and he had to go back to Frances before his daughter and *her* daughter had to go home. That's the nine-year-old, Emma she's called. Anyway, he calmed down after a bit and then he said he couldn't live without Frances, he couldn't imagine life without her, he'd kill himself . . ."

"Ah," I said.

"Ah, nothing. That had nothing to do with it. Frances went back into the hospital soon after that. They were trying some new kind of chemotherapy on her. Tom hadn't any faith in it. By then he only had faith in Tarsis. He was having daily talk sessions with her. He'd taken leave from his job, and he'd spend an entire morning talking to Tarsis, mostly about his feelings for Frances, I gather, and how he felt about the rest of his family, and how he and Frances had met, and so on. She'd make him go over and over it, and the more he repeated himself the more approving she was.

"Frances came home and she was very ill, thin, with no appetite. Her hair began to fall out. She could barely walk. The side effects from the chemo were the usual ghastly thing, nausea and faintness and ringing in the ears and all that. Tarsis came round and took a look at her, said the chemo was a mistake but, in spite of it, she thought she could heal Frances completely. Then came the crunch. I didn't know this at the time, Tom didn't tell me until—oh, I don't know, two or three months afterward. But this is what Tarsis said to him.

"They talked while Frances was asleep. Tarsis said, 'What would you give to make Frances live?' Well, of course, Tom asked what she meant, and she said, 'Whose life would you give in exchange for Frances's life?' Tom said that was nonsense, you couldn't trade one person's life for another, and Tarsis said, oh yes, you could. The power of thought could do that for you. She'd trained Tom in practicing the power of thought, and now all he had to do was wish for Frances to live. Only he had to offer someone else up in her place.

"That was when he started to see her for what she was. A charlatan. But he played along, he said. He wanted to see what she'd do. Called her bluff, was what he said, but he was deceiving himself in that. He still half believed. Who would he offer up, she asked him. 'Oh, anyone you like,' he said, and he laughed. She was deadly serious. That day she'd met Tom's elder daughter and the granddaughter Emma. Tom said—he hated telling me this, but on the other hand he was really past caring what he told anyone—he said Emma hadn't been very polite to Davina Tarsis. She'd sort of stared at her, at the tight leggings and the sun on her tunic and sneered a bit, I suppose, and then she'd said it wasn't Tarsis but the chemo that was doing her grandmother good, it stood to reason that was what it was."

I interrupted her. "What do you mean, he hated telling you?"

"Wait and see. He had good reason. It was after Emma and her mother had gone and Frances was resting that they had this talk. When Tom said it could be anyone she liked, Tarsis said it wasn't what she liked but what Tom wanted, and then she said, 'How about that girl Emma?' Tom told her not to be ridiculous, but she persisted and at last he said that, well, yes, he supposed so, he would give Emma, only the whole thing was absurd. The fact was that he'd give anyone to save Frances's life if it were possible to do that, so of course, yes, he'd give Emma."

"It must have put him off this Davina Tarsis, surely?"

"You'd think so. I'm not sure. All this was about nine or ten months ago. Frances started to get better. Oh, yes, she did. You needn't look like that. It was just an amazing thing. The doctors were amazed. But it wasn't unheard-of, it wasn't a miracle, though people said it was. Presumably, the chemo worked. All the things that should get right got right. I mean, her blood count got to be normal, she put on weight, the pain went, the tumors shriveled up. She simply got a bit better every day. It wasn't a remission, it was a recovery."

"Tom must have been over the moon," I said.

Penelope made a face. "He was. For a while. And then Emma died."

"*What?*"

"In a road crash. She died."

"You're not saying this witch woman, this Davina Tarsis. . . ?"

"No, I'm not. Of course I'm not. At the time of the crash Tarsis and Tom were together in Tom's house with Frances. Besides, there was no mystery about the accident. It *was* indisputably an accident. Emma was on a school bus with the rest of her class, coming back from a visit to some stately home. There was ice on the road, the bus skidded and overturned, and three of the pupils were killed, Emma among them. You must have read about it, it was all over the media."

"I think I did," I said. "I can't remember."

"It affected Tom—well, profoundly. I don't mean in the way the death of a grandchild would affect any grandparent. I mean he was racked with guilt. He had such faith in Tarsis that he really believed he'd done it. He believed he'd given Emma's life in exchange for Frances's. And another awful thing was that his love for Frances simply vanished, all that great love, that amazing devotion that was an example to us all really, it disappeared. He came to dislike her. He told me it wasn't that he had no feeling for her anymore—he actively disliked her.

"So there was nothing for him to live for. He believed he'd ruined his own life and ruined his daughter's and destroyed his love for Frances. One night after Frances was asleep he drank a whole bottle of liquid morphine she'd had prescribed but hadn't used with twenty paracetomol and a few brandies. He died quite quickly, I believe."

"That's terrible," I said. "The most awful tragedy. I'd no idea. And poor Frances. One's heart goes out to Frances."

Penelope looked at me and took another cigarette. "Don't feel too sorry for her," she said. "She's as fit as a fiddle now and about to start a new life. Her G.P. lost his wife about the time he diagnosed her cancer, and he and Frances are getting married next month. So you could say that all's well that ends well."

"I wouldn't go as far as that," I said.

THE WINK

T HE WOMAN IN RECEPTION gave her directions: Go through the dayroom, then the double doors at the back, turn left, and Elsie's in the third room on the right. Unless she's in the dayroom.

Elsie wasn't but the Beast was. Jean always called him that, she had never known his name. He was sitting with the others watching television. A semicircle of chairs was arranged in front of the television, mostly armchairs but some wheelchairs, and some of the old people had fallen asleep. He was in a wheelchair and he was awake, staring at the screen where celebrities were taking part in a game show.

Ten years had passed since she had last seen him but she knew him, changed and aged though he was. He must be well over eighty. Seeing him was always a shock, but seeing him in here was a surprise. A not unpleasant surprise. He must be in that chair because he couldn't walk. He had been brought low; his life was coming to an end.

She knew what he would do when he saw her. He always did. But possibly he wouldn't see her, he wouldn't turn around. The game show would continue to hold his attention. She walked as softly as she could, short of tiptoeing, around the edge of the semicircle. Her mistake was to look back just before she reached the double doors. His eyes were on her and he did what he always did. He winked.

Jean turned sharply away. She went down the corridor and found Elsie's room, the third on the right. Elsie was asleep, sitting in an armchair by the window. Jean put the flowers she had brought on the bed and sat down on the only other chair, an upright one without arms. Then she got up again and drew the curtain a little to keep the sunshine off Elsie's face.

Elsie had been at Sweetling Manor for two weeks, and Jean knew she would never come out again. She would die here—and why not? It was clean and comfortable and everything was done for you and probably it was ridiculous to feel as Jean did, that she would prefer anything to being here, including being helpless and old and starving and finally dying alone.

They were the same age, she and Elsie, but she felt younger and thought she looked it. They had always known each other, had been at school together, had been each other's bridesmaids. Well, Elsie had been her matron of honor, having been married a year by then. It was Elsie she had gone to the pictures with that evening, Elsie and another girl whose name she couldn't remember. She remembered the film, though. It had been Deanna Durbin in *Three Smart Girls.* Sixty years ago.

When Elsie woke up Jean would ask her what the other girl was called. Christine? Kathleen? Never mind. Did Elsie know the Beast was in here? Jean remembered then that Elsie didn't know the Beast, had never heard what happened that night—no one had, she had told no one. It was different in those days, you couldn't tell because you would get the blame. Somehow, ignorant though she was, she had known that even then.

Ignorant. They all were, she and Elsie and the girl called Christine or Kathleen. Or perhaps they were just afraid. Afraid of what people would say, would think of them. Those were the days of blame, of good behavior expected from everyone, of taking responsibility, and often punishment, for one's own actions. You put up with things and you got on with things. Complaining got you nowhere.

Over the years there had been extraordinary changes. You were no longer blamed or punished, you got something called empathy. In the old days what the Beast did would have been her fault. She must have led him on, encouraged him. Now it was a crime, *his* crime. She read about it in the papers, saw about things called helplines on television, and counseling and specially trained women police officers. This was to avoid your being marked for life, traumatized, though you could never forget.

That was true, that last part, though she had forgotten for weeks on end, months. And then, always, she had seen him again. It came of living in the country, in a small town, it came of her living there and his going on living there. Once she saw him in a shop, once out in the street;

another time he got on a bus as she was getting off it. He always winked. He didn't say anything, just looked at her and winked.

Elsie had looked like Deanna Durbin. The resemblance was quite marked. They were about the same age, born in the same year. Jean remembered how they had talked about it, she and Elsie and Christine-Kathleen, as they left the cinema and the others walked with her to the bus stop. Elsie wanted to know what you had to do to get a screen test and the other girl said it would help to be in Hollywood, not Yorkshire. Both of them lived in town, a five minutes' walk away, and Elsie said she could stay the night if she wanted. But there was no way of letting her parents know. Elsie's had a phone but hers didn't.

Deanna Durbin was still alive, Jean had read somewhere. She wondered if she still looked like Elsie or if she had had her face lifted and her hair dyed and gone on diets. Elsie's face was plump and soft, very wrinkled about the eyes, and her hair was white and thin. She smiled faintly in her sleep and gave a little snore. Jean moved her chair closer and took hold of Elsie's hand. That made the smile come back, but Elsie didn't wake.

The Beast had come along in his car about ten minutes after the girls had gone and Jean was certain the bus wasn't coming. It was the last bus, and she hadn't known what to do. This had happened before—the driver just hadn't turned up and had got the sack for it, but that hadn't made the bus come. On that occasion she had gone to Elsie's and Elsie's mother had phoned her parents' next-door neighbors. She thought that if she did that a second time and put Mr. and Mrs. Rawlings to all that trouble, her dad would probably stop her from going to the pictures ever again.

It wasn't dark. At midsummer it wouldn't get dark till after ten. If it had been she mightn't have gone with the Beast. Of course he didn't seem like a Beast then but young, a boy really, and handsome and quite nice. And it was only five miles. Mr. Rawlings was always saying five miles was nothing, he used to walk five miles to school every day and five miles back. But she couldn't face the walk and, besides, she wanted a ride in a car. It would only be the third time she had ever been in one. Still, she would have refused his offer if he hadn't said what he had when she'd told him where she lived.

"You'll know the Rawlings then. Mrs. Rawlings is my sister."

It wasn't true, but it sounded true. She got in beside him. The car wasn't really his—it belonged to the man he worked for; he was a chauffeur—but she found that out a lot later.

"Lovely evening," he said. "You been gallivanting?"

"I've been to the pictures," she said.

After a couple of miles he turned a little way down a lane and stopped the car outside a derelict cottage. It looked as if no one could possibly live there but he said he had to see someone, it would only take a minute, and she could come too. By now it was dusk but there were no lights on in the cottage. She remembered that he was Mrs. Rawlings's brother. There must have been a good ten years between them, but that hadn't bothered her. Her own sister was ten years older than she was.

She followed him up the path, which was overgrown with weeds and brambles. Instead of going to the front door, he led her around the back, where old apple trees grew in waist-high grass. The back of the house was a ruin, half its rear wall tumbled down.

"There's no one here," she said.

He didn't say anything. He took hold of her and pulled her down in the long grass, one hand pressed hard over her mouth. She hadn't known anyone could be so strong. He took his hand away to pull her clothes off and she screamed, but the screaming was just a reflex, a release of fear, and otherwise useless. There was no one to hear. What he did was rape. She knew that now—well, had known it soon after it happened, only no one called it that then. Nobody spoke of it. Nowadays the word was on everyone's lips. Nine out of ten television series were about it. Rape, the crime against women. Rape, which these days you went into court and talked about. You went to self-defense classes to stop it happening to you. You attended groups and shared your experience with other victims.

At first she had been most concerned to find out if he had injured her. Torn her, broken bones. But there was nothing like that. Because she was all right and he was gone, she stopped crying. She heard the car start up and then move away. Walking home wasn't exactly painful, more a stiff achy business, rather the way she had felt the day after she and Elsie had been learning to do the splits. She had to walk anyway—she had no choice. As it was, her father was in a rage, wanting to know what time she thought this was.

"Anything could have happened to you," her mother said.

Something had. She had been raped. She went up to bed so they wouldn't see she couldn't stop shivering. She didn't sleep at all that night. In the morning she told herself it could have been worse, at least she wasn't dead. It never crossed her mind to say anything to anyone about what had happened. She was too ashamed, too afraid of what they would think. It was past, she kept telling herself, it was all over.

One thing worried her most. A baby. Suppose she had a baby. Never in all her life was she so relieved about anything, so happy, as when she saw that first drop of blood run down the inside of her leg a day early. She shouted for joy. She was all right! The blood cleansed her and now no one need ever know.

Trauma? That was the word they used nowadays. It meant a scar. There was no scar that you could see and no scar she could feel in her body, but it was years before she would let a man come near her. Afterward she was glad about that, glad she had waited, that she hadn't met someone else before Kenneth. But at the time she thought about what had happened every day, she relived what had happened, the shock and the pain and the dreadful fear, and in her mind she called the man who had done that to her the Beast.

Eight years went by and she saw him again. She was out with Kenneth. He had just been demobbed from the air force and they were walking down the High Street arm in arm. Kenneth had asked her to marry him, and they were going to buy the engagement ring. It was a big jewelers they went to, with several aisles. The Beast was in a different aisle, quite a long way away, on some errand for his employer, she supposed, but she saw him and he saw her. He winked.

He winked, just as he had ten minutes ago in the dayroom. Jean shut her eyes. When she opened them again Elsie was awake.

"How long have you been there, dear?"

"Not long," Jean said.

"Are those flowers for me? You know how I love freesias. We'll get someone to put them in water. I don't have to do a thing in here, don't lift a finger. I'm a lady of leisure."

"Elsie," said Jean, "what was the name of that girl we went to the pictures with when we saw *Three Smart Girls*?"

"What?"

"It was nineteen thirty-eight. In the summer."

"I don't know, I shall have to think. My memory's not what it was. Bob used to say I looked like Deanna Durbin."

"We all said you did."

"Constance, her name was. We called her Connie."

"So we did," said Jean.

Elsie began talking of the girls they had been at school with. She could remember all their Christian names and most of their surnames. Jean found a vase, filled it with water, and put the freesias into it because they showed signs of wilting. Her engagement ring still fitted on her finger, though it was a shade tighter. How worried she had been that Kenneth would be able to tell she wasn't a virgin! They said men could always tell. But of course, when the time came, he couldn't. It was just another old wives' tale.

Elsie, who already had her first baby, had worn rose-colored taffeta at their wedding. And her husband had been Kenneth's best man. John was born nine months later and the twins eighteen months after that. There was a longer gap before Anne arrived, but still she had had her hands full. That was the time, when the children were little, that she thought less about the Beast and what had happened than at any other time in her life. She forgot him for months on end. Anne was just four when she saw him again.

She was meeting the other children from school. They hadn't had a car then; it was years before they got a car. On the way to the school they were going to the shop to buy Anne a new pair of shoes. The Red Lion was just closing for the afternoon. The Beast came out of the public bar, not too steady on his feet, and he almost bumped into her. She said, "Do you mind?" before she saw who it was. He stepped back, looked into her face, and winked. She was outraged. For two pins she'd have told Kenneth the whole tale that evening. But of course she couldn't. Not now.

"I don't know what you mean about your memory," she said to Elsie. "You've got a wonderful memory."

Elsie smiled. It was the same pretty teenager's smile, only they didn't use that word *teenager* then. You were just a person between twelve and twenty. "What do you think of this place, then?"

"It's lovely," said Jean. "I'm sure you've done the right thing."

Elsie talked some more about the old days and the people they'd known and then Jean kissed her good-bye and said she'd come back next week.

"Use the shortcut next time," said Elsie. "Through the garden and in by the French windows next door."

"I'll remember."

She wasn't going to leave that way, though. She went back down the corridor and hesitated outside the dayroom door. The last time she'd seen the Beast, before *this* time, they were both growing old. Kenneth was dead. John was a grandfather himself, though a young one, the twins were joint directors of a prosperous business in Australia, and Anne was a surgeon in London. Jean had never learned to drive, and the car was given up when Kenneth died. She was waiting at that very bus stop, the one where he had picked her up all those years before. The bus came and he got off it, an old man with white hair, his face yellowish and wrinkled. But she knew him; she would have known him anywhere. He gave her one of his rude stares and he winked. That time it was an exaggerated, calculated wink, the whole side of his face screwed up and his eye squeezed shut.

She pushed open the dayroom door. The television was still on, but he wasn't there. His wheelchair was empty. Then she saw him. He was being brought back from the bathroom, she supposed. A nurse held him tightly by one arm. The other rested heavily on the padded top of a crutch. His legs, in pajama trousers, were half-buckled, and on his face was an expression of agony as, wincing with pain, he took small tottering steps.

Jean looked at him. She stared into his tormented face and his eyes met hers. Then she winked. She winked at him as he had winked at her that last time, and she saw what she had never thought to see happen to an old person. A rich dark blush spread across his withered face. He turned away his eyes. Jean tripped lightly across the room toward the exit, like a sixteen-year-old.

CATAMOUNT

T HE SKY WAS THE BIGGEST she had ever seen. They said the skies of Suffolk were big and the skies of Holland, but those were small, cozy, by comparison. It might belong on another planet, covering another world. Mostly a pale soft azure or a dark hard blue, it was sometimes overcast with huge rolling cumulus clouds, swollen and edged with sharp white light, from which rain roared without warning.

Chuck and Carrie's house was only the second built up there, under that sky. The other was what they called a modular home, which Nora thought of as a prefab, a frame bungalow standing on a bluff between the dirt road and the ridge. The Johanssons, who lived there, kept a few cows and fattened white turkeys for Thanksgiving. It was—thank God, said Carrie—not visible from her handsome log house, built of yellow Montana pine. She and Chuck called it Elk Valley Ranch, a name Nora had thought pretentious when she'd read it on their headed notepaper but not when she saw it. The purpose of the letter was to ask her and Gordon to stay, and she could hardly believe it—it seemed too glorious, the idea of a holiday in the Rocky Mountains, though she and Carrie had been best friends for years. That was before Carrie had married a captain in the U.S. Air Force stationed at Bentwaters and went back home to Colorado with him.

It was August when they went the first time. The little plane from Denver took them to the airport at Hogan, and Carrie met them in the Land Cruiser. The road ran straight and long, parallel with the Crystal River, which was also straight, like a canal, with willows and cottonwood trees along its banks. Beyond the flat flowery fields the mountains rose, clothed in pine and scrub oak and aspen, mountains that were dark, almost black, but with green sunlit meadows bright between the trees. The sun shone and it was hot, but the sky looked like a winter sky in England, very pale, the clouds stretched across it like torn strips of chiffon.

There were a few small houses, many large barns and stables. Horses were in the fields, one chestnut mare with a newborn foal. Carrie turned in toward the western mountains and through a gateway with ELK VALLEY RANCH carved on a board. It was still a long way to the house. The road wound through curves and hairpin bends, and as they went higher the mountain slopes and the green canyons opened out below them, mountain upon mountain and valley upon valley, a herd of deer in one deep hollow, a golden eagle perched on a spar. By the roadside grew yellow asters and blue Michaelmas daisies, wild delphiniums, pale pink geraniums and the bright red Indian paintbrush, and above the flowers brown and yellow butterflies hovered.

"There are snakes," Carrie said. "Rattlesnakes. You have to be a bit careful. One of them was on the road last night. We stopped to look at it and it lashed against our tires."

"I'd like to see a porcupine." Gordon had his Rocky Mountains wildlife book with him, open on his knees. "But I'd settle for a raccoon."

"You'll very likely see both," Carrie said. "Look, there's the house."

It stood on the crown of a wooded hill, its log walls a dark gamboge, its roof green. A sheepdog came down to the five-barred gate when it saw the Land Cruiser.

"You must have spectacular views," Gordon said.

"We do. If you wake up early enough, you see fabulous things from your window. Last week I saw a cougar."

"What's a cougar?"

"Mountain lion. I'll just get out and open the gate."

It wasn't until she was home again in England that Nora had looked up the cougar in a book about the mammals of North America. That night and for the rest of the fortnight she had forgotten it. There were so many things to do and see: walking and climbing in the mountains; fishing in the Crystal River; picking a single specimen of each flower and pressing it in the book she bought for the purpose; photographing hawks and eagles; watching the chipmunks run along the fences; driving down to the little town of Hogan, where on their way to Telluride, Butch Cassidy and Sundance had stopped to rob the bank; visiting the hotel where the Clanton Gang had left bullets from their handguns in the bathroom wall; shopping; sitting in the hot springs and swimming in the cold pool; eating in Hogan's restaurant, where elk steaks and rattlesnake burgers were specialities, and drinking in the Last Frontier Bar.

Carrie and Chuck said to come back next year, or come in the winter, when the skiing began. That was at the time when Hogan Springs was emerging as a ski resort. Or come in the spring, when the snows melted and the alpine meadows burst into bloom, miraculous with gentians and avalanche lilies. And they did go again, but in late summer, a little later than in the previous year. The aspen leaves were yellowing, the scrub oak turning bronze.

"We shall have snow in a month," Carrie said.

A black bear had come with her cubs and eaten Lily Johansson's turkeys. "Like a fox at home," Gordon said. They went up to the top of Mount Opie in the new ski lift and walked down. It was five miles through fields of blue flax and orange gaillardias. The golden ridge and the pine-covered slopes looked serene in the early autumn sunshine; the skies were clear until late afternoon, when the clouds gathered and the rain came. The rain was torrential for ten minutes, and then it was hot and sunny again, the grass and wild flowers steaming. A herd of elk came close up to the house, and one of them pressed its huge head and stubby horns against the window. They saw the black bear and her cubs through Chuck's binoculars, loping along down in the green canyon.

"One day I'll see a cougar," Nora said, and Gordon asked if cougars were an endangered species.

"I wouldn't think so," Chuck answered. "There are supposed to be mountain lions in every state of the United States, but I guess most are here. You ought to talk to Lily Johansson—she's often seen them."

"There was a boy got killed by one last fall," Carrie said. "He was cycling and the thing came out of the woods, pulled him off his bike, and, well—ate him, I suppose. Or started to eat him. It was scared off. They're protected, so there was nothing to be done."

Cougar stories abounded. Everyone had one. Some of them sounded like urban—rural, rather—myths. There was the one about the woman out walking with her little boy in Winter Park who came face to face with a cougar on the mountain. She put the child on her shoulders and told him to hold up his arms so that, combined, they made a creature eight feet tall, which was enough to frighten the animal off. The boy in the harness shop in Hogan had one about the man out with his dog. To save himself he had to let the cougar kill and eat his dog while he got away. In town Nora bought a reproduction of Audubon's drawing of a cougar, graceful, powerful, tawny, with a cat's mysterious, closed-in face.

"I thought they were small, like a lynx," Gordon said.

"They're bigger than a lynx, about the size of an African lion—well, lioness. That's what they look like, a lioness."

"I shall frame my picture," Nora said, "and one day I'll see the real thing."

They came back to Hogan year after year. More houses were built, but not enough to spoil the place. Once they came in winter but, at their age, it was too late to learn to ski. Seventeen feet of snow fell. The snowplow came out onto the roads on Christmas Eve and cleared a passage for cars, making ramparts of snow where the flowers had been. Nora wondered about the animals. What did they live on, these creatures? The deer ate the twigs of trees. Chuck put cattle feed out for them.

"The herds have been reduced enough by mountain lions," he said. "You once asked if they were endangered. There are thousands of them now, more than there have ever been."

Nora worried about the golden eagle. What could it find to feed on in this white world? The bears were hibernating. Were the cougars also? No one seemed to know. She would never come again in winter, when everything was covered, sleeping, waiting, buried. It was one thing for the skiers, another for a woman, elderly now, afraid to go out lest she slip on the ice. The few small children they saw had colored balloons tied to them on long strings so that their parents could see and rescue them if they sank too deep down in the snow. All Christmas Day sun blazed, melting the snow on the roof, and by night frost held the place in its grip, so that the gutters around the house grew a fringe of icicles.

The following spring Gordon died. Lily Johansson wrote a letter of sympathy, and when Jim Johansson died the next Christmas, Nora wrote one to her. She delayed going back to the mountains for a year, two years. Driving from the airport with Carrie, she noticed for the first time something strange. It was a beautiful landscape but not a comfortable one, not easeful, not conducive to peace and tranquillity. There was no lushness and, even in the heat, no warmth. Lying in bed at night or sitting in a chair at dawn, watching for elk or a cougar, she tried to discover what was not so much wrong—it was far from wrong—but what made this feeling. The answer came to her uncompromisingly. It was fear. The countryside was full of fear, and the fear, while it added to the grandeur and in a strange way to the beauty, denied peace to the observer. Danger informed it; it threatened while it smiled. Always something lay in wait for you around the corner, though it might be only a beautiful butterfly. It never slept, it never rested even under snow. It was alive.

Lily Johansson came around for coffee. She was a large heavy woman with callused hands who had had a hard life. Six children had been born to her, two husbands had died. She was alone, struggling to make a living from hiring out horses, from a dozen cows and turkeys. Every morning she got up at dawn, not because she had so much to do but because she couldn't sleep after dawn. A cougar, passing the night high up in the mountains, came down many mornings past Lily's fence to hunt along the green valley. It might be days before she came back to her mountain hideout, but she would come back and lope down the rocky path between the asters and the Indian paintbrush past Lily's fence.

"Why do you call it 'she'?" Nora asked. Was this an unlikely statement of feminist principles?

Lily smiled. "I guess on account of knowing she's a mother. There was weeks went by when I never saw her, and then one morning she comes down the trail with two young ones. Real pretty kittens they was."

"Do you ever speak to her?"

"Me? I'm scared of her. She'd kill me as soon as look at me. Sometimes I says to her, 'Catamount, catamount,' but she don't pay me no attention. You want to see her, you come down and stop over and maybe we'll see her in the morning."

Nora went a week later. They sat together in the evening, the two old widows, drinking Lily's root beer and talking of their dead husbands. Nora slept in a tiny bedroom, with linen sheets on the narrow bed and a picture on the wall of (appropriately) Daniel in the lion's den. At dawn Lily came in with a mug of tea and told her to get up, put on her robe, and they'd watch.

The eastern sky was black with stripes of red between the mountains.

The hidden sun had colored the snow on the peaks rosy pink. All the land lay still. Along the path where the cougar passed, the flowers were still closed up for the night.

"What makes her come?" Nora whispered. "Does she see the dawn or feel it? What makes her get up from her bed and stretch and maybe wash her paws and her face and set off?"

"Are you asking me? I don't know. Who does? It's a mystery."

"I wish we knew."

"Catamount, catamount," said Lily. "Come, come, catamount."

But the cougar didn't come. The sun rose, a magnificent spectacle, almost enough to bring tears to your eyes, Nora thought, all that purple and rose and orange and gold, all those miles and miles of serene blue. She had coffee and bread and blueberry jam with Lily and then she went back to Elk Valley Ranch.

"One day I'll see her," she said to herself as she stroked the sheepdog and went to let herself in by the yard door.

But would she? She had almost made up her mind not to come back next year. This was young people's country and she was getting too old for it. It was for climbers and skiers and mountain bikers, it was for those who could withstand the cold and enjoy the heat. Sometimes when she stood in the sun, its power frightened her—it was too strong for human beings. When rain fell it was a wall of water, a cascade, a torrent, and it might drown her. Snakes lay curled up in the long grass, and spiders were poisonous. If anything could be too beautiful for human beings to bear, this was. Looking at it for long made her heart ache, filled her with strange, undefined longings. At home once more in the mild and gentle English countryside, she looked at her Audubon and thought how this drawing of the cougar symbolized for her all that landscape, all that vast green and gold space, yet she had never seen it in the flesh, the bones, the sleek tawny skin.

Two years passed before she went back. It would be the last time. Chuck was ill, and Elk Valley was no place for an old, sick man. He and Carrie were moving to an apartment in Denver. They no longer walked in the hills or skied on the slopes or ate barbecue on the bluff behind the house. Chuck's heart was bad, and Carrie had arthritis. Nora, who had always slept soundly at Elk Valley Ranch, now found that sleep eluded her. She lay awake for hours with the curtains drawn back, gazing at the black velvet starry sky and listening to the baying of the coyotes at the mountain's foot. Sleepless, she began getting up earlier, and on the second morning, tiptoeing to the kitchen, she found that Carrie had gotten up early too. They sat together, drinking coffee and watching the dawn.

The night of the storm she slept and awoke and slept till the thunder woke her at four. The storm was like nothing she had ever known, and she who had never been frightened by thunder and lightning was afraid now. The lightning lit the room with searchlight brilliance, and while it lingered, dimming and brightening, for a moment too bright to look at, the thunder rolled and cracked as if the mountains themselves moved and split. Into the ensuing silence, the rain broke. If you were out in it, you couldn't defend yourself against it; it would beat you to the ground.

Carrie's calling fetched her out of her room. No lights were on. Carrie was feeling her way about in the dark.

"What is it?"

"Chuck's sick," Carrie said. "I mean very sick. He's lying in bed on his back with his mouth all drawn down to one side and when he speaks his voice isn't like his voice—it's slurred, he can't form the words."

"How do you phone the emergency services? I'll do it."

"Nora, you can't. I've tried calling them. The phone's down. Why do you think I've no lights on? The power's gone."

"What shall we do? I don't suppose you want to leave him, but I could do something."

"Not in this rain," Carrie said. "When it stops, could you take the Land Cruiser and drive into Hogan?"

Then Nora had to admit she had never learned to drive. They both went to look at Chuck. He seemed to be asleep, breathing noisily through his crooked mouth. A crash from somewhere overhead drove the women into each other's arms, to cling together.

"I'm going to make coffee," Carrie said.

They drank it, sitting near the window, watching the lightning recede, leap into the mountains. Nora said, "The rain's stopping. Look at the sky."

The black clouds were streaming apart to show the dawn. A pale tender sky, neither blue nor pink but halfway between, revealed itself as the banks of cumulus and the streaks of cirrus poured away over the mountain peak into the east. The rain lifted like a blind rolled up. One moment it was a cascade, the next it was gone, and the coming light showed gleaming pools of water and grass that glittered and sparkled.

"Try the phone again," Nora said.

"It's dead," said Carrie and, realizing what's she'd said, shivered.

"Do you think Lily's phone would be working? I could go down there and see. If her phone's down too, maybe she'd drive me into Hogan."

"Please, Nora, would you? I can't leave him."

The air was so fresh, it made her dizzy. It made her think how seldom most people ever breathe such air like this or know what it is, but that once the whole world's atmosphere was like this, as pure and as clean. The sun was rising, a red ball in a sea of pale lilac, and while on the jagged horizon black clouds still massed, the huge deep bowl of sky was scattered over with pink and golden cirrus feathers. Soon the sun would be hot and the land and air as dry as a desert.

She made her way down the hairpin bends of the mountain road, aware of how poor a walker she had become. An ache spread from her thighs into her hips, particularly on the right side, so that in order to make any progress she was forced to limp, shifting her weight onto the left. But she was near Lily Johansson's house now. Lily's two horses stood placidly by the gate into the field.

Then, suddenly, they wheeled around and cantered away down the meadow as if the sight of her had frightened them. She said aloud, "What's wrong? What's happened?"

As if in answer the animal came out of the flowery path onto the surface of the road. She was the size of an African lioness, so splendidly loose-limbed and in control of her long fluid body that she seemed to flow from the grass and the asters and the pink geraniums. On the road she stopped and turned her head. Nora could see her amber eyes and the faint quiver of her golden cheeks. She forgot about making herself tall, putting her hands high above her head, advancing menacingly. She was powerless, gripped by the beauty of this creature, this cougar she had longed for. And she was terribly afraid.

"Catamount, catamount," she whispered, but no voice came.

The cougar dropped onto her belly, a quivering cat flexing her muscles, as she prepared to spring.

WALTER'S LEG

W HILE HE WAS TELLING THE STORY about his mother taking him to the barber's, the pain in Walter's leg started again. A shooting pain—appropriate, that—and he knew very well what caused it. He shifted Andrew onto his other knee.

The story was about how his mother and he, on the way to get his hair cut, stopped on the corner of the High Street and Green Lanes to talk to a friend who had just come out of the fishmonger's. His mother was a talkative lady who enjoyed a gossip. The friend was like-minded. They took very little notice of Walter. He disengaged his hand from his mother's, walked off on his own down Green Lanes and into Church Road, found the barber's, produced sixpence from his pocket, and had his hair cut. After that he walked back the way he had come. His mother and the friend were still talking. The five-year-old Walter slipped his little hand into his mother's, and she looked down and smiled at him. His absence had gone unnoticed.

Emma and Andrew marveled at this story. They had heard it before, but they still marveled. The world had changed so much; even they knew that, at six and four. They were not even allowed to stand outside on the pavement on their own for two minutes, let alone go anywhere unaccompanied.

"Tell another," said Emma.

As she spoke a sharp twinge ran up Walter's calf to the knee and pinched his thigh muscle. He reached down and rubbed his bony old leg.

"Shall I tell you how Moultry shot me?"

"Shot you?" said Andrew. "With a gun?"

"With an airgun. It was a long time ago."

"Everything's that happened to you, Granddad," said Emma, "was a long time ago."

"Very true, my sweetheart. This was sixty-five years ago. I was seven."

"So it wasn't as long ago as when you had your haircut," said Emma, who already showed promise as an arithmetician.

Walter laughed. "Moultry was a boy I knew. He lived down our road. We used to play down by the river, a whole bunch of us. There were fish in the river then, but I don't think any of us were fishing that day. We'd been climbing trees. You could get across the river by climbing willow trees—the branches stretched right across.

"And then one of us saw a kingfisher, a little, tiny bright blue bird it was, the color of a peacock, and Moultry said he was going to shoot it. I knew that would be wrong, even then I knew. Maybe we all did except Moultry. He had an airgun—he showed it to us. I clapped my hands, and the kingfisher flew away. All the birds went, we'd frightened them away with all the racket we were making. I had a friend called William Robbins—we called him Bill, he was my best friend—and he said to Moultry that he'd bet he couldn't shoot anything, not aim at it and shoot it. Well, Moultry wasn't having that and he said, yes, he could. He pointed to a stone sticking up out of the water and said he'd hit that. He didn't, though. He shot me."

"Wow," said Andrew.

"But he didn't mean to, Granddad," said Emma. "He didn't do it on purpose."

"No, I don't suppose he did, but it hurt all the same. The shot went into my leg, into the calf, just below my right knee. Bill Robbins went off to my house. He ran as fast as he could—he was a very good runner, the best in the school—and he fetched my dad and my dad took me to the doctor."

"And did the doctor dig the bullet out?"

"A pellet, not a bullet. No, he didn't dig it out." Walter rubbed his leg, just below the right knee. "As a matter of fact, it's still there."

"It's still *there?*"

Emma got off the arm of the chair and Andrew got off Walter's lap and both children stood contemplating his right leg in its gray flannel trouser leg and gray-and-white argyle sock. Walter pulled up the trouser leg to the knee. There was nothing to be seen.

"If you like," said Walter, "I'll show you a photograph of the inside of my leg next time you come to my house."

The suggestion was greeted with rapture. They wanted "next time" to be now but were told by their mother that they would have to wait till Thursday. Walter was glad he'd come in the car. He wouldn't have fancied walking home, not with this pain. Perhaps he'd better go back to his G.P., get a second opinion, ask to be sent to a—what would it be called?—an orthopedic surgeon, presumably. Andrew, surely, had had the right idea when he'd asked if the doctor had dug the pellet out of his leg. Out of the mouths of babes and sucklings, thought old-fashioned Walter, hast thou ordained strength. It was hard to understand why the doctor hadn't dug it out sixty-five years ago, but in those days, so long as something wasn't life threatening, they tended to leave well—or ill—alone. Ten years ago the specialist merely said he doubted if it was the pellet causing the pain; it was more likely arthritis. Walter must accept that he wasn't as young as he used to be.

Back home, searching for the X-rays through his desk drawers, Walter thought about something else Andrew had said. No, not Andrew, Emma. She'd said Moultry hadn't done it on purpose, and he'd said he didn't suppose he had. Now he wasn't so sure. For the first time in sixty-five years he re-created in his mind the expression on Moultry's face that summer's evening when he'd boasted he could hit the stone.

Bill Robbins was sitting on the riverbank, two other boys whose names he had forgotten were up in the willow tree, while he, Walter, was down by the water's edge, looking up at the kingfisher, and Moultry was higher up with his airgun. The sun had been low in a pale blue July sky. Walter had clapped his hands then and, when the kingfisher flew away, turned his head to look at Moultry. And Moultry's expression had been resentful and revengeful too because Walter had scared the bird away. That was when he'd started boasting about hitting the stone. So perhaps he had meant to shoot him, shot him in the leg because he'd been balked of his desire. He didn't think of that at the time, though, Walter thought. He took it for an accident, and so did everyone else.

"I'm imagining things," he said aloud, and he laid the X-rays on top of the desk, ready to show them to Emma and Andrew. On Thursday, their mother brought the children along after school.

The pictures were admired and a repetition of the story demanded. In telling it, Walter said nothing about the revengeful look on Moultry's face.

"You forgot the bit about Bill running to your house and being the best runner in the school," said Emma.

"So I did, but now you've put it in yourself."

"What was his other name, Granddad? Moultry what?"

"It must have been a case of what Moultry," said Walter, and he thought, as he often did, of how times had changed. It would be incomprehensible to these children that one might have known someone only by his surname. "I don't know what he was called. I can't remember."

The children suggested names. In his childhood the ones they knew would have been unheard-of (Scott, Ross, Damian, Liam, Seth) or, strangely enough, too old-fashioned for popular use (Joshua, Simon, Jack, George). He put up some ideas himself, appropriate names for the time (Kenneth, Robert, Alan, Ronald), but none of them was right. He'd know Moultry's name when he heard it.

His daughter Barbara was looking at the X-rays. "You'll have to go back to the doctor with that leg, Dad."

"It does give me jip." Walter realized he'd used an expression that had been out of date even when he was a boy. It was a favorite of his own father's. "It does give me jip," he said again.

"See if they can find you a different consultant. They must be able to do something."

When Barbara and the children had gone he looked Moultry up in the phone book. The chances were that Moultry wouldn't be there, not in the same place after sixty-five years, and he wasn't. No Moultrys were in it. Walter's leg began to ache dreadfully. He tried massaging it with some stuff he'd bought when he'd pulled a muscle in his back. It heated the skin but did nothing for the pain. He tried to remember Moultry's first name. It wasn't Henry, was it? No, Henry was old-fashioned in the twenties and not revived till the eighties. David? It was a possibility, but Moultry hadn't been called David.

Bill Robbins had known Moultry a lot better than he had. The Moultrys and the Robbinses had lived next door but one to each other. Bill was dead—he'd died ten years before—but up until his death he and Walter had remained friends, played golf together, and been fellow members of the Rotary Club, and Walter still kept in touch with Bill's son. He phoned John Robbins.

"How are you, Walter?"

"I'm fine but for a spot of arthritis in my leg."

"We're none of us getting any younger." This was generous from a man of forty-two.

"Tell me something. D'you remember those people called Moultry who lived near your grandparents?"

"Vaguely. My gran would."

"She's still alive?"

"She's only ninety-six, Walter. That's nothing in our family, barring my poor dad."

John Robbins said it would be nice to see him and to come over for a meal and Walter said thanks very much, he'd like to. Old Mrs. Robbins was in the phone book, in the same house she'd lived in since she'd gotten married, seventy-three years before. She answered the phone in a brisk spry voice. Certainly she remembered the Moultrys, though they'd been gone since 1968, and she particularly remembered the boy with his airgun. He'd taken a potshot at her cat, but he'd missed.

"Lucky for the cat." Walter rubbed his leg.

"Lucky for Harold," said Mrs. Robbins grimly.

"That was his name, Harold," said Walter.

"Of course it was. Harold Moultry. He disappeared in the war."

"Disappeared?"

"I mean he never came back here, and I wasn't sorry. He was in the army—never saw active service, of course not. He was in a camp down in the west country somewhere for the duration, took up with a farmer's daughter, married her, and stopped there. I reckon he thought he'd come in for the farm, and maybe he has. Why don't you ever come and see me, Walter? You come over for a meal and I'll cook you steak and chips—you were always partial to that."

Walter said he would once he'd had his leg seen to.

He got an appointment with an orthopedic surgeon, a different one, who looked at the new X-rays and said Walter had arthritis. *Everyone* of Walter's age had arthritis somewhere. The children liked the new X-rays, and Emma said they were an improvement on the old ones. Andrew asked for one of them to put on his bedroom wall along with a magazine cutout of the Spice Girls and his *Lion King* poster.

"You ought to get a second opinion on that leg, Dad," said Barbara.

"It would be a third opinion by now, wouldn't it?"

"Tell about Moultry, Granddad," said Andrew.

So Walter told it all over again, this time adding Moultry's Christian name. "Harold Moultry pointed at a stone in the water and said he'd shoot that, but he shot me."

"And Bill Robbins who was the fastest runner in the whole school ran to your house and fetched your dad," said Emma. "But Harold didn't mean to do it, he didn't mean to hurt you, did he?"

"Who knows?" said Walter. "It was a long time ago."

They were all going away on holiday together, Barbara and her husband, Ian, and the children and Walter. It was a custom they'd established after Walter's wife died five years before. If he'd been completely honest, he'd have preferred not to go. He didn't much like the seaside or the food in the hotel, and he was embarrassed about exposing his skinny old body in the swimming pool. And he suspected that if they were completely honest—perhaps they were, secretly, when alone together—Barbara and Ian would have preferred not to have him with them. The children liked him there; he was pretty sure of that, and that was why he went.

The night before they left he went around to old Mrs. Robbins's. John was there and John's wife, and they all had steak and chips and tiramisu, which Mrs. Robbins had become addicted to in extreme old age. They all asked about Walter's leg, and he had to tell them nothing could be done. A discussion followed on how different things would be these days if a child of seven had been shot in the leg by another child. It would have got into the papers and Walter would have had counseling. Moultry would have had counseling too, probably.

Driving down to Sidmouth with Emma beside him, trying to keep in convoy with Ian and Barbara and Andrew in the car ahead, Walter asked himself if Moultry had ever said he was sorry. He hadn't. There had been no opportunity, for Walter was sure he'd never seen Moultry again. Suddenly he thought of something. Ever since the pain in his leg had started, he'd thought about Moultry every single day. He was becoming obsessed with Moultry.

"I'm bored, Granddad," said Emma. "Tell me a story."

Not Moultry. Not the visit to the barber, which for some reason reminded him of Moultry. "I'll tell you about our dog Pip who stole a string of sausages from the butcher's and once bit the postman's hand when he put it through the letter box."

Another world it was. Sausages no longer came in strings and supermarkets were more common than butcher's. These days the postman would have had counseling and a tetanus injection and Pip would have been threatened with destruction, only his parents would have fought the magistrates' decision and taken it to the High Court and Pip's picture would have been in the papers. Walter was tired by the time they got to Sidmouth, while Emma was as fresh as a daisy and raring to go. He had related the entire history of his childhood to her, or as much as he could recall, several times over.

His leg ached. He still thought exercise better for him than rest. While the others went down to the beach, he took a walk along the seafront and through streets of Georgian houses. He hardly knew what made him glance at the brass plate on one of the pillars flanking a front door—perhaps the brilliant polish on it caught the sun—but he did look and there he read: JENKINS, MOULTRY, HALL, SOLICITORS AND COMMISSIONERS FOR OATHS. It couldn't be his Moultry, could it? Harold Moultry as a solicitor was a laughable thought.

After dinner and a drink in the bar he went early to his room. Leave the young ones alone for a bit. He looked for a telephone directory and finally found one inside the wardrobe behind a spare blanket. Jenkins, Moultry, Hall were there and so was Moultry, A.P. at an address in the town. Under this appeared: Moultry, H., Mingle Valley Farm, Harcombe. That was him, all right. That was Harold Moultry. The solicitor with the initials A.P. would be his son. Why don't I phone him, thought Walter, lying in bed, conjuring up pictures in the dark. Why don't I phone him in the morning and ask him over for a drink? Meeting him will take him off my mind. I bet if I had counseling I'd be told to meet him. Confront him, that would be the expression.

An answering machine was what he got. Of course the voice wasn't recognizable. Not after all these years. It didn't say it was Harold Moultry but that this was the Moultry Jersey Herd and to leave a message after the tone. Walter tried again at midday and again at two. After that they all went to Lyme Regis and he had to leave it.

When he got back he expected the message light on his phone to be on, but there was nothing. And nothing next day. Moultry had chosen not to get in touch. Briefly, Walter thought of phoning the son, the solicitor, but dismissed the idea. If Moultry didn't want to see him, he certainly didn't want to see Moultry. That evening Walter sat with the children while Ian and Barbara went out to dinner, and on the following afternoon, because it was raining, they all went to the cinema and saw *The Hunchback of Notre Dame*.

On these holidays Walter always behaved as tactfully as he could, doing his share of looking after the children and sometimes more than his share, but also taking care not to be intrusive. So it was his policy, on at least one occasion, to take himself off for the day. This time he had arranged to visit a cousin who lived in Honiton. Hearing he was coming to Sidmouth, the cousin had invited him to lunch.

On the way back, approaching Sidbury, he noticed a sign to Harcombe. Why did that ring a bell? Of course. Harcombe was where Moultry lived, he and his Jersey herd. Walter had taken the Harcombe turning almost before he knew what he was doing. In the circumstances it would be ridiculous to be so near and not go to Mingle Valley Farm, an omission he might regret for the rest of his life.

Beautiful countryside, green woods, dark red earth where the harvested fields had already been plowed, a sparkling river that splashed over stones. He saw the cattle before he saw the house, cream-colored elegant beasts, bony and mournful-eyed, hock-deep in the lush grass. Hundreds of them—well, scores. If he said "scores" to Emma and Andrew they wouldn't know what he was talking about. On a gatepost, lettered in black on a white board, he read: MINGLE VALLEY FARM, THE MOULTRY JERSEY HERD and under that, TRESPASSERS WILL BE PROSECUTED.

He left the car. Beyond the gate was only a path, winding away between flowery grass verges and tall trees. A pheasant made him jump, uttering its harsh rattling cry and taking off on clumsy wings. The path took a turn to the left, the woodland ended abruptly, and there ahead of him stretched lawns and, beyond them, the house. It was a sprawling half-timbered place, very picturesque, with diamond-paned windows. On the lawn rabbits cropped the grass.

He had counted fifteen rabbits when a man came out from behind the house. Even from this distance Walter could tell he was an old man. He could see too that this old man was carrying a gun. Six decades fell away, and instead of a green Devon lawn, Walter saw a sluggish river on the outskirts of London, willow trees, a kingfisher. He did as he had done then and clapped his hands.

The rabbits scattered. Walter heard the sharp crack of the shotgun, expected to see a rabbit fall but fell himself instead. Rolled over as pain stabbed his leg. It was his left leg this time, but the pain was much the same as it had been when he was seven. He sat up, groaning, blood all over his trousers. A man was standing over him with a mobile phone in one hand and the gun bent over in the middle—broken, did they call it?—in the other. Walter would have known that resentful glare anywhere, even after sixty-five years.

In the hospital they took the shot out and for good measure—"Might as well while you're in here"—extracted the pellet from his right leg. With luck, the doctor said, he'd be as good as new.

"Remember, we're none of us getting any younger."

"Really?" said Walter. "I thought I was."

Moultry didn't come to see him in the hospital. He told Barbara her father was lucky not to have been prosecuted for trespassing.

THE PROFESSIONAL

T HE GIRLS HAD THE BEST OF IT. Dressed in models from the Designer Room, they disposed themselves in one of the windows that fronted onto the High Street, one in a hammock from *House & Garden,* another in an armchair from *Beautiful Interiors,* holding best-sellers from the book department and pretending to read them. Small crowds gathered and stared at them, as if they were caged exotic animals.

The boys had seats inside, between Men's Leisurewear and Perfumery, facing the escalators. Anyone coming down the escalators was obliged to look straight at them. They sat surrounded by the materials of their craft, ten pairs of brushes each, thirty kinds of polishes and creams and sprays, innumerable soft cloths, all of different colors, all used just once, then discarded. Customers had comfortable leather chairs to sit in and padded leather footrests for their feet. A big notice said: LET OUR PROFESSIONALS CLEAN YOUR SHOES TO AN UNRIVALED HIGH STANDARD, £2.50.

It was a lot harder work than what the girls did. Nigel resented the girls, lounging about doing bugger all, getting to wear the sort of kit they'd never afford in their wildest dreams. But Ross pointed out to him that the boys would do better out of it in the long run. After all, it was a load of rubbish Karen and Fiona thinking this was the first step to a modeling career. As if it were Paris (or even London), as if they were on the catwalk instead of in a department-store window in a city that had one of the highest rates of unemployment in the country.

Besides, he and Nigel were trained. They'd both had two weeks of intensive training. When he had been at his pitch at the foot of the escalator a week, Ross's parents came in to see how he was getting on. Ross hadn't much liked that; it was embarrassing, especially as his father thought he could get his shoes cleaned for free. But his mother understood.

"Professional," she said, nudging his father, "you see that. That's what it says, 'our professionals.' You always wanted him to get some real training and now he's got it. For a profession."

The W. S. Marsh Partnership got a subsidy for taking them on. Sixty pounds a week per head, someone had told him. And a lot of praise and a framed certificate from the Chamber of Commerce for their "distinguished contribution to alleviating youth unemployment." The certificate hung up on the wall at the entrance to Men's Leisurewear, which Ross privately thought rather too close for comfort. Still, it was a job and a job for which he was trained. He was twenty and it was the first employment he'd had since he left school, four years before.

At school, when he was young and didn't know any better, he was ambitious. He thought he could be a pilot or something in the media.

"Yeah, or a brain surgeon," said Nigel.

But of course it turned out that any one of those was as unlikely as the others. His aims were lower now, but at least he could have aims. The job with the W. S. Marsh Partnership had made that possible. He'd set his sights on the footwear trade. Manager of a shoeshop. How to get there he didn't know, because he didn't know how managers of shoeshops got started, but still, he thought he had set his foot on the lowest rung of the ladder. While he cleaned shoes he imagined himself fitting on shoes or, better still, calling to an assistant to serve this customer or that. In these daydreams of his the assistant was always Karen, obliged to do his bidding, no longer favoring him with disdainful glances as he walked by her window on his way to lunch. Karen, though, not Fiona. Fiona sometimes lifted her head and smiled.

The customers—Nigel called them "punters"—mostly treated him as if he didn't exist. Once they'd paid, that is, and said what they wanted done. But no, that wasn't quite right. Not as if he didn't exist—more as if he were a machine. They sat down, put their feet on the footrest, and nodded at him. They kept their shoes on. Women always took their shoes off, passed him the shoes, and left their slender and delicate stockinged feet dangling. They talked to him, mostly about shoes, but they talked. The women were nicer than the men.

"Yeah, well, you know what they're after, don't you?" said Nigel.

It was a good idea, but Ross didn't think it was true. If he had asked any of those pretty women who showed off their legs in front of him what they were doing that evening or did they fancy a movie, he'd have expected to get his face smacked. Or be reported. Be reported and probably sacked. The floor manager disliked them anyway. He was known to disapprove of anything that seemed designed to waylay or entrap customers. No assistants stood about in Perfumery spraying passing customers with scent. Mr. Costello wouldn't allow it. He even discouraged assistants from asking customers if they might help them. He believed in the total freedom of everyone who entered W. S. Marsh's doors. Short of shoplifting, that is.

Every morning, when Ross and Nigel took up their positions facing the escalators ten minutes before the store opened at nine, Mr. Costello arrived to move them back against the wall, to try to reduce their allotted space, and to examine both of them closely, checking that they were properly dressed, that their hair was short enough and their hands clean. Mr. Costello himself was a model of elegance, six feet tall, slender, strongly resembling Linford Christie, if you could imagine Linford Christie dressed in a black suit, ice-white shirt, and satin tie. When he spoke he usually extended one long—preternaturally long—well-manicured sepia forefinger in either Nigel's direction or Ross's and wagged it as if beating time to music.

"You do not speak to the customers until they speak to you. You do not say 'hi,' you do not say 'cheers.'" Here the unsmiling glance was turned on Nigel and the finger wagged. "'Cheers' is no substitute for 'thank you.' You do not attract attention to yourselves. Above all, you do not catch customers' eyes or seem to be trying to attract their attention. Customers of the W. S. Marsh Partnership must be free to pay *untrammeled* visits to this store."

Mr. Costello had a degree in business studies, and "untrammeled" was one of his favorite words. Neither Ross nor Nigel knew what it meant. But they both understood that Mr. Costello would prefer them not to be there. He would have liked an excuse to be rid of them. Once or twice he had been heard to say that no one had paid an employer to take him on when he was twenty; he had been obliged to take an evening job to make ends meet at college. Any little thing would be an excuse, Ross thought, any stepping out of line in the presence of a customer.

But they had few customers. After those early days when he and Nigel had been a novelty, business ceased to boom. Having your shoes cleaned at W. S. Marsh was expensive. Out in the High Street you could get it done for a pound, and guests in the hotels used the electric shoe polisher for nothing. Mostly it was the regulars who came to them, businessmen from the big office blocks, women who had nothing to do but go shopping and had time on their hands. This worried Ross, especially since in Mr. Costello's opinion, sixty pounds a week or no sixty pounds, no commercial concern was going to keep them on in idleness.

"It's not as if you are an ornament to the place," he'd said with an unpleasant smile.

And they were often idle. After the half dozen who came first thing in the morning, there'd be a lull until, one by one and infrequently, the women appeared. It was typical of the women to stand and look at them, to consider, maybe discuss the matter with a companion, smile at them, and pass on into Perfumery. Ross sat on his stool, gazing up the escalator. If you did what Nigel did and stared at the customers at ground level, if you happened to eye the girls' legs, you got a reprimand. Mr. Costello walked round the ground floor all day, passing the foot of the escalators once an hour, observing everything with his Black & Decker drill eyes. When there was nothing to do Ross watched the people going up the escalator on the right-hand side and coming down the escalator on the left. And he watched them with his face fixed into a polite expression, careful to catch no eyes.

Karen and Fiona seldom came to get their shoes cleaned. After all, they only wore their own shoes to come in and go home in. But sometimes, on wet days, at lunchtime, one or the other of them would present herself to Ross to have a pair of damp or muddy loafers polished. They didn't like the way Nigel looked at them, and both preferred Ross.

Karen didn't open her mouth while he cleaned her suede boots. Her eyes roved round the store as if she were expecting to see someone she knew. Fiona talked, but still he couldn't believe his luck when, extending a slim foot and handing him a green leather brogue, she asked him if he'd like to go for a drink on the way home. He nodded—he couldn't speak—and looked deep into her large turquoise eyes. Then she went, her shoes sparkling, turning once to flash him a smile. Nigel pretended he hadn't heard, but a flush turned his face a mottled red. Ross, his heart thudding, gazed away to where he always gazed, the ascending and descending escalators.

He was getting somewhere. He was trained, a professional. It could only lead onward and to better things. Fiona, of the kingfisher eyes and the cobweb-fine feet, was going to have a drink with him. He gazed upward, dreaming, seeing his future as the escalator that ceaselessly and endlessly climbed. Then he saw something else.

At the top of the escalator stood a woman. She was holding on to the rail and looking back over one shoulder toward the man who came up behind her. Ross recognized the man; he had once or twice cleaned his shoes and actually been talked to and smiled at and thanked. And once he had seen him outside, giving a passing glance at Fiona and Karen's window. He was about forty but the woman was older, a thin, frail woman in a very short skirt that showed most of her long bony legs. She had bright hair, the color of the yellow hammock Fiona reclined in. As she turned her head to look down the escalator, as she stepped onto it, Ross saw the man put out one hand and give her a hard push in the middle of her back.

Everything happened very fast. She fell with a loud protracted scream. She fell forward, just like someone diving into deep water, but it wasn't water—it was moving metal, and halfway down as her head caught against one of the steps she rolled over in a perfect somersault. All the time she was screaming.

The man behind her was shouting as he ran down. People at the top of the escalator shrank back from it as the man went down alone. Ross and Nigel had sprung to their feet. The screaming had fetched assistants and customers running from Perfumery and Men's Leisurewear, but it had stopped. It had split the air as an earthquake splits rock, but now it had stopped and for a moment there was utter silence.

In that moment Ross saw her, lying spread at the foot of the escalator. A funny thought came to him, that he'd never seen anyone look so relaxed. Then he understood she looked relaxed because she was dead. He made a sound, a kind of whimper. He could no longer see her—she was surrounded by people—but he could see the man who had pushed her. He was so tall, he towered above everyone, even above Mr. Costello.

Nigel said, "Did you see her shoes? Five-inch heels, at least five-inch. She must have caught her heel."

"She didn't catch her heel," Ross said.

A doctor had appeared. There was always a doctor out shopping, which was the reason the National Health Service was in such a mess, Ross's mother said. The main doors burst open and an ambulance crew came running in. Mr. Costello cleared a path among the onlookers to let them through and then he tried to get people back to work or shopping or whatever they'd been doing. But before he had got very far a voice came over the public-address system telling customers the south escalators would be out of service for the day and Perfumery and Men's Leisurewear closed.

"What d'you mean, she didn't catch her heel?" said Nigel.

Ross ought to have said then. This was his first chance to tell. He nearly told Nigel what he'd seen. But then he got separated from him by the ambulance men carrying the woman out on a stretcher, pushing Nigel to one side and him to the other, the tall man walking behind them, his face white, his head bowed. Mr. Costello came up to them.

"I suppose you thought you could skive off for the rest of the day," he said. "Sorry to disappoint you. We're making you a new pitch upstairs in Ladies' Shoes."

This was his second chance. Mr. Costello stood there while they packed their materials into the cases. Nigel carried the notice board that said LET OUR PROFESSIONALS CLEAN YOUR SHOES TO AN UNRIVALED HIGH STANDARD, £2.50. The escalators had stopped running, so they followed Mr. Costello to the lifts and Ross pressed the button and they waited. Now was the time to tell Mr. Costello what he had seen. He should tell Mr. Costello and through Mr. Costello the top management and through them, or maybe before they were brought into it, the police.

"I saw the man that was with her push her down the escalator."

He didn't say it. The lift came and took them up to the second floor. The departmental manager, a woman, showed them their new pitch, and they laid out their things. No one had their shoes cleaned, but a girl Nigel knew who worked in the stockroom came over and told them that the woman who fell down the escalator was a Mrs. Russell, the tall man with her was her husband, and they had a big house up on The Mount, which was the best part of town, where all the nobs lived. They were good customers of the Marsh Partnership and were often in the store; Mrs. Russell had an account there and a Marsh Partnership Customer Card. Ross went off for his lunch, and when he returned Nigel went off for his, coming back to add more details that he had picked up in the cafeteria. Mr. and Mrs. Russell had only been married a year. They were devoted to each other.

"Mr. Russell is devastated," said Nigel. "They're keeping him under sedation."

When the departmental manager came along to see how they were getting on, Ross knew that this was his third chance and perhaps his last. She told them everything would be back to normal next day, they'd be back at the foot of the escalator between Perfumery and Men's Leisurewear, and now he should tell her what he had seen. But he didn't and he wouldn't. He knew that now because he saw very clearly what would happen if he told.

He would attract attention to himself. In fact, it was hard to think of any way to attract *more* attention to himself. He would have to describe what he had seen, identify Mr. Russell—a customer, a good customer!— and say he had seen Mr. Russell put his hand in the middle of his wife's back and push her down the escalator. He alone had seen it. Not Nigel, not the customers, but himself alone. They wouldn't believe him; he'd get the sack. He had had this job just six weeks and he would get the sack.

So he wouldn't tell. At least, he wouldn't tell Mr. Costello. There was only one person he really wanted to tell, and that was Fiona, but when they met and had their drink and talked and had another drink and she said she'd see him again the next night, he didn't say anything about Mr. Russell. He didn't want to spoil things, have her think he was a nut or maybe a liar. Once he was at home he thought about telling his mother. Not his father—his father would just get on to the police—but his mother, who sometimes had glimmerings of understanding. But she had gone to bed, and the next morning he wasn't in the mood for talking about it.

Something strange had happened in the night. He was no longer quite sure of his facts. He had begun to doubt. Had he really seen that rich and powerful man, that tall middle-aged man, one of the few men who had ever talked to him while he had his shoes cleaned, had he really seen that man push his wife down the escalator? Was it reasonable? Was it *possible?* What motive could he have had? He was rich, he had only recently married, he was known for being devoted to his wife.

Ross tried to re-create the sight in his mind, to rewind the film, so to speak, and run it through once more. To stop it at that point and freeze the frame. With his eyes closed, he attempted it. He could get Mrs. Russell to the top of the escalator, he could turn her head around to look back at her approaching husband, he could turn her head once more toward the escalator, but then came a moment of darkness, of a blank screen, as had happened once or twice to their TV set when there was a power cut. His power cut lasted only ten seconds, but when the electricity came on again it was to show Mrs. Russell plunging forward and to transmit the terrible sound of her scream. The bit where Mr. Russell had put his hand on her back and pushed her had vanished.

They were back that morning at the foot of the escalator. Things were normal, as if it had never happened. Ross could hardly believe his ears when Mr. Costello came by and said he wanted to congratulate them, him and Nigel, for keeping their heads the day before, behaving politely, not attracting unnecessary attention to themselves. Nigel blushed at that, but Ross smiled with pleasure and thanked Mr. Costello.

Business picked up wonderfully from that day onward. One memorable Wednesday afternoon there was actually a queue of customers waiting to have their shoes cleaned. The accident had been in all the papers and someone had got a photograph. Just as there is always a doctor on hand, so is there always someone with a camera. People wanted to have their shoes cleaned by the two professionals who had seen Mrs. Russell fall down the stairs, who had been there when it was all happening.

Fall down the stairs, not "get pushed down." The more Ross heard the term "fall down," the more "pushed down" faded from his consciousness. He hadn't seen anything, of course he hadn't. It had been a dream, a fantasy, a craving for excitement. He was very polite to the customers. He called them "sir" and "madam" with every breath, but he never talked about the accident beyond saying how unfortunate it was and what a tragedy. When they asked him directly he always said, "I'm afraid I wasn't looking, madam. I was attending to a customer."

Mr. Costello overheard approvingly. Three months later, when there was a vacancy in Men's Shoes, he offered Ross the job. By that time Ross and Fiona were going steady, she had given up all ideas of modeling in favor of hairdresser training, and they had moved in together into a studio flatlet. Karen had disappeared. Fiona had never known her well: Karen was a deep one, never talked about her personal life, and now she was gone and the window where they had sat and pretended to read best-sellers from the book department had been given over to Armani for Men.

While in Men's Shoes, Ross managed to get into a day-release scheme and took a business-studies course at the metropolitan college. His mother was disappointed because he wasn't a professional anymore, but everyone else saw all this as a great step forward. And so it was, because two weeks before he and Fiona got engaged, he was taken on as assistant manager at a shop in the precinct called The Great Boot Sale, at twice the salary he was getting from the Marsh Partnership.

In all that time he had heard very little of Mr. Russell beyond that he had let the house on The Mount and moved away. It was his mother who told Ross he was back and having his house done up before moving into it with his new wife.

"It's a funny thing," she said, "but I've noticed it time and time again. A man who's been married to a woman a lot older than him will always marry a woman a lot younger than him the second time around. Now why is that?"

No one knew. Ross thought very little of it. He had long ago convinced himself that the whole escalator incident had been in his imagination, a kind of daydream, probably the result of the kind of videos he had been watching. And when he encountered Mr. Russell in the High Street he wasn't surprised the man didn't recognize him. After all, it was a year ago.

But to see Karen walk past with her nose in the air did surprise him. She tucked her hand into Mr. Russell's arm—the hand with the diamond ring on it and the wedding ring—and turned him around to look where she was looking, into the jeweler's window. Ross looked at their reflections in the glass and shivered.

THE BEACH BUTLER

T HE WOMAN WAS THIN AND STRINGY, burned dark brown, in a white bikini that was too brief. Her hair, which had stopped looking like hair long ago, was a pale dry fluff. She came out of the sea, out of the latest crashing breaker, waving her arms and crying, screaming of some kind of loss. Alison, in her solitary recliner, under her striped hood (hired at $6 a morning or $10 a whole day), watched her emerge, watched people crowd about her, heard complaints made in angry voices but not what was said.

As always, the sky was a cloudless blue, the sea a deeper color. The Pacific but not peaceable. It only looked calm. Not far from the shore a great swell would bulge out of the sea, rise to a crest, and crash on whoever happened to be there at the time, in a cascade of overwhelming, stunning, irresistible water, so that you fell over before you knew what was happening. Just such a wave had crashed on the woman in the white bikini. When she had struggled to her feet she had found herself somehow damaged or bereft.

Alone, knowing nobody, Alison could see no one to ask. She put her head back on the pillow, adjusted her sunglasses, returned to her book. She had read no more than a paragraph when she heard his gentle voice asking her if there was anything she required. Could he get her anything?

When first she heard his—well, what? his title?—when first she heard he was called the beach butler it had made her laugh; she could hardly believe it. She thought of telling people at home and watching their faces. The beach butler. It conjured up a picture of an elderly man with a paunch wearing a white dinner jacket with striped trousers and pointed patent shoes like Hercule Poirot. Agustin wasn't like that. He was young and handsome, he was wary and polite, and he wore shorts and white trainers. His T-shirts were always snow white and immaculate; he must go through several a day. She wondered who washed them. A mother? A wife?

He stood there, smiling, holding the pad on which he wrote down orders. She couldn't really afford to order anything—she hadn't known the package didn't include drinks and midday meals and extras like this recliner and hood. On the other hand, she could hardly keep pretending she never wanted a drink.

"A Diet Coke then," she said.

"Something to eat, ma'am?"

It must be close on lunchtime. "Maybe some crisps." She corrected herself. "I mean, chips."

Agustin wrote something on his pad. He spoke fairly good English but only, she suspected, when food was the subject. Still, she would try.

"What was wrong with the lady?"

"The lady?"

"The one who was screaming."

"Ah. She lose her..." He resorted to miming, holding up his hands, making a ring with his fingers round his wrist. "The ocean take her—these things."

"Bracelet, do you mean? Rings?"

"All those. The ocean take. Bracelet, rings, these..." He put his hands to the lobes of his ears.

Alison shook her head, smiling. She had seen someone go into the sea wearing sunglasses and come out having lost them to the tide. But jewelry...!

"One Diet Coke, one chips," he said. "Suite number, please?"

"Six-oh-seven—I mean, Six-zero-seven."

She signed the chit. He passed on to the couple sitting in chairs under a striped umbrella. It was all couples here, couples or families. When they'd decided to come, she and Liz, they hadn't expected that. They'd expected young unattached people. Then Liz had got appendicitis and had to cancel and Alison had come alone. She'd paid, so she couldn't afford not to come, and she'd even been excited at the prospect. Mostly Americans, the travel agent had said, and she had imagined Tom Cruise look-alikes. American men were all tall, and in the movies they were all handsome. On the long flight over she had speculated about meeting them. Well, about meeting one.

But there were no men. Or, rather, there were plenty of men of all ages, and they were tall enough and good-looking enough, but they were all married or with partners or girlfriends and most of them were fathers of families. Alison had never seen so many children all at once. The evenings were quiet, the place gradually becoming deserted, as all these parents disappeared into their suites—there were no rooms here, only suites—to be with their sleeping children. By ten the band stopped playing, for the children must be allowed to sleep, and the restaurant staff brought the tables indoors, the bar closed.

She had walked down to the beach that first evening, expecting lights, people strolling, even a barbecue. It had been dark and silent, no one about but the beach butler, cleaning from the sand the day's litter, the drinks cans, the crisp bags, and the cigarette butts.

Now he brought her Diet Coke and her crisps. He smiled at her, his teeth as white as his T-shirt. She had a sudden urge to engage him in conversation, to get him to sit in a chair beside her and talk to her, so as not to be alone. She thought of asking him if he had had his lunch, if he'd have a drink with her, but by the time the words were formulated he had passed on. He had gone up to the group where sat the woman who had screamed.

Alison had been taught by her mother and father and her swimming teacher at school that you must never go into sea or pool until two hours have elapsed after eating. But last week she had read in a magazine that this theory was now old hat, that you could go swimming as soon as you liked after eating. Besides, a packet of crisps was hardly a meal. She was very hot; it was the hottest time of the day.

Looking at herself in one of the many mirrors in her suite, she'd thought she looked as good in her black bikini as any woman there. Better than most. Certainly thinner, and she would get even thinner because she couldn't afford to eat much. It was just that so many on the beach were younger than she, even the ones with two or three children. Or they looked younger. When she thought like that, panic rushed upon her, a seizure of panic that gripped her like physical pain. And the words that came with it were *old* and *poor.* She walked down to the water's edge. Showing herself off, hoping they were watching her. Then she walked quickly into the clear, warm water.

The incoming wave broke at her feet. By the time the next one had swollen, reared up, and collapsed in a roar of spray, she was out beyond its range. There were sharks, but they didn't come within a thousand yards of the beach, and she wasn't afraid. She swam, floated on the water, swam again. A man and a woman, both wearing sunglasses, swam out together, embraced, began a passionate kissing while they trod water. Alison looked away and up toward the hotel, anywhere but at them.

In the travel brochure, the hotel had looked very different, more golden than red, and the mountains behind it less stark. It hadn't looked like what it was, a brick-red building in a brick-red desert. The lawns around it weren't exactly artificial, but they were composed of the kind of grass that never grew and so never had to be cut. Watering took place at night. No one knew where the water came from, because there were no rivers or reservoirs and it never rained. Brilliantly colored flowers, red, pink, purple, orange, hung from every balcony, and the huge tubs were filled with hibiscus and bird-of-paradise. But outside the grounds the only thing that grew was cactus, some like swords and some like plates covered with prickles. And through the desert went the white road that came from the airport and must go on to somewhere else.

Alison let the swell carry her in, judged the pace of the waves, let one break ahead of her, then ran ahead through the shallows, just in time before the next one came. The couple who had been kissing had both lost their sunglasses. She saw them complaining and gesticulating to Agustin, as if he were responsible for the strength of the sea.

The tide was going out. Four little boys and three girls began building a sand castle where the sand was damp and firm. She didn't like them— they were a nuisance, and the last thing she wanted was for them to talk to her or like her—but they made her think that if she didn't hurry up she would never have children. It would be too late; it was getting later every minute. She dried herself and took the used towel to drop it into the bin by the beach butler's pavilion. Agustin was handing out snorkeling equipment to the best-looking man on the beach and his beautiful girlfriend. Well, the best-looking man after Agustin.

He waved to her, said, "Have a nice day, ma'am."

The hours passed slowly. With Liz there it would have been very different, despite the lack of available men. When you have someone to talk to, you can't think so much. Alison would have preferred not to keep thinking all the time, but she couldn't help herself. She thought about being alone and about apparently being the only person in the hotel who was alone. She thought about what this holiday was costing, some of it already paid for, but not all.

When she had arrived they had asked for an imprint of her credit card and she had given it—she didn't know how to refuse. She imagined a picture of her pale blue-and-gray credit card filling a computer screen and every drink she had and slice of pizza she ate and every towel she used and recliner she sat in and video she watched depositing a red spot on its pastel surface, until the whole card was filled up with scarlet. Until it burst or rang bells and the computer printed NO, NO, NO across the screen.

Back in her room, she lay down on the enormous bed and slept. The air-conditioning kept the temperature at the level of an average January day in England, and she had to cover herself up with the thick quilt they called a comforter. It wasn't much comfort but was slippery and cold to the touch. Outside the sun blazed onto the balcony and flamed on the glass so that looking at the windows was impossible. Sleeping like this kept Alison from sleeping at night, but there was nothing else to do. She woke in time to see the sunset. The sun seemed to sink into the sea or be swallowed up by it, like a red-hot iron plunged in water. She could almost hear it fizz. A little wind swayed the thin palm trees.

After dinner, pasta and salad and fruit salad and a glass of house wine, the cheapest things on the menu, after sitting by the pool with the coffee that was free—they endlessly refilled one's cup—she went down to the beach. She hardly knew why. Perhaps it was because at this time of the day the hotel became unbearable with everyone departing to their rooms, carrying exhausted children or hand in hand or arms round each other's waists, so surely off to make love it was indecent.

She made her way along the pale paths, under the palms, between the tubs of ghost-pale flowers, now drained of color. Down the steps to the newly cleaned sand, the newly swept red rocks. Recliners and chairs were all stacked away, umbrellas furled, hoods folded up. It was warm and still, the air smelling of nothing, not even of salt. Down at the water's edge, in the pale moonlight, the beach butler was walking slowly along, pushing ahead of him something that looked from where she stood like a small vacuum cleaner.

She walked toward him. Not a vacuum cleaner: a metal detector.

"You're looking for the jewelry people lose," she said.

He looked at her, smiled. "We never find." He put his hand into the pocket of his shorts. "Find this only."

Small change, most of it American, a handful of sandy nickels, dimes, and quarters.

"Do you get to keep it?"

"This money? Of course. Who can say who has lost this money?"

"But jewelry, if you found that, would it be yours?"

He switched off the detector. "I finish now." He seemed to consider, began to laugh. From that laughter she suddenly understood so much, she was amazed at her own intuitive powers. His laughter, the tone of it, the incredulous note in it, told her his whole life: his poverty, the wonder of having this job, the value to him of five dollars in small change, his greed, his fear, his continuing amazement at the attitudes of these rich people. A lot to read into a laugh, but she knew she had got it right. And at the same time she was overcome by a need for him that included pity and empathy and desire. She forgot about having to be careful, forgot that credit card.

"Is there anything to drink in the pavilion?"

The laughter had stopped. His head a little on one side, he was smiling at her. "There is wine, yes. There is rum."

"I'd like to buy you a drink. Can we do that?"

He nodded. She had supposed the pavilion was closed and he would have to unlock a door and roll up a shutter, but it was still open. It was open for the families who never came after six o'clock. He took two glasses down from a shelf.

"I don't want wine," she said. "I want the rum."

He poured alcohol into their glasses and soda into hers. He drank his down in one gulp and poured himself a refill.

"Suite number, please," he said.

It gave her a small, unpleasant shock to be asked. "Six-zero-seven," she said, not caring to read what it cost, and signed the chit. He took it from her, touching her fingers with his fingers. She asked him where he lived.

"In the village. It is five minutes."

"You have a car?"

He started laughing again. He came out of the pavilion carrying the rum bottle. When he had pulled down the shutters and locked them and locked the door, he took her hand and said, "Come." She noticed that he had stopped calling her "ma'am." The hand that held hers went around her waist and pulled her closer to him. The path led up among the red rocks, under pine trees that looked black by night. Underfoot was pale dry sand. She had thought he would take her to the village, but instead he pulled her down onto the sand in the deep shadows.

His kisses were perfunctory. He threw up her long skirt and pulled down her panties. It was all over in a few minutes. She put up her arms to hold him, expecting a real kiss now and perhaps a flattering word or two. He sat up and lit a cigarette. Although it was two years since she had smoked, she would have liked one too, but she was afraid to ask him—he was so poor, he probably rationed his cigarettes.

"I go home now," he said, and he stubbed out the cigarette into the sand he had cleaned of other people's butts.

"Do you walk?"

He surprised her. "I take the bus. In poor countries are always many buses." He had learned that. She had a feeling he had said it many times before.

Why did she have to ask? She was half-afraid of him now, but his attraction for her was returning. "Shall I see you again?"

"Of course. On the beach. Diet Coke and chips, right?" Again he began laughing. His sense of humor was not of a kind she had come across before. He turned to her and gave her a quick kiss on the cheek. "Tomorrow night, sure. Here. Same time, same place."

Not a very satisfactory encounter, she thought as she went back to the hotel. But it had been sex, the first for a long time, and he was handsome and sweet and funny. She was sure he would never do anything to hurt her, and that night she slept better than she had since her arrival.

· · ·

All mornings were the same here, all bright sunshine and mounting heat and cloudless sky. First she went to the pool. He shouldn't think she was running after him. But she had put on her new white swimming costume, the one that was no longer too tight, and after a while, with a towel tied round her sarong-fashion, she went down to the beach.

For a long time she didn't see him. The American girl and the Caribbean man were serving the food and drink. Alison was so late getting there that all the recliners and hoods had gone. She was provided with a chair and an umbrella, inadequate protection against the sun. Then she saw him, leaning out of the pavilion to hand someone a towel. He waved to her and smiled. At once she was elated, and leaving her towel on the chair, she ran down the beach and plunged into the sea.

Because she wasn't being careful, because she had forgotten everything but him and the hope that he would come and sit with her and have a drink with her, she came out of the water without thinking of the mountain of water that pursued her, without any awareness that it was behind her. The great wave broke, felled her, and roared on, knocking out her breath, drenching her hair. She tried to get a purchase with her hands, to dig into the sand and pull herself up before the next breaker came. Her eyes and mouth and ears were full of salt water. She pushed her fingers into the wet, slippery sand and encountered something she thought at first was a shell. Clutching it, whatever it was, she managed to crawl out of the sea while the next wave broke behind her and came rippling in, a harmless trickle.

By now she knew that what she held was no shell. Without looking at it she thrust it into the top of her swimming costume, between her breasts. She dried herself, dried her eyes, which stung with salt, felt a raging thirst from the brine she had swallowed. No one had come to her aid, no one had walked down to the water's edge to ask if she was all right. Not even the beach butler. But he was here now beside her, smiling, carrying her Diet Coke and packet of crisps as if she had ordered them.

"Ocean smack you down? Too bad. I don't think you lose no jewels?"

She shook her head, nearly said, "No, but I found some." But now wasn't the time, not until she had had a good look. She drank her Diet Coke, took the crisps upstairs with her. In her bathroom, under the cold tap, she washed her find. The sight came back to her of Agustin encircling his wrist with his fingers when he told her of the white bikini woman's loss. This was surely her bracelet or some other rich woman's bracelet.

It was a good two inches wide, gold set with broad bands of diamonds. They flashed blindingly when the sun struck them. Alison examined its underside, found the assay mark, the proof that the gold was eighteen carat. The sea, the sand, the rocks, the salt had damaged it not at all. It sparkled and gleamed as it must have done when first it lay on blue velvet in some Madison Avenue or Beverly Hills jeweler's shop.

She took a shower, washed her hair and blew it dry, put on a sundress. The bracelet lay on the coffee table in the living area of the suite, its diamonds blazing in the sun. She had better take it downstairs and hand it over to the management. The white bikini woman would be glad to have it back. No doubt, though, it was insured. Her husband would already have driven her to the city where the airport was (Ciudad Something) and bought her another.

What was it worth? If those diamonds were real, an enormous sum. And surely no jeweler would set any but real diamonds in eighteen-carat gold? Alison was afraid to leave it in her suite. A safe was inside one of the cupboards. But suppose she put the bracelet into the safe and couldn't open it again? She put it into her white shoulderbag. The time was only just after three. She looked at the list of available videos, then, feeling reckless, at the room-service menu. Having the bracelet—though of course she meant to hand it in—made her feel differently about that credit card. She picked up the phone, ordered a piña colada, a half bottle of wine, seafood salad, a double burger and french fries, and a video of *Shine*.

Eating so much didn't keep her from a big dinner four hours later. She went to the most expensive of the hotel's three restaurants, drank more wine, ate smoked salmon, lobster thermidor, raspberry pavlova. She wrote her suite number on the bill and signed it without even looking at the amount. Under the tablecloth she opened her bag and looked at the gold and diamond bracelet. Taking it to the management now would be very awkward. They might be aware that she hadn't been to the beach since not long after lunchtime; they might want to know what she had been doing with the bracelet in the meantime. She made a decision. She wouldn't take it to the management; she would take it to Agustin.

The moon was bigger and brighter this evening, waxing from a sliver to a crescent. Not quite sober, for she had had a lot to drink, she walked down the winding path under the palms to the beach. This time he wasn't plying his metal detector but sitting on a pile of folded beach chairs, smoking a cigarette and staring at the sea. It was the first time she had seen the sea so calm, so flat and shining, without waves, without even the customary swell.

Agustin would know what to do. There might be a reward for the finder, almost sure to be. She would share it with him—she wouldn't mind that, so long as she had enough to pay for those extras. He turned around, smiled, extended one hand. She expected to be kissed but he didn't kiss her, only patted the seat beside him.

She opened her bag, said, "Look."

His face seemed to close up, grow tight, grow instantly older. "Where you find this?"

"In the sea."

"You tell?"

"You mean, have I told anyone? No, I haven't. I wanted to show it to you and ask your advice."

"It is worth a lot. A lot. Look, this is gold. This is diamond. Worth maybe fifty thousand, hundred thousand dollar."

"Oh, no, Agustin!"

"Oh, yes, yes."

He began to laugh. He crowed with laughter. Then he took her in his arms, covered her face and neck with kisses. Things were quite different from the night before. In the shadows, under the pines, where the rocks were smooth and the sand soft, his lovemaking was slow and sweet. He held her close and kissed her gently, murmuring to her in his own language.

The sea made a soft lapping sound. A faint strain of music, the last of the evening, reached them from somewhere. He was telling her he loved her. *I love you, I love you.* He spoke with the accents of California and she knew he had learned it from films. *I love you.*

"Listen," he said. "Tomorrow we take the bus. We go to the city ..." Ciudad Something was what he said, but again she didn't catch the name. "We sell this jewel, I know where, and we are rich. We go to Mexico City, maybe Miami, maybe Rio. You like Rio?"

"I don't know. I've never been there."

"Me too. But we go. Kiss me. I love you."

She kissed him. She put her clothes on, picked up her shoulderbag. He watched her, said, "What are you doing?" When she began to walk down the beach, he called after her, "Where are you going?"

She stood at the water's edge. The sea was swelling into waves now. It hadn't stayed calm for long, its gleaming, ruffled surface black and silver. She opened her bag, took out the bracelet, and threw it as far as she could into the sea.

His yell was a thwarted child's. As he plunged into the water, she turned and began to walk away, up the beach toward the steps. When she was under the palm trees she turned to look back and saw him splashing wildly, on all fours scrabbling in the wet sand, seeking what surely could never be found again. As she entered the hotel the thought came to her that she had never told him her name and he had never asked.

THE ASTRONOMICAL SCARF

I T WAS A VERY LARGE SQUARE, silk in the shade of blue called midnight, which is darker than royal and lighter than navy, and the design on it was a map of the heavens. The Milky Way was there and Charles's Wain, Orion, Cassiopeia, and the Seven Daughters of Atlas. A young woman who was James Mullen's secretary saw it in a shop window in Bond Street, draped across the seat of a (reproduction) Louis Quinze chair with a silver chain necklace lying on it and a black picture hat with a dark blue ribbon covering one of its corners.

Cressida Chilton had been working for James Mullen for just three months when he sent her out to buy a birthday present for his wife. Not jewelry, he had said. Use your own judgment, I can see you've got good taste—but not jewelry. Cressida could see which way the wind was blowing there.

"Not jewelry" were the fateful words. Elaine Mullen was his second wife and had held that position for five years. Office gossip had it that he was seeing one of the management trainees in Foreign Securities. I wish it were me, thought Cressida, and she went into the shop and bought the scarf—appropriately enough, for an astronomical price—and then, because no shops gift-wrapped in those days, into a stationer's around the corner for a sheet of pink-and-silver paper and a twist of silver string.

Elaine knew the meaning of the astronomical scarf. She knew who had wrapped it up, too, and it wasn't James. She had expected a gold bracelet, and she could see the writing on the wall as clearly as if James had turned graffitist and chalked up something to the effect of all good things coming to an end. As for the scarf, didn't he know she never wore blue? Hadn't he noticed that her eyes were hazel and her hair light brown? That secretary, the one who was in love with him, had probably bought it out of spite. Elaine gave it to her blue-eyed sister, who happened to come around and saw it on the dressing table. It was the very day she was served with her divorce papers under the new law, Matrimonial Causes Act, 1973.

Elaine's sister wore the scarf to a lecture at the Royal Society of Lepidopterists, of which she was a fellow. Cloakroom arrangements in the premises of learned societies are often somewhat slapdash, and here, in a Georgian house in Bloomsbury Square, fellows, members, and their guests were expected to hang up their coats themselves on a row of hooks in a dark corner of the hall. When all the hooks were in use, coats had to be either placed over those already there or hung up on the floor. Elaine's sister, arriving rather late, took off her coat, threaded the astronomical scarf through one sleeve, in at the shoulder and out at the cuff, and draped the coat over someone's very old ocelot.

Sadie Williamson was a world authority on the genus *Argynnis,* its global distribution and habitats. She was also a thief. She stole something nearly every day. The coat she was wearing she had stolen from Harrods, and the shoes on her feet from a friend's clothes cupboard after a party. She was proud to say (to herself) that she had never given anyone a present she had had to pay for. Now in the dim and deserted hall, on the walls of which a few eighteenth-century prints of British butterflies were just visible, Sadie searched among the garments for some trifle worth picking up.

An unpleasant smell arose from the clothes, compounded of dirty cloth, old sweat, mothballs, cleaning fluid, and something in the nature of wet sheep. Sadie curled up her nose distastefully. She would have liked to wash her hands, but someone had hung an Out of Order sign on the washroom door. Not much worth bothering about here, she was thinking, when she saw the hand-rolled and hemstitched corner of a blue scarf protruding from a coat sleeve. She gave it a tug. Rather nice, she decided, and quickly tucked it into her coat pocket because she could hear footsteps coming from the lecture room.

The next day she took it around to the cleaners. Most things she stole she had dry-cleaned, even if they were fresh off a hanger in a shop. You never knew who might have tried them on.

"The zodiac," said the woman behind the counter. "Which sign are you?"

"I don't believe in it, but I'm a Cancer."

"Oh, dear," said the woman. "I never think that sounds very nice, do you?"

Sadie put the scarf into a box that had contained a pair of tights she had stolen from Selfridges, wrapped it up in a piece of paper that had wrapped a present given to *her,* and sent it to her godchild for Christmas. The parcel never got there. It was one of those lost in the robbery of a mail train traveling between Norwich and London.

Of the two young men who snatched the mailbags, it was the elder who helped himself to the scarf. He thought it was new; it looked new. He gave it to his girlfriend. She took one look and asked him who he thought she was, her own mother? What was she supposed to do with it, tie it round her head when she went to the races?

She meant to give it to her mother but accidentally left it in the taxi in which she was traveling from Kilburn to Acton. It was found, along with a carton of two hundred cigarettes, two cans of Diet Coke, and a copy of *Playboy,* the lot in a rather worn Harrods carrier, by the taxi driver's next fare. She happened to be Cressida Chilton, who was still James Mullen's secretary but who failed to recognize the scarf because it was enclosed in the paper wrapped around it by Sadie Williamson. Besides, she was still in a state of shock from what she had read in the paper that morning: the announcement of James's imminent marriage, his third.

"This was on the floor," she said, handing the bag over with the taxi driver's tip.

"They go about in a dream," he said. "You wouldn't believe the stuff they leave behind. I had a full set of Masonic regalia left in my cab last week, and the week before that it was a baby's pot, no kidding, and a pair of wellies. How am I supposed to know who the stuff belongs to? They'd leave themselves behind, only they have to get out when they pay, thank God. I mean, what is it this time? Packets of fags and a dirty book..."

"I hope you find the owner," said Cressida, and she rushed off through the revolving door and up in the lift to be sure of getting there before James did, to be ready with her congratulations, all smiles.

"Find the owner, my arse," said the taxi driver to himself.

He drew up at the red light next to another taxi whose driver he knew and, having already seen this copy, passed him the *Playboy* through their open windows. The cigarettes he smoked himself. He gave the Diet Cokes and the scarf to his wife. She said it was the most beautiful scarf she had ever seen and she wore it every time she went anywhere that required dressing up.

Eleven years later her daughter Maureen borrowed it. Repeatedly the taxi driver's wife asked for it back, and Maureen meant to give it back, but she always forgot. Until one day when she was about to go to her mother's and the scarf came into her head, a vision inspired by a picture in the *Radio Times* of the night sky in September. Her flat was always untidy, a welter of clothes and magazines and tape cassettes and full ash-trays. But once she had started looking she really wanted to find the scarf. She looked everywhere, grubbed about in cupboards and drawers, threw stuff on the floor and fumbled through half-unpacked suitcases. The result was that she was very late in getting to her mother's but she had not found the astronomical scarf.

This was because it had been taken the previous week—borrowed, she too would have said—by a boyfriend who was in love with her but whose love was unrequited. Or not as fully requited as he wished. The scarf was not merely intended as a sentimental keepsake but to be taken to a clairvoyant in Shepherds Bush who had promised him dramatic results if she could only hold in her hands "something of the beloved's." In the event, the spell or charm failed to work, possibly because the scarf belonged not to Maureen but to her mother. Or did it? It would have been hard to say who its owner was by this time.

The clairvoyant meant to return the scarf to Maureen's boyfriend at his next visit, but that was not due for two weeks. In the meantime she wore it herself. She was only the second person into whose possession it had come to look on it with love and admiration. Elaine Mullen's sister had worn it because it was obviously of good quality and because it was *there;* Sadie Williamson had recognized it as expensive; Maureen had bor-rowed it because the night had turned cold and she had a sore throat. But only her mother and now the clairvoyant had truly appreciated it.

This woman's real name was not known until after she was dead. She called herself Thalia Essene. The scarf delighted her, not because of the quality of the silk, nor its hand-rolled hem, nor its color, but because of the constellations scattered across its midnight blue. Such a map was to her what a chart of the Atlantic Ocean might have been to some early navigator—essential, enrapturing, mysterious, indispensable, lifesaving. Its stars were the encyclopedia of her trade, the impenetrable spaces between them the source of her predictions. She sat for many hours in meditative contemplation of the scarf, which she spread on her lap, stroking it gently and sometimes murmuring incantations. When she went out she wore it along with her layers of trailing garments, her black cloak, and her pomander of asafetida grass.

Roderick Thomas had never been among her clients. He was a neighbor, having just moved into one of the rooms below her flat in the Uxbridge Road. Years had passed since he had done any work or anyone had shown the slightest interest in him, wished for his company or paid attention to what he said, let alone cared about him. Thalia Essene was one of the few people who actually spoke to him, and all she said when she saw him was "Hi" or "Rain again."

One day, though, she made the mistake of saying a little more. The sun was shining out of a cloudless sky.

"The goddess loves us this morning."

Roderick Thomas looked at her with his mouth open. "You what?"

"I said, the goddess loves us today. She's shedding her glorious sunshine onto the face of the earth."

Thalia smiled at him and walked on. She was on her way to the shops in King Street. Roderick Thomas started shambling after her. For some years he had been on the lookout for the Antichrist, who he knew would come in female form. He followed Thalia into Marks & Spencer's and the cassette shop, where she was in the habit of buying music as background for her fortune-telling sessions. She was well aware of his presence and, growing increasingly angry, then nervous, went home in a taxi.

Next day he hammered on her door. She told him to go away.

"Say that about the sunshine again," he said.

"It's not sunny today."

"You could pretend. Say about the goddess."

"You're mad," said Thalia.

A client who had been having his palm read and had heard it all gave her a funny look. She told him his life line was the longest she had ever seen and he would probably make it to a hundred. When she went downstairs Roderick Thomas was waiting for her in the hall. He looked at the scarf.

"Clothed in the sun," he said, "and upon her head a crown of twelve stars."

Thalia said something so alien to her philosophy of life, so contrary to all her principles, that she could hardly believe she'd uttered it. "If you don't leave me alone, I'll call the police."

He followed her just the same. She walked up to Shepherds Bush Green. Her threats gave her a dark aura, and he saw the stars encircling her. She fascinated him, though he was beginning to see her as a source of danger. In Newcastle, where he had been living until two years before, he had killed a woman he had mistakenly thought was the Antichrist because she'd told him to go to hell when he spoke to her. For a long time he expected to be sent to hell, and although the fear had somewhat abated, it came back when he was confronted by manifestly evil women.

A man was standing on one of the benches on the green, preaching to the multitude. Well, to four or five people. Roderick Thomas had followed Thalia to the tube station, but there he had to abandon pursuit for lack of money to buy a ticket. He wandered onto the green. The man on the bench stared straight at him and said, "Thou shalt have no other gods but me!"

Roderick took that for a sign—you'd have to be daft not to get the message—but he asked his question just the same.

"What about the goddess?"

"For Solomon went after Ashtoreth," said the man on the bench, "and after Milcom, the abomination of the Ammonites. Wherefore the Lord said unto Solomon, I will surely rend the kingdom from thee and will give it to thy servant."

That was fair enough. Roderick went home and bided his time, listening to the voice of the preacher, which had taken over from the usual voice he heard during his waking hours. It told him of a woman in purple sitting on a scarlet-colored beast, full of names of blasphemy, having seven heads and ten horns. He watched from his window until he saw Thalia Essene come in, carrying a large recycled paper bag in a dull purple with CELESTIAL SECONDS printed on its side.

Thalia was feeling happy because she hadn't seen Roderick for several hours and believed she had shaken him off. She was going out that evening to see a play at the Lyric, Hammersmith, in the company of a friend who was a famous water diviner. To this end she had bought herself a new dress or, rather, a "nearly new" dress, purple Indian cotton with mirrorwork and black embroidery. The blue starry scarf, which she had taken to calling the *astrological* scarf, went well with it. She draped it around her neck, lamenting the coldness of the night. A shawl would be inadequate, and all this would have to be covered by her old black coat.

A quick glance at her engagement book showed her that Maureen's boyfriend was due for a consultation the next morning. The scarf must be returned to him. She would wear it for the last time. As it happened, Thalia was wearing all these clothes for the last time, doing everything she did for the last time, but clairvoyant though she was, of her imminent fate she had no prevision.

She walked along, looking for a taxi. None came. She had plenty of time and decided to walk to Hammersmith. Roderick Thomas was behind her, but she had forgotten about him and she didn't look around. She was thinking about the water diviner, whom she hadn't seen for eighteen months but who was reputed to have split up from his girlfriend.

Roderick Thomas caught up with her in one of the darker spots of Hammersmith Grove. It wasn't dark to him but illuminated by the seven times seventy stars on the clothing of her neck and the sea of glass like unto crystal on the hem of her garment. He spoke not a word but took the two ends of the starry cloth in his hands and strangled her.

After they had found the body, her killer was not hard to find. There was little point in charging Roderick Thomas with anything or bringing him up in court, but they did. The astronomical scarf was Exhibit A at the trial. Roderick Thomas was found guilty of the murder of Noreen Blake, for such was Thalia's real name, and committed to a prison for the criminally insane.

The exhibits would normally have ended up in the Black Museum, but a young police officer called Karen Duncan, whose job it was to collect together such memorabilia, thought it all so sad and distasteful, that poor devil should never have been allowed out into the community in the first place, that she put Thalia's carrier bag and theater ticket in the shredder and took the scarf home with her. Although it had been dry-cleaned, the scarf had never been washed. Karen washed it in cold-water gel for delicates and ironed it with a cool iron. Nobody would have guessed it had been used for such a macabre purpose; there wasn't a mark on it.

But an unforeseen problem arose. Karen couldn't bring herself to wear it. It wasn't the scarf's history that stopped her so much as her fear that other people might recognize it. There had been some publicity for the Crown Court proceedings, and much had been made of the midnight-blue scarf patterned with stars. Cressida Chilton had read about it and wondered why it reminded her of James Mullen's second wife, the one before the one before his present one. She didn't think she could face a fourth divorce and fifth marriage; she'd have to change her job. Sadie Williamson read about the scarf, and for some reason there came into her head a picture of butterflies and a dark house in Bloomsbury.

After some inner argument, reassurance countered by denial and self-rebuke, Karen Duncan took the scarf round to the charity shop, where they let her exchange it for a black velvet hat. Three weeks later it was bought by a woman who didn't recognize it, though the man who ran the charity shop did and had been in a dilemma about it ever since Karen had brought it in. Its new owner wore it for a couple of years. At the end of that time she got married to an astronomer. The scarf shocked and enraged him. He explained to her what an inaccurate representation of the heavens it was, how it was quite impossible for these constellations to be adjacent to each other or even visible at the same time, and if he didn't forbid her to wear it that was because he wasn't that kind of man.

The astronomer's wife gave the scarf to the woman who did the cleaning three times a week. Mrs. Vernon never wore the scarf—she didn't like scarves, could never keep them from slipping off—but it wouldn't have occurred to her to say no to something that was offered to her. When she died, three years later, her daughter came upon it among her effects.

Bridget Vernon was a silversmith and a member of a celebrated craft society. One of her fellow members made quilts and was always on the lookout for likely fabrics to use in patchwork. The quiltmaker, Fenella Carbury, needed pieces of blue, cream, and ivory silks for a quilt that had been commissioned by a millionaire businessman well known for his patronage of arts and crafts and for his charitable donations. No charity was involved here. Fenella worked hard, and she worked long hours. The quilt would be worth every penny of the two thousand pounds she was asking for it.

For the second time in its life the scarf was washed. The silk was as good as new, its dark blue unfaded, its stars as bright as they had been twenty years before. From it Fenella was able to cut forty hexagons, which, interspersed with forty ivory damask diamond shapes and forty sky-blue silk lozenge shapes from a fabric shop cutoff, formed the central motif of the quilt. When it was finished it was large enough to cover a king-size bed.

James Mullen allowed it to hang on exhibition in Chelsea at the Chenil Gallery for precisely two weeks. Then he collected it and gave it to his new bride for a wedding present, along with a diamond bracelet, a cottage in Derbyshire, and a Queen Anne four-poster to put the quilt on.

Cressida Chilton had waited through four marriages and twenty-one years. Men, as Oscar Wilde said, marry because they are tired. Men, as Cressida Mullen said, always marry their secretaries in the end. It's dogged as does it, and she had been dogged, she had persevered, and she had her reward.

Before getting into bed on her wedding night, she contemplated the £2,000 quilt and told James it was the loveliest thing she had ever seen.

"The middle bit reminds me of you when you first came to work for me," said James. "I should have had the sense to marry you then. I can't think why it reminds me, can you?"

Cressida smiled. "I suppose I had stars in my eyes."

HIGH MYSTERIOUS UNION

1

B EFORE BEN, I'd never lent the house to anyone. No one had ever asked. By the time Ben asked I had doubts about its being the kind of place to inflict on a friend, but I said yes because if I'd said no I couldn't have explained why. I said nothing about the odd and disquieting things, only that I hadn't been there myself for months.

I'm not talking about the house. The house was all right. Or it would have been if it hadn't been where it was. A small gray Gothic house with a turret would have been fine by a Scottish loch or in some provincial town, only this one, mine, was in a forest. To put it precisely, on the edge of the great forest that lies on the western borders of—well, I won't say where. Somewhere in England, a long drive from London. It was for its position that I'd bought it. This beautiful place, the village, the woods, the wetlands, changed very little while everything else all around was changing. My house was about a mile outside the village, at the head of a large man-made lake. And the western tip of the forest enclosed house and lake in a curved sweep with two embracing arms, the shape of a horseshoe.

It was the village that was wrong: right for the people and wrong for the others, a place to be born in, to live and die in, not for strangers.

• • •

B en had been there once to stay with me. Just for the weekend. His wife was to have come too but cried off at the last moment. Ben said later she took her chance to spend a night with the man she's with now. It was July and very hot. We went for a walk, but the heat was too much for us and we were glad to reach the shade of the trees on the lake's eastern side.

Then we saw the bathers. They must have gone into the water after we'd started our walk, for they were up near the house, had gone in from the little strip of gravel I called "my beach."

The sky was cloudless and the sun hot in the way it is only in the east of England, brilliant white, dazzling, the clean hard light falling on a greenness that is so bright because it's well watered. The lake water, absolutely calm, looked phosphorescent, as if a white fire burned on the flat surface. And out of that blinding fiery water we saw the bathers rise and extend their arms, stand up, and, with uplifted faces, slowly rotate their bodies to and away from the sun.

It hurt the eyes but we could see. They wanted us to see, or one of them did.

"They're children," I said.

"She's not a child, Louise."

She wasn't, but I knew that. We're all inhibited about nudity, especially when we come upon it by chance and in company, when we're unprepared. It's all right if we can see it when alone and ourselves unseen. Ben wasn't especially prudish, but he was rather shy and he looked away.

The girl in the burning water, entirely naked, became more and more clearly visible to us, for we continued to walk toward her, though rather slowly now. We could have stopped and at once become voyeurs. Or turned back and provoked—I knew—laughter from her and her companions. And from God knows who else, hidden for all I could tell among the trees.

They were undoubtedly children, her companions, a boy and a girl. The three of them stretched upward and gazed at the dazzling blueness while the sun struck their wet bodies. That was another thing that troubled me, *that* sun, inflicting surely a fierce burning on white skin. For they were all white, white as milk, as white lilies, and the girl's uplifted breasts, raised by her extended arms, were like plump white buds, tipped with rosy pink.

What Ben thought of it I didn't quite know. He said nothing about it till much later. But his face flushed darkly, reddening as if with the sun, as those bodies should have reddened but somehow, I knew, would not— would stay, by the not always happy magic of this place, inviolable and unstained. He had taken his hands from his eyes and was feeling with his fingertips the hot red of his cheeks.

He didn't look at the bathers again. He kept his head averted, staring into the wood as if spotting there an array of interesting wildlife. They waded out of the water as we approached, the children running off to the shelter of the trees. But the girl stood for a moment on the little beach, no longer exposing herself to us but rather as if—there is only one word I can use, only one that gives the real sense of how she was—as if *ashamed*. Her stance was that of Aphrodite on her shell in the painting, one hand covering the pale fleece of hair between her thighs, the other, the white arm glittering with water drops, across her breasts. But Aphrodite gazes innocently at the onlooker. This girl stood with hanging head, her long white-blond hair dripping, and, though there was nothing to detain her there, remained in her attitude of shame as might a slave exhibited in a marketplace.

Yet she was enjoying herself. She was acting a part and enjoying what she acted. You could tell. I thought even then, before I knew much, that she might equally have chosen to be the bold visitor to the nude beach or the flaunting stripper or the shopper surprised in the changing room, but she had chosen the slave. It was a game, yet it was part of her nature.

When we were some twenty yards from her, she lifted her head and behaved as if she had only just seen us. We were to think, for it can't have been sincere, that until that moment she had been unconscious of our approach, of our being there at all. She gave a little artificial shriek, then a laugh of shocked merriment, waving her arms in a mime of someone grasping at clothes, seizing invisible garments out of the air and wrapping them around her, as she ran into the long grass, the low bushes, and at last into the tall, concealing trees.

"I don't know who that was," I said to him as we went into the house. "One of the village people, perhaps."

"Why not a visitor?" he said.

"No, I'm sure. One of the village people."

I was sure. There were ways of telling, though I hardly ever went near the village. Not by that time. Not to the church or the pub or the shop. And I didn't take Ben there. The place was gradually becoming less and less attractive to me, Gothic House somewhere I thought I ought occasionally to go to but put off visiting. You could only reach it with ease by driving through the village, and I avoided that village as much as I could.

By the time he asked me if he could borrow it, I had already decided to sell the house.

. . .

His wife had left him. Or made it plain to him that she expected him to leave *her*—leave her, that is, the house they lived in. He'd bought a flat in London, but before he'd ever lived in it he'd had a kind of breakdown from an accumulation of causes but mainly Margaret's departure. He wanted to get away somewhere, to get away from everyone and everything he knew, the people and places and things that reminded him. And he wanted to be somewhere he could work in peace.

Ben is a translator. He translates from French and Italian, fiction and nonfiction, and was about to embark on the biggest and most complex work he'd ever undertaken, a book called *The Golden Apple* by a French psychoanalyst that examined from a Jungian viewpoint the myths attendant on the Trojan War, Helen of Troy and Paris, Priam and Hecuba and the human mind. He took his word processor with him, his Collins-Robert French dictionary, his Liddell and Scott Greek dictionary, and Graves's *The Greek Myths.*

I gave him a key to Gothic House. "There are only two in existence. Sandy has the other."

"Who's Sandy?"

"A sort of odd-job man. Someone has to be able to get in in case of fire or, more likely, flood."

Perhaps I said it unhappily, for he gave me an inquiring look, but I didn't enlighten him. What was there to say without saying it all?

. . .

There was nothing sinister about the village and its surroundings. It is important that you understand that. It was the most beautiful place, and in spite of all the trees, the crowding forest that stretched to the horizon, it wasn't dark. The light even seemed to have a special quality there, the sky to be larger and the sun out for longer than elsewhere. I am sure there were more unclouded skies than to the north and south of us. Mostly, if you saw clouds, you saw them rolling away toward that bluish wooded horizon. Sunsets were pink, the color of a bullfinch's breast.

I don't know how it happened that the place was so unspoiled. Trunk roads passed within ten miles on either side, but the two roads into the village and the three out were narrow and winding. New building had taken place but not much, and what there was by some lucky chance was tasteful and plain. The old school still stood, no industry had come there, and no row of pylons marched across the fields of wheat and the fields of grazing beasts. Nothing interrupted the view everyone in the village had of the green forest of oak and ash and the black forest of fir and pine. The church had a round tower like a castle, but its surface was of cut flints.

That is not to say there were no strangenesses. I am sure there was much that was unique in the village and that much of what happened there happened nowhere else in England. Well, I know it now, of course, but even then, when I first came and in those first years...

• • •

I told Ben some of it before he left. I thought I owed him that.

"I shan't want to socialize with a lot of middle-class people," he said.

"You won't be able to. There aren't any."

His lack of surprise was due, I think, to his ignorance of country life. I had told him that the usual mix of the working people whose families had been there for generations with commuters, doctors, solicitors, retired bank managers, university professors, schoolteachers, and businessmen wasn't to be found. A parson had once been in the rectory, but for a couple of years the church had been served by the vicar of a parish some five miles away, who held a service once a week.

"I'd never thought of you as a snob, Louise," said Ben.

"It isn't snobbery," I said. "It's fact."

There were no county people, no "squire," no master of foxhounds or titled lady. No houses existed to put them in. A farmer from Lynn had bought the rectory. The hall, a pretty Georgian manor house of which a print hung in my house, had burned down in the fifties.

"It belongs to the people," I said. "You'll see."

"A sort of ideal communism," he said, "the kind we're told never works."

"It works. For them."

Did it? I wondered, after I'd said it, what I'd meant. Did it really belong to the people? How could it? The people there were as poor and hard-pressed as anywhere else; there was the same unemployment, the

same number living on benefit, the same lack of work for the agricultural
laborer driven from the land by mechanization. Yet another strange thing
was that the young people didn't leave. There was no exodus of school
graduates and the newly married. They stayed, and somehow there were
enough houses to accommodate them. The old people, when they
became infirm, were received, apparently with joy, into the homes of
their children.

* * *

Ben went down there one afternoon in May, and he phoned that night
to tell me he'd arrived and all was well. That was all he said then. Nothing
about Sandy and the girl. For all I knew he had simply let himself into the
house without seeing a soul.

"I can hear birds singing," he said. "It's dark, and I can hear birds. How
can that be?"

"Nightingales," I said.

"I didn't know there were such things anymore."

And though he didn't say, I had the impression that he put the phone
down quickly so that he could go outside and listen to the nightingales.

* * *

The front door was opened to him before he had a chance to use his key.
They had heard the car or seen him coming from a window, having plenty
of opportunity to do that, for he had stopped for a while at the point
where the road comes closest to the lake. He wanted to look at the view.

He'd left London much later than I thought he would, not till after six,
and the sun was setting. The lake was glazed with pink and purple, reflecting the sky, and it was perfectly calm, its smooth and glassy surface broken only by the dark green pallets of water-lily pads. Beyond the farther
shore the forest grew black and mysterious as the light withdrew into that
darkening sky. He'd been depressed, "feeling low," as he put it, and the
sight of the lake and the woodland, the calmness and the colors, if they
hardly made him happy, comforted him and steadied him into a kind of
acceptance of things. He must have stood there gazing, watching the light
fade, for some minutes, perhaps ten, and they must have watched him
and wondered how long it would be before he got back into the car.

The front door came open as he was feeling in his pocket for the key. A girl stood there, holding the door, not saying anything, not smiling, just holding the door and stepping back to let him come in. The absurd idea came to him that this was the *same* girl, the one he had seen bathing, and for a few minutes he was sure it was; it didn't seem absurd to him.

He even gave some sort of utterance to that thought. "You," he said. "What are you. . . ?"

"Just here to see everything's all right, sir." She spoke deferentially but in a practical way, a sensible way. "Making sure you're comfortable."

"But haven't I—no. No, I'm sorry." He saw his mistake in the light of the hallway. "I thought we'd"—*met* was not quite the word he wanted—"seen each other before."

"Oh, no." She looked at him gravely. "I'd remember if I'd seen you before."

She spoke with the broad up-and-down intonation they have in this part of the country, a woodland singsong burr. He saw now in the lamplight that she was much younger than the woman he had seen bathing, though as tall. Her height had deceived him, that and her fairness and her pallor. He thought then that he had never seen anyone who was not ill look so delicate and so fragile.

"Like a drawing of a fairy," he said to me, "in a children's book. Does that give you an idea? Like a mythological creature from this book I'm translating, Oenone, the fountain nymph, perhaps. Tall but so slight and frail that you wonder that she can have a physical existence."

She offered to carry his luggage upstairs for him. It seemed to him the most preposterous suggestion he had ever heard, that this fey being, a flower on a stalk, should be able to lift even his laptop. He fetched the cases himself and she watched him, smiling. Her smile was intimate, almost conspiratorial, as if they shared some past unforgettable experience. He was halfway up the stairs when the man spoke. It froze Ben, and he turned around.

"What were you thinking of, Lavinia, to let Mr. Powell carry his own bags?"

Hearing his own name spoken like that, so casually, as if it were daily on the speaker's lips, gave him a shock. Come to that, to hear it at all. . . . How did the man know? Already he knew there would be no explanation.

He would never be able to fetch out an explanation, now or at any time—not, that is, a true one, a real, factual, honest account of why anything was or how. Somehow he knew that.

"Alexander Clements, Mr. Powell. Commonly known as Sandy."

The girl followed him upstairs and showed him his bedroom. I'd told him to sleep where he liked, that he had the choice of four rooms, but the girl showed him to the big one in the front with the view of the lake. That was his room, she said. Would he like her to unpack for him? No one had ever asked him that before. He had never stayed in the kind of hotel where they did ask. He shook his head, bemused. She drew the curtains and turned down the bedcovers.

"It's a nice big bed, sir. I put the clean sheets on for you myself."

The smile returned, and then came a look of a kind he had never seen before—well, he had, but in films, in comedy westerns and a movie version of a Feydeau farce. At any rate, he recognized it for what it was. She looked over her shoulder at him. Her expression was one of sweet naughty coyness, her head dipped to one side. Her eyebrows went up and her eyes slanted toward him and away.

"You'll be lonely in that big bed, won't you?"

He wanted to laugh. He said in a stifled voice, "I'll manage."

"I'm sure you'll *manage,* sir. It's just Sandy I'm thinking of—I wouldn't want to get on the wrong side of Sandy."

He had no idea what she meant, but he got out of that bedroom quickly. Sandy was waiting for him downstairs and the table was laid for one, cold food on it and a bottle of wine.

"I hope everything's to your liking, Mr. Powell?"

He said it was, thank you, but he hadn't expected it, he hadn't expected anyone to be here.

"Arrangements were made, sir. It's my job to see things are done properly, and I hope they have been. Lavinia will be in to keep things shipshape for you and see to any necessary cookery. I'll be on hand for the more masculine tasks, if you take my meaning, your motor and the electricals, et cetera. Never underrate the importance of organization."

"What organization?" I said when he told me. "I didn't arrange anything. I knew Sandy Clements still had a key, and I've been meaning to ask for it back. Still, as for asking him to organize anything, to make 'arrangements' ..."

"I thought you'd got them in, Sandy and the girl. I thought she came in to clean for you and you'd arranged it that she'd do the same for me. I didn't want her, but I hardly liked to interfere with your arrangement."

"No," I said, "no, I see that."

They stood there until he was seated at the table and unfolding the white napkin Lavinia had presumably provided. I don't know where it came from; I haven't any white table linen. Sandy opened the bottle of wine, which Ben saw to his dismay was a supermarket Riesling. The horror was compounded by Sandy's pouring an inch of it into Ben's wineglass and watching while Ben tasted it.

He said he was almost paralyzed by this time, though seeing what he thought then was "the funny side." After a while he didn't find anything particularly funny, but he did that evening. They had cheered him up. He saw the girl as a sort of stage parlor maid. She was even dressed somewhat like that, a white apron with its sash tied tightly around her tiny waist, a white bow on her pale blond hair. He thought they were trying to please him. These unsophisticated rustics were doing their best, relying on an experience of magazines and television, to entertain the visitor from London in the style to which he was accustomed.

Once he'd started eating, they left. It was quite strange, the manner in which they left. Lavinia opened the door and let Sandy pass through ahead of her, looking back to give him another of those conspiratorial naughty looks. She delayed for longer than was necessary, her eyes meeting his until his turned away. A fleeting smile and then she was gone, the door and the front door closing behind her.

Only a few seconds passed before he heard the engine of Sandy's van. He got up to draw the curtains and saw the van moving off down the road toward the village, its red taillights growing small and dimmer until they were altogether swallowed up in the dark. A bronze-colored light that seemed to be slowly ascending showed through the treetops. It took him a little while before he realized it was the moon he was looking at, the coppery-golden disk of the moon.

He ate some of the ham and cheese they had left him and managed to drink a glass of the wine. The deep silence that prevailed after Sandy and the girl had gone was now broken by birdsong, unearthly trills of sound he could hardly at first believe in, and he went outside to try to confirm that he had really heard birds singing in the dark.

The rich yet cold singing came from the nearest trees of the wood; it was clear and unmistakable, but it seemed unreal to him, on a par somehow with the behavior he had just witnessed, with the use of his name, with the fountain nymph's coy glances and come-hither smiles. Yet when he came inside and phoned me, it was the nightingales' song he talked about. He said nothing of the man and the girl, the food, the bed, the "arrangements."

"Why didn't you?" I asked him when I came down for a weekend in June. "Why didn't you say?"

"I don't know. I consciously made up my mind I wouldn't. You see, I thought they were ridiculous, but at the same time I thought they were your—well, help, your cleaner, your handyman. I felt I couldn't thank you for making the arrangement with Lavinia without laughing about the way she dressed and the way Sandy talked. Surely you can see that?"

"But you never mentioned it. Not ever till now."

"I know," he said. "You can understand why, can't you?"

2

When I first came to Gothic House, Sandy was about twenty-five, so by the time Ben went there he would have been seven years older than that, a tall, fair man with very regular features who still escaped being quite handsome. His eyes were too pale, and the white skin of his face had reddened, as it does with some of the locals after thirty.

He came to me soon after I'd bought Gothic House, offering his services. I told him I couldn't afford a gardener or a handyman and I didn't need anyone to wash my car. He held his head a little to one side. It's an attitude that implies total understanding of the other person's mind, and indulgence, even patience.

"I wouldn't want paying."

"And I wouldn't consider employing you without paying you."

He nodded. "We'll see how things go then, shall we? We'll leave things as they are for now."

"For now" must have meant a couple of weeks. The next time I went to Gothic House for the weekend, the lawn in front of the house that slopes down to the wall above the lakeshore had been mowed. A strip of blocked gutter on the back that I had planned to see to had been cleared. If Sandy had presented himself while I was there, I would have repeated my refusal of his services, and done so in definite terms, for I was angry. But he didn't present himself, and at that time I had no idea where he lived or even his name.

On my next visit I found part of the garden weeded. Next time the windows had been cleaned. It was only when I came down and found a window catch mended, a repair that could only have been done after entry to the house, that I went down into the village to try to find Sandy.

That was my first real exploration of the village, the first time I noticed how beautiful it was and how unspoiled. Its center, the green, was a triangle of lawn on which the trees were the kind generally seen on parkland, cedars and unusual oaks and a swamp cypress. The houses and cottages either had rendered walls or were faced with flints, their roofs of slate or thatch. It was high summer, and the gardens, the tubs, the window boxes were full of flowers. Fuchsia hedges had leaves of a deep, soft green, spangled with sharp red blossoms. The whole place smelled of roses. It was the sort of village television-production companies dream of finding when they film Jane Austen serials. The cars would have to be hidden, but otherwise it looked unchanged from an earlier century.

A woman in the shop identified Sandy for me and told me where he lived. She smiled and spoke about him with a kind of affectionate admiration. Sandy, yes, of course, Sandy was much in demand. But he wouldn't be at home that morning, he'd be up at Marion Kirkman's. This was a cottage facing the pretty green and easily found. I recognized Sandy's van parked outside, opened the gate, and went into the garden.

By this time my anger had cooled—the shopwoman's obvious liking for and trust of Sandy had cooled it—and I asked myself if I could legitimately go up to someone's front door, demand to see her gardener, and harangue him in front of her. In the event, I didn't have to do that. I walked round to the back, hoping to find him alone there, and I found him—with her.

They had their backs to me, a tall, fair man and a tall, fair woman, his arm around her shoulders, hers around his waist. They were looking at something, a flower on a climber or an alighted butterfly perhaps, and then they turned to face each other and kissed. A light, gentle, loving kiss such as lovers give each other after desire has been satisfied, after desire

has been satisfied many times over months or even years, a kiss of acceptance and trust and deep mutual knowledge.

It was not so much the kiss as their reaction to my presence that
decided me. They turned around. They were not in the least taken aback,
and they were quite without guilt. For a few moments they left their
arms where they were while smiling at me in innocent friendliness. And
I could see at once what I'd stumbled upon—a long-standing loving relationship and one that, in spite of Marion Kirkman's evident seniority,
would likely result in marriage.

Two women, then, in the space of twenty minutes, had given their
accolade to Sandy. I asked him only how he had got into my house.

"Oh, I've keys to a good many houses around here," he said.

"Sandy makes it his business to have keys," Marion Kirkman said. "For
the security, isn't it, Sandy?"

"Like a neighborhood watch, you might say."

I couldn't quite see where security came into it, understanding as I
always had that the fewer keys around, the safer. But the two of them, so
relaxed, so smiling, so firm in their acceptance of Sandy's perfect right of
access to anyone's house, seemed pillars of society, earnest upholders of
social order. I accepted Marion's invitation to a cup of coffee. We sat in a
bright kitchen, all its cupboards refitted by Sandy, I was told, the previous year. It was then that I said I supposed it would be all right, that of
course he must come and do these jobs for me.

"You'll be alone in this village otherwise," said Marion, laughing, and
Sandy gave her another kiss, this time planted in the center of her smooth
pink cheek.

"But I'm going to insist on paying you."

"I won't say no," said Sandy. "I'm not an arguing man."

And after that he performed all these necessary tasks for me, regularly,
unobtrusively, efficiently, winning my trust, until one day things (as he
might have put it) changed. Or they would have changed, had Sandy had
his way. Of course they changed anyway; life can never be the same
between two people after such a happening. But though Sandy kept my
key he was no longer my handyman, and I ceased paying him. I believed
that I was in control.

So why did I say nothing of this to Ben before he went to Gothic

House? Because I was sure, for reasons obvious to me, that the same sort of thing couldn't happen to him.

•   •   •

The therapist Ben had been seeing since his divorce had advised him to keep a diary. He was to set down his thoughts and feelings, his emotions and his dreams, rather than the actual events of each day. Now, Ben had never done this, he had never "got around to it," until he came to Gothic House. There, perhaps because—at first—he had few distractions and there wasn't much to do once he'd worked on his translation and been out for a walk, he began a daily noting down of what passed through his mind.

This was the diary he later allowed me to see part of; other entries he read aloud to me, and he had it by him to refer to when he recounted the events of that summer. It had its sensational parts, but to me much of it was almost painfully familiar. At first, though, he confined himself to descriptions of his state of mind, his all-pervading sadness, a feeling that his life was over, and the beauties of the place, the lake, the woodland, the sunshine, the huge blue cirrus-patterned sky, somehow remote from him, belonging to other people.

He walked daily: around the lake, along a footpath high above damp meadows crossed by ditches full of watercress; down the lane to a hamlet where there was a green and a crossroads and a pub, though he never at that time ventured into the forest. Once he went to the village and back, but saw no one. Though it was warm and dry, nobody was about. He knew he was watched—he saw eyes looking at him from windows—but that was natural and to be expected. Villagers were always inquisitive about and even antagonistic to newcomers; that was a cliché that even he, as a townee, had grown up with. Not that he met with antagonism. The postman, collecting from the pillar-box, hailed him and wished him good morning. Anne Whiteson, the shopwoman, was friendly and pleasant when he went into the shop for tea bags and a loaf. He supposed he couldn't have a newspaper delivered? He could. Indeed he could. He had only to say what he wanted and "someone" would bring it up every morning.

The "someone" turned out to be Sandy, arriving at eight-thirty with his

Independent. Lavinia Fowler had already been twice, but this was the first time he had seen Sandy since that first evening. Though unasked, Lavinia brought tea for both of them, so Ben was obliged to put up with Sandy's company in the kitchen while he drank it. How was he getting on with Lavinia? Was she giving satisfaction?

Ben thought this a strange, almost archaic term. Or should another construction be put on it? Apparently it should, for Sandy followed up his inquiry by asking if Ben didn't think Lavinia a most attractive girl. The last thing Ben intended to do, he told me, was enter into this sort of conversation with the handyman. He was rather short with Sandy after that, saying he had work to do and to excuse him.

But he found it hard to settle down to *The Golden Apple.* He had come to a description of the contest between the three goddesses, when Paris asks Aphrodite to remove her clothes and let fall her magic girdle, but he could hear sounds from the kitchen, once or twice a giggle, the soft murmur of voices. Too soft, he said, too languorous and cajoling, so in spite of himself, he got up and went to listen at the door.

He heard no more and shortly afterward saw Sandy's van departing along the lakeshore. But as a result of what Sandy had said, he found himself looking at Lavinia with new eyes. Principally, she had ceased to be a joke to him, and when she came in with his midmorning coffee he was powerfully aware of her femininity, that fragile quality of hers, her vulnerability. She was so slender, so pale, and her thin white skin looked— these were his words, the words he put in his diary—as if waiting to be bruised.

Her fair hair was as fine and soft as a baby's but longer than any baby had ever had, a gauzy veil, almost waist length, very clean and smelling faintly of some herb. Thyme, perhaps, or oregano. As she bent over his desk to put the cup down, her hair just brushed his cheek, and he felt that touch with a kind of inner shiver just as he felt the touch of her finger. For he put out his hand to take the coffee mug while she still held it. Instead of immediately relinquishing her hold she left her forefinger where it was for a moment, perhaps thirty seconds, so that it lay alongside his own forefinger and skin delicately touched skin.

Again he thought, before he abruptly pulled his hand away, of skin waiting to be bruised, of how it would be if he took that white wrist, thin as a child's, blue veined, in a harsh grip and squeezed, his fingers more than meeting, overlapping and crushing until she cried out. He had never had such thoughts before, never before about anyone, and they made him uncomfortable. Departing from the room, she again gave him one of those over-the-shoulder glances, but this time wistful—disappointed?

Yet she didn't attract him, he insisted on that. He was very honest with me about all of it. She didn't attract him except in a way he didn't wish to be attracted. Oenone, the shepherdess and daughter of the river, was how he saw her. Her fragility, her look of utter weakness, as of a girl to be blown over by the wind or felled by a single touch, inspired in him only what he insisted it would inspire in all men, a desire to ravish, to crush, to injure, and to conquer.

"Ravish" was his word, not "rape."

"You really felt all that?" I asked.

"I thought about it afterward. I don't say I felt that at the time. I thought about it and that's how I felt about her. It didn't make me happy, you know—I wasn't proud of myself. I'm trying to tell you the honest truth."

"She was"—I hesitated—"offering herself to you?"

"She had been from the first. Every time we encountered each other she was telling me by her looks and her gestures that she was available, that I could have her. And, you know, I'd never come across anything quite like that before."

Since the separation from his wife he had been celibate. And he could see no end to his celibacy; he thought it would go on for the rest of his life, for the step that must be taken to end it seemed too great for him to consider, let alone take. Now someone else was taking that step for him. He had only to respond, only to return that glance, let his finger lie a little longer against that finger, close his fingers around that wrist.

Any of these responses were also too great to make. Besides, he was afraid. He was afraid of himself, of those horrors that presented themselves to him as his need. His active imagination showed him how it would be with him when he saw her damaged and at his hands, the bruised whiteness, the abraded skin. But her image came into his consciousness many times throughout that day and visited him in the night like a succubus. He stood at the open window listening to the nightingales, and felt her come into the room behind him, could have sworn one of those transparent fingers of hers softly brushed his neck. When he spun round no one was there, nothing was there but the faint herby smell of her, left behind from that morning.

That night was the first time he dreamed of the lake and the tower.

The lake was as it was in his conscious hours, a sheet of water that took twenty minutes to walk around, but the tower on Gothic House was immensely large, as high as a church spire. It had absorbed the house— there was no house, only this tall and broad tower with crenellated top and oeil-de-boeuf windows, as might be part of a battlemented castle. He had seen the tower and then he was on the tower, as is the way in dreams, and Lavinia, the river god's daughter, was walking out of the lake, water streaming from her body and her uplifted arms. She came to the tower and embraced it, pressing her wet body against the stone. But the curious thing, he said, was that by then *he* had become the tower, the tower was himself, stone still but about to be metamorphosed, he felt, into flesh that could respond and act. He woke up before that happened and he was soaking wet, as if a real woman had come out from the lake and embraced him.

"Sweat," he said, "and—well, you can have wet dreams even at my age."

"Why not?" I said, though at that time, in those early days, I was still surprised by his openness.

"Henry James uses that imagery, the tower for the man and the lake for the woman. *The Turn of the Screw,* isn't it? I haven't read it for a hundred years, but I suppose my unconscious remembered."

Lavinia didn't come the next day. It wasn't one of her days. That Friday he prepared himself for her coming—nervous, excited, afraid of himself and her, recalling always the dream and the feel against his body of her wet, slippery skin, her small, soft breasts. He put in the diary that he remembered water trickling down her breasts and spilling from the nipples.

She was due at eight-thirty. By twenty to nine, when she still hadn't come—she was never late—he knew he must have offended her. His lack of response she saw as rejection. He reminded himself that the woman in the dream was not Lavinia but an imagined figment. The real woman knew nothing of his dreams, his fears, his terrible self-reproach.

She didn't come. No one did. He was relieved but at the same time sorry for the hurt he must have done her. Apart from that, he was well content; he preferred his solitude, the silence of the house. Having to make his own midmorning coffee wasn't a chore but a welcome interruption of the work, to which he went back refreshed. He was translating a passage from Eustathius on Homer that the author cited as early evidence of sexual deviation. Laodamia missed her husband so much when he set sail for the Trojan War that she made a wax statue of him and laid it in the bed beside her.

It was an irony, Ben thought, that the first time he'd been involved since the end of his marriage in any amorous temptation happened to coincide with his translating this disturbingly sexy book. Or did the book disturb him only because of the Lavinia episode? He knew he hadn't been tempted by Lavinia because of the book. And when he went out for his walk that afternoon he understood that he was no longer tempted; the memory of her, even the dream, had no power to stir him. All that was past.

But it—and perhaps the book—had awakened his long-dormant sexuality. He had lingered longer than he needed over the passage where Laodamia's husband, killed in the war, comes back as a ghost and inhabits as her lover the wax image. It had left him prey to an undefined, aimless, undirected desire.

That evening his diary entry was full of sexual imagery. And when he slept he dreamed flamboyantly, the dreams full of color, teeming with luscious images, none approximating anything he'd known in life. Throughout the day he was restless, working automatically, distracted by sounds from outside: birdsong, a car passing along the road, the arrival of Sandy, and then by the noise of the lawn mower. He couldn't bring himself to ask what had happened to Lavinia. He didn't speak to Sandy at all, disregarding the man's waves and smiles and other meaningless signals.

It occurred to him when he was getting up the next Monday that Lavinia might come. She might have been ill on Friday or otherwise prevented from coming. Perhaps those signs that Sandy had made to him had indicated a wish to impart some sort of information about Lavinia. It was an unpleasant thought. He dreaded the sight of her.

He had already begun work on the author's analysis of a suggestion that the real Helen had fled to Egypt while it was only a simulacrum that Paris took to Troy, when distantly he heard the back door open and close and footsteps cross the tiles. It was not Lavinia's tread; these were not

Lavinia's movements. For a moment he feared Sandy's entry into his room, Sandy with an explanation or, worse, Sandy *asking* for an explanation. Somehow he felt that was possible.

Instead a girl came in, a different girl. She didn't knock. She walked into his room without the least diffidence, confidently, as if it were her right.

"I'm Susannah, I've taken over from Lavinia. You won't mind, will you? We didn't think you'd mind. It's not as if it will make a scrap of difference."

•   •   •

I know the girl he meant, this Susannah. Or I think I do, though perhaps it's one of her sisters that I know, that I have seen in the village outside her parents' house. Her father was one of those rarities not native to the place, but a newcomer when he married her mother, a man for some reason acceptable and even welcomed. There were a few of such people, perhaps four. As for the girl...

"She was so beautiful," he said.

"There are a lot of good-looking people in the village," I said. "In fact, there's no one you could even call ordinarily plain. They're a handsome lot."

He went on as if I hadn't spoken. Her beauty struck him forcibly from that first moment. She had golden looks, film-star looks. If that had a vulgar sound, I was to remember that this particular appearance was only associated with Hollywood *because* it was the archetype, because no greater beauty could be found than the tall blonde with the full lips, straight nose, and large blue eyes, the plump breasts and narrow hips and long legs. Susannah had all that and a smile of infinite sweetness.

"And she didn't throw herself at me," he said. "She cleaned the house and made me coffee and she wasn't—well, servile, the way Lavinia was. She smiled. She talked to me when she brought the coffee and before she left, and she talked sensibly and simply, just about how she'd cycled to the house and the fine weather and her dad giving her a Walkman for her birthday. It was nice. It was *sweet*. Perhaps one of the best things was that she didn't mention Sandy. And there was something *curative* about her coming. I didn't dream the dreams again, and as for Lavinia—Lavinia vanished. From my thoughts, I mean. That weekend I felt something quite new to me: contentment. I worked. I was satisfied with my rendering of *The Golden Apple.* I was going to be all right. I didn't even mind Sandy turning up on Sunday and cleaning all the windows inside and out."

"Young Susannah must be a marvel if she could do all that," I said.

He didn't exactly shiver, but he hunched his shoulders as if he was cold. In a low voice he began to read from his diary entries.

3

She seemed very young to him. The next time she came and the next he wanted to ask her how old she was, but he had a natural aversion to asking that question of anyone. He looked at her breasts—he couldn't help himself; they were so beautiful, so perfect. The shape of a young woman's breasts was like nothing else on earth, he said, there was nothing they could be compared to and all comparison was vulgar pornography.

At first he told himself he looked at them so because he was curious about her age—was she sixteen or seventeen or more?—but that wasn't the reason, that was self-deception. She dressed in modest clothes, or at least in clothes that covered most of her—a high-necked T-shirt, a long skirt—but he could tell she wore nothing underneath, nothing at all. Her navel showed as a shallow declivity in the clinging cotton of the skirt, and the material was lifted by her mount of Venus (his words, not mine). When he thought of these things as well as when he looked, the blood pumped loudly in his head and his throat constricted. She wore sandals that were no more than thongs, which left her small, high-instepped feet virtually bare.

It never occurred to him at that time that he was the object of some definite strategy. His mind was never crossed even by the suspicion that Susannah might have taken Lavinia's place because he'd made it plain he didn't find Lavinia desirable; that it would be most exceptional for two young girls, coming to work for him in succession, to both—immediately—make attempts to fascinate him, indeed to seduce him.

There should have been no doubt in his mind, after all, for all he had said about Susannah not throwing herself at him, that in the ordinary usages of society a girl doesn't come to work for and be alone with a man stark naked under her skirt and top unless she is extending an invitation.

But he didn't see it. He saw the movement of her breasts under that thin stuff, but he saw only innocence. He saw the cotton stretched across her belly, close as a second skin, and put down her choice of dressing like this to juvenile naïveté. The blame for it was his—and Lavinia's. Lavinia, he told himself, had awakened an amorousness in him that he would have been happy never to feel again. Instead, he had lost all peace and contentment; with her stupid coyness, her posturing and her clothes, she had robbed him of that. And now he was in thrall to this beautiful, simple, and innocent girl.

She was subtle. Not for her the blatant raising of her arms above her head to reach a high shelf, still less the climbing onto a chair or up a pair of steps, stuff of soft pornography. He asked her to sit and have her coffee with him and she demurred but finally agreed, and she sat so modestly, taking extravagant care to cover not only her knees but her legs, almost to those exquisite ankles. She even tucked her skirt round her legs and tucked it tightly, thus revealing—he was sure in utter innocence— as much as she concealed. While she talked about her family—her mother, who had been a Kirkman, her father, who came from a hundred miles away, from Yorkshire, her big sister and her little sister—she must have seen the direction his eyes took, for she folded her arms across her breasts.

It dismayed him. He wasn't that sort of man. Before his wife he had had girlfriends, but there had been nothing casual, no pickups, no one-night stands. He might almost have said he had never made love to a woman without being, or in a fair way to being, in love with her. But this feeling he had was lust. He was sure that it had nothing to do with "being in love," though it was as strong and as powerful as love. And it was her beauty alone that was to blame—he said "to blame"—for he couldn't have said if he liked her; liking didn't come into it. Her appearance, her presence, the aura of her stunned him but at the same time had him desperately staring. It was an amazement to him that others didn't see that desperation.

Not that there were others, with the exception, of course, of Sandy.

While Ben was working, Sandy, if he was outside, would sometimes appear at the window to smile and point up his thumbs. Ben would be working on some abstruse lining up of Jungian archetypes with Helen and Achilles and be confronted by Sandy's grinning face. If the weather was fine enough for the window to be open, Sandy would put his head inside and inquire if everything was all right.

"Things going okay, are they?"

Ben moved upstairs. He took his word processor and his dictionary into a back bedroom with an inaccessible window. And all this time he thought these people were my servants, "help" paid by me to wait on him. He couldn't dismiss them, he felt, or even protest. I was charging him no rent; he paid only for his electricity and the telephone. It would have seemed to him the deepest ingratitude and impertinence to criticize my choice. Yet if he had been free to do so he would have got rid of not only Sandy but Susannah also. He could scarcely bear her in his presence. Yet he wondered what grayness and emptiness would replace her.

I must not give the impression that all of this went on for long. No more than three weeks, perhaps, before the change came and his world was overturned. He thought afterward that the change was helped along by his taking his work upstairs. She might not have done what she did if he had been in the room on the ground floor with its view of the lake— affording a view to other people driving by the lake and to window-cleaning, lawn-mowing, flower-bed-weeding Sandy.

She always came into his room to tell him when she was leaving. He had reached the point where the sound of her footsteps ascending the stairs heated his body and set his blood pounding. The screen of the word processor clouded over, and his hands shook above the keyboard. That's how bad it was.

One of the things that terrified him was that she might touch him. Playfully, or in simple friendliness, she might lay her hand on his arm or even, briefly, take his hand. She never had; she wasn't a "toucher." But if she did, he didn't know what he would do. He felt he couldn't be responsible for his own actions; he might do something outrageous or his body, without his volition, something shameful. The strange thing was that in all this it never seemed to have occurred to him that she might want *him,* or at least be acquiescent. She came into the room. His desire blazed out of him, but he was long beyond controlling it.

"I'll be off then, sir."

How he hated that "sir"! It must be stopped and stopped now, whatever I might require from my "help."

"Please don't call me that. Call me Ben."

It came from him like a piteous cry. He might have been crying to her that he had a mortal illness or that someone close to him was dead.

"Ben," she said. "Ben." She said it as if it were new to her or distantly exotic instead of, as he put it, the name of half the pet dogs in the district. "I like it." And then she said, "Are you all right?"

"It doesn't matter," he said. "Ignore me."

"Why would I want to do that, Ben?"

The burr in her voice was suddenly more pronounced. She spoke in a radio rustic's accent. Perhaps she had experience of men in Ben's condition; probably it was a common effect of her presence, for she knew exactly what was wrong with him. What was *right* with him?

She said, "Come here."

He got up, mesmerized, not yet believing, a long way still from believing. But she took his hands and laid them on her breasts. It was her way to do that, to take his hands to those soft hidden parts of her body where she most liked to feel his touch. She put her mouth up to his mouth, the tip of her tongue on his tongue; she stood on tiptoe, lifting her pelvis against him. Then, with a nod, with a smile, she took him by the hand and led him into his bedroom.

4

Before Ben went to Gothic House it had been arranged that I should go down myself for a weekend in June. I'd decided to put the house on the market as soon as Ben left, and there were matters to see to, such as what I was going to do about the furniture, which of it I wanted to keep and which to sell. As the time grew near I felt less and less like going. To have his company would be good—perhaps rather more than that—but I could have his company in London. It was the place I didn't care to be in. In the time I'd been away from it my aversion had grown. If that was possible, I felt even worse about it than when I'd last been there.

At this time, of course, I knew almost nothing of what Ben was doing. We'd spoken on the phone just once after the nightingale conversation, and he had said only that the change of air was doing him good and the translation was going well. The girls weren't mentioned and neither was

Sandy, so I knew nothing of Susannah beyond what I'd seen of her some two or three years before.

That was when I'd had my encounters with her parents. Peddar, they were called, and they had three young daughters, Susannah, Carol, and another one whose name I couldn't remember. I couldn't even remember which was the eldest and which the youngest. Of course I have plenty of cause to do so now. I'd been to the village quite a lot by that time and even taken a small part in village life, attended a social in the village hall and gone to Marion Kirkman's daughter's wedding.

The villagers were guarded at first, then gradually friendlier. Just what one would expect. I went to the wedding and to the party afterward. In spite of all that has happened since, I still think it was the nicest wedding I've ever been to, the best party, the handsomest guests, the best food, the greatest joy. Everyone was tremendously nice to me. If I had the feeling that I was closely watched, rather as if the other people there were studying me for a social survey, I put that down to imagination. They were curious, that was all. They were probably shy of my middle-classness, for I had noticed by that time that there were no professional people in the village: agricultural laborers, mechanics, shopworkers, and cleaners (who went to their jobs elsewhere), plumbers, electricians, builders, thatchers and pargeters, a hairdresser, and, because even there modern life intruded, a computer technician, but no one who worked otherwise than with his or her hands.

I think now I was a fool. I should have kept myself to myself. I should have resisted the seductions of friendliness and warmth. Instead, because I'd accepted hospitality, I decided to give a party. It would be a Sunday-morning drinks party, after church. I invited everyone who had invited me and a good many who hadn't but whom I had met at other people's gatherings. Sandy offered to serve the drinks and in the event did so admirably.

They came and the party happened. Everyone was charming; everyone seemed to know that if you go to a party you should endeavor to be entertaining, to talk, to listen, to appear carefree. What was lacking was middle-class sophistication, and it was a welcome omission. The party resulted in an invitation, just one, from the Peddars, who delivered it as they were leaving, a written invitation in an envelope, evidently prepared beforehand with great care. Would I come to supper the following

Friday? And I need not bother to drive: John Peddar would collect me and take me home.

It must have been about that time that I noticed another oddity—if good manners and friendliness can be called that—about the village and its people. I'd already, of course, observed my own resemblance to the general appearance of them, a sort of look we had in common. I was tall and fair with blue eyes, and so were they. Not that they were all the same, not clonelike, I don't mean that. Some were shorter, some less slender; eyes varied from midnight blue through turquoise to palest sky and hair from flaxen to light brown; but they had a certain look of all belonging to the same tribe. Danes used to look like that, I was once told, before the influx of immigrants and visitors; if you sat outside a café on Strøhet you saw all these blue-eyed blondes pass by, all looking like members of a family. Thus it was in the village, as if their gene pool was small, and I might have been one of them.

So might Ben, though I didn't think of it then. Why should I?

I wrote a note to the Peddars, saying I'd be pleased to come on Friday.

• • •

It sounds very cowardly, what I'm about to say. Well, it will have to sound that way. Although I'd much have preferred to postpone going to Gothic House till the Saturday, I'd told Ben I'd come on the Friday, and I kept to that. But I drove down in the evening so as to pass through the village in the dark, and since, in June, it didn't start getting dark till after nine-thirty, I was late arriving.

I braced myself, even took a deep breath, as I reached the corner where the first house was, some half mile from the rest, Mark and Kathy Gresham's house. There were lights on but no windows open, though it was a warm night. I drove on quickly. A dozen or so teenagers had assembled with their bikes by the bus shelter; they were the only people about. The light from the single lamp in the village street shone on their fair hair. They turned as one as I passed, recognizing the car, but not one of them waved.

An estate agent's For Sale board was up outside the Old Rectory. So the farmer from Lynn hadn't been able to stand it either. Or they hadn't been able to stand him. I slowed and, certain no one was about, stopped. No lights were on in the big handsome Georgian house. It was in darkness and it was deserted. You can always tell from the outside if a house is empty—no wonder burglars are so successful.

No doubt he spent as little time there as possible. He hadn't been there long, perhaps two years, and I'd known him only by sight, a big dark man with a pretty blond wife, much younger than he. As I started the car again I wondered what they had done to him and why.

The sky was clear but moonless. In the dark, glassy lake whole constellations were reflected and a single bright planet shining like a torch held under the water. A little wind had got up, and the woodland trees rustled their heavy weight of leaves. In my headlights Gothic House had its fairy-tale-castle look, gray but bright, its lighted windows orange oblongs with arched tops, the crenellated crown of the turret the only part of it reflected in the water. Ben and I had never kissed. But now he took me in his arms and kissed me with great affection.

"Louise, how wonderful that you're here. Welcome to your own house!"

I thought him a changed man.

. . .

It was only half an hour since Susannah had left him and gone home to her father's house. He told me that while we sat drinking whiskey at the window with its view of the lake. The moon had risen, a bright full moon whose radiance was nearly equal to winter sunshine. Its silver-green light painted the tree trunks like lichen.

"Susannah Peddar?" I was finding an awkwardness in saying it, already remembering.

"Why the surprise?" he said. "You employ her. And, come to that, Sandy."

I told him I used to employ Sandy but no longer. As for Susannah. . . . She wasn't quite the last person from that village I'd have wanted in my house, but nearly. I didn't say that. I said I was glad he'd found someone to look after him. He went on talking about her, already caught up in the lover's need to utter repeatedly the beloved's name, but I didn't know that then. I only wondered why he dwelt so obsessively on the niceness, the cleverness, and the beauty of someone I still thought of as a village teenager.

That night he said nothing of what had happened between them but went off to bed in a pensive mood, still astonished that Susannah wasn't employed by me. I, who had been relaxed, moving into a quiet sleepy frame of mind, was now unpleasantly wide awake, and I lay sleepless for a long time, thinking of the Peddars and of other things.

•   •   •

The evening with John and Iris Peddar was very much what I'd expected it would be, or the early part was. They lived in one of the newer houses, originally a council house, but they had done a great deal of work on it, building an annex and turning the two downstairs rooms into one.

I'd calculated, in my middle-class way, my deeply English class-conscious way, that they would dress up for me. He would wear a suit, she a dress with fussy jewelry, and the three little girls frilly frocks. So I decided to dress up for them and did that rare thing, wore a dress and stockings and shoes with heels. When John Peddar arrived to collect me I was surprised to see him in jeans and an open-necked check shirt but supposed that he intended to change when we got to his house.

Everyone looks better in informal clothes, in my opinion. Something of the absurd is inseparable from gowns and jewels and men's dark suits. But I didn't expect them to feel this. I was astonished when Iris came out to greet me in jeans and a striped T-shirt. The children too wore what they'd worn at school that day, or what they'd changed into after the greater formality of school.

Even now, knowing what I know, I marvel at the psychology of it, at their knowledge of people and taste. They *knew* I wouldn't necessarily be easier with them dressed like that, but that I would unquestionably find one or all of them more attractive. They were a good-looking family, John especially—tall, thin, fair, with a fine-featured face and inquiring eyes, eyebrows that went up often, as if commenting with secret laughter on the outrageous. Iris was pretty, with commonplace Barbie-doll looks, but the three little girls were all beauties, two of them golden blondes who favored their father, the third unlike either parent, the image of a Millais child with nut-brown hair and soulful eyes.

We drank sherry before the meal. John drank as much as Iris and I did and as much wine. I think I must have known by that time that in the village you drank as much as you liked before driving. The police who drove their little car around the streets every so often would never stop a villager, still less breath-test him. Two P.C.'s lived here, after all, and one was Jennifer Fowler's brother.

We had avocado with prawns, chicken casserole, and chocolate mousse. That, at any rate, was what I'd expected. The children went to bed, the eldest one last, as was fair. Iris called me upstairs to see her bedroom, which she and John had newly decorated, and I went—it was still light, though dusk, the soft violet dusk that comes to woodland places—and there, while I admired the wallpaper, she tucked her arm into mine and stood close up against me.

It was friendliness, the warm outgoing attitude of one woman to another that she finds congenial. So I thought as she squeezed my arm and pressed her body against mine. She had had a great deal to drink. Her inhibitions had gone down. I still thought that when she moved her arm to my shoulders and, slowly turning me to her, brought her lips to within an inch of mine. I stepped aside, I managed a small laugh. I was anxious, terribly anxious in that moment, to avoid her doing anything she might bitterly regret the next morning. We all know the feeling of waking to horrified memory, to the what-have-I-done self-inquiry that sets the blood pounding.

About an hour later he drove me home. She was all pleasantness and charm, begging me to come again, it was delightful that we'd got to know each other at last. This time I had no choice but to allow the kiss; it was no more than a cool pecking of the air around my cheek. John showed no signs of the amount he'd drunk. But neither, then, had she, apart from that bedroom overture I was sure now came from nothing more than a sudden impulse of finding she liked me.

In the car, sitting beside me, he told me I was a beautiful woman. It made me feel uncomfortable. All possible rejoinders were either coy or vulgar, so I said nothing. He drove me home and said he'd come in with me—he wouldn't allow me to go alone into a dark, empty house. It was late, I said, I was tired. All the more reason for him to come in with me. Once inside I put on a lot of lights, and I offered him a drink. He had seated himself comfortably, as if at home.

"Won't Iris wonder where you are?"

He looked at me and those eyebrows rose. "I don't think she will."

It was clear what he meant. I was revolted. His intrigues must be so habitual that his wife accepted with resignation that if he was late home he was with a woman. It explained her overture to me, a gesture born of loneliness and rejection.

He began talking about her, how he would never do anything to hurt her or imperil their marriage. Nothing *could* imperil it, he insisted. Most women have heard that sort of thing from men at some time or other; it is standard philanderer-speak. Yet if he hadn't said it, if he'd been a little different, less knowing, less confident, and, yes, less rustic, I might have felt his attraction, at least the attraction of his looks. I'd have done nothing because of her, but I might have felt like doing something. As it was, I was simply contemptuous. But I didn't want trouble, I didn't want a scene. Was I afraid of him? Perhaps a little. He was a tall, strong man who had had a lot to drink, and I was alone with him.

In the end, when he'd had a second whiskey, I stood up and said I was desperately tired, I was going to have to turn him out. I know now that physical violence was quite foreign to his nature, but I didn't then, and I hated it when he put his hand under my chin, lifted my face, and kissed me. You could just—only just—have called it a friendly, social kiss.

Just as Ben was later to have those dreams, so did I. Something in the air? Or, more subtly, the atmosphere of the place? The first of my dreams was that night. John Peddar was different in the dream, looking the same but more my kind of man. *Civilized* is the word that comes to mind, yet it's not quite the right one. Gentler, more sensitive, less crude in his approach. I suppose that the I who was dreaming arranged all that, but whatever it was I didn't repulse him; I began to make love with him, I began to enjoy him in a luxuriating way, until the dawn chorus of birds awoke me with their singing.

He came back in the morning—the real man, not the dream image.

It was a dull morning of heavy cloud. I've said the sky was always clear and the sun always shining, but of course it wasn't. All that is fantasy, myth, and magic. The house was quite dark inside. Before the dream came I had slept badly. That was the beginning of sleeping badly at Gothic House, of bad nights and, later, total insomnia. I came downstairs in my dressing gown, thinking it must be Sandy at the door. He came in and— I don't know how to put this—took the door out of my hands, took my hands from it, closed it himself, and shot the bolt across it.

I was taken aback by this appropriation of actions that should be exclu-

sively mine. I stared. He took me into his arms in a curious caressing gesture, a sweeping of light gentle hands down my arms, my body, my
thighs. He drew me close to him, murmuring "darling" and "darling"
again and "sweetheart," his voice thick and breathless. Before his mouth
could touch mine I pushed him away with a great shove, and he staggered
back against the wall.

"Please go," I said. "I can't stand this. Please go."

I expected trouble, excuses that I'd invited him, defenses that he could
sense my desire, accusations finally of frigidity. But there was nothing. For
a moment he looked at me inquiringly. Then he nodded as if something
suspected had been confirmed. He even smiled. My front door, which he
had previously taken possession of, he opened; he let himself out and
closed it quietly and very carefully behind him.

• • •

Ben told me about Susannah. He told me all those things I have already
told you and more than that. We sat out in the garden. There was a stone
table, a bench, and chairs on the lawn in front of the house under a mul-
berry tree, and we sat there in the heat of the day. The fallen fruit lay
about on the grass like spoonfuls of crimson jam.

The tree gave enough shade to make sitting there pleasant. You could
no more look at the lake than you could at a mirror with the full sun shining on it. A few cars passed along the road, village people off to shop in
the town supermarkets, and the drivers waved. At Ben, of course; they
wouldn't wave at me. He told me how his early lovemaking with
Susannah had become a full-blown love affair.

No inhibition held him back from telling me about it. He had to tell
someone. I'd never known him so open, so revelatory.

"I'm glad it's making you happy," I said.

What lies we tell for the sake of social accord!

"It won't last, of course, I know that. It's entirely physical." (I'm always
skeptical when people say that. What do they mean? Do they know what
they mean?) "She's years younger than I am."

"Yes." Oh, yes, she was. "How old *is* she?"

"Eighteen, I suppose."

"And you wouldn't"—I tried to put it tactfully—"exactly call her an
educated person, would you?"

"What does that matter? I'm not going to marry her, I'm not going to settle down with her for life. It's not as if I were in love with her. I'm having—oh, something I've never had with anyone in my life before, something I've only read about: pure, uncomplicated, beautiful sex. Sex without questions, without pain, without consequences. It's as if we're mythical beings at the beginning of the world, we're Paris and Helen, mutually exulting in the sweetest and most innocent pleasure known to mankind."

"My goodness," I said.

"I suppose you think that very high-flown, Louise, but it's an accurate expression of my feelings."

Why didn't I warn him then? Why didn't I tell him about Susannah's father and Sandy and Roddy Fowler and meetings in the village hall? Or my suspicions about the farmer's wife from Lynn? Quite simply because I thought *the difference of gender made the difference.* He was a man. I thought men would be exempt. But later that day, after I'd made a rough inventory of the furniture I'd keep and noted the few small repairs the house needed before it could be put up for sale, I found myself looking at him, assessing things about him.

I was very fond of him, had started to grow fond after he'd separated from his wife, but it was very much for his mind and his manner. His gentleness pleased me, as did his thoughtfulness, his sensitivity and modesty. Pointless to pretend that he was much to look at, though I liked his looks, the intelligence in his face and the perceptiveness, his expressions of understanding and of pondering. But he was somewhat below medium height and very thin, with an unfit, slack-muscled thinness. He looked older than his age—thirty-seven? thirty-eight?—and his face was lined as thin, fair faces soon become with time, his hair fast receding.

I knew what I saw in him but not what Susannah did. The older man, perhaps, a father figure, though she had a perfectly adequate father of her own, very little older than Ben. They marry early in the village. But who can account for love? Even for attraction?

We went out for our dinner that evening to a restaurant ten miles away. During the meal he asked me if he should be paying Sandy. Wasn't there something wrong about Sandy working for him without payment?

"If you don't pay him," I said, "maybe he'll get the message and go away. He's a pest and a nuisance." I said nothing about Sandy's attempts to make love to me after the John Peddar incident and my outrage. I would have if I'd thought it would make a difference.

"But for him," he said, "I suppose I'd never have met Susannah."

He would have, but I didn't know it then.

"When are you seeing her again?" I meant this joke question seriously, and that was how he took it.

"On Monday morning. It's a bit awkward her going on cleaning the house, and paying her is very awkward. I shall have to try to get someone else. Of course we meet in the evenings—well, she comes to the house. I can't exactly go to her father's house."

I had nothing to say to that. From what I knew of her father's house, an orgy in the front room in broad daylight wouldn't have been unacceptable. I had revised my sympathy for Iris when at a village dance she had tried to introduce me, with unmistakable motive, to her younger unattached brother, Roddy. For some reason the Peddar family had done their best to find me a sexual partner, and apparently anyone would do, if not either of them or a relation of theirs, some other villager. Sandy, I supposed, had been put up to it by them. After all, I knew him already, and in their eyes perhaps that was the only necessary prerequisite.

While showing me something he'd done in the garden he'd put his arm around me. I'd told him not to do that. He'd looked sideways at me and asked why not.

"Because," I'd said. "Because I don't want you to. Isn't that enough?"

"Come on, Louise, it's not natural, a nice-looking woman like yourself, never with a man."

"None of this is any business of yours." How ridiculous one sounds when offended!

"Is it women that you fancy? You can say, you needn't be shy. I know about those things, I've been around."

"You needn't be around here anymore, that's for sure," I'd said. "I don't want you working for me any longer. Please go and don't come back."

Ben wouldn't have been interested in any of that, so I didn't tell him. We went home to Gothic House, and next day I said I thought I might put it on the market at the end of August.

"You'll have finished your translation by then, won't you?"

"Yes, I'm sure I will." He looked rather dismayed. "I said three months, didn't I? It's so beautiful here, and the situation of the house, this village—won't you regret getting rid of it?"

"I come here so seldom," I said, "it's really not worth keeping it up."

5

It was strange how seldom those people went out in the evenings. They visited each other, I know that now, but they hardly ever left the village after six. I spent two weeks there once, when I was trying to teach myself to like the place, and not a single car passed along the road by the lake in the evenings. I might not have seen cars if they had passed, but I would have seen the beams from their headlights sweep across my ceilings. They stayed at home. They preferred their isolation.

I believe I was their principal concern at that time. No doubt they had a meeting in the village hall, called especially for the discussion of *me*. I'd blundered into one of those meetings one night, having mistaken it for a teenage fund-raiser for cancer research. Utter silence had prevailed as I'd walked in; they had heard or sensed my coming. Mark Gresham had come down the hall to me, explained my mistake, and escorted me out with such care and exquisite politeness that the thinnest skinned couldn't have taken offense.

Sometimes, in those days, the last of those days, the watchers in the windows waved to me. There was never any question of concealing from me that they *were* watching. They waved or they smiled and nodded. And then, suddenly, all smiles and waving ceased, all friendliness came to an end. When Ben came down for that weekend and we saw the bathers, they were still amiably inclined toward me. Next time I came everything had changed, and the antagonism was almost palpable.

• • •

Ben fell in love with her.

Perhaps he'd really been in love from the first but had refused to allow himself to admit it, and all that insistence on matters between them being "entirely physical" was self-deception. Whatever it was, by the middle of

July he was in love—"deeply in, in up to my neck," as he told me—
utterly, obsessively, committed to love.

Not that he told me *then*. That came much later. At the time, though I
heard from him, he did not mention Susannah. He wrote to ask if I was
sincere about selling Gothic House and if I was, would I sell it to him. His
former wife had found a buyer for the home they had shared, and under
the terms of the divorce settlement half the proceeds were to be his.
Gothic House might, even so, be beyond his means, and if this was the
case he would look for some cottage in the village. In a mysterious,
oblique sentence he wrote that he thought "living elsewhere might not be
acceptable to everyone concerned."

Why live there? He was a Londoner. He had lived abroad but never
other than in a big city. The answer was that in the short time he'd been
there he'd become very attached to the place. He loved it. How could he
return to London and its painful memories? As a translator he could live
anywhere. The village was a place in which he thought he could be happy
as he had never been before.

Perhaps I was slow, but I attached no particular significance to any of
this. The truth was that I felt it awkward. It was a principle of mine,
which had never before needed to be acted on, that one does not sell a
house, a car, or any large valuable item or object, maybe anything at all,
to a friend. The passing of money will break the friendship, or that was
the theory.

I waited a few days before replying. The seriousness of this, the pro-
jected sale or refusal to sell, caused me to write rather than phone. If I
had phoned I might have learned more. But at last I wrote to say that, as
I'd told him, I wasn't intending to sell yet. Let us wait till the end of
August. Didn't he really need more time before committing himself? If
by then he still wanted to live in the village and still wanted Gothic
House, then we could talk about it.

No answer came to my letter. I found out later that Ben, exasperated
by my delaying tactics, had gone the next day to an estate agent to inquire
about cottages. He didn't much care what he lived in, what roof was over
his head, so long as he could live there with Susannah.

When it was all over and we were talking, when he poured out his
heart to me, he told me that love had come to him in a moment, with an

absolute suddenness. From being a contented man with a beautiful young lover whose body he enjoyed more than perhaps he'd ever enjoyed any woman's, he became lost, at once terrified and exalted, obsessed, alone, and desperate. Yet it came to him when she was out of his sight, when she was at home in her father's house.

They had made love in his bed at Gothic House, had eaten a meal and drunk wine and gone back to bed to make love again. And then quite late, but not as late as midnight, he had done what he was now in the habit of doing: he had driven her home, discreetly dropping her at the end of the street. Useless, all this secrecy, as I could have told him. Everyone would have known. They would have known from the first kiss that passed between those two. But to him the love affair was a secret that—since almost as soon as he recognized his feelings for what they truly were, he wanted everything out in the open—he wanted the world to know.

He walked about the house, putting dishes in the sink, drinking the last of the wine, and suddenly he found himself longing for her. A pain caught him in the chest and shoulders. Like a heart attack, he said, or what he imagined a heart attack would be. He hugged himself in his arms. He sat down and said aloud, "I'm in love and I know I've never been in love before."

The pain flowed out of him and left him tired and spent. He was filled with what he called "a glory." He saw her in his mind's eye, naked and smiling, coming to him so sweetly, so tenderly, to put her arms around him and touch him with her lips. The wrench of it was so bad that he said he didn't know how he continued to sit there, how he resisted jumping in the car and rushing back to her, beating on her father's door to demand her release into his arms. And he did get up but only to pace the room, the house, speaking her name, *Susannah,* and uttering into that silent place, "I love you, oh, I love you."

The next day he told her. She seemed surprised. "I know," she said.

"You know?" He gazed at her, holding her hands. "How clever you are, my love, my sweetheart, to know what I didn't know. Do you love *me?* Can you love me?"

She said with the utmost tranquillity, "I've always loved you. From the first. Of course I love you."

"Do you, darling Susannah?"

"Did you think I'd have done those things we've done if I didn't love you?"

He was chastened. He should have known. She was no Lavinia. Yet I suppose some caution, some vestige of prudence or perhaps just his age and the remembrance of his marriage, prevented his asking her there and then to marry him. For that was what he had wanted from the first moment of his realization, to marry her. It was what you did, he said to me, when you were in love like that, irrevocably, profoundly; you didn't want any trial time, you wanted commitment for life. Besides, she was half his age, she was very young; it wasn't as if he were a fellow teenager and the two of them experimenting with passion. Honorably, he must marry her.

"But you didn't ask her?" I said.

"Not then. I intended to wait a week. She was so sweet that week, Louise, so loving, I can't tell you how giving she was, how passionate. Of course I wouldn't tell you, it's not something I'd speak of. I wrote some of it down in my diary. You can see the diary. Why should I care now?"

She had shown him, when they made love, things he wouldn't have suspected she knew. Things he had hardly known himself. She was adventurous and entirely uninhibited. He was even, once, quite shocked.

"Oh, I wouldn't do it," she said serenely, "if I didn't love you so much."

She still came to clean the house. His suggestion that it was no longer suitable, that he must find someone else, was met with incredulity, with laughter. Of course she would come to clean the house, and she did so, regularly, without fail. Only sometimes she came to him away from her work to kiss him or hold her arms around his neck and lay her cheek sweetly against his.

It was a Saturday when she made that remark about loving him so much, and he expected her on the Monday morning. No, that is to put it too tamely. He hadn't seen her for thirty hours, and he yearned for her. Waiting for the appointed hour, eight-thirty, he paced the house, watching for her from window after window.

She didn't come.

After a half-hour of hell—in which he speculated every possible disaster, a road accident, her father's wrath—when he at last decided he must phone the Peddars' house, Lavinia came.

She had no explanation to offer him beyond saying Susannah couldn't be there and had sent her as a substitute. Susannah had come around to her mother's very early and asked if Lavinia would do the Gothic House duty that day. Only today? he had asked, and she said as far as she knew. She, at any rate, doubted if she would be coming again herself. But when she said this she gave him one of her coy looks over her thin, white shoulder, somehow making him understand that future visits could happen, might be contingent on his response. He was disgusted and angry. He did his best to ignore her, put her money downstairs on the kitchen table, and fled to his room upstairs. Susannah would come that evening; they had an arrangement for her to come at seven, and then all would be well, all would be explained.

Soon after Lavinia left, the estate agent phoned. A cottage had just been put on the market. It was in the heart of the village. Would he be interested? If so, the estate agent would meet him outside the cottage at three and show him around. The owner was a Mrs. Fowler, an old lady growing infirm, who intended to move in with her son and his wife.

Ben walked to the village. It was a lovely day. The sun was brighter for him than for others, the lake bluer and its waters more sparkling, the flowers in the gardens more scented and more brilliant and the air sweeter—because he was in love. Sometimes "the glory" came back to him, and when that happened he wanted to leap and sing, he wanted to prostrate himself on the ground and cry aloud to whoever or whatever had given him the joy of love, had given him Susannah. All this was in his diary. A phrase from the Bible kept coming back to him: "And sorrow and sighing shall flee away." He said it to himself as he walked along—there shall be no more pain, and sorrow and sighing shall flee away. He didn't think the word in the text was "pain," but he couldn't really remember.

Mrs. Fowler's was a tiny cottage, two up and two down, with a thatched roof. The frowsty little bedroom—low-ceilinged, the floor piled with layers of rugs, the bed with layers of dingy whitish covers, fringed or lacy, and now inhabited by sleeping cats—he saw as it would be when transformed, when occupied by himself and Susannah. A four-poster they would have, he thought, and he imagined her kneeling naked on the quilt, drawing back the curtains to disclose herself to him, the two of them sinking embraced into that silky, shadowy, scented warmth...

He looked out of the window and faces looked back at him, one in each of the windows opposite. A curtain dropped; another pair of eyes appeared. Mrs. Fowler said comfortably, "Everyone likes to know your business down here."

She was a tiny, upright woman, still handsome in extreme age, hawk-faced and no doubt hawk-eyed, those eyes a sparkling pale turquoise.

"My granddaughter does for you," she said.

He thought for some reason she meant Lavinia, but she didn't.

"Susannah Peddar."

There was the suspicion of a smile at the corners of her mouth when she said the name. She looked conspiratorial. In that moment he longed to tell her. An overpowering desire to tell her seized him, to come out with it. He wanted to say that this was why he needed a house in the village, a home to which he could bring his bride, a bower for Susannah, among her own people, a stone's throw from her mother. How splendid it was, how serendipitous, that the very house in the whole village that might seem almost home to Susannah was the one he could buy.

He managed to suppress that desire, but all ideas of purchasing Gothic House vanished. This was the house for him, the only one. He would have offered her double what she was asking, anything to possess it and present it to Susannah. Probably it was as well he had been cautioned only to make his offer through the estate agent.

"At least I was saved from making a total fool of myself," he wrote in his diary.

The agent, he discovered, had his own home in the village. He was a villager born and bred. Mrs. Fowler would very likely take an offer, he said. Anyway, there would be no harm in trying.

"I wouldn't want to lose it," Ben said.

The estate agent smiled. "No fear of that. Think about it and come back to me."

Rather late in the day Ben reflected that he should have asked Susannah first. She should have been asked if she wanted to live in a house that had belonged to her grandmother. He would ask her that night. He would propose marriage to her and he had no doubt she would accept, since she had told him she loved him. Then he'd tell her about the cottage. She was, he told himself, a simple country girl. Of course she was a goddess, his Helen and Oenone and Aphrodite, an ideal woman, a queen, the perfect paramour, but she was a country girl also, only eighteen, and one who would have no latter-day urban preferences for cohabitation over marriage or any nonsense of that sort.

At seven-thirty she still hadn't come. He was mad with worry and terror. He didn't want to phone her father's house; he'd never done so, and he'd got it into his head—without any evidence for so doing—that the Peddars disapproved of him. Perhaps she was ill. He had a moment's comfort from thinking that. (Thus do lovers console themselves, deriving peace of mind from the beloved's incapacity.) He had forgotten for the moment that she had gone out "very early" to Lavinia's house, hardly the behavior of someone too ill to go to work. He would phone, he had to.

Her voice was always magical to him, soft, sweet, with the lilting accent he had come to hear as pretty and, of course, seductive. He had never heard it on the phone, but somehow he knew that when he did hear it he would be silenced, for seconds he would be unable to reply, he would have to listen, be captured by her voice and feel it run into his blood and take away his breath. He dialed the number and waited, waited for *her.* It was the first time in his life he had ever suffered the awfulness of hearing the ringing tone repeated and repeated while longing, praying, for an answer.

Someone answered at last. It was a young girl's voice, soft, sweet, with that same accent, but without the power to stir him, a voice immediately recognizable as not hers. One of the sisters, he supposed. She didn't say.

"Sue's gone 'round to Kim's."

It sounded like a code to him, a spatter of phonemes. He had to ask her to repeat it.

"Sue," she said more slowly, "has gone 'round to Kim's house, okay?"

"Thank you," he said.

He realized he knew nothing of her friends, nothing of her life away from him. He had supposed her so young and artless as to be satisfied with the company of her parents and her sisters, remaining at home in the evenings until he rescued her from this rustic domesticity. But of course she had friends, girls she had been to school with, the daughters of neighbors. None of that accounted for her failure to come to him, and he racked his mind for reasons. Had he inadvertently said something to hurt her feelings?

Could it be that, after taking thought, she found herself offended by his inquiry as to her sexual adventurousness? But she had replied that she would only do these things with someone she loved and she loved him so much. That had been almost the last thing she had said to him when they'd parted on the previous Friday a hundred yards from her father's house, that she loved him so much. He was driven to think—he *wanted* to think—that it was that father and that mother who, having discovered the truth from Susannah, her heart too full to keep love to herself, had taken a heavy line and sent her to spend the evening not at Gothic House but with a girlfriend.

Night is the enemy of the unhappy lover, for it's then that fearful thoughts come and horrible forebodings. It would have been better if the night had been dull and wet, but it was warm with a yellow moon rising, a moon fattening to the full. He walked out and down to the lake, expecting to hear the nightingales, not knowing that they cease to sing once early June is past. The moonlight was almost golden, laying a pale sheen on the water and on the lilies, closed into buds for the hours of darkness. He wrote about that in his diary, the things he observed and the sounds he heard, a single cry from the woods as of an animal attacked by a fox, a disturbance of lily pads as a roosting moorhen shifted and folded its wings. Above him the sky was a clear bright opal, the stars too weak to show in the light of that moon.

He thought about Susannah, perhaps lying in her bed wakeful and longing for him as he longed for her. He lay down on the dry turf of the shoreline, facedown, his arms outstretched, and whispered her name into the sand, *Susannah, Susannah.*

•   •   •

The following morning he tried to work. Over and over he read the last passage he had translated, of Hecuba's dream that she had given birth to a burning brand that split into coils of fiery serpents. The French text swam before his eyes like tadpoles, meaningless black squiggles. He spent the rest of the day trying to reach Susannah.

He phoned and no one answered. He tried again, and still there was no reply. Her job at Gothic House wasn't the only one she had, he knew that. She cleaned for someone else somewhere, she minded the children of one of the schoolteachers, she washed hair and swept up for the hairdresser who operated from two rooms over the shop. The irony escaped him that in London, in his old life, he would never have considered taking out for a drink a woman who earned her living by performing such menial tasks, still less been intent on marrying her.

He had very little idea when and where she went to these jobs. The hairdresser's perhaps, he could find that number and try that. Anne Whiteson at the shop gave him the number. It was his imagination, it must be, but he had an uncomfortable sense that she knew something he didn't know or was humoring him, was playing along with him in some indefinable way. A great deal to read into a woman's voice asking after his health and giving him a phone number, but, as he said, his imagination was very active, was pulsating with theories and suspicions and terrors.

Susannah wasn't at the hairdresser's. She wasn't expected there till Wednesday afternoon. He phoned her father's house again, and again there was no reply. He imagined phones unplugged by determined parents. Nothing more was done on the translation that day, and in the late afternoon he drove down to her home, anxious, very apprehensive, not in the least wanting to confront John Peddar or Iris but seeing no other way.

A little girl came to the door. That was how he described her, Julie, the youngest one, who must have been fourteen or fifteen but whom he saw as a child.

"They've all gone to the seaside. They won't be back till late."

It wasn't the voice on the phone. He thought she was lying but could hardly tell her so.

"Why didn't you go, then?" This was the nearest to an accusation he could get.

"I was at school, wasn't I?"

By then he had noticed how seldom people left the village but to work or shop. The seaside story strained his credulity. He thought they must all be hidden in the house, Susannah perhaps a prisoner in the house, and that evening, in his misery, he sat in the window watching for the Peddar van to pass along the lake road, that being the way the family would be obliged to return from the coast. But only two cars passed, and they were both sedans.

He dreamed of Susannah, naked and chained like Andromeda, who appeared briefly in the preface to *The Golden Apple,* on her dragon-menaced rock. He struck off the chains and they fell from her at a single blow, but when he took her into his arms and felt the smooth resilience of her breasts and thighs press against him, the flesh began to melt and pour through his hands in a scented, sticky flood, like cream or some cosmetic fluid. He woke up crying out, put his head in his hands, then saw the time and knew that Lavinia would soon come. Or would she? Hadn't she said she had no plans to come on Wednesday? Was it possible that after everything *Susannah* would come?

The girl who let herself into the house and came into the kitchen, where he stood staring, his fists clenched, his teeth set, was the one whose voice he had heard the only time one of his calls was answered.

"Sue won't be coming today."

He said rudely, "Who are you?"

"Carol," she said. "I'm the middle one."

She opened the cupboard where the cleaning things were kept, pulled out the vacuum cleaner, inspected a not very clean duster, and sniffed it. He could hardly believe what he was seeing. It was as if the whole family had united and conspired together to control him, keep an eye on him, *handle* him, and keep him from Susannah. He was a man of thirty-seven, an intellectual, a highly respected linguist taken over by a bunch of peasants of whom this pert sixteen-year-old blonde was the representative. No doubt we say such things to ourselves when we are desperately unhappy and frightened. Ben wouldn't normally have talked about peasants, nor about himself as belonging to an elite. Besides, his Susannah was one of them . . .

"I want an explanation," he said.

She smiled, about to leave the room. "Do you?"

He took her by the wrist. "You have to tell me. I want you to tell me— now. What's going on? Why can't I see Susannah?"

She looked at his hand gripping her wrist. "Let me go."

"All right," he said. "But you can sit down, sit down here at the table, and tell me."

"I came to tell you, as a matter of fact," she said calmly. "I thought I'd get your bits and pieces done and then I'd tell you over a coffee."

"Tell me now."

She smiled comfortably. It was the smile of a woman much older than she was, a middle-aged smile, as of a mother speaking of some gratifying event, a daughter's wedding, for instance. Yet she was a smooth-faced, pink-cheeked adolescent, full-mouthed, her lips as red as lipstick but unpainted, not a line or mark on her velvety skin.

"You can see Sue again, of course you can. There's no question of anything else. But not all the time. You can't"—she brought the word out as if someone had taught it to her that morning—"monopolize her. You can't do that. Don't you see?"

"I don't see anything," he said. "I love Susannah, and she loves me." He might as well tell her. It must all come into the open now. "I want to marry Susannah."

She shrugged. She said the unbelievable thing. "Sue's engaged to Kim Gresham."

His voice almost went. He said hoarsely, "I don't know what you mean."

"Sue's been engaged to Kim for a year now. They'll be getting married in the spring." She got up. "There are plenty of other girls, you know."

6

On a warm September evening I saw the bathers in the lake outside my house. Not the young woman and the two children who'd appeared to us when Ben was staying with me for that weekend, but a whole group who arrived to swim from "my" beach. This was after I'd repulsed John Peddar and after I'd dismissed Sandy but before the really alarming things happened.

They were all women and all good to look at. I suppose it was then that I realized there were no grossly fat women in the village, none who was misshapen, and that even as they grew older their bodies seemed not pulled down by gravity or ridged with wrinkles or marked with distorted veins. These things are very much a matter of genes. I had plenty of chance to observe the results of a good gene pool when I watched the women from my front garden in that soft twilight.

It wasn't quite warm enough to bathe. Not strictly. If I'd gone closer, I expect I should have seen gooseflesh on limbs. But I didn't go closer, though they evidently wanted me to. They waved. Jennifer Fowler called out, "It's lovely in the water!"

They swam among the lilies. Those lilies were like a Monet painting, red and pink and white cups floating among their flat, duck-green leaves on the pale water. One of the women picked a red lily and tucked its brown snaky stem into the knot of yellow hair she had tied up on top of her head. The wife of the farmer from Lynn was there, floating on her back beside Jennifer on the calm, gleaming surface, her outstretched hand clasping Jennifer's hand.

Have I said they were naked, every one of them? They swam, but mostly they played in the shallow water by the shore, splashing one another, then lying down and submerging themselves, except for their uplifted, laughing faces and long hair spread on the rippling water. The farmer's wife whose name I never knew stood up and, in a gesture at once erotic and innocent—didn't that sum them all up?—lifted her full breasts, one cupped in each hand, while Kathy Gresham splashed her with handfuls of water.

All the time they were glancing at me, smiling at me, giving me smiles of encouragement. It was plain they wanted me to come in too. I didn't disapprove; I didn't mind what they did—the lake was free and as much theirs as anyone's. But I did object to an attitude they all had, unmistakable though hard to define. It was as if they were laughing at me. It was as if they were saying, and probably were saying to one another, that I was a fool, inhibited, shy, perhaps ashamed of my own body. Go in there with them and all that would change. But I didn't want to go in there. It's not an excuse to say that it was really by this time quite cold. I got up and went into the house.

Later I saw them all emerge from the woods where their clothes were, fully dressed, still laughing, slowly dancing homeward along the lakeshore, some of them holding hands. It was dusk by then, and all I could see as they receded into the distance were shadowy forms, still dancing and no doubt still laughing, coming together and parting as if taking part in some elegant pavane.

• • •

If any bathers came to display themselves to Ben, he didn't mention them in his diary. But there was a lot he left out. I suppose he couldn't bear to put it down or perhaps look at it on the page after he'd written it. Some of it he told me, but there must have been a lot he didn't, a great deal I shall never know.

The actions of others he faithfully recorded. It was his own that he became, for a few days, reticent about. For example, he didn't seem to mind putting on paper that Carol Peddar had offered herself to him. After she said that about there being plenty of other girls, she looked into his eyes and, smiling, said there was herself. Didn't he like her? A lot of men thought she was prettier than her sister.

"Try me," she said, and then, "touch me," and she reached for his hand. He told her to go, to get out, and never to come back. He still believed, you see, that it was a family conspiracy that was trying to separate him from Susannah, a plot in which every Peddar was involved, and Carol with them.

"I even believed the engagement was an arranged thing," he told me. "I thought they'd fixed it up. Perhaps that was the way marriages happened in that village. I knew something strange was going on, and I thought there must be a tradition of arranged marriages. Susannah and this Kim Gresham had been destined for each other from babyhood, like something in India or among the Habsburgs. You see, I knew it was me she wanted, I knew it as I know you and I are sitting here together now."

"You thought you did," I said.

"Later on, when I really knew, I tried telling myself I'd only known her for a couple of months, so it couldn't be real, it must be sex and infatuation, whatever that is. I told myself what you told me that weekend, that she wasn't an educated person and that she was too young for me."

"Did I say that?"

"You meant it whether you said it or not," he said. "I told myself all that and I asked myself what we had in common. Would she even understand what I did for a living, for instance? That sort of thing ought to matter, but it didn't. I was in love with her. I'd never felt for anyone what I felt for her, not even for Margaret when we were first married. I'd have given the whole world, I'd have given ten years of my life, for her to have walked in at that moment and said the engagement story was nonsense, made up by her family, and it was I she was going to marry."

Ten years of his life, in those circumstances, was the last thing he should have thought of giving. Still, he wasn't called on to give anything. He went to the Peddars' house that evening, demanded admittance, and got it. John and Iris were at home with Carol and Julie, but there was no sign of Susannah. She was out, Iris said. No, she didn't know where, she didn't think a person of eighteen ought to have to account to her parents for everywhere she went.

"Especially in this village," John said. "This is a safe place. Horrible things don't happen here, never have and never will."

He sounded absolutely sure of himself, Ben said. He was smiling. Had I ever noticed how much they smiled in that village? The men always had a grin on their faces and the women sunny smiles.

"Now that you mention it," I said, "I suppose I have." Until they changed toward me and all smiles stopped.

Ben was tremendously angry. He thought of himself—and others thought of him—as a quiet, reserved sort of man, but by then he was angry. How did he know she wasn't in the house, that they hadn't got her hidden somewhere?

"You're welcome to look," Iris said, and then, incredibly, the self-conscious housewife, "It's not very tidy upstairs, I'm afraid."

Of course he didn't look. They wouldn't have given him the chance to look if she'd been there. John was eyeing him up and down as if summing him up for some purpose. Then he asked him why he wanted Susannah. What did he want her *for?*

Carol, no doubt, had reported back their conversation of the morning, so they must have known about himself and Susannah, that he wanted to marry her. He told them so then and there, he repeated what he'd said.

"It takes two to agree to that," Iris said comfortably.

"We are two," he said. "She loves me, she's told me often enough. I don't know what you're doing, how you're controlling her or coercing her, but it won't work. She's eighteen. She doesn't need your consent, she can please herself."

"She has pleased herself, Ben." It was the first time anyone from the village but Susannah had called him by his given name. "She's pleased herself and chosen Kim."

"I don't believe it," he said. "I don't believe *you.*"

"That's up to you," said John. "You can believe what you like."

He said it serenely; he was smiling. Ben said then what I'd often thought, that they were so happy in that village, as if they'd found the secret of life, always smiling, never ruffled, calm, forbearing. They were mostly quite poor: a lot of them were unemployed, and a few were on the edge of being comfortably off, that was all. But they didn't need material things; they were happy without them.

"As if they were all in love," Ben said bitterly. "All in love all the time."

"Perhaps," I said, "in a way they were."

After he'd told Ben he could believe what he liked and added that that was his privilege, John said why be so set on marrying Susannah. Why not, for instance, Carol?

"This I don't believe," Ben said.

"Ah, but you'll have to change your way of thinking. That's the point, don't you see? If you're going to live here, if you're going to take on my mother-in-law's place."

"There are no secrets in this village," said Iris. "But you know that."

John nodded. "Carol's as lovely in her way as Susannah, and she likes you. I wouldn't be saying any of this if she didn't like you. That's not our way. Stand up, Carol."

The girl stood. She held her head high and slowly turned to show herself in profile, then fully frontal. Like a slave for sale, Ben thought, and he remembered the bather emerging from the lake. She put up her arms and untied the ribbon that confined her hair in a ponytail. It was thick, shiny hair, the color of the corn they'd begun cutting that day.

"You could be engaged to Carol if you like," said Iris.

He got up and walked out of the house, slamming the front door behind him.

At the house next door he rang the bell hard. He didn't know who lived there—that hardly mattered. The young woman who answered the door he recognized at once. Later on he found out she was Gillian Atkins, but all he knew then was that she was the bather he had seen when with me and had been thinking of only a moment before. It gave him, he said, a horrible feeling of having stumbled into another world, a place of dreams and magic and perhaps science fiction. Or into the French analyst's myths where goddesses appeared out of clouds and where gods, in order to seduce, disguised themselves as swans and bulls and showers of gold.

She was smiling, of course. He stared, then he asked her if she knew where Kim Gresham lived. That made her smile again. As if she wouldn't know that, as if anyone in this place wouldn't know a thing like that. She told him to go to the house on the outskirts of the village.

When he got there the house was shut up. He knew, as one does, that there was no one at home. It was a lovely place, like a cottage on an old-fashioned calendar or a chocolate-box lid, thatch coming down over eyelid dormers, a pheasant made of straw perched on the roof. Roses climbed over the half-timbering and a white-flowering climber with them that gave off a rich, heavy scent. It made him feel sick.

The evening was warm, the sky lilac and pink. Birds flew homeward in flocks as dense as swarms of bees. He walked back to where he'd left his car, passing the cottage he meant to buy, he still at that time meant to buy. Old Mrs. Fowler was taking the air, sitting on the wooden bench in the front garden beside an old man. They were holding hands, and they waved to him and smiled. He said that though he was in a turmoil, he was profoundly aware of them and that he had never seen such a picture of tranquillity.

He knew where Susannah would be the next day. On Wednesday afternoons she went to work for the hairdresser. He expected Lavinia to come in the morning—it surely wouldn't be Carol after what had happened—but instead a stranger arrived, brought to his door by Sandy.

"We didn't want to let you down," Sandy said, "did we, Teresa? This is Teresa, she's taking Susannah's place."

"Teresa what?" he said.

"Gresham," the woman said. "Teresa Gresham. It's my husband's nephew that Susannah's engaged to."

She was probably thirty-five, shorter and plumper than the girls, browner-skinned and with light brown hair, an exquisitely pretty face, her eyes the bright dark blue of delphiniums. The summer dress she wore he had learned to think of as an old-fashioned garment. This one was pink with white flowers on it. Her legs were bare, and she had white sandals on her strong brown feet.

"They tried everything," I said when he told me.

"I suppose they did. But she wasn't flirtatious like Lavinia or blatant like Carol. I suppose you could say she was—*maternal*. She talked to me in a soothing way, she was cheerful and comforting—or she thought she was being comforting. Of course the whole village knew about Susannah and me by then, and they knew what had happened. Teresa made me coffee and brought it up. I was still working upstairs, still hiding from Sandy's grins and gestures, and she brought the coffee in and said not to be unhappy, life was too short for that. Smiling all the time, of course, need I say? She didn't tell me there were plenty more girls in the village—she said there were more fish in the sea than ever came out of it."

Sandy knocked on the back door at one to take her home in his van. Ben had suspected there was something between those two, he had sensed a close, affectionate intimacy, but then Sandy announced he was getting married in ten days' time and would Ben like to come? The village church at twelve noon. He didn't say whom he was marrying, but it couldn't be Teresa because she had talked of a husband, and Marion Kirkman also was married. Almost anything could have been believed of the villagers by that time, he thought, but no doubt they drew the line at bigamy.

He said he didn't know if he could accept—he didn't know where he'd be on the Saturday that week, he'd have to see.

"Oh, you'll come," Sandy said airily. "Things'll work out, you'll see. Everything'll be coming up roses by then."

You had to pass through the shop to get to the hairdresser's, through the shop and up the stairs. Anne Whiteson, behind the counter, detained him too long, smiling, friendly, asking after his health, his work, his opinion of the enduring hot weather. He heard Susannah's voice while he was climbing the steep staircase, and as much as he longed to see her, he stood for a moment experiencing the pleasure and the pain, not knowing which predominated, of those soft sweet tones, that rustic burr, the sunny warmth that informed everything she said. Not that she was saying anything particularly worth hearing, even he knew that, though it was poetry to him. It was something about a kind of shampoo she was discussing and whether it really made a perm last longer, but it thrilled him so that he was both shivering and awestruck.

The door was open, but as he came to it two hair dryers started up simultaneously. He walked in. All the women had their backs to him: Angela Burns, the hairdresser, and her assistant, Debbie Kirkman—he learned their names later—plus two older women, with their gray hair wound up onto pink plastic curlers, and Gillian Atkins, whose long blond curls were at that moment being liberated from a battery of rollers by

Susannah herself. He was beginning to see Gillian Atkins as some kind of evil genius who dogged his steps and appeared at crucial moments of his life. Aphrodite or Hecate.

Although the windows were open the place was very hot, and when Susannah turned around her cheeks were flushed and her hair curled into tendrils around her face like one of Botticelli's girls. He thought she had never looked more beautiful. In front of them all she came up to him, put her arms around his neck, and kissed him. Over her shoulder he could see five pairs of eyes watching them, heads all turned around to see. In front of them he couldn't speak, but she could.

"It's all right," she said. "It's going to be fine. Trust me. I'll come to you tomorrow evening."

Someone laughed. The five women started clapping. They clapped as at a play or a show put on for their benefit. Horribly embarrassed, he muttered something and ran down the stairs and out through the shop. But she'd restored him, he was better now, she had told him to trust her. He could see it all: the arranged marriage, the established engagement, two sets of parents and a bunch of siblings all wanting the marriage, everyone set on it but the promised bride, who was set on *him*.

That evening he managed to do some good work. The French was about sacrifice as propitiation of the gods, Agamemnon's killing of Iphigenia and the sacrifice of Polyxena on Achilles' tomb, and the subject demanded a similarly elegant grave prose. He worked upstairs in that room that had a view of the forest, not the lake, and when he reached Polyxena's burial, a wind sprang up like that which had risen while the Greeks waited to embark from Rhoetea. The forest trees bent and fluttered in this freakish wind, which blew and howled and died after half an hour.

Once he had the Greeks embarked for Thrace, he abandoned the translation and turned to write in his diary instead, the diary that had been untouched for almost a week. He wrote about Susannah and how she had reassured him and about the dark forest too and the strange sounds he could hear as he sat there with the dark closing in. "A yelping like a puppy," he wrote, unaware that what he heard must have been the cry of the little owl out hunting.

He slept soundly that night, and the next day, at lunchtime, on a whim, he walked down to the pub. Have I mentioned there was a pub? I don't think I have, but there was one and it was kept by Jean and David Stamford. It should have been called by some suitable name in that village, the Cupid's Bow, perhaps, or the Maiden's Prayer, Ben said, but it wasn't, it was called the Red Lion. Like almost every house along the village street and around the green, it was a pretty building, half-timbered, with flowers climbing over it and flowers in tubs outside. Ben went in there to lunch off a beer and a sandwich for no better reason than that he was happy.

You could always tell strangers from the village people. They looked different. Ben said brutally that strangers were fat or dark or ugly or all those things together. There were several couples like that in the bar. He had noticed their cars parked outside. They were passing through—all they would be permitted to do, he said, though in fact the Red Lion did have rooms available, and visitors had been known to stay a few nights or even a week.

The farmer from Lynn was sitting by himself up at the bar. It's a measure of the way the village people regarded him and had for quite a long time regarded him that no one ever uttered his name or called him by it, which is why even now I don't know what it was. He sat in miserable solitude while the rest of the clientele enjoyed themselves, greeting Ben enthusiastically, the old man he had seen holding hands with Mrs. Fowler actually slapping him on the back. No doubt, the farmer had come in there out of defiance, refusing to be browbeaten. He drank his beer and, after sitting there a further five minutes, staring at the bottles behind the bar, got down from his stool and left.

To Ben's astonishment everyone laughed and clapped. It was like the scene in the hairdresser's all over again. When the applause died down Jean Stamford announced to the assembled company that a little bird had told her the Old Rectory was sold. Everyone seemed to know that the little bird was the village's resident agent and her brother-in-law. Mrs. Fowler's friend asked how much the farmer had got for it, and Jean Stamford named a sum so large that the customers could only shake their heads in silence.

"Who's bought it?" Ben asked.

They seemed to like his intervention. There was a kind of hum of approval. It was apparently the right inquiry put at the right time. But no one knew who had bought the Old Rectory, only that it was nobody from the village.

"More's the pity," said the old man.

"And a pity for them," David Stamford said strangely, "if they don't suit."

Ben walked home. All this talk of houses as well as the prospect of his reunion with Susannah prompted him to ring up the estate agent and make an offer for Mrs. Fowler's house. The agent assured him it would be accepted, no doubt about it.

The combination of the beer, the walk, and the sunshine sent him to sleep. It was gone five before he woke, and he immediately set about putting wine in the fridge and preparing a meal for Susannah and himself, avocados and chicken salad and ice cream. He wrote all this down in his diary the next morning while she still slept. It was the first time she had ever stayed a whole night with him.

From his bedroom window he'd watched for her to come. She hadn't said a time and he watched for her for an hour, quietly going mad, unable to remain still. When at last she arrived it was in her father's van, which she was driving herself. The sight of it filled him with joy, with enormous exhilaration. All the suspense and terrors of the past hour were forgotten. If she could come in her father's own car this must mean that, miraculously, her parents had given their approval, minds had changed, and he was to be received, the accredited lover.

She was wearing nothing underneath her thin, almost transparent silk trousers and a loose top of lilac-colored silk. He had never been so aware of the beauty of her young body, her long legs and very slightly rounded belly, in which the navel was a shallow well. Her loose hair covered her breasts as if spread there from modesty. She lifted to him her warm red lips and her tongue darted against the roof of his mouth.

"Susannah, I love you so. Tell me you love me."

"I love you, dear Ben."

He was utterly consoled. Those were the words he wrote down the next morning. She shared the wine with him, she ate. She talked excitedly of Sandy Clements's wedding to Rosalind Wantage, the present her parents had bought, the dress she would wear to the ceremony. And Ben must come with her—they would go together. He would, wouldn't he?

Ben laughed. He'd have gone to the ends of the earth with her, let alone to the village church.

His laughter died, and he asked her about Kim Gresham. She was to tell him there was nothing in it or at least that it was over. He could bear an old love, a love from the past.

She said seriously, "Let's not talk about other people," and, as if repeating a rule, "We don't. Not here. You'll soon learn, darling Ben."

They made love many times that night. Ben wrote that there had never been such a night in all his life. He didn't know it could be like that; he had read of such things and thought they existed only in the writer's imagination. And one of the strange things was that those actions of hers he had previously thought of as adventurous, even as shocking, weren't indulged in, or if they were they became *unmemorable,* for something else had happened. It was as if in the midst of this bodily rapture they had somehow become detached from their physical selves; it was sex made spirit and all the stuff of sex transcended. They were taken from themselves to be made angels or gods, and everything they did took on the aspect of acts of grace or sacred rituals, yet at the same time made a continuum of pleasure.

He wrote that in his diary in the morning. He couldn't have brought himself to tell it to me in words.

She slept with her head on his pillow and her hair spread out—"rayed out," was how he put it, "like the sun in splendor." He watched her sleeping and he remembered her telling him to trust her. He couldn't therefore account for his terror, his awful fear. What was he afraid of?

Teresa Gresham came at eight-thirty to clean the house, and at nine Susannah woke up.

7

Dodging Teresa, avoiding knowing glances, he made coffee for Susannah and set a tray with orange juice, toast, and fruit. But when he took it up to her she was already dressed, sitting on the edge of the bed combing her hair. She smiled at him and held out her arms. They held each other and kissed and he asked her when they could be married.

She gave him a sidelong look. "You've never asked me to marry you."

"Haven't I?" he said. "I've told almost everyone else it's what I want."

"Anyway, darling Ben..." She always called him that, "dear Ben" or "darling Ben," and it sat oddly—charmingly to him—with her rustic accent. But what she had to say wasn't charming. "Anyway, darling Ben, I can't because I'm going to marry Kim."

He didn't believe he'd heard that, he literally didn't believe his ears. She must have asked if he'd thought she was marrying Kim. He asked her what she'd said, and she repeated it. She said, "You know I'm engaged to Kim. Carol said she'd told you."

"This is a joke, isn't it?" he said.

She took his hand, kissed it, and held it between her breasts. "It's nice that you want to marry me. Marriage is very important, you only do it once, so I think it's lovely that you want to be with me like that forever and ever. But that's the way I'm going to be with Kim. Live in the same house and share the same bed and bring up children together. It can't be changed, darling Ben. But I can still see you, we can be like we were last night. No one will mind. Did you think they would mind?"

She was his dear love, his adored Susannah, but she was a madwoman too. Or a child who understood nothing of life. But he knew that wasn't so. She was eighteen, but the depths of her eyes weren't; they were as old as her grandmother's, as knowledgeable, in her own way as sophisticated.

He took his hand away. It didn't belong there. She picked up her coffee cup and repeated what she'd said. She was patient with him, but she didn't know what it was he failed to understand. It seemed as clear as glass to her.

"Look, I'm not good at this," she said. "Ask Teresa."

The last person he wanted at that moment was Teresa Gresham, but Susannah went to the door and called her, and Teresa came upstairs. She looked quite unembarrassed; she wasn't even surprised.

"We all do as we please here," she said. "Marriage is for life, of course, just the once. But lovemaking, that's another matter. Men go with who they like, and so do women. There's only been one divorce in this village in thirty years," she said. "And before that no one got divorced, anyway. No one outside here—in the world, that is."

It made him shudder to hear the village talked of as if it were heaven or some utopian planet. "In the world," out there, two miles away...

"I couldn't believe it," he said to me. "Human beings wouldn't stand

for it, not as a theory of life. It may be all right in a commune, a temporary thing, but for everyone of all ages, a whole village community in
England? I asked her about jealousy. Teresa, I mean. I asked her. She said
they used to say jealousy wasn't in their blood, but now they thought it
was rather that a gene of jealousy had been left out of them. After all, they
were all more or less the same stock, they came out of the same gene
pool." He asked me, "Did you know about all this?"

"I? No, I didn't know."

"Not the green-eyed monster," he said, "but the blue-eyed fairy. You
didn't know when you came down for that weekend?"

"I knew there was something. I thought it was because I was a woman,
and it wouldn't happen to a man."

"We sat in that bedroom, Susannah and Teresa and I, and Teresa told
me all about it. She'd known it all her life, it was part of everyone's life,
and as far as they knew it had always been so, perhaps for hundreds of
years. When new people tried to live in the village they judged whether
they'd be acceptable or not, did they have the right physical appearance,
would they *join in.*"

"You mean take part in this sexual free-for-all?"

"They tested them. John Peddar passed the test. If they didn't pass
they—got rid of them. Like they were getting rid of the man from Lynn.
He wouldn't, Teresa said, but his wife would, and naturally the poor man
didn't want her to."

"And I wouldn't," I said, "and you wouldn't."

"They knew enough to be aware that new genes ought to be intro-
duced sometimes, though no defects ever appeared in the children. As to
who their fathers were, it just as often wasn't the mother's husband, but
he'd have children elsewhere, so no one minded. If a man's children
weren't his they were very likely a brother's or a cousin's."

"How about accidental brother-and-sister incest?"

"Perhaps they didn't care," he said, and then he said, "I've told you all
this as if I believed it when I was first told. But I didn't believe it. I
thought Susannah had been brainwashed by her parents and Teresa roped
in because she was articulate, a suitable spokeswoman. You see, it wasn't
possible for me to take this in after—well, after the way Susannah had
been with me and the things she'd said. Teresa hadn't been there, thank
God—what did she know? I thought the Peddar family had instructed

Susannah in what to say and they and Teresa had concocted this tale to make me back off."

"It was true, though, wasn't it?"

He said, "Even the Olympian gods were jealous. Hera persecuted the lovers of Zeus. Persephone was jealous of the King of the Underworld." Then he answered me. "Oh, yes, it was true."

After Susannah had gone and Teresa had followed her, for he had told Teresa to get out of the house and never to come back, he shifted the blame from the Peddar family onto Teresa and onto Kim Gresham. Wasn't she, after all, Kim Gresham's aunt? (Or cousin or second cousin or even sister.) Kim Gresham was holding Susannah to her engagement even though she loved him, Ben. In the light of what he'd just heard this wasn't a logical assumption, but he was beyond logic.

He would go to the Greshams' house and see Kim, have it out with him, drive down to the village and find out where he worked. But something strange happened while he was locking up, getting the car out. It was another beautiful day, sunny and warm, the blue sky flecked with tiny clouds like down. A pair of swans had appeared on the lake to swim on the calm, glassy water among the lily pads. The forest was a rich, velvety green, and for a moment he stood staring at the green reflected in the blue.

He found himself thinking that if, as he put it, "all things had been equal," if he hadn't been in love with Susannah, how idyllic would be the life Teresa had presented to him: unlimited love and pleasure without jealousy or recrimination, without fear or risk, free love in all senses, something to look forward to all day and look back on every morning. Love of which one never wearied because if one did it could without pain or damage be changed. An endless series of love affairs in this beautiful place where everyone was kind and warm and liked you, where people clapped at the sight of kisses. He thought of his wife, whom he hated because she had been unfaithful to him. Here he would have given her his blessing, and they would still be together.

If he believed what Teresa said. But he didn't. The sun didn't always shine. Jealousy hadn't been left out of his genetic makeup nor, he was sure, out of Susannah's. It hadn't occurred to him before this that she might have slept with Kim Gresham, but now it did, and the green of the forest turned red, the sky blazed with a hard yellow light, passion roared inside his head, and he forgot about idylls and blessings and unlimited love.

He drove to the village, parked the car, and went into the shop, the source of all his supplies of food and information. Anne Whiteson was less friendly than usual, and it occurred to him that Teresa might already have begun spreading the tale of her expulsion from Gothic House. She was less friendly, but it was no worse than that, and she was quite willing to tell him where Kim Gresham was to be found: at home with his parents in their house on the village outskirts. He had lost his job as a mechanic in a garage four miles away and was, until he found another, on the dole.

Scorn was now added to Ben's rage against Kim. Those Peddars were willing for their daughter to marry an unemployed man who couldn't support her. They preferred that man to him. He made his way to the Greshams' house, that pretty house a little way outside the village with the roses round the door. Kathy opened it and let him in, and he found Kim sprawled in the front room in front of the television. In his eyes, that compounded the offense.

Kim got up when Ben came in and, all unsuspecting, smiling—how they all smiled and smiled!—held out his hand. He was a tall, well-built young man, very young, perhaps twenty, several inches taller than Ben and probably two stone heavier. Ben ignored the hand. It suddenly came to him that it wouldn't do to have a row in Kim's parents' house, as he had no particular quarrel with the parents, and he told Kim to come outside.

Though obviously in the dark about all this, Kim followed Ben out into the front garden. I suppose he thought Ben wanted to show him some-thing—possibly there was something wrong with his car. After all, he was a motor mechanic. Outside, among the flowers, standing on a lawn with a birdbath in the middle of it, Ben told him he was in love with Susannah and she with him, there was no room for Kim in that relationship, he'd been replaced, his time with Susannah was past. Did he understand?

Kim said he didn't know what Ben was talking about. "I'm going to marry Susannah," he said, and he said it with no show of emotion, in the tone he might have used to say he was going bowling or down to the pub. "The wedding's been fixed for September. Second Saturday in September. You can come if you want. I know you like her, she's said, and that's okay with me. She's told me all about it—we don't have secrets."

Ben hit him. He said it was the first time in his life he'd ever hit any-one, and it wasn't a very successful blow. He had lashed out and struck Kim on the neck below the jawbone, and he hit him again with the other fist, this time striking his head, but neither punch seemed to have much effect. Unlike adversaries in films, Kim didn't reel back or fall over. He got hold of Ben around his neck, in that armlock the police are advised not to use on people they arrest, and propelled him down the path and out of the gate, where Ben collapsed and sat down heavily on the ground. Ben told me all this quite openly. He said he was utterly humiliated.

Kim Gresham, who probably watched a lot of television, said to Ben not to try anything further or he might "be obliged to hurt him." Then he asked him if he was all right and, when Ben didn't answer, went back into the house and closed the front door quietly behind him.

Because the Gresham house stood alone with fields on either side of it—Greshams, someone had told me, always liked to live a little way away from the village—there were no witnesses. Ben got up and rubbed his neck and thought that, with luck, no one else would know of his defeat and humiliation. His ignorance of the village and its ways was still sublime. He still thought there were things he could do outside his own four walls and no one would know.

He walked back to the village to where he had parked. In his absence his car had received attention. Someone had printed on the windscreen in a shiny red substance, probably nail varnish: GO AWAY. Even then he knew they didn't just mean go away for now, don't park here. The village street was empty. It often was, but if people were about this was the time they would be, eleven in the morning. There was no one to be seen. Even the front gardens were empty, and on this fine August day all the front doors and windows were closed. Eyes watched him. No one made any pretense that those eyes weren't watching.

Back at Gothic House he cleaned the printed letters off with nail-varnish remover he found in the bathroom cabinet. Deterred by what had happened but willing himself to be strong, he phoned the Peddars. A woman answered, Iris, he supposed, for the voice didn't belong to Susannah or her sisters.

He said, "This is Ben Powell."

Without another word, she put the receiver down. In the afternoon he phoned the hairdresser. Before the horrible things began to happen, on the previous evening when he and Susannah had been so happy, she'd told him she worked for the hairdresser on Friday afternoons as well. He phoned at two. Angela Burns answered, and when he said who it was, she put the receiver down.

That shook him, because it seemed to him to prove that Kim Gresham or his mother had talked of what had happened. Teresa had talked. It was one thing telling the Peddars, but the news had spread to the hairdresser. His defeat of the morning made him feel he had to be brave. If he was to achieve anything, overcome these people and secure Susannah for himself exclusively, he had to have courage now. He drove back to the village, but this time he parked the car directly outside the shop.

When Anne Whiteson saw him she said straight out she wasn't going to serve him. Then she walked into the room at the back and shut the door behind her. Ben went to the staircase, but before he'd gone up half a dozen stairs Susannah appeared at the top. She came down and met him halfway. Or, rather, she stood two stairs above him. He put out his hand to her.

She shook her head and said very softly, so that no one else should hear, "It's over, Ben."

"What do you mean?" he said. "What do you mean, over? Because of what these people say and do? The rest of the world isn't like this, Susannah. You don't know that but I do, I've seen, believe me."

"It's over," she said, and now she was whispering. "I thought it needn't be, I thought it could go on, because I do love you, but it has to be over because of what you've done and, Ben, because of what you *are*."

"What I am?"

"You're not like my dad, not many are. You're like the man who lives in the rectory, you're like the lady Gothic House belongs to. I didn't think you were, but you are."

"This is all nonsense." He wasn't going to whisper, no matter what she might do. "It's rubbish, it's irrelevant. Listen, Susannah, I want us to go away. Come away with me." He forgot about her grandmother's cottage. "I've got a place in London. We can go there tonight—we can go there *now*."

"You must go, Ben. I'm not going anywhere. This is where I live and I always will, you know. The people who live here never want to go away." She reached down from her higher stair and touched him on the arm. It was electric, that touch; he felt the shock of it run up his arm and rattle his body. "But you must go," she said.

"Of course I'm not going," he shouted. "I'm staying here, and I'm going to get you away from these people."

He meant it. He thought he could. He ran back to his car and drove home to Gothic House, where he began composing a letter to Susannah's parents and another, for good measure I suppose, to Susannah's grandmother. Perhaps he was thinking of her in the capacity of a village elder. Then by one of those coincidences, just as he was writing "Dear Mrs. Fowler," the phone rang. It was the estate agent to tell him Susannah's grandmother had received a better offer than his for her house.

"What is it?" he said. "I'll match it." Recklessness, which can be as much the effect of terror as of happiness, made him say, "I'll top it."

"Mrs. Fowler has already accepted the offer."

He tore up the letter he'd started writing. The one he'd written to the Peddars remained on his desk. But he intended to send it. He intended to fight. This time he refused to allow himself to become despondent. He pushed away the longings for her that came, the desire that was an inevitable concomitant of thinking of her. He would fight for her, he would think of that. What did the loss of the cottage matter? They couldn't live in this village, anyway.

He refused to let her become part of what he saw as an exceptionally large commune, where wife-swapping was the norm and husbands couldn't tell which were their own offspring. For a moment he had seen it, very briefly he'd seen it, as the ideal that all men, and women too perhaps, would want. But that had been a moment of madness. These people had made a reality out of a common fantasy, but he was not going to be drawn into it and nor was Susannah. Nor was he going to leave the village until it was to take her with him.

8

They got rid of me. I had no idea of the reason for my expulsion—no, that's not true. I did have ideas, they just weren't the right ones. I did have explanations of a kind. I was a "foreigner," so to speak, born and bred a long way off with most of my life lived elsewhere. I'd sacked Sandy. When

I asked myself if it also had something to do with my repudiation of John Peddar I was getting near the truth, but I thought it too far-fetched. Aware that I had somehow offended, I could never believe that I had done anything reprehensible enough to deserve the treatment I got.

The day after the bathers had extended their invitation to me—the final overture, as it happened, from any of them—I went to church. I tried to go to church. It was Saint John's day and the church's dedication was to Saint John, and I had noticed that a special service was always held on that day, whether it fell during the week or on a Sunday. They had a wonderful organist at Saint John's, a Burns who came from a village some miles away but was, I suppose, a cousin of that Angela, the hairdresser. The visiting clergyman preached a good sermon, and everyone sang the hymns lustily.

One of the sidesmen or wardens—I don't know what he was but he was a Stamford, I knew that—met me in the church porch. He was waiting for me. They knew I'd come, and they'd despatched him to wait for me.

"The service is private this morning," he said.

"What do you mean, private?"

"I'm not obliged to explain to you," he said, and he stood with his back against the heavy old door, barring my way.

There wasn't much I could do. There was nothing I could do. I couldn't get involved in a struggle with him. I went back to my car and drove home, indignant and humiliated. I wasn't frightened then, not yet, not by then.

A week later I came down again. I came on the Friday evening, as I often did when I could make it. Of course I'd thought a lot about what had happened when I'd tried to get into the church, but the incident became less a cause for rage and indignation the more I considered it. Perhaps I'd asked my question aggressively and Stamford, also being inclined to belligerence, had answered in kind. Perhaps he was having a bad day, was already angry. It was nonsense, I decided, to suppose "they" had sent him; it was paranoia. He happened to be there, was probably just arriving himself, when I arrived.

All this, somewhat recycled and much reviewed, was passing through my mind as I reached the village at dusk that Friday evening. They knew I would come, knew too approximately what time I'd come, and besides that, I had to pass the Greshams' house two minutes before I entered the village proper. They used the phone and their own grapevine.

It was like pictures that one sees of streets that royalty or some other celebrity is about to pass through. They were all outside, standing in front of their houses. They stood in front gardens if they had them, on the road itself if they didn't. But those waiting to welcome someone famous are preparing to smile and wave, even to cheer. These people, these Kirkmans and Burnses, Stamfords and Wantages, Clementses and Atkinses and Fowlers, all of them, some with children in their arms, tall, fair, handsome people, stood and stared.

As I approached I saw their eyes all turned in my direction, and as I passed I've no doubt their eyes followed, for in my driving mirror I could see them staring after me. All down that village street they were outside their houses, waiting for me. Not one of them smiled. Not one of them even moved beyond turning their eyes to follow me. Outside the last house three old people stood, a woman between two men, all holding hands. I don't know why this hand-holding particularly unnerved me. Perhaps it was the implication of total solidarity it conveyed. Now I think it symbolized what I had rejected: diffused love.

A little way down the road I slowed and saw in the mirror the three of them turn and go back into the house. I drove to Gothic House, and when I got out of the car I found that I was trembling. They had done very little, but they had frightened me. I hadn't much food in the house and I'd meant to go to the village shop in the morning, but now I wouldn't go. I'd take the road that didn't pass through the village to the town four miles away.

• • •

I've since wondered if they approached every newcomer to the village or if they applied some system of selection. Would they, for instance, tolerate someone for the sake of a spouse, as in the case of the farmer from Lynn? Would elderly retired people be welcome? I thought not, since their principal motivation was to draw in new genes to their pool and the old were past breeding.

I should therefore, I suppose, have been flattered, for I was getting on to forty. Did they hope I would settle there, would *live* there, *marry* some selected man? I shall never know. I shall never know why they wanted

Ben, although it has occurred to me that it might have been for his intellect. He had a good mind, and perhaps they thought that brains too might
be passed on. Perhaps whoever decided these things—all of them in con-
cert? like a parliament?—discerned a falling intelligence quotient in the
village.

He too tried to go to church. It was Sandy's wedding, and Susannah
had said they would go to it together. His mind had magnified her invitation to a firm promise, and he still believed she'd honor it. He stuck for
a long while to his belief that, having said and said many times that she
loved him, she would come to him and stay with him.

He wasn't, then, frightened of the village the way I was. He walked
there boldly and knocked on the Peddars' door. Carol opened it. When
she saw who it was she tried to shut the door, but he put his foot in the
way. He pushed past her into the house, and she came after him as he
kicked the door open and burst into their living room. There was nobody
there: all the Peddars but Carol had already gone to the wedding. He
didn't believe her, and he ran upstairs, going into all the rooms.

"Where's Susannah?"

"Gone," she said. "Gone to the church. You'll never get her—you
might as well give up. Why don't you go away?"

Leave the house was what he thought she meant. He didn't, then, take
in the wider implication. Sandy was just arriving at the church when he
got there, Sandy in a morning coat and carrying a topper, looking completely different from the handyman and window cleaner Ben knew. His
best man was one of the Kirkmans, similarly dressed, red-faced, very
blond, self-conscious. Ben stood by the gate and let them go in. Then he
tried to get in himself, and his way was barred by two tall men who came
out of the porch and simply marched at him. Ben didn't recognize them,
though they sounded from his description like George Whiteson and
Roger Atkins. They marched at him, and he stood his ground.

For a moment. It's hard to do that when you're being borne down
upon, but Ben did his best. He walked at them, and there was an impasse
as he struggled to break through the high wall their bodies made and they
pushed at him with the flat of their hands. They were determined not to
assault him directly, Ben was sure of that. He, however, was indifferent as
to whether he assaulted them or not. He said he beat at them with his

fists, and that was when other men joined in: John Peddar, who came out of the church, and Philip Wantage, who had just arrived with his daughter, the bride. They pinned Ben's arms behind him, lifted him up, and dropped him onto the grass on the other side of the wall.

With these indignities heaped on him, he sat up in time to see Rosalind Wantage in white lace and streaming veil proceed up the path with a bevy of pink-clad Kirkman and Atkins and Clements girls behind her. He tried to go after them but was once more stopped at the porch. Another tall, straight-backed guardian gave him a heavy push that sent him sprawling and retreated into the church. Ben sprang at the door in time to hear a heavy bolt slide across it on the inside.

The more of this they did, the more he believed that they might be acting on Susannah's behalf but not with her consent. It was a conspiracy to keep her from him. He sat on the grass outside the church gate and waited for the wedding to be over. It was a fine, sunny day and such windows in the church as could be opened were open. Hymns, swelling from the throats of almost the entire village, floated out to him, "Love Divine, All Loves Excelling" and "The Voice That Breathed o'er Eden."

"For dower of blessed children,
For love and faith's sweet sake,
For high mysterious union
Which nought on earth may break."

No one should break the union he had with Susannah and, sitting out there in the sunshine, perhaps he thought of the night they had spent, of transcendence and sex made spirit, which he had written of in his diary. It didn't occur to him then, though it did later, that a high mysterious union was what that village had, what those village people had.

They began coming out of the church, bride and bridegroom first, then bridesmaids and parents. Susannah came out with her parents and Carol. He said that when he saw her he saw no one else. Everyone else became shadows, gradually became invisible, when she was there. She came down the path, let herself out of the gate. What the others did he said he didn't know, if they stared after her or made to follow her, he had no eyes for them.

Susannah was in a pale blue dress. If she had stood against the sky, he said, it would have disappeared into the blueness, it was like a thin scanty slip of sky. She pushed back her hair with long pale fingers. He wanted to fall at her feet, her beautiful white feet, and worship her.

"You must go away, Ben," she said to him. "I've told you that before, but you didn't hear me."

"They've put you up to this," he said. "You're wrong to listen. Why do you listen? You're old enough to make up your own mind. Don't you understand that away from here you can have a great life? You can do anything."

"I don't want us to have to hurt you, Ben." She didn't say "them," she said "us." "We needn't do that if you go. You can have a day. You don't have to go till Monday, but you must go on Monday."

"You and I will go on Monday." But her use of that "us" and that "we" had shaken him. "You're coming with me, Susannah," he said, but his doubts had at last begun.

"No, Ben, you'll go. You'll have to." She added, as if inconsequentially, but it was a consequence, it was an absolute corollary, "Sandy's buying the cottage, Grandma's cottage, for him and Roz to live in."

• • •

I haven't said much about the forest.

The forest surrounded the lake in a horseshoe shape with a gap on the side where the road left its shores and turned toward the village. Behind the arms of the horseshoe it extended for many miles, dense and intersected only by trails or as a scattered sprinkling of trees with healthy clearings between them. It was protected, and parts of it were a nature reserve, the habitat of the little owl and the greater spotted woodpecker. If I haven't mentioned it much, if I've avoided referring to it, it's because of the experience I had within its depths, the event that drove me from the village and made me decide to sell Gothic House.

Already, by then, the place was losing its charms for me. I avoided it for a whole month after that Friday night drive through the village, confronted as I'd been by the silent, staring inhabitants. But I still liked the house and its situation, I loved the lake and walking in the forest, the nightingales in spring and the owl calling in winter, the great skies and the swans and water lilies. Unwilling to face that silent hostility again, I drove down very late. I passed through half an hour before midnight.

No one was about, but every light was on. They had turned on the lights in every room in the front of their houses, upstairs and down. The village was ablaze. And yet not a face showed at any of those bright windows. It was if they had turned on their lights and left, departed somewhere, perhaps to be swallowed up by the forest. I think those lights were more frightening than the hostile stares had been, and then and there I resolved not to pass through the village again, for, as I slowed and turned to look, the lights were one after another turned off; all died into darkness. No one had departed: they were there, and they had done their work.

I wouldn't pass through the village again, not at least until they had got over whatever it was, had come to accept me again. I really believed then that this would happen. But not passing through hardly meant I had to stay indoors. There is, after all, little point in a weekend retreat in the country if you never go out of it.

On Saturday afternoons I was in the habit of going for a walk in the forest. If I had a guest I asked that guest to go with me; if I was alone I went alone. They knew I was alone that weekend. If I hadn't seen them behind their lights they had seen me, alone at the wheel in an otherwise empty car.

At three in the afternoon I set out into the forest. It was May, just one year before Ben went there, not a glorious day but fine enough, the sun coming out for half an hour, then retreating behind fluffy white clouds. A little wind was blowing, not then much more than a breeze. Ten minutes into the forest and I saw the first of them. I was walking on the wide path that ran for several miles into the forest's heart. He stood close to the silver-gray trunk of a beech tree. I recognized him as George Whiteson, but if he recognized me—and of course he did, I was why he was there—he gave no sign of it. He wasn't staring this time, but looking at the ground around his feet.

A hundred yards on, three of them were sitting on a log, Kirkmans or Kirkmans and an Atkins, I forget and it doesn't matter, but I saw them and they affected not to see me, and almost immediately there were more, a man and a woman on the ground embracing—a demonstration for my benefit, I suppose—then two children in the branches of a tree, a knot of women—those bathers, standing in a ring, holding hands.

The sun was shining onto a clearing, and it was beautiful in there, all the tiny wildflowers in blossom in the close heathy turf, crab-apple trees flowering, and the sunlight flitting, as the wind drove clouds across it and bared it again. But it was terrible too, with those people, the whole village it seemed, there waiting for me but making no sign they'd seen me. They were everywhere, near at hand or in the depths of the forest, close to the path or just discernible at the distant end of a green trail, Burnses and Whitesons, Atkinses and Fowlers and Stamfords, men and women, young and old. And as I walked on, as I tried to stick it out and keep on, I became aware that they were following me. As I passed they fell into silent step behind, so that when I turned around—it was quite a long time before I turned around—I saw behind me this stream of people padding along quietly on the sandy path, on last year's dry, fallen leaves.

It was as if I were the Pied Piper. But the children I led were not in happy thrall to me, not following me to some paradise, but dogging my steps with silent menace, driving me ahead of them. To what end? To what confrontation in the forest depths?

I was terribly afraid. It's not an exaggeration to say I feared for my life. The whole tribe of them, as one, had gone mad, had succumbed to spontaneous psychopathy, had conceived some fearful paranoiac hatred of me. They would surround me in some dark green grove and murder me. In their high mysterious union. In silence.

But I never quite came to believe that. If I wanted to crouch on the ground and cover my head and whimper to them to let me go, to leave me alone, I didn't do that either. By some sort of effort of will that I achieved, God knows how, I turned, clenched my fists, set one foot before the other, and began walking back the way I'd come.

This brought me face to face with the vanguard of them, with John Peddar and one of his daughters, Susannah herself for all I know. They fell back out of my path. It was gracefully done; one by one they all yielded, half bowing, as if this were some complicated ritual dance and they giving place to the principal dancer, who must now pass with prescribed steps down the space between them. Only I had no partner in this minuet; I was alone.

No one spoke. I didn't speak. I wanted to, I wanted to challenge them, to ask why, but I couldn't. I suppose I knew I wouldn't get an answer or perhaps that no voice would come when I tried to speak. The speechlessness was one of the worst things, that and the closed faces and the silent movements. Another was the sound of the rising wind.

They followed me all the way back. While I was in the forest the wind could be heard but not much felt. It met me as I emerged onto the lakeshore and even held me back for a moment, as if pushing me with its hands. The surface of the lake was ruffled into waves, and the tree branches were pulled and stretched and beaten. By the shore the people who followed me let me go and turned aside, two hundred of them I suppose, at least two hundred.

From having been perfectly silent, they broke into talk and laughter as soon as they were separated from me and, buffeted by the wind, made their way homeward. I ran into my house. I shut myself inside, but I could still hear their voices, raised in conversation, in laughter, and at last in song. It would be something to chronicle, wouldn't it, if they'd sung an ancient ballad, a treasure for an anthropologist, something whose words had come down unbroken from the time of Langland or Chaucer? But they didn't. The tune I heard carried by the wind, receding, at last dying into silence, was "Over the Rainbow."

That evening the gale became a storm. Trees went down on the edge of the woodland and four tiles blew off the roof of Gothic House. The people of the village weren't to blame, but that was not how it seemed to me at the time, as I cowered in my house, as I lay in bed listening to the storm, the crying of the wind and the crash of falling tree branches. It was just a lucky happening for them that this gale blew up immediately after their slow, dramatic pursuit of me in the forest. But that night I could have believed them all witches and magicians, *wicca* people who could control the elements and raise a wind.

9

They had something else in store for Ben.

"I was determined not to go," he said. "I would have gone immediately if Susannah had come too, but without her I was going to stay put. On the Sunday I went back to the village to try to find her, but no one would answer their doors to me, not just the Peddars, no one."

"It was brave of you to try," I said, and that was when I told him what had happened to me, the silent starers, the blazing lights, the pursuit through the forest.

"I'd stopped being a coward," Ben said. "Well, I thought I had."

The next morning someone was due to come and clean the house. Which girl would they send? Or was it possible Susannah might come? Of course he hadn't slept much. He hadn't really slept for four nights, and exhaustion was beginning to tell on him. If he managed to doze off it would be to plunge into dreams of Susannah, always erotic dreams but deeply unsatisfying. In them she was always naked. She began making love with him, kissing him, placing his hands on her body as was her habit, kissing his fingers and taking them to the places she loved to be touched. Then, suddenly, she would spring out of his arms and run to whoever had come into the room, Kim Gresham or George Whiteson or Tom Kirkman, it could be any of them, and in a frenzy begin stripping off their clothes, nuzzling them, gasping with excitement. He'd reached a point where he didn't want to sleep for fear of those dreams.

By eight-thirty the next morning he'd been up for more than two hours. He'd made himself a pot of coffee and drunk it. His head was banging, and he felt sick. The time went by, nine o'clock went by, and no one came. No one would come now, he knew that.

The weather had changed and become dull and cool. He went outside for a while and walked about, he couldn't say why. There wasn't anyone to be seen—there seldom was—but he had a feeling that he was being watched. He took his work into the ground-floor front room because he knew it would be impossible for him to stay upstairs in the back. If he did that, sat up there where he could only see the rear garden and the forest, something terrible might happen in the front, by the lake, some awful event take place that he ought to witness. It was an unreasonable feeling, but he gave in to it and moved into the living room.

The author of *The Golden Apple* was analyzing Helen, her narcissism, her choice of Menelaus declared by hanging a wreath round his neck, her elopement with Paris. Ben tried to concentrate on translating this, first to understand which events stemmed in the writer's estimation from destiny and which from character, but he couldn't stop himself from constantly glancing up at the window. Half an hour had passed, and he had translated only two lines, when a car came along the road from the village. It parked by the lake in front of Gothic House.

I suppose there was about a hundred yards between the house and the little beach, and the car was on the grass just above the beach. He

watched and waited for the driver or the driver and passenger to get out
of it and come up to the house. No one did. Nothing moved. Then about
ten minutes later the car windows were wound down. He saw that the
driver was Kim Gresham and his passenger an unknown woman.

He tried to work. He translated the lines about Helen taking one of
her children on the elopement with her, then read what he had written
and saw that the prose was barely comprehensible and the sense lost.
There was no point in working in these conditions. He wondered what
would happen if he tried to go out and felt sure that if he attempted a
walk to the village those two would stop him. They would seize hold of
him and frog-march him back to the house.

"I thought of calling the police," he said.

"Why didn't you?"

"The man they'd have sent lived in the police house in the village. He's
one of them, he's called Michael Wantage. If anyone else had come, what
could I have said? That two people were sitting in a parked car admiring
the view? I didn't call the police. I got my car out of the garage."

He put his work aside and decided to drive to the town four miles
away and do his weekly shopping. He watched them watching him as he
backed the car out.

"I think they were hoping I'd fetch out suitcases and the word processor and my books. Then they'd know I was being obedient and leaving.
They'd just have let me go, I'm sure of that. A sigh of relief would have
been heaved and they'd have gone back to the village."

As it was, they followed him. He saw the car behind him all the way.
They made no attempt at secrecy. In the town he left his car and went to
the supermarket but, as far as he knew, they remained in theirs. When he
got back they were still sitting in their car, and when he drove home they
were behind him.

In the early afternoon a second car arrived and the first one left. They
were operating a shift system. From Ben's description it seemed that
Marion Kirkman was driving the second car. He had no doubt as to the
identity of her passenger. It was Iris Peddar. Later on another car replaced
it and was still there when darkness came.

Perhaps a car was there all night. He didn't know. By then he didn't
want to know; he just desperately hoped this surveillance would have
ceased by morning. Just after sunrise he pulled back the curtains and

looked out. A car was there. He couldn't see who was inside it. It was then that he told himself he could be as strong and as resolute as they. He could stick it out. He simply wouldn't look. He'd do what seemed impossible the day before, work in the back, not look, ignore them. They meant him no harm; they only mounted this guard to stop him from going to the village to find Susannah. But there must be other ways of reaching Susannah. He could do a huge circular detour via the town and come into the village from the other direction. He could park *his* car outside her father's house. But if he did that, all that, any of that, they would follow him . . .

All that day he stayed indoors. He couldn't work, he couldn't read, he didn't want to eat. At one point he lay down and slept, only to dream of Susannah. This time he was in a tower, tall and narrow with a winding stair inside like a windmill, and he was watching her from above, through a hole in the floor. He heard her footsteps climbing the stairs, hers and another's, and when she came into the room below she was with Sandy Clements. Sandy began to undress her, taking the bracelet from her arm and the necklace from her neck and held one finger of her right hand as she stepped naked out of the blue dress. She looked up to the ceiling and smiled, stretching out her hands, one to him, one to Sandy, turning her body languorously for them to gaze at and worship. He awoke with a cry and, forgetting his resolve, stumbled into the front room to look for the car. A red one this time, Teresa Gresham's. She was alone in it.

At about seven in the evening, long before dark, she got out of the car and came up to the house. He'd forgotten he'd left the back door unlocked. She walked in. He asked her what the hell she thought she was doing.

"You asked me to come up and do your ironing," she said.

"That's rubbish," he said. "I asked you nothing. Now get out."

She had apparently been gone five minutes when he saw, in the far distance, a bicycle approaching. The very first time she came Susannah had been on a bicycle, and that was who he thought it was. The surveillance was over: she had persuaded them to end it, and she was coming to him. She had told them they couldn't prevent her from being with him, she was over age, she loved him. He opened the front door and stood on the doorstep waiting for her.

It wasn't Susannah. It was the younger of her two sisters, the fourteen-year-old Julie. Disappointment turned inside his body as love does, with a wrench, an apparent lurching of the heart. But he called out a greeting to her. She rested her bicycle against the garden wall and fastened a chain and padlock to its front wheel—the good girl, the responsible teenager. Who did she think would steal it out here? He let her into the house, certain she must have a message for him, perhaps a message from Susannah, who was allowed to reach him in no other way.

She was a pretty little girl—his words—who was much shorter than her sisters, who clearly would never reach Susannah's height, with a very slight, childish figure. She wore a short skirt and a white sweatshirt, ankle socks, and white trainers. Her straw-colored hair was shoulder-length, and she had a fringe.

"She looked exactly like the girl in the Millais painting, the one who's sitting up in bed and looking surprised but not unhappy."

"I know the one," I said. "It's called *Just Awake.*"

"Is it?" he said. "I wonder what Millais meant by 'awake.' D'you think a double meaning was intended?"

Julie sat down sedately in my living room. He asked her if she had a message for him from Susannah, and she shook her head.

"You asked me to come," she said. "You phoned up an hour ago and said if I'd come over you'd let me have those books you told Susannah I could have."

"What books?" He had no idea what she meant.

"For my schoolwork. For my English homework."

It was at this point that he had the dreadful feeling they had sent her as the next in the progression. They'd decided it was still worth trying to keep him and make him one of them. He didn't want Lavinia or Carol; stubbornly, he still wanted monogamy with Susannah. But since he'd rejected the more mature Teresa, wasn't it possible he'd be attracted by her antithesis, by this child?

Of course he was wrong there. They weren't perverse. In their peculiar way, they were innocent. But by this time he'd have believed anything of them, and he did, for a few minutes, believe they'd sent her to tempt him. He'd been sitting down but he jumped up, and she too got up.

"Why are you really here?"

She forgot about the books. "I'm to tell you to go away," she said. "I'm to say it's your last chance."

"This is ridiculous," he said. "I'm not listening to this."

"You can stay here tonight." She said it airily, as if it were absolutely her province to give him permission. "You can stay here tonight, but you must go tomorrow. Or we'll make you go."

He didn't once touch her. She didn't touch him. She left the house, unlocked the padlock on her bicycle chain, and got on the bicycle. It's almost impossible for a practiced cyclist to fall off a bicycle, but she did. She fell off in the road, and the machine fell on her. He lifted the bicycle off her, put out his hand to help her up, pulled her to her feet. She jumped on the bicycle and rode off, turning around to call something after him, but he didn't hear what it was. He returned to the house and thought that in the morning he'd go to the village and get into her parents' house, even if that meant breaking a window or kicking the door in.

In the morning the car was back. It was parked at the lakeshore. The driver was David Stamford and the passenger Gillian Atkins.

• • •

If he went to the town and from there by the back way into the village, they would follow him. He had no doubt that they would physically prevent him from driving or walking along the lakeshore road. It was harassment, their simply being there was harassment, but imagine telling this tale to the police, imagine proving anything.

Working on his translation was impossible. Attempting to find Susannah would be difficult, but he tried. He phoned the Peddars, Sandy Clements, the shop, the pub, Angela Burns. One after the other, when they heard his voice, they put the phone down. It was deeply unnerving, and after Angela's silence and the click of the receiver going into its rest, he stopped trying.

But there was some comfort to be drawn from these abortive phone calls. He'd been able to make them. They hadn't cut his phone line. It's some measure of the state he was getting into that he even considered they might. This negativity, this absence of some hypothetical action, told him there would be no violence used against him. He hadn't exactly been afraid of violence, but he'd been apprehensive about it.

He sat down, in the back of the house where he couldn't see that car, and thought about what they'd done. Not so very much, really. They'd stopped him from going to a wedding and followed his car and sent him to the town. Surely he could stick it out if that was all that was going to happen? If he had Susannah he could. He had to stay at Gothic House for her sake, he had to stay until he got her away.

"I thought of going out to them," he said to me, "to those two, Stamford and the Atkins woman, and later on to the people who replaced them, the Wantages, Rosalind's parents, of going out to them and asking what they wanted of me. Of course I knew really, I knew they wanted me to leave, but I wanted to hear someone say it, and not a child of fourteen. And then I thought I'd say, Okay, I'll leave but I'm taking Susannah with me."

By now he couldn't bear to leave his observers unobserved, and he sat in the front window watching them while they watched him. He still hadn't been able to bring himself to carry out his intention. He just sat there watching and thinking of how to put his question and what words to choose to frame his resolution. In the middle of the afternoon a terrible thing happened. He had calculated that the Wantages' shift would end at four—that was the state he had got into, that he was measuring his watchers' shifts—and, sure enough, at five to four another car arrived. The driver was an unknown man, his passenger Susannah.

The car was parked so that its near side, and therefore the passenger's seat, was toward Gothic House. He looked out into Susannah's eyes and she looked back, her face quite expressionless. There are times when thinking is dismissed as useless, when one stops thinking and just acts. He had thought enough. He walked, marched, out there, calling her name.

She wound down the window. The face she presented to him, he said, was that of a woman in a car of whom a stranger has asked the way. It was as if she had never seen him before. The man in the driver's seat didn't even turn around. He was staring at the lake with rapt attention. He looked, Ben said, as if he'd seen the Loch Ness Monster.

"Please get out of the car and come inside, Susannah," he said to her.

She was silent. She went on staring as if he really was that stranger and she was considering what directions to give him.

"We can talk about all this, Susannah. Come inside and talk, will you please? I know you don't want to leave this place, but that's because you don't know anywhere else. Won't you come with me and try?"

Slowly she shook her head. "You have to go," she said.

"Not without you."

"I'm not coming. You have to go alone."

She touched her companion's arm, and he turned his head. From that touch, intimate but relaxed, Ben somehow knew this young fair-haired man was her lover as he had been her lover, and for a moment the sky went black and a sharp pain pierced his chest. She watched him as if calculating all this. Then she said, "Why don't you go now? You'll go if you've any sense."

The young man beside her said, "I'd advise you to leave before dark."

"We'll follow you through the village," said Susannah. "Then you'll be safe. Pack your bags and put them in the car."

"Shall we say an hour?" That was the young man, in his coarse, rustic voice.

Ben went back into the house. He had no intention of packing, but at the same time he didn't know what to do next. The idea came to him that if he could only get Susannah alone all would be well. He could talk to her, remind her, persuade her. The question was, how to do that? Not at the hairdresser's, he'd tried that. She baby-sat for Jennifer Fowler one evening a week, an evening she'd never been able to come to him, a Wednesday—those few Wednesdays, how bereft and lonely he'd felt. Tomorrow, then, he'd somehow get to the village and Jennifer Fowler's house. They'd only kept up their surveillance till dark the night before, and it would be dark by nine . . .

He sat inside the window watching Susannah for a long time. It was marginally better to see her, he'd decided, than to be in some other part of the house, not seeing her but knowing she was there. To gaze and gaze was both pleasure and pain. The strange thing was, he told me, that watching her was never boring, and he couldn't imagine that applying to any other person or object on earth.

He also watched, in sick dread, to see if she and the man with her touched each other or moved toward each other or gave any sign of the relationship he had at first been sure was theirs. But they didn't. As far as he could tell, they didn't. They talked and, of course, he wondered what they said. He saw Susannah's head go back against the headrest on the seat and her eyes close.

The afternoon was calm and dull, white-skied. Because there was no wind, the surface of the water was quite smooth and the forest trees were still. He went into the back of the house to watch the sunset, a bronze-and-red spectacular sunset striped with black-rimmed thin clouds. These signs of time going by seemed to bring the following night closer,

Wednesday night, when he could be alone with her. He began planning how to do it.

When he went back to the front window the car was moving, turning around prior to leaving. And no other had come to replace it. He began to feel a lightness, something that was almost excitement. They couldn't keep her from him if they both wanted to be together, and if they could influence her, how much more could he? Any relationship between her and her companion in the car had been in his imagination. Probably, at some time or other, she had slept with Kim Gresham, but that was only to be expected. He had never had any ideas of being the first with her or even desired to be.

After a little while he poured himself a drink. Never much of a drinker, he had nevertheless had to stop himself from having recourse to whiskey these past few days. But at eight o'clock at night he could indulge himself. He began thinking of getting something to eat, but he hadn't been outside all day except to speak those few brief words to Susannah, and at about nine, when the twilight was deepening, he walked down to the lake.

Flies swarmed a few inches above its surface and fish were jumping for them. The water bubbled and broke as a slippery body leapt, twisted, gleaming silver in the last of the light. He watched, growing calm and almost fatalistic, resigning himself to the hard struggle ahead, but knowing that anyone as determined as he would be bound to win.

Because their lights were off and dusk had by now fallen, because they drove quietly and in convoy, he didn't see the cars until the first of them was almost upon him.

10

He went back into the house. He didn't quite know what else to do. They parked the cars on the little beach and on the grass. There were about twenty of them, and he said it was like people going to some function in a village hall and parking on the green outside. Only they didn't get out of their cars until he was indoors, and then not immediately.

You have to understand that it was all in darkness, or absence of light, for it wasn't quite dark. The cars were unlit, and so was the house. Once he was inside he tried putting lights on, but then he couldn't see what they meant to do. He put on the light in the hall and watched them through the front-room window.

They sat inside their cars. He recognized the Wantages' car and Sandy Clements's and, of course, John Peddar's white van. There was just enough light left to see that. He thought then of phoning the police—he often had that thought—and he always came to the same conclusion, that there was nothing he could say. They had a right to be there. For all he knew, they'd explain their presence by saying they'd come fishing or owl-watching. But by now he was frightened. He was also determined not to show his fear, whatever they did.

The doors of the white van opened and the four people inside it got out, Susannah and her parents and one of the sisters. He stepped back from the window and moved into the hall. One after the other he heard car doors slamming. It seemed as if an hour passed before the front door-bell rang, though it was probably less than a minute. He breathed in slowly and out slowly and opened the door.

John Peddar pushed his way into the house or, rather, he pushed his daughter Julie into the house and followed behind her. Next came his wife and Susannah. Ben saw about forty people in the front garden and on the path and the doorstep, and once he had let Susannah in he tried to shut the door, but his effort was useless against the steady but entirely nonviolent onslaught. They simply pushed their way in, close together, a body of men and women, a relentless shoving crowd. He retreated before them into the living room, where the Peddars already were. He backed against the fireplace and stood there with his elbows on the mantelpiece, because there was nowhere farther that he could go, and faced them, feeling that now he knew how it was to be an animal at bay.

My small front room was full of people. He thought at this moment literally that they meant to kill him, that as one they had gone mad. He thought as I had thought in the wood, that the collective unconscious they seemed to share had taken a turn into madness and they had come there to do him to death. And the worst thing was, one of the worst things, that he now grouped Susannah with them. Suddenly he lost his feeling for her. She became one of them, and his passion evaporated with his fear. He could look at her, and did, without desire or tenderness or even nostalgia, but with distaste and the same fear as he had for her family and her neighbors.

At first he couldn't speak. He swallowed; he cleared his throat. "What do you want?"

John Peddar answered him. He said something Ben couldn't believe he'd heard aright.

"What?"

"You heard, but I'll say it again. I told you you could have my Carol, but not my little girl, not my Julie."

Ben said, his voice strengthening, "I don't know what you mean."

"Yes, you do. D'you know how old Julie is? She's not fourteen." He was still holding the girl in front of him, and now he pushed her forward, displaying her. "See the bruises on her? See her leg? Look at that blue all up her arms."

There was a murmur that seemed to swell all around him, like the buzzing of angry bees. His eyes went to Susannah, and he thought he saw on that face that was no longer lovely to him the hint of a tiny malicious smile.

"Your daughter fell off her bicycle," he said. "She hurt her leg falling off her bicycle. The bruises on her arm I may have made, I don't know. I may have made them when I helped her to her feet, that's all."

The child said, in a harsh unchildish voice, "You were going to rape me."

"Is that why you've come here?" he said. "To accuse me of that?"

"You tried to rape me." The accusation, slightly differently phrased, was repeated. "I fell over when I ran out of the house. Because you were trying to do it."

"This is rubbish," he said. "Will you please go." He looked at Susannah. "All of you, please leave."

"We've a witness," said Iris. "Teresa saw it all."

"Teresa wasn't in the house," he said.

"That's not true," Teresa Gresham said. "I'd been there an hour when Julie came. I expect you'd forgotten—there was a lot you forgot once you got to touch her." She said to the Peddars, "I came out of the kitchen and I saw it all."

"What do you want of me?" he said again.

"We don't want to go to the police," John Peddar said.

His wife said, "It's humiliating for our little girl."

"Not that it's in any way her fault. But we'll go to them if you don't go. You go tonight and this'll be the last you hear of it. Go now or we get the police. Me and Julie and her mother and Teresa. You can phone them on his phone, Iris."

He imagined the police coming and his having absolutely no defense except the truth, which would collapse in the face of Julie's evidence and the Peddars' and Teresa's. If that wasn't enough, they'd no doubt produce Sandy Clements, who would have also have been there watching, cleaning the windows perhaps or weeding the garden. Sandy he could pick out of the crowd packed into the room, just squeezed in, leaning against the closed door beside his new wife.

"None of this is true," he said. "It's lies, and you know it."

They didn't try to deny it. They weren't interested in whether something was true or not, only in their power to control him. None of them smiled now or looked anything but grim. One of the strangest things, he said, was that they were all perfectly calm. There was no anxiety. They knew he'd do as they asked.

"This is a false accusation, entirely fabricated," he said.

"Iris," said John Peddar, "phone the police."

"Where's the phone?"

Teresa Gresham said, "It's in the back room. I'll come with you."

Sandy moved away from the door and opened it for them. The crowd made a passage, squeezing back against one another in a curiously intimate way, not seeming to resist the pressure of other bodies. Breasts pushed against arms, hips rested against bellies, without inhibition, without awkwardness. But perhaps that wasn't curious, perhaps it wasn't curious at all. They stood close together, crushed together, as if in some collective embrace, cheek to cheek, hand to shoulder, thigh to thigh.

Then Teresa went out of the room. Iris, following her, had reached the door when Ben said, "All right. I'll go."

He was deeply humiliated. He kept his head lowered so that he couldn't meet Susannah's eyes. His shame was so great that he felt a burning flush spread across his neck and face. But what else could he have done? One man is helpless against so many. In those moments he knew that every one of those people and those left behind in the village would stand by the Peddars. No doubt, if need was, they would produce other evidence of his proclivities, and he remembered how, once, he had taken hold of Carol Peddar by the wrist.

"I'll go now," he said.

They didn't leave. They helped his departure. He went upstairs and they followed him, pushed their way into his bedroom. One of them found his suitcases; another set them on the bed and opened their lids. Teresa Gresham opened the wardrobe and took out his clothes. Kathy Gresham and Angela Burns folded them and packed them in the cases. No one touched him, but once he was in that bedroom, he was their prisoner. They packed his hairbrush and his shoes. John Peddar came out of the bathroom with his sponge bag and his razor and toothbrush. All the time, Julie, the injured one, sat on the bed and stared at him.

Sandy Clements and George Whiteson carried the cases out of the room. One of the women produced a carrier bag and asked him if they'd got everything of his. When he said they had but for his dressing gown and the book he'd been reading in bed, she put those items in the bag, and then they let him leave the room.

If they were enjoying themselves, there was no sign of it. They were calm, unsmiling, mostly silent. Teresa led a group of them into the back room, where he had worked on his translation, admitted him, and closed the door behind him. Gillian Atkins—she was bound to be there, his nemesis—brought two plastic bags with her, and into these they cleared his table of books and papers. They did it carefully, lining up the pages, clipping them together, careful not to crease or crumple. A man Ben didn't recognize, though his coloring, height, and manner were consistent with the village people, unplugged his word processor and put it into its case. Then his dictionary went into the second bag.

Again he was asked if there was anything they'd forgotten. He shook his head, and they let him go downstairs. Gillian Atkins went into the kitchen and came back with a bag containing the contents of the fridge.

"Now give me the door key," Kevin Gresham said.

Ben asked why. Why should he?

"You won't need it. I'll send it back to the present owner."

Ben gave him the key. He really had no choice. He left the house in the midst of them. Their bodies pressed against him, warm, shapely, herbal-smelling. They eased him out, nudging and elbowing him, and, when the last of them had left and turned out the hall light, closed the door behind them. His cases and bags were already in the boot of his car, his word processor in its case carefully placed on the floor in front of the back seat. He looked for Susannah to say good-bye, but she had already left; he could see the red taillights of the car she was in receding into the distance along the shore road.

They accompanied him in convoy through the village, two cars ahead of him and all the rest behind. Every light was on, and some of the older people, the ones who hadn't come to Gothic House, were in their front gardens to see him go. Not all the cars continued on. Some fell away when their owners' homes were reached, but the Peddars and the Clementses continued to precede him, and Gillian Atkins with Angela Burns continued to follow him, as did, he thought, the Greshams, but he wasn't sure of that because he couldn't see the car color in the dark.

After ten miles, almost at the approach to an A road, Gillian Atkins cut off his further progress the way a police car does, by overtaking him and pulling sharply ahead of him. He was forced to stop. The car behind stopped. Those in front already had. Gillian Atkins came around to his window, which he refused to open. But he'd forgotten to lock the door, and she opened it.

"Don't come back," was all she said.

They let him go on alone.

He had to stop for a while on the A road in a lay-by because his hands were shaking and his breathing erratic. He thought he might choke. But after a while things improved and he was able to drive on to London.

11

My key came home before he did.

There was no note to accompany it. I knew where it had come from only by the postmark. No one answered the phone, either at Gothic House or at Ben's London flat. I drove to Gothic House, making the detour through the town to reach it, and found it empty, all Ben's possessions gone.

I phoned the estate agent and put the house up for sale.

. . .

A month passed before Ben surfaced. He asked if he could come over, and once with me, he stayed. The translation was done. He had worked on it unremittingly, thinking of nothing else, closing off his mind, until it was finished.

"Helen went back to her husband," he said. "He took her home to Sparta, and she brought the heroes nepenthe in a golden dish, which made them forget their sorrows. My author got a lot of analytical insights out of that."

"What was nepenthe?" I said.

"No one knows. Opium? Cannabis maybe?" He was silent for a while, then suddenly vociferous. "Do you know what I'd like? I've thought a lot about this. I'd like them to build a road right through that village, one of those bypasses there are all these protests about. They never work, the protests, do they? The road gets built. And that's what I'd like to hear, that some town nearby has to be bypassed and the village is in the way, the village has to be cut in half, split up, destroyed."

"It doesn't seem very likely," I said, thinking of the forest, the empty, arable landscape.

After that he never mentioned the place, so when I heard, as I did from time to time, how my efforts to sell Gothic House were proceeding, I said nothing to him. I didn't tell him when I heard, from the same source, that old Mrs. Fowler had died and had left, in excess of all expectations, rather a large sum.

By then he'd shown me the diary and told me his story. In the details he told me far more than I often cared to hear. He was still sharing my house, though he often talked of buying somewhere for himself, and one evening, when we were alone and warm and I felt very close to him, when the story was long told, I asked him—more or less—if we should make it permanent, if we should change the sharing to a living together, with its subtle difference of meaning.

I took his hand and he leaned toward me to kiss me absently. It was the sort of kiss that told me everything: that I shouldn't have asked or even suggested, that he regretted I had, that we must forget it had ever happened.

"You see," he said, after a few moments, in which I tried to conquer my humiliation, "it sounds foolish, it sounds absurd, but it's not only that I've never got over what happened, though that's part of it. The sad, dreadful thing is that I want to be back there, I want to be with them. Not just Susannah—of course I want *her,* I've never stopped wanting her for more than a few minutes—but it's to be with all of them that I want, and in that place. Sometimes I have a dream that I am—back there, I mean. I said yes to the offers, I was accepted, and I stayed."

"You mean you regret saying no?"

"Oh, no. Of course not. It wouldn't have worked. I suppose I mean I wish I were that different person it might have worked for. And then sometimes I think it never happened, that I only dreamed that it happened."

"In that case, I dreamed it too."

He said some more, about knowing that the sun didn't always shine there, it wasn't always summer, it couldn't be eternally happy, not with human nature the way it was, and then he said he'd be moving out soon to live by himself.

"Did you manage to sell Gothic House?"

I shook my head. I couldn't tell him the truth, that I'd heard the day before that I had a buyer, or rather a couple of buyers with an inheritance to spend, Kim Gresham and his wife. Greshams have always liked to live a little way outside the village.